James Roberts Gilmore

On the Border

James Roberts Gilmore

On the Border

ISBN/EAN: 9783337346553

Printed in Europe, USA, Canada, Australia, Japan

Cover: Foto ©Andreas Hilbeck / pixelio.de

More available books at **www.hansebooks.com**

BY

EDMUND KIRKE,

AUTHOR OF "AMONG THE PINES," "LIFE OF JESUS," "PATRIOT BOYS AND PRISON PICTURES," ETC.

BOSTON:

LEE AND SHEPARD.

1867.

CAMBRIDGE: STEREOTYPED BY JOHN STONE.

BOSTON: PRINTED BY GEORGE C. RAND & AVERY.

To

WILLIAM LEE,

This Volume

IS AFFECTIONATELY DEDICATED,

BY

THE AUTHOR.

(III)

PREFACE.

THE facts which form the groundwork of the following story were communicated to the writer during a visit which he made to the "Army of the Cumberland" in the spring of 1863. Their romantic interest at once fascinated his imagination, and he readily listened to the suggestion, which was then made him, to write the history of Garfield's campaign in Eastern Kentucky. In pursuance of this purpose he opened a correspondence with the principal actors in that "eventful history," and within the following eighteen months accumulated a mass of material that would, of itself, make a respectable volume. A careful examination of this material, however, showed him that many of the statements of his correspondents were so inconsistent and so contradictory, that no reliable history could be compiled from it without an amount of sifting and research which he had not the time to make. In these circumstances, he decided not to write a history, but a story, that should embrace, and be founded on, the acknowledged facts of the campaign.

In following out this plan he has endeavored to relate events as accurately as possible. Whenever he speaks of known and living men he writes authentic history, and only in describing subordinate characters and circumstances does he give any play to his imagination. The events related of Jordan are mainly facts; but are not all facts true of him. This one man, as he appears in the story, is a combination of two men, — one of them named John Jordan, the other, Joseph Sowards. The adventurous ride, and the midnight visit to Marshall's camp on the eve of the battle of Middle Creek, are true of Jordan; the killing of Cecil, the double outlawry, and the unparalleled patriotism which made him, while under sentence of death from both his friends and his enemies, do such great services to his country, are true of Sowards.

In a pretty wide reading the writer has met with no such character, and the proverbial ingratitude of republics only can account for the fact that this brave man and pure patriot went to his grave unknown and unwept save among his native mountains.

CONTENTS.

CHAPTER I.

PAGE

ANCESTRY, ... 11

CHAPTER II.

THE SHADOWS OF COMING EVENTS, ... 24

CHAPTER III.

AFTER TWENTY YEARS, ... 52

CHAPTER IV.

THE FUNERAL, ... 75

CHAPTER V.

RACHEL'S MARRIAGE, ... 95

CHAPTER VI.

A WINTER NIGHT, ... 108

CHAPTER VII.

A CHRISTMAS IN FEBRUARY, ... 124

(VII)

CHAPTER VIII.

A Tragedy, ... 141

CHAPTER IX.

"The Beginning of the End," 155

CHAPTER X.

The Husband and Wife Together, ... 167

CHAPTER XI.

A Midnight Ride, ... 187

CHAPTER XII.

A March and a Battle, ... 197

CHAPTER XIII.

Results, ... 205

CHAPTER XIV.

The Removal, ... 210

CHAPTER XV.

A Trial and a Temptation, ... 216

CHAPTER XVI.

A New Actor on the Scene, ... 222

CHAPTER XVII.

Communications Opened, ... 231

CHAPTER XVIII.

A March in Mid-Winter, ... 243

CHAPTER XIX.

A Battle, ... 257

CHAPTER XX.

Bradley Brown Again, ... 266

CHAPTER XXI.

Retribution, ... 270

CHAPTER XXII.

Condemnation, ... 275

CHAPTER XXIII.

Another Escape, ... 278

CHAPTER XXIV.

A Midnight Meeting, ... 287

CHAPTER XXV.

The Children of One Father, ... 294

CHAPTER XXVI.

Midnight Duty, ... 304

CHAPTER XXVII.

The Pound Gap Expedition, ... 315

CHAPTER XXVIII.

The Death of "Beauty," 323

CHAPTER XXIX.

The "Last of Earth," 329

ON THE BORDER.

CHAPTER I.

ANCESTRY.

ISTORY, it is said, repeats itself; but this can hardly be, unless the world be moving in a circle, and not, as we suppose, in an unending spiral "onward and upward." But, however this may be, it is certain that man reproduces himself, — that, throwing aside his worn-out periwig and shoe-buckles, he issues from the grave after sleeping soundly, perhaps, for centuries, and stalks abroad again in stove-pipe hat and patent-leathers, to act once more a part in the great drama of human existence. To credit this we need not believe the doctrine of the transmigration of souls, but only accept the evident truth, that the father impresses his nature on the son, the grandsire on the grandson, and thus sends him into the world bound hand and foot with all his cast-off passions and propensities, only to do over again, it may be, the deeds which made his ancestor execrated in his day and generation. In this way, if in no other, history repeats itself; and in view of it how inestimable is the birthright of which Cowper boasted! Who would not rather inherit the virtues of a peasant than the vices of a king? And yet, how we look

down upon peasants and up to kings, never once asking
whether one or the other have either virtues or vices.

The young rustic who is the principal actor in this short
history was descended from a long line of peasants; and in
glancing back at his ancestors it is curious to notice how more
than one of them, though comfortably dead and buried for
nearly two hundred years, managed to reappear and act again
in his brief career.   The first of these ancestors, of whom
there is any historical mention, was the John Brown who so
heroically met death at the hands of Claverhouse, during the
civil war which distracted Scotland in 1685.   He lived at
Priesthill, in Lanarkshire; and, though but an humble carrier,
was a man of such shining virtues that he obtained honorable
mention in the annals of that dark period.   Led by convictions of duty to join the Rebellion, he was out with the in-
surgents at Bothwell Bridge, and was thus included in the
sweeping sentence of outlawry which followed that disastrous
battle.   The sentence was executed upon him by Claverhouse
under circumstances of savage cruelty; but he met it with a
fortitude that showed him possessed of such stuff as even kings
are seldom made of.   The circumstance forms a most wild
and picturesque story, and it is related by the old chronicle*
with such rude and touching eloquence, that I am tempted to
transcribe it.

* The extract is from " Walker's Life of Peden," which was published in
Edinburgh in 1724.   The account is briefly quoted by Macaulay in Vol. II.
page 74 of his history; and, more at length, by Sir Walter Scott, in " The
Tales of a Grandfather."   The story took strong hold of the poetical imagination and large heart of the great novelist, as is shown by his weaving some
of its most affecting incidents into the beautiful episode of Bessie Maclure, in
Chapter VI. of " Old Mortality."

The narrative is as follows: "Between five and six in the morning, the said John Brown, having performed the worship of God in his family, was going, with a spade in his hand to make ready some peat-ground. The mist being very dark, he knew not until the cruel and bloody Claverhouse compassed him with three troop of horse, brought him to his house, and there examined him, who, though he was a man of a stammering speech, yet answered him distinctly and soberly, which made Claverhouse to examine those whom he had taken to be his guides through the muirs, if ever they heard him preach ? They answered, 'No, no; he was never a preacher.' He said, 'If he has never preached, mickle has he prayed in his time.' He said to John, 'Go to your prayers, for you shall immediately die.'

"When he was praying, Claverhouse interrupted him three times. One time that he stopped him, he was pleading that the Lord would spare a remnant, and not make a full end in the day of his anger. Claverhouse said, 'I gave you time to pray, and ye are begun to preach.' John turned upon his knees, and said, 'Sir, you know neither the nature of preaching or praying, that calls this preaching.' Then he continued without confusion. When ended, Claverhouse said, 'Take good-night of your wife and children.' His wife, standing by with her child in her arms that she had brought forth to him, and another child of his first wife's, he came to her and said, 'Now, Marian, the day is come that I told you would come, when I spake first to you of marrying me.' She said, 'Indeed, John, I can willingly part with you.' Then he said, 'This is all I desire. I have no more to do but to die.'

"He kissed his wife and bairns, and wished purchased and

2

promised blessings to be multiplied upon them, and his bless-
ing. Claverhouse ordered six soldiers to shoot him. The
most part of the bullets came upon his head, which scattered
his brains upon the ground. Claverhouse said to his wife,
'What thinkest thou of thy husband now, woman?' She
said, 'I ever thought much of him, and now more than
ever.' He said, 'It were but justice to lay thee beside him.'
She said, 'If you were permitted, I doubt not your crueltie
would go that length; but how will ye make answer for this
morning's work?' He said, 'To man I can be answera-
ble; and for God, I will take him in my own hand.' Claverhouse mounted his horse, and marched, and left her with the
corpse of her dead husband lying there. She set the bairn on
the ground, and gathered his brains and tied up his head, and
straighted his body, and covered him in her plaid, and sat
down and wept over him.

"It being a very desert place, where never victual grew,
and far from neighbors, it was some time before any friends
came to her. The first that came was a very fit hand, — that
old, singular Christian woman in the Cummerhead, named
Elizabeth Menzies, three miles distant, who had been tried
with the violent death of her husband at Pentland, afterwards
of two worthy sons, — Thomas Weir, who was killed at Drum-
clog, and David Steel, who was suddenly shot after being
taken. The said Marian Brown, sitting upon her husband's
grave, told me that before that she could see no blood, except
she was in danger to faint, but she was helped to be a witness
to all this without either fainting or confusion; only when the
shots were let off her eyes dazzled."

The infant, who was thus an unconscious witness to its

father's bloody death, grew to womanhood, and became the wife of one John Jordan, a Cameronian minister of the same little parish of Priesthill, and the son of another Cameronian minister, who gave his life for the Prince of Orange at Dunkeld. The name of this man has not gone into history, but tradition has kept his memory alive among his descendants to this day; and, if one half that it tells of him be true, he deserved the almost superstitious veneration in which he is still regarded.

It is not to my purpose to recount the incidents of his career; and, indeed, if I did, I should be in danger of confounding truth with fiction, for the two seem inextricably blended in the traditions which have been handed down in his family. This much, however, is certain. He was a man of stern integrity, of singular religious insight, and of wonderful power as a preacher, and, though only "a man of the people," wielded an influence among his clansmen second only to that of their hereditary chieftain.

Inheriting his father's hatred of the English Union, he was easily lured into the Rebellion of 1715, and mustering a body of his parishioners, led them to the help of the Chevalier St. George at Sheriffmuir. For his valor in that battle he was made, on the field, a captain in the regular forces under the Earl of Mar. He followed the fortunes of the Pretender until his defeat at Prestonpans, when he was taken prisoner, and, with a score of others who had been conspicuous in the rebellion, was condemned to be shot at daybreak on the following morning. The rest suffered death at once; but Jordan's execution was delayed, and he was offered life and freedom on condition that he would acknowledge allegiance to the reign-

ing monarch by publicly crying, "God save King George!"
This he refused to do, and then his enemies, bent on saving
him, — whether from admiration of his character, or because
they desired his conciliatory offices with the other Cameroni-
ans, tradition does not state, — adopted a novel mode of execution which, while keeping death before him for hours, gave
him opportunity to retreat from his fate at the very last moment.

Taking him to the bank of the Forth, they chained him to
a stake driven into the sand at low-water mark. It was the
fall of the year, and the water was as cold as in midwinter.
It came up to his knees, to his waist, to his armpits, and at
last, with an icy embrace, encircled his neck and shoulders.
His executioners from the shore had from time to time urged
him to utter the few words that would save his life, and they
now cried out, "For God's sake, mon, speak! Say the words,
an' ye wad na do self-murder!"

He looked at his wife, who was standing near, but made no
answer. For a moment she seemed to hesitate; then, lifting
her eyes to his, she hoarsely whispered, —

"John, ye wat that God is aboon ye; that the angels are
waiting."

"Yea, lass, my only thoctht is of yoursel and the bairns!"

"Think na' of us," she answered. "He is Father to the
fatherless — husband to the widow!" and she sank upon her
knees, her arms stretched upward.

"Then my fecht is done," he answered. "But, be of good
cheer, Jennie. In the dark days I will be with ye."

The water was now even with his nostrils, and, raising himself on the tips of his toes, he cried to her, —

"Bid John be worthy of his ancestors." Then he sank again to his feet, and the swelling wave swept over him.

Of this woman — the Jennie Brown whose father suffered martyrdom at the hands of Claverhouse — many marvellous stories are told. She is said to have had the strange faculty of "second-sight," of which such frequent mention is made in the traditions of Scotland, and to have possessed the power of healing by a word, or by the laying on of hands after the manner of the early Christians. On one occasion, says tradition, she entered the house of a woman who had been bedridden for many years, and, looking upon her, said, —

"In the name of the Lord, I say to thee, Rise!"

The woman, it is said, rose, and lived in good health to the age of eighty.

At another time, it is also said, she restored a child who had lain apparently dead a dozen hours; and almost numberless instances are related of her curing, by a touch, those sick of divers diseases, and those wounded in battle.

But still more marvellous was her strange power of "second-sight." If the tradition be true, she not only saw into the unseen world which lies, an invisible cloud, all about us, but with mortal eye read in the shadows of coming events the far-off and mysterious future. She is said to have witnessed, in a series of visions, the defeat and misfortunes of the Pretender, long before he set foot in Scotland, and to have foretold, months before the event, the fate which overtook her husband.

"John," she said to him, "I see ye chained to a stake, and the waters rising round ye! But, stand fast; die like a Christian."

2 *

Her son, the third John Jordan of whom the family has knowledge, inherited the peculiarities of both his father and mother. He had her delicate organization and wonderful gift of spirit-vision, and his force of character and religious fervor and insight. He, too, was a Cameronian minister, and, like his father, met death at the hands of the ruling aristocracy. Engaging in the Rebellion of 1745, he was taken prisoner, condemned, and executed, after being offered life if he would swear allegiance to the English government. His aged mother stood beside the block to cheer his last moments, and, as the axe was about to descend, told him of a vision she had of the waiting angels.

This woman, who thus witnessed the execution of her father, her son, and her husband, lived to a great age, and died at last in the arms of a grandson, revered by all who knew her, and leaving a name which even now is only spoken with uncovered head by her remote descendants.

The year 1745 saw the end of civil commotions in Scotland, and after that the Jordans — father, son, and grandson — walked in peaceful ways, and died in their beds like other Scotchmen. They all were of the Cameronian faith, and all preachers in good standing; but tradition makes especial mention of only one of them. He was minister at Stirling, and on him the mantle of the old Seeress and the Cameronian captain seems to have fallen. He was a man of iron mould, powerful in word and deed, and with ungloved hand he tore aside the veil before the very Holy of Holies. With that strange gift of "second-sight" he read the Apocalypse. To him it seemed not a revelation of things "coming on the earth," but a history of the spirit world, from the birth of

Adam to the day when the last man shall look up at the sky, and amid the wreck of a dissolving universe, cry, "It is finished." The book he left behind on the subject is full of genius, and indicates that if his mind had not been cramped by a narrow Calvinism, he might have uttered words that would have "been music to the listening ages."

The grandson of this man — the seventh in regular descent from the old Cameronian — was born at Sterling in the year 1795, and, being the oldest son, was baptized by the name of John, and destined for the hereditary office of preacher. But when he began to talk, it was discovered that he had inherited the stammering tongue of his great ancestor. This shut him out from the ministry, and the "keys of heaven" descended to a younger brother.

This Jordan received a respectable education, and adopted, when he grew up, the profession of land surveyor. But an old country affords little scope for such a pursuit, and, at the close of the war of 1812, he emigrated to America.

At first he joined the Scotch settlers who had located at Fayetteville in North Carolina, but soon afterward removed to Virginia, where, at the age of thirty-six, he married a woman who, how truly I know not, claimed direct descent from the James-river Huguenots. She was fifteen years younger than himself, and a family might grow up about him; so, with Scotch foresight, he sought a home in a newer district, where every one of his posterity might become the lord of a thousand acres. He removed to Paintville, a little town in the "Piedmont region" of Kentucky.

This is a district larger than the whole of Massachusetts; but is as little known to the people of this generation as was the Garden of Eden to the races of men who, some geologists tell us, made their graves in the strata of the earth fifty thousand years ago. Though in the world, it is not of the world, — not, at least, of this world, which drives stage-coaches, builds railroads, talks across wide oceans, and wends its way to the other life through the marble aisles of churches whose spires, it may be, come no nearer to heaven than the famous tower once builded to furnish man an easy ascent to the celestial country.

It is a rugged, rocky region, broken into high hills and narrow valleys, and covered — except where dotted with little plantations of wheat and Indian corn — with vast forests of oak and maple, and the honey-locust, grown gray with the gathered moss of many centuries. In the hilly portion the soil is stony and sterile; but along the valleys it is of amazing fertility, yielding most abundantly of the fruits of the earth ; and in these valleys dwell the aristocracy of the district; for even in this primitive region, shut out as it is by a sort of Chinese wall from the rest of the world, are people who somehow have imbibed the civilized notion that a man's own blood is of somewhat better quality than that of his neighbors. Aside from this class, — who, being of a superior race, may properly be excluded from any general census of a country, — the district has a population of about one hundred thousand whites and four thousand blacks, a brave, hardy, rural people, with few schools, scarcely any churches, and only one newspaper, but with the simple virtues which grow among mountains, and now and then clothe even barren hillsides with a moral beauty that is something akin to the bloom of their own wild flowers.

In the very heart of this region is the little town I have mentioned, and there Jordan rented a small house, and put up a small sign, which told all the world — as plainly as a small sign in a retired locality could tell it — that he was a "Surveyor and Draughtsman of Legal Instruments." The latter part of the inscription the rustic denizens of the district, after a while, managed to make out by dint of hard spelling; but the former altogether baffled their comprehension. Legal meant law, and so, Jordan was a lawyer; and survey meant to look, so Jordan was a lawyer looking for land; and of that there were square miles for sale at his very door-way. Before a month passed at least a million acres of stony field and barren mountain were trundled up to his door, and offered to him "at haff thar valu." He explained that he was a measurer not a buyer of terra-firma, and then the honest rustics said to him: "Wall, stranger, ye hev brung yer eggs to a pore market. We buy land by the lump, — so much, more or less, — and we reckon we kin guess 'bout as nigh as other men kin measure."

Jordan was a man of decision and energy, and he at once determined to return to Virginia. He was about to set out with his wife, and his small store of worldly wealth, when one evening a stranger came to see him. He was a man of middle age, blunt and rather imperious in manner, and he accosted the Cameronian somewhat as follows : —

"Your name, they tell me, is Jordan."

"It is, sir," said Jordan.

"Are you an honest man?" asked the other.

".I am a Scotchman," said Jordan, probably thinking that a full answer to the question.

The other laughed, and said, good-humoredly, "Well, I've known a good many Scotchmen who were fools; but none who were scoundrels. I reckon you will do. I want you to take the oversight of my plantation."

Upon this Jordan asked the stranger to be seated, and the latter, accepting the somewhat tardy civility, went on to say that his name was Weddington, — 'Squire Weddington, attorney-at-law, member of the House, and, in short, the first man of the district. He closed a brief but rather egotistical account of himself by saying: "I have married a wife. She is twenty years younger than I am, and to bridge over the distance between us, I've promised her a tour in Europe. I want an honest man to look after my affairs while I am away. I'll give you five hundred a year, a house to live in, and as much as you can eat from the plantation."

The proposition actually dazzled Jordan. He saw in it education, perhaps wealth, for his unborn children; but his Scotch honesty suggested some obstacles. He explained that he knew nothing of planting, and that he had a natural antipathy to the negro.

The 'Squire met these objections as follows: "Planting! Why, the hands do that. And as for the nigger, I wouldn't give a continental dime for·an overseer who didn't hate the very continent of Africa."

His objections so easily disposed of, Jordan very soon took possession of the vine-clad cabin, which, for a dozen years, had been occupied by the overseers of the 'Squire's plantation.

The plantation was located near the head-waters of a small stream called the Blaine, which empties into the Big Sandy, not far from the town of Louisa, in Kentucky; and the cabin

was a rude structure of logs, laid up in clay; but it was so
overgrown with vines and creeping-plants, that one half of its
natural ugliness was hidden from the eye, and it seemed to
have sprung from the ground, a ready-made human habita-
tion. In other respects it was not unlike thousands of log
dwellings that are so plentifully scattered all over the Southern country. It had two rooms on the ground floor, separated
by an open passage-way, an unfurnished loft, approached by a
couple of rickety ladders, a low roof falling down at the eaves
so as to form the covering of a wide veranda, and two enormous chimney-stacks rising at either gable like mud models
of the Egyptian pyramids.

Located in the very heart of the forest, the great trees
crowded around it so closely that their branches overhung its
very roof, and only a small patch of tilled land, sloping down
in its front to a little stream at the foot of the hill, allowed it
any view of the outside world. But this view was broad and
picturesque. Far away a long mountain range rose against
the sky, and far below, an extended valley, dotted here and
there with little farms and broad plantations, lay spread out
like a map; and through this valley wound the narrow road,
which, like a slender thread, held this rustic region to the rest
of creation.

In this rude cabin, on the tenth of September, A. D. 1832,
just as the moon was breaking through the clouds of a somewhat murky midnight, was born another John Jordan, — the
eighth in descent from the old Cameronian, — and with his
birth our little history has its proper beginning.

CHAPTER II.

HE antipathy of Jordan to the negroes was deeper than even he had imagined. They proved a perpetual trial to him; but he was a man who would have cut off his right hand, if it had come in the way of his duty; and he set about his new vocation with the same self-devotion that made martyrs of his ancestors. Soon his management worked miracles, as genuine as any that are reported of the old Seeress. It transformed a hundred idle, eye-serving, dissolute wretches, into as many industrious, faithful, and respectable men and women. They had been driven hard all the week, and even denied religious services on Sunday; but Jordan allowed them Saturdays to work for themselves, and built for them a log church on a distant corner of the plantation.

After an absence of about three years the 'Squire returned from his European tour, and had a reckoning with his overseer. He had received frequent accounts from him, but was not prepared for the final result of his balance-sheet.

"Why, Jordan," he exclaimed, "you've paid the expenses of my journey over and above the ordinary yield of the plantation! Here's my check for an extra five hundred; and I'll give you a deed of the cabin and a hundred acres, if you'll stay with me five years longer."

These terms being agreed upon, Jordan was about taking his leave, when the 'Squire, who was in a liberal mood, called him back, saying, " Jordan, about that boy who has come to your house since I've been away. Give him my name, and I'll see that he has an education."

" I thank you, 'Squire," answered Jordan; " he is already named, — John, after his ancestors."

" D—n his ancestors! What can they do for him ? Call him after me, and I'll make him a congress-man."

Jordan's gray eyes flashed ; but he answered, coolly, —

" Sir, the boy inherits his name from men whose blood helped to give freedom to Scotland. Not for all your money would I change it."

" Well, well," said the 'Squire, " you Scotch are a queer set ; but I'm d—d if you aren't honest. There's my hand, Jordan ; take no offence — I meant none."

Jordan took his hand, and tried, honestly tried, to forgive him ; but the insult rankled within him, and was not for a long time forgotten. The two men, however, never but once came in collision. This occurred two years afterward, and may as well be mentioned, as it has some bearing on the future of this narrative.

The 'Squire was a luxurious liver, and from his youth up had been sadly given to the " gentlemanly " vices of gaming, drinking, and horse-racing. Of these vices his friends predicted that matrimony would cure him ; but it seemed to have a contrary effect, for, on his return from Europe, he plunged deeper than ever into dissipation. It soon was whispered

3

about that he and his wife did not live happily together;
that he had learned the truth of the old adage, "A young
maid's heart is not bought by an old man's money," and was
trying to drown his disappointment in the bottle. But this
was only conjecture. Nothing certain was known, except the
evident fact that the 'Squire was making rapid progress downward.

He was, as has been said, a member of the Legislature, and
every winter he went, with his wife, to Lexington, returning
home at the close of the session. One spring, the next after
his return from abroad, he came back to the mansion bringing
with him a gentleman named Irving, who remained during
the summer. Irving was a dark, silent man, many years the
'Squire's junior, but the two seemed on a footing of the most
intimate friendship. They rode, drank, smoked, and gambled together, and it was said that large sums were often lost
and won between them in the little billiard-room at the farther end of the mansion. In the course of the summer the
'Squire was called North on business, and invited Irving to go
with him; but the latter declined, alleging that he had taken
oath never again to set foot on abolition territory. This, to
the 'Squire, seemed a natural feeling for a Southern gentleman,
and he went away, leaving Irving behind with Mrs. Weddington. After a few weeks he returned, and then the two
friends resumed their intimacy.

The 'Squire's marriage had been barren; but in the following summer he was blessed with an heir, — a fine boy, who
was boisterously welcomed by the whole plantation. The
coming of a young stranger is usually a happy event in any
family; but it promised to be peculiarly happy in this family.

It wrought an entire revolution in Weddington. He threw off his bad habits as other men throw off their worn-out garments, went about again among his neighbors, looked into the condition of his slaves, and one night even came to Jordan's cabin to examine his accounts, and see how affairs for the previous year had been managed.

Jordan had not yet forgotten his allusion to his venerated ancestry; but he was a true man, and such a change in any one would have given him exquisite gratification. On this occasion he could not repress his feelings, and when they had gone over the accounts together, he said to the 'Squire, —

"Mr. Weddington, I must tell you how glad I am to see you again a man."

Not heeding the bluntness of the remark, the 'Squire answered, warmly, —

"Why, bless your soul! don't you know? I've something now to live for!"

At the close of the summer Irving reappeared at the mansion; but after a few weeks went away again, taking with him one of the 'Squire's negroes.

This negro, whose name was Ezekiel, had been brought up with Weddington from boyhood, and his sale was a matter of astonishment to Jordan. He was the preacher of the plantation, and wielded a great influence over the other negroes, — so great that his absence bred a spirit of discontent among them, which soon became troublesome to the overseer. Jordan mentioned this to Weddington, and suggested that he should buy Ezekiel back; but the 'Squire answered him rather testily, —

"Let me manage my own affairs, Mr. Jordan. 'Zeke can't come again upon the plantation."

He did, however, come again — the next summer, with his master; but he lodged in Jordan's barn, and carefully avoided being seen by Weddington. Then Jordan learned why he had been sold; but he kept the reason secret, even from his wife, saying only, —

"'Zekiel, presuming on his long connection with his master, gave him some unwholesome advice, and, to punish his presumption, the 'Squire sold him to Irving."

That night Jordan went to the mansion. What passed between him and Weddington on the occasion is not known; but on his return to the cabin, he said to his wife, —

"Ruth, the 'Squire and I have had words. Shall we go back to Virginia?"

"Where ye will, John," she answered. "Yer country ar' my country, yer God my God;" and, strange to say, she asked no questions.

Early the next morning the negro and his master went away, and a few nights afterward the 'Squire came to Jordan's cabin. His face was pallid, his beard long, his hair dishevelled. He looked like a man just recovering from a deep debauch or a long sickness. Half-walking, half-staggering into the room, he held out his hand to Jordan.

"I've come to ask your pardon," he said. "What you said was false, — false as hell; but you're a true man, and I ask your pardon."

Jordan took his hand, and said with an unusual degree of warmth, for his temperament was as cool as the north of Scotland, "Say nothing of it, 'Squire. It is all forgotten. I am sorry to see you've suffered."

With this the 'Squire's composure forsook him, and, sinking into a chair, he covered his face with his hands, and groaned audibly. Turning to his wife, Jordan asked her to take the child — the younger John, who was playing on the floor — into another room; and then the two men were, for more than an hour, alone together.

When the 'Squire had gone, Jordan said to his wife, —

"Ruth, we must go to the mansion for a while. The 'Squire is obliged to go away, and the mistress is taken suddenly ill, and needs your nursing."

"As ye will, John," answered Ruth, and again the wonderful woman asked no questions.

On the following day the 'Squire went away, and Jordan, his wife and child, took up their abode at the mansion. Mrs. Weddington was suffering severely from a nervous disorder, but she steadily refused to have a physician. Day and night she walked the room, wringing her hands and uttering piercing cries, and, at times, grovelling on the floor like a mad woman. She scarcely ate or slept, and soon had dwindled to a skeleton. Then Ruth became alarmed, and said to her husband, "John, if we longer heed her whims, her death'll be on us. Ye must go for a doctor."

He went for one immediately. The village was twelve miles away, and he did not return till nightfall; but then his wife met him at the door, and, with a smiling face, said, —

"She's a deal better, — a deal better, John! Mr. Irving has been here, and ever since she's been mending." The cool

3 *

Scotchman started back; his face grew suddenly pale; even his sandy hair took on an ashen color.

"What do ye say, woman?" he exclaimed. "Irving here!"

"Why, yes," answered his astonished wife. "Ye'd not been gone two hours. He asked for the lady, and she come down to see him; and ever since she's been better, — a deal better. I hope it warn't no harm."

Jordan made no answer, but told a servant to show the physician to the lady's apartment. In a few moments the medical man came downstairs, saying that Mrs. Weddington was sleeping soundly, and had better not be disturbed. He would remain over night, and see her in the morning.

During the night the attendant with the lady came to the physician's room, and called him to the bedside of her mistress.

He found her delirious and in a high fever. After that he did not leave the mansion for a fortnight, and then Mrs. Weddington had sunk into that deep sleep which on this earth has no awaking.

As soon as she was known to be in danger, Jordan wrote to her husband, stating her condition. He was supposed to be at Lexington, and distant only two days' journey; but he did not arrive at the plantation until four days after the death of his wife, and then, the weather being warm, she had been two days buried.

He came just in the edge of evening, and, entering Jordan's room in the dim twilight, said to him in a collected way, "My friend, I am glad to see you." Then he sat down, rested his head upon his hand, and said nothing for some minutes.

At last, without looking up, he asked, —

"How is the mistress?"

"She is well," answered Jordan, with the feeling which makes a strong man's voice as soft as that of a woman. "It is well with her, I hope, forever."

"It is well!" answered Weddington. Then, rising from his seat, he added, "Be good enough to give me a candle. I will go to my room."

In the morning breakfast was sent up to him, and soon afterward the servant came down, saying that his master would see "Massa Jordan."

Jordan found him by an open window, smoking a cigar.

"Jordan," he said, more kindly than usual, "I want to go away for a while; have you any money? Somebody has robbed me."

"Robbed you!" echoed Jordan, turning instinctively to an iron safe which stood in a corner of the apartment.

"Yes, I had twenty-five Kentucky Sixes when I went away. They are gone now; and, when I looked for them this morning, the key was in the safe."

"The key in the safe! Where have you kept it?" asked Jordan.

"Behind some books, on a shelf, in that closet."

Obeying a natural impulse, Jordan opened the safe, and began to look over the contents. They were a few account-books, and a quantity of loose papers, scattered about in some confusion. Taking out the books, one by one, he had begun to examine the papers, when the 'Squire said, —

"It is useless to look. They are gone. They were tied up with red tape, and in the upper drawer."

Jordan opened the drawer. It was empty, but a piece of red tape lay among the disordered papers. Taking it up he found one of the ends coiled loosely about some neatly-folded documents. Unfolding one of them, his eye fell on the broad seal of Kentucky; and, rising suddenly to his feet, he exclaimed, —

"Here they are! Safe, after all! The thief must have dropped them."

"It is strange," said the 'Squire, taking the papers, and passing them mechanically through his fingers. In a moment, in the same indifferent way as before, he added, "But here are only fifteen, — I had twenty-five."

"Only fifteen!" echoed Jordan, taking the bonds, and counting them hurriedly. Then, kneeling down, he began to look carefully among the remaining papers.

The 'Squire lighted another cigar and gazed, for a time, vacantly out at the window; then he rose suddenly to his feet, thrust his hands into his hair, and paced rapidly up and down the apartment. Jordan stood for a moment fixed to the floor with amazement; at last he said, —

"'Squire, don't take on. You have the numbers. The thief can't possibly pass them without detection."

"D—n the bonds! Let them go. Leave me! Leave the room, I tell you!" cried the 'Squire, stamping violently on the floor.

At the hour of noon the servant, going to his master's door with dinner, found it locked; but heard footsteps pacing rapidly up and down the room. Again at supper-time he found the door locked, and coming away told Jordan that his master must be dying, for he was no longer walking about, but groaning heavily. Jordan and his wife rushed upstairs, and tried to enter the apartment; but the door resisted their efforts. Then Jordan bent down and listened; but soon he turned, and led his wife away, saying, —

"Let us leave him alone — alone with his great sorrow."

In the morning Weddington's bell rang a little after daybreak, and Jordan, without waiting for a servant, went up to his apartment. He was seated by a window, fully dressed, and his boots were wet and muddy. He had evidently been out of doors in the night-time. He turned round as the overseer entered, and, half rising from his seat, said, —

"Ah! Jordan, I'm glad you've come. Sit down — here — close by me. Look me in the face. Do I look like a villain?"

Jordan smiled, as he answered, —

"You know I'm a peaceable man, 'Squire; but my Scotch temper would be tried if any man should say that of you."

"But you're an honest man. I want to know — if I look like a villain?"

"No, 'Squire! Like anything but a villain."

"That's enough," said Weddington. "Now, let what's happened here rest between us."

"As you say, 'Squire," answered Jordan, "but you're not well. Keep quiet for a few days. I'll track the bonds."

"Let the bonds go, I tell you! I'll manage them," said the 'Squire, somewhat impatiently. "I mean you shall say nothing of the robbery. Do you understand?"

"Yes — yes," stammered the overseer.

"Well," said the 'Squire, "I shall go away to-morrow.

To-day I want to be alone. You may send me some breakfast."

Jordan saw no more of Weddington during that day; but
on the following morning he went again to his apartment.
He had already risen, and a small portmanteau, ready
strapped, stood by his bedside. His eye lighted up as Jordan
entered the room.

"Ah! Jordan," he said; "sit down — here, by the table.
I am going away; where, and for how long, I don't know.
Here are some papers which, if I don't come back, you will
open. They leave you in possession of the plantation till
Jackson comes of age. I owe some debts. Here is the list.
You will pay them with the avails of these bonds. There
will be a balance left, and that, whether I return or not, I
want you to consider your own."

The faithful Scotchman had his eyes bent on the schedule,
vainly trying to make out the sum of the liabilities. A mist
had gathered between him and the paper, and the figures
would not be deciphered; but at this remark he looked up and
said, "No, no, 'Squire! I'll not take it."

"It's your due; you have earned it, and more."

"No, 'Squire, I've had my due. I should despise myself
if I took advantage of the good feeling of a man who is —
who is crushed as you are."

The 'Squire's face grew a shade paler, and the corners of
his mouth twitched nervously, as, grasping the Scotchman
suddenly by the hand, and wringing it violently, he said,
"Jordan, among all the men and women I ever knew, you
are the only one who has been true to me. I thought you
merely honest; but by ——, you've a soul in you."

Jordan, rising to his full height, took a step or two backward, and said, solemnly, " 'Squire, the hand of God is on you, — in love it's on you. Speak not lightly of the Great Father!"

The other also rose and paced the room for a while, saying nothing. Then he came to Jordan, put his arm about his neck, and his head on his shoulder; and then, — the strong man wept bitterly. For many minutes they stood thus, neither of them speaking. Then Jordan said, and his voice sounded like a woman's, — "He answers prayer. Let us pray to Him."

Long he prayed, wrestling with God, as Jacob wrestled with the angel; and when they rose from their knees the 'Squire was another man. The clouds had broken away about him, and into his soul had come a ray of the ineffable light that streams down from the Infinite. An hour afterward he had left the plantation.

A fortnight later, a gentleman came to the mansion, with a note from Weddington, which directed that the child — Jackson — and his nurse, should be sent to Lexington, to the sister of the child's mother.

Then another fortnight went away. Mrs. Weddington had been a month dead, and, it was thought, quietly sleeping in the little graveyard at the rear of the mansion; but soon it began to be whispered about that some of the negroes, out after hours, had seen her, draped in a long black robe, and walking the lonely cemetery by moonlight.

The rumor at last reached the ears of Jordan. Though a Scotchman, he had no faith in ghosts, and concluding that it was the 'Squire, returned, and venting his grief in secret at the grave of his wife, he determined to explore the mystery.

He went there one midnight. When he came back his face was ghastly pale; but to his startled wife he only said, "It *is* a spirit, Ruth, — an evil spirit; but not that of the mistress." Of old it was thought that a saint could lay the worst demon in creation. Beyond a doubt this is true; for Jordan was a saint, and it is certain that he laid this ghost so effectually that it was never seen or heard of afterward.

Not many months later the 'Squire returned to the plantation, — another man, truly. His form was wasted, his face wrinkled, his black hair turned to an iron-gray; twenty years seemed to have gone over him. He went into the room where Jordan was alone, and, sitting down near him, said, "John, I've come back to die with you."

That night he went upstairs to sleep in his own apartment, — the one adjoining that of the dead woman, — but in the morning Jordan, rising before daybreak, found him lying on a sofa in the library.

"I can't sleep in this house," he said; "there is something in its air that stifles me."

In this enlightened age no one believes that the dead revisit their earthly abodes; but may not some of that spiritual emanation which goes out from the human soul linger behind them, and fill the homes they have left with a portion, as it were, of their living presence?

The next night they made the 'Squire a bed in Jordan's cabin, and soon afterward built for him the little room under the rear veranda, which has been already mentioned. Jordan then went back to his home, and the mansion was closed, never again to be opened during the 'Squire's lifetime.

His life after this was sad, and yet, somehow, it was beautiful. He seemed to have begun the world anew, and to be living over again his childhood. The young heir to so much Scotch royalty — now a bright lad of about six years — became, day and night, his constant companion. In pleasant weather, the two would roam the old woods, sit together under the great tree in the little court-yard, or wander along the margin of the narrow stream, writing strange stories in the sand, or singing the wild songs which the 'Squire had learned from his old nurse, who came from Africa. Once in a while the negroes would come upon them kneeling in some shady place, their hands clasped together, and they talking to God as if he were a father to such little children. Then the poor slaves would go away with wet eyes, and say to one another, " Pore, pore massa! "

In winter they would build great houses in the snow, and, feigning they were old Scottish castles, would arm themselves with pine claymores, and have long combats before them ; and the woods would ring again with the boy's shouts when the man, after a hard fight, would fall mortally wounded. Then the boy, covering the man up in the snow, would play he was dead and buried, and preach over him a funeral sermon.

And so two summers and winters went away, — this once strong, proud man, living over again his childhood.

One sunny afternoon, toward the close of the second summer, they went together to a little nook they had fashioned in the wood, near the little streamlet. Here they sat down, and

4

the man wrote in the sand some of his strange stories. As fast as one was written the boy would rub it out, and the man would write another ; but at last he wrote one shorter than the rest, and when it was done, said, —

"Don't rub this out, Johnny. Let it stay till to-morrow I'm tired now. Come, let us take a nap in the wigwam."

It was a little nook between two spreading trees, and two summers before they had planted Virginia creepers, so as to make of it a natural arbor. Its floor was carpeted with the long leaves of the pine, and on these leaves they lay down beside each other, and fell into quiet slumbers. After awhile the boy woke, and moving quietly away, so as not to wake the man, sat down on the ground near him. His face was pale, — very pale ; but a smile was on it, gentle and sweet as the earliest dream of childhood. Tiring of this at last, the boy rose, and went out to the bank of the little streamlet. He sat down there, and read over again the legend the man had written in the sand.

"The Spirit and the Bride say, Come. And let him that heareth say, Come. And whosoever will, oh ! let him freely come, and freely drink the stream of life, — 'tis Jesus bids him come."

"I wonder what this means ? How queer uncle is !" said the boy, taking up a pebble, and casting it into the stream. It sank almost noiselessly into the still water ; but the tiny waves it raised circled round, growing wider and wider, and dying away only at the very edge of the streamlet.

"Uncle says that when a good man dies, he leaves just such waves behind him," said the boy again, thinking aloud, and throwing another stone into the water. "I mean to be a good man, and then, maybe, when I die I shall raise bigger waves than these, — as big as a great rock going down in a great river."

So the boy sat there, throwing stones into the water, until the sun began to sink below the trees which fringed the opposite mountain.   Then he rose, and saying, "It's time we were home, I must wake uncle," he went into the little wigwam.

He shook the man by the shoulder, but he did not awaken. He was usually roused by the slightest touch; but now the boy shook him again and again, crying out, "Uncle! uncle! wake up! wake up!   Mother'll scold if we're out after sundown;" but still he did not awaken.   At last a strange fear came over the boy, and he ran to the cabin for his father.

The two came, and, kneeling down by the side of the 'Squire, Jordan put his finger upon his wrist.   His pulse was still. Then he thrust his hand into his side.   His heart had ceased beating.

Among the 'Squire's papers was found a will, which had been executed when he was away on his last journey.   It was brief, and read as follows :

"Know all men by these presents, That I, Richard Weddington, of the county of Johnson, and State of Kentucky, gentleman, being of sound and disposing mind and memory, do make and publish this, my only will and testament.

"*First*, I hereby appoint my friend, John Jordan, to be my sole executor.

"*Second*, I direct that the mansion-house on my plantation, with its furniture, and one hundred acres of contiguous land, shall be sold at public auction as soon as may be after my death, and that the proceeds shall be appropriated by the said Jordan, to settling in some free State such a number of my slaves, not exceeding fifty, as he may deem fit for freedom.

" *Third*, I give and devise to the son of the said Jordan, who is also named John, three bonds of the State of Kentucky, numbered respectively 11,718, 11,719, 11,720, which are contained in my safe at the mansion. Said bonds to be held in trust by the boy's father till he shall be of age, and to become the property of his mother in case the boy should die before attaining his majority.

" *Fourth*, I give and devise to the said John Jordan the gold watch and chain which I wear, and which were given me by my father, and I request that he will wear them always. I give him no more. What I owe him cannot be paid with money.

" The residue of my estate, real and personal, after my debts shall be paid, I bequeath to my next of kin, with this condition, that all the said residue shall remain in the undisturbed control of the said John Jordan until the first day of January, 1859.

" For his services, under this will, the said Jordan is to receive such compensation as, to him, shall seem right and reasonable."

The will was duly signed and attested according to the laws of Kentucky, and, within a fortnight, Jordan presented it to the proper officer for probate. Before he had entered upon his duties under it, or his grief for the 'Squire had grown cold, just after noon, one September day, a gentleman rode up to his cabin. Jordan was seated with his son under the great maple which shaded his doorway, and a vacant chair was beside them. The stranger dismounted, tied his horse to a tree, and then approaching said, "Good-morning." He was a stout, squarely-built man, with dark sunken eyes, bushy hair and beard, and heavy eyebrows.

Jordan, rising, answered, "Good-morning."

"My name is Cecil," said the stranger, "Judge Cecil, of Piketon."

Jordan recognized the name as that of the leading man of the district, — the politician who had stepped into the shoes of Weddington.

"I have heard of you," said Jordan, whose manner to the stranger was something like that of an iceberg to a befogged mariner.

"I have business with you. I have ridden far. I will take a seat," said Cecil, advancing a step or two, and laying his hand on the arm of the vacant chair.

"Not this! not this!" cried the boy, springing up and clutching the chair in absolute terror. "This is uncle's!"

The stranger looked astonished, and Jordan, brought to a sense of common courtesy, said, "Excuse the boy; this is the 'Squire's chair. He sat in it, under this tree, every pleasant day until he died."

"Never mind, never mind; no apologies are needed," said Cecil; to whom the emotion of the lad was as much of a mystery as the origin of the Pyramids.

Jordan bade his son bring a chair from the cabin, and then the stranger sat down beside them.

"I have come to see you, Mr. Jordan," he said, "about that will of 'Squire Weddington's. It is a singular document."

4 *

"It *is* singular," answered Jordan. "It surprised me greatly."

"It makes no provision for the education of his son. It does not even mention him," said Cecil.

"No, it does not. It speaks of his next of kin," said Jordan.

"It throws away one-half of his property, and gives you undisturbed control of the remainder for eighteen years, allowing you to fix your own compensation," said Cecil. "Why, sir! in that time your charges might swallow up the whole estate!"

Jordan looked at the other for a moment, his cold gray eye glittering with a sort of spiritual phosphoresence. Then he said, —

"Come to the point, sir! Let me know your business."

The lawyer was taken somewhat aback by the bluntness of this address, but he answered coolly, —

"Very well, I will. I represent the relatives of Mrs. Weddington. The 'Squire was imbecile, — that is notorious. He has robbed his only son of one-half of his property. If you press it to probate we shall contest the will."

"That would be expensive," answered Jordan, "and it would be a quarrel over a dead man's grave."

"It need not be a quarrel, unless you insist that the will shall go to probate," said Cecil. "I am authorized to offer you satisfactory terms."

"I understand you, sir," answered Jordan, very deliberately, looking at the other with his cold, phosphorescent eye. "I feel interested in the execution of the will for only three reasons: First, it is the will of the 'Squire, — made when he was as sane as I am; and I would see his wishes carried out.   Second, it will enable me to educate my son for the ministry, — and his ancestors have been ministers for more than two hundred years; and, third, it provides for the freedom of fifty men and women, who are as fit for it as I, or, — you are, sir."

This remark was placing a white man, whose pedigree went back, it may be, to the time of Adam, — or Cain, — on a par with vermin littered only yesterday in a kennel; but the judge did not perceive, or did not choose to notice, the implied insult.   He replied, eagerly, —

"I see, I see!   You can be satisfied, Mr. Jordan.   We will allow you the three bonds for your son, and five thousand dollars for yourself; and, if you choose, let you manage the estate till the boy, Jackson, comes of age."

"And what will you do about the fifty slaves that the will liberates?" asked Jordan.

"Why, let them remain as they are; they do not want their freedom."

"About that, sir, I am a better judge than you," answered Jordan, speaking quickly, and again looking at the lawyer, his eyes now blazing like firebrands, or rather like jets of white flame.   "Your proposition is an insult, sir, and allow me to tell you, that you are a scoundrel."

The judge bounded to his feet as if struck by a rifle-bullet. His face flushed, and his eyes flashed as he said, "What do you say?   Do you know who I am?"

"Oh, yes!" answered Jordan, without moving a muscle, or rising from his seat.   "I've *heard* of you.   You are a man who lives by sucking the veins of dead men, — a ghoul,

we should call you in Scotland.   But I always deal with the
devil fairly.   Sit down, sir, and I'll tell you something you
don't know.   Johnny, go into the house."

The boy went into the cabin, and Cecil, as if moved by
some mechanical force, took the vacant chair by the side of
Jordan.   What passed between the two is not known;
but in ten minutes the judge mounted his horse, and rode
away, his face overcast with something strongly resembling a
thunder-cloud.

The threat to contest the will made Jordan nervously
anxious to effect the sale of the mansion, — that being a necessary preliminary to the manumission of the negroes.   He
pressed forward the legal proceedings, and, at last, the auction took place one cloudy day in October.   The house and
furniture were put up separately; but both went to one purchaser, — the dark, silent man whose shadow had already
darkened the doorway of Weddington.   Together they
brought the sum of ten thousand dollars.

Directly after the sale Irving approached Jordan.

"I understood the auctioneer to say," he said, "that the
purchaser would have the right to select any one hundred
acres lying contiguous to the mansion."

"That is what the auctioneer said, sir."

"I will then, if you please, have the north line run to a
point beyond the cedar grove, in the rear of the mansion; and
the east line on a course parallel with the middle of the highway."

"It will be done as you say, sir," answered Jordan; "but I
tell you, frankly, you will get some of the poorest land on the

plantation. The soil at the south of the road is far better."

"I prefer the north side; it is more heavily timbered."

"But the line run precisely as you direct, would include the family cemetery. That, of course, you do not want," said Jordan.

"I do, sir," answered the other, quickly; "I prefer a square plat of ground."

The eyes of the two men met at this moment, and said something which was Greek to the bystanders.

"You will, at least, allow me to remove the bodies of the dead," said Jordan, his breath grating against his teeth.

"Yes, sir," answered Irving, "the bones of Mr. Weddington." And then he added quickly, as if to change the subject, "When will the deed be ready?"

"By to-morrow noon, — that is, if you will take my measurement. I am a professional surveyor."

"It will be satisfactory. I will wait for it. You will allow me a bed to-night at the mansion?"

"I — I — am sorry to have to say it, sir," stammered Jordan; "but I prefer to keep possession until the papers have passed between us."

"Very well, sir," answered Irving, without the slightest sign of vexation. "I will be here at twelve to-morrow."

Mounting his horse, he then rode away, — twelve miles for a night's lodging.

The papers were passed on the following noon, and Irving took the key of the mansion. He remained shut up in the house during the day, but, soon after dark, was seen walking moodily along the northern boundary of his hundred acres.

In the morning he was gone, no one knew whither. A fort-night later he returned with his wife, the man Ezekiel, and an old negress who bore a young infant in her arms, and took possession of the mansion.

Jordan, knowing that Ezekiel's return would be the signal for great rejoicing among the negroes, decided to give them a general holiday on the occasion. As soon as he arrived, therefore, he called them together, and told them they were free the rest of the day, except for an hour after dark, when they would meet him at the little meeting-house.

" Leff de preachin' gwo for to-day, massa," said one of the more bold of the negroes.

"I have something to say to you," answered Jordan; " but I'm not going to preach. I give you preaching enough on Sundays."

This was probably true. Since the sale of Ezekiel, he had conducted their religious services, and no doubt had given them quite as much Calvinism as they were able to bear.

The morning was a time of general jollification, but in the evening the negroes gathered together at the little church in the forest. They had an indefinite notion that something good was coming; for, though the fact that freedom had been given to a portion had been carefully kept from them, it had got whispered about that the 'Squire had mentioned them in his will. They were, therefore, wofully disappointed when, on assembling, they found nothing to eat or drink in the whole church, — nothing but a big Bible, two rows of hard benches, and a couple of flaming pine torches, which were throwing a dim light around the dismal building.

Ezekiel opened the meeting with prayer, and then Jordan

advanced to the front of the platform, on which stood the rude pulpit, and addressed the negroes. He spoke of his long connection with them, of their cheerful obedience, and general good conduct, and of the mournful pleasure it had given him to witness their sincere grief for the death of their master. That master, had he lived and recovered his faculties, would have filled their lives with so many blessings that they would have desired nothing, not even freedom ; but though he was dead, he had not forgotten them. He had so provided by his will, that none of them could be sold away from the plantation, — at least not for nearly twenty years, — and to fifty had given freedom, and enough to begin life in a free country.

Here Jordan was interrupted by a shout that shook the rude building, and echoed through the dense woods like the noise of a waterfall. It was long before the uproar subsided, and when it did, one after another began to cry out, " Am it me, Massa Jordan ? Am it me ? "

" Be as quiet as you can," said Jordan ; " I don't expect you to be altogether quiet ; but be as quiet as you can."

When order was somewhat restored, he went on to say, that the 'Squire had left to him the selection of the fifty who should receive freedom ; that making the selection had been the most difficult duty of his life ; but he had devoted to it much thought and prayer, and had at last the manumission papers ready for delivery. He had been guided, he said, by a desire not to separate families, and not to throw upon their own resources those not in every way able to provide for themselves. And he said that those who remained must not think he considered them unworthy of freedom. He only

thought they needed his care more than the others, and his
care they should have ; for, if his life were spared, he should
remain among them until the time fixed by the 'Squire for the
passing of the estate into the hands of his kindred.   Finally,
he told them, he desired those who were freed to prepare
for removal as soon as they could, for there had been some
threats of an attempt to break the will.   Hence he had
pressed forward the sale of the mansion, and now wanted to
see them, as soon as possible, in a Free State, where they
would be beyond the reach of all the lawyers, and all the
courts, in Kentucky.

Then, one by one, he called over the names of the freed
negroes; and one by one, as the roll was called, they came up
to the platform, and received their manumission papers, while
a stillness, like that of death, reigned throughout the rude
building.   A half dozen had received the " charter of liberty," and returned to their seats, when a tall, stalwart man,
coal-black, and of about middle age, came forward.   He held
out his hand hesitatingly at first, but suddenly withdrew it,
saying, " No, no, massa, I don't want to leab you."   Turning
then to the assemblage, he added, " And I tell you, all you
brack folks, you wont neber agin be nigh so well off away up
Norf dar.   You'll git froze to death ; and dar haint anoder
such a massa as Massa Jordan in all dis worle, — not in all
dis worle."

At once from all parts of the house, a confused murmur of
voices arose, saying, " Dat's a fac' ; " " I don't want no freedom ; " " I wont leab Massa Jordan, nohow ; " and one woman,
who had already received a paper, came tremblingly forward
with it in her hand.

Jordan was visibly affected, but rising to his feet he said, "You are wrong,—you are not to be turned upon the world empty-handed. You are to have all that the mansion has sold for, and that divided among you will be two hundred dollars for every one who is freed. I advise you to take your freedom. I will go to a Free State with you, and try to settle you comfortably."

Then again a confused murmur ran through the house; but now the voices said, "We will go;" "We'll do what Massa Jordan say."

There was no further interruption, and soon all the papers were distributed. Then Jordan, saying "Good-night to all of you," left the building.

But the negroes remained. That number of white men awarded so priceless a boon, might have made night hideous with wild shouts and drunken revelry; but these simple souls, knowing no better, went upon their knees, and, until far into the night, sent up, from overflowing hearts, grateful songs and thanksgivings to the Great Father, who so tenderly cares for the meanest of his earthly children.

The negroes had dispersed to their several homes, and it was the dark hour which always precedes the morning, when Jordan's wife awoke him by crying out, "John! John! See! That great light down in the valley!"

Springing hastily out of bed, Jordan went to the window; and, as he began to hurriedly throw on his clothes, said, "Don't be frightened, Ruth. The mansion is on fire."

When he reached the scene, the flames were climbing the roof, and rising, in lurid jets, far above the tall chimneys of

the great building. Nothing could be done. The house was
already beyond saving.

A hundred negroes were standing about in frightened
groups, and pacing to and fro before the fire, his head bent
down, his face ghastly white, was the man, Irving. Jordan
went directly up to him.

"Your wife and child," he said, — "are they safe?"

He looked vacantly at Jordan for a moment, then, without
speaking, resumed his walk in front of the burning building.

At this moment the negro, Ezekiel, emerged from the rear
of the mansion, and came toward Jordan.

"Are they safe?" asked the white man, eagerly, — "the
mistress and the child?"

"Oh, yas, massa, — safe. Dey's safe in one ob de cabins."

"How did it happen?" asked Jordan.

"'Taint 'zackly clar, massa," answered the negro, "but I
reckon 'twas dis away. Ye sees, I leff de church long ter de
mornin', and, comin' yere, seed the flames a bustin' out ob de
back winders. I run in and woke massa and missus, and den
got out de old nuss and little Rachel. But I wan't a minnit
too soon, fur de fire was a blazin' in de hall, and I hed to leff
'em down fru de winder. Massa 'peared like he was struck
wid de palsy, but, wid two or free as had come, I went ter
wuck, and toted out a few cheers, a bed or two, and a bureau;
and den we couldn't wuck no more, for de fire was all ober de
mansion. De nuss, she say she leff a candle a burnin' fur
me in de room off de library. She sot it on a cane-cheer,
and it was a yaller-dip, so I reckon it cracked, drapped down,
and so sot de cheer a fire in no time. What would de poor

'Squar' say if he knowd de ole house war sich a brack ruination as it'll be to-morrer ? "

"He would be sorry, 'Zekiel, — the more sorry if he had just sold it, and had the money, as I have," answered Jordan.

He stood with the negro, watching the flaming rafters, as one by one they fell upon the blazing pile below, when Irving paused in his hurried walk, and came toward them. His eyes gave out a strange light, as if his soul were on fire with some such flame as that which was devouring his dwelling.

"That safe!" he said, in a husky voice, — "all I have in the world is in it! Is it fire-proof ? "

"I'm afraid not," answered Jordan. "It was said to be ; but I fear it is not to be trusted."

Three days afterwards the safe was exhumed from the smoking ruins, and, being deluged with water, was finally opened. A handful of cinders was all that it contained. On these cinders this man had built a life of ease, and with them had meant to laugh at destiny!

CHAPTER III.

ONCE knew a man who set about building a house, and, having laid the foundation and put up the framework, left it exposed, like a ship riding at anchor under bare poles, to the wind and the rain for half a generation. Like the man in the Gospels, he began to build and was not able to finish. In the course of years, however, he did add here and there a joist, and nail on here and there a weather-board; but it was not till his youngest boy had grown to be a man that the skeleton-house became a finished building. Then, to the merry music of the saw and the plane, it sprang up from a confused heap of boards and beams, all at once, as if by enchantment.

As it was with the man's house, so it is with our story. Having laid its foundation, and set up its framework, we are obliged to leave it in the wind and the rain for twenty years, adding only here and there a joist or a weather-board. Nobody has died, nobody been married, and the great world has been moving round just as if none of its characters were in existence. And yet they all have lived, all have been growing older, and, it may be, wiser, and all have been in training in that school of silent events by which God fits every man to act his part, great or small, in the long drama of the centuries.

(52)

It was late one night in the winter of 1860, when a man was slowly wending his way along the narrow road which leads from the site of the burned mansion, to the little cabin on the hill-side. He walked with a shambling, uncertain step, as if lost in thought, or wearied with a long journey; but he paused when he reached the foot of the little clearing, and looked off into the forest. A ruddy light was streaming from the windows of the cabin, and the long shadows it cast on the opposite woods, swayed by the flickering fire, were dancing about among the trees, as ghosts are supposed to dance about in graveyards. It was these shadows, or the thoughts that they awakened, which arrested the steps of the man, and made him — sitting down on the low fence which bordered the clearing — look again, long and moodily, off into the forest. "How strange they are!" he said, as if speaking to some one beside him. "I wonder if his soul is at rest, or wandering, like them, among the shadows?"

After a time he rose, and, with a steadier tread, ascended the narrow pathway which led to the cottage. Before the window he paused again, and looked back at the weird creatures of the night that were making such wild revelry in the forest. As he moved between them and the fire-light, they seemed, for a moment, to dance more wildly, and then to steal up the hill, as if to clutch him in their airy arms and bear him away to the shadowy realm beyond the rivulet. But as he turned and opened the door of the cabin, they gave up the chase, raced again down the hill, and began again their ghostly minuet in the valley.

As the man entered the room, a woman rose from a seat

5 *

near the fire, and came toward the door-way. "Ye is late,
John," she said.   "It's arter two in the mornin'."

"I know," he answered ; "I couldn't come sooner. He
is dead."

"Dead!" echoed the woman, in a startled way.

"Yes, dead.   He went just at midnight," replied the man,
standing with his hand on the latch of the door.   "But look
there, mother, — down there by the run! See those black
things a-dancing! Don't they make you think of the dark
spirits they say come out o' nights to take the souls of bad
men down to the under-world?"

"Hush, John; don't ye speak so! Them is only the
shadders from the fire through the winder."

"I know, I know, mother; but to-night they seem to me
living things, — dark spirits who have taken on the shadows
so our eyes may see them. I know it isn't so; but — I hope
his soul isn't among them."

"Among 'em! Why, John, how you tork! Israel warn't
a bad man, — he never done nothin' to send him among the
dark sperets."

"Not that you know, mother; not that you know," answered the man, barring the door, and coming forward into the
fire-light; "but he's told me things to-night that have froze
my blood in hearing."

He sat down by the fire, and the blaze of the burning logs
lit up his features. He was a man of about twenty-eight,
with a tall, gaunt, somewhat awkward frame, and a sallow,
sun-browned complexion. He had large hands and feet,
long, bony arms, and shoulders which, though square and
broad, had a singular stoop that almost amounted to de-

formity. He was dressed in common homespun, and wore the
shapeless slouched hat which, time out of mind, has covered
every male head in the district; but, when he lifted this uncouth head-gear from the mass of soft, jet-black hair which
fell in wavy folds almost to his shoulders, he disclosed an
open, intensely white forehead, thickly interlaced with those
fine blue lines that always denote a mind of great power
and sensibility. With his hat on, and, as he usually wore it,
slouched down, so as to half hide his face, he would have
passed unnoticed as a common rustic; but with it off, and the
light falling upon his broad head, expanded and flexible nostrils, wide and strong jaws, and singularly regular and handsome features, he would have arrested attention anywhere as
a man of no ordinary character. Over his features he had
a strange control; for, as he sat now in the fire-light, they
wore a quiet, dreamy expression, blended with a certain look
of trust and gentleness, which seemed habitual to them ; and
yet a wild, white, ghastly light came out of his great gray
eyes that drove the color from the woman's face, and made
her half-stagger into the seat beside him.

"What was it, John?" she cried. "Was it murder?"

"Hush, mother!" he said, laying his hand suddenly on
her arm, and speaking in a hoarse, broken whisper. "Where
is father and Robin?"

"Asleep these five hours," she answered, in the same
broken whisper. "No 'un kin yere ye. What did he do,
John? Tell me!"

The man glanced down at the fire, and said nothing for a
few moments; then, without looking up, he answered, "Nothing, mother, — nothing that can be told."

"It *war* suthin', John, — suthin' dreadful ; for I never seed that look in yer eyes afore.   And yet I can't b'lieve Israel ever done ary wrong, — he, as was allers so quiet and so patient like, in all the trouble as was ever a follerin' him."

" The trouble was the fruit of his crimes," said the man. "The Lord has so fixed the order of things that even dumb nature works against the wrong-doer.   I never thought he put any special sentence upon Cain.   It was the spirit of his evil deed that haunted him, and made him a wanderer in the world, — his hand against every man, and every man's hand against him."

"I knows, John, I knows; but ye's allers a preachin'. What was it ? " again asked the woman, in a tone of slight impatience, and drawing her chair nearer to the man's.

This was the same woman who, twenty years before, had seemed not to know how to ask a question ; but now she addressed her son, and then her husband ; and, too, the dark, silent man of whom they were speaking, had, all those years, been to her among the strangest of mysteries.

" I'd like to tell you, mother," answered the man ; " it would ease my mind ; but I can't.   It's a dead man's secret."   Then after a pause, he added, " It's very late.   You ought to go to bed and get some rest.   Rachel will need you to-morrow."

He turned away, and looked again at the fire, and neither spoke for many minutes.   While they are thus silent, we may as well glance around the apartment.

It is somewhat larger than an ordinary sitting-room, and is evidently the best apartment in the cabin.   It opens by one door upon the covered passage-way already mentioned; by another into a small bedroom, formed by inclosing a portion of the rear veranda; and it has plastered walls, and a tongued-and-grooved ceiling, through which project the naked beams that support the upper story. A rag carpet covers the floor, except in front of the fire-place, which is deep and wide, and surmounted by a broad mantle of unpainted oak, on which a Yankee clock is ticking. In one corner stands a spinning-jenny, in another a cushioned settle, and opposite the fireplace is a large bureau of natural maple, on which rests an unpainted violin, evidently of home manufacture. Over against the door-way is a small table, covered with a patch-work cloth, and holding a few books, among which are the Bible, "The Course of Time," a large dictionary, Watts' Hymns, an odd volume of Shakespeare, and the "Heaven and Hell" of Swedenborg. These books are all well worn, as if handled by a whole neighborhood, or often read by some one individual. The latter, however, is the more likely supposition; for the neighborhood is not of a literary turn of mind; and this supposition may account for the fact that the young man employs so little of the uncouth dialect of the region. Long pondering on these books has probably made their language even more natural and familiar to him than the rude accents he has learned from the lips of his mother.

A half-dozen chairs, with rustic frames and deer-skin coverings, arranged somewhat regularly about the floor, and a few other articles comprise the remaining furniture of the apartment; but among these other articles are some which, more than anything I have enumerated, reveal the character of the man who has been speaking.

They are several paintings in oak frames, which are hanging on the walls. They are coarsely done in oil, and evident-

ly by one with no educated knowledge of art; but they show
a natural perception of the beautiful; and one is a picture
that would arrest the attention of the most careless observer.
It covers the whole blank space over the bureau, and repre-
sents several mountain ranges, rising one above another in
more than Alpine grandeur. In the foreground, at the foot
of the mountains is a broad, arid plain, dotted here and
there with little oases, which are watered by small rivulets, and thickly covered with verdure. On these oases are
vine-embowered cottages, around which groups of children
are playing, and men and women are gathered in little knots,
or two by two in various occupations. Some are tilling the
ground, some felling the trees, some tending the flowers, and
others looking up with rapt faces at the high mountain summits; but all are engaged in some act of work or devotion.
They are of graceful form and comely feature, and many of
them bear small bunches of flowers in their hands, and the
bloom on their hearts seems as fresh as that on the roses they
carry. Their clothing is mean and poor, and some have
scarcely any covering; but the rude breath of spring, and the
cold wind of winter, never comes to them; for these are they
who are clothed in the garments of salvation.

Around these leafy Edens is a different landscape. It is a
broad, arid plain, and over it the drifting sand, lifted by the
fierce simoon, is rising in dense clouds that well-nigh shut out
the vision. But through the hazy air one may discern, in
dim outlines, the dwellers in this desert. They are a count-
less multitude, — countless as the leaves on the trees, — and
of every imaginable shape and complexion; but all have some
lineament of manhood. Here, with the form of a man, the

face of a lamb, and the feet of a bird of prey, is a priest, in white robe and surplice; yonder, in a brass mask, with a huge boulder for a heart, is a judge, arrayed in the ermine; and about in various places are divers others, — a king in rags and tatters; a politician kissing the feet of a toper; a black-smith hammering away at a naked heart; a miser sinking under a load of gold, and a scholar with a head like a dried pumpkin, and bearing the significant inscription: "Lofts to Let." Every character has its peculiar features. Some have the faces of wolves, of panthers, owls, foxes or hyenas; others the claws of vultures, and the bodies of all manner of creep-ing things, and all are preying and making war on one other.

But the most striking figures are directly in the fore-ground. They are an ape in a dandy's coat and trousers, who is dancing and grimacing on the very brink of an abyss which seems unfathomable; and a woman with a serpent's body, who is coiling her slimy length round the dandy's waist, and luring him down the precipice. Down this abyss one may catch a glimpse of the under-world, into which no ray of light enters, and where sin holds its high carnival for-ever.

But the sand-clouded air clears away at the foot of the first mountain, and there various figures can be seen climbing a broken and rocky ascent. They seem weary and bent, as with some great life-burden; but on they are going through the briers and thistles that strew the steep and flinty way; and as they go, their faces lose the lineaments of beasts and birds of prey, and take on those of a radiant manhood. Passing in and out among them are shining figures, clad in white, who are guiding the weary wayfarers, and pointing them to the sun-illumined plateau toward which they are journeying.

This plateau is an evergreen land, bathed in a sunshine that is softened, not obscured, by the misty clouds which over-hang the whole lower part of the mountain. It is like the earth, only far more beautiful. In it are rolling hills, and running streams, and verdant plains, and waving fields, rich with growing grains, and fruitful trees, and blooming flowers. Around are cosey cottages and gorgeous palaces, and great cathedrals, on whose spires a light is resting that seems a glory from the Infinite. The scene is all alive with singing-birds, and all overflowing with ethereal beings, floating in the dreamy air, or resting in the leafy woods, as if life to them were only one long day of joy and sunshine.

Beyond this mountain is another, sloping up through ver-dant fields and flowery meads; and along its sides are moving figures, clad in shining robes, and resembling the angels of the old painters. They are aiding the toilers from below, as these are aiding the pilgrims from the desert-region. Above this mountain another rises through the mist, until three in all are seen, — the three heavens, it may be, that Paul saw in his vision.

But the striking feature of all the striking picture is at the summit of the loftiest mountain. There, on the top-most peak, beneath the great sun which gives light and warmth to all these radiant regions, and encircled by a count-less throng, who are kneeling, as if in adoration, is a way-worn man, laying a heavy cross upon the ground. His form is wasted, his hands and feet are torn and bleeding, and on his face are traces of an infinite sorrow. It is the Man of

Calvary. Up all the toilsome way he has borne the weary load, and now he is laying it down at the feet of the Infinite, while over his head a belt of stars, new-created to celebrate the hour, are with their new-born rays writing on the sky: " THIS IS MY BELOVED SON, IN WHOM I AM WELL PLEASED."

A singular picture this to be found in a wilderness, and a singular man must he be whose untutored art has painted so gorgeous a panorama of the eternal pilgrimage ! What unseen hand has drawn aside for him the veil that divides this life from the other ? or what angel-voice whispered in his soul the sublime truth that the Man of Calvary bore the cross of Self-Sacrifice up to the highest heaven, before he received the homage of the angels, and was crowned the " LORD OF ALL ? "

But the woman speaks, and we will turn again to those two who are seated there in the fire-light. Her eyes, like the man's, have been bent on the fire ; but now she looks up and a smile, half of wonder, half of doubt, is on her features. They are pleasant features, and though they lack some of the intellect, and all of the dreamy expression which is in the man's, they show — if one's life may be shown in one's face — that her life has been a summer day, or a gentle stream, rippling down through quiet ways, and singing as it goes to the great, ever-singing ocean.

" But John," she said, " how did he come to tell ye ? "

" He sent for me expressly to tell me," he answered, leaning back in his chair, and drawing a long breath, as if speech were a relief to the thoughts which his eyes showed were working within him. " When I went thar, just after

6

dark, Zeke was doing up his evening chores at the barn. I stopped to say a few words to him, when Rachel came running out, saying her father wanted me to come at once into the cabin. She said he'd seemed better during the day than for months going; but, when I went into the room, he asked them all out, and told me that he was dying. I thought it couldn't be so; for his face was flushed, and his voice strong and husky; but I asked him if I hadn't better call back his wife and daughter. He shook his head and said : 'No, no! Not yet! Thar's time enough for that. I must talk to you first. I've something on my mind, John, that I must tell before I die; and I can tell it to no one but you, — for I can trust no one but you never to use it against Rachel or her mother.' I said he could trust me; and then, in a broken way, stopping often for breath, and for more strength to face the terrible thing, he told me the story."

Here the man paused, and gazed again for a while at the fire, and the woman said: "It must have been dreadful, John — dreadful. I know it by the look that's in yer eyes this minnit."

"It *was* dreadful, mother," said the man, looking up, and a different light coming into his great gray eyes. It must have been this new light which shut from his view the hideous vision that seemed rising before the mind of the woman, — as a strong blaze will illumine a room, while a weaker flame will only fill it with gloomy shadows. At any rate, he went on : "It *was* dreadful, — too dreadful for you to hear, or for me to tell. It showed me the real nature of evil. Evil is like fire, mother, — a good thing if kept under, but, allowed to get the mastery, a very devil of destruction."

"Why, John! How kin ye say so? How kin ye call evil good?"

"It isn't good in itself, — it's only good in its way. It is useful, and, it may be, necessary for our development. If it was not, it wouldn't exist; for God would allow nothing to be that was not for the final happiness of his creatures. This always puzzled me, — how God, who is all goodness, could permit evil, — until one day when I was down at the village, before the new court-house was finished. I had heard it was to be the finest building in all Kentucky; and I went to see it. It was only half-way up; all about it was a rough scaffolding, and all around were loose bricks, and mortar, and rough plank, and the upturned earth, on which not a blade of grass was growing. I sat down on the other side of the way, and said to myself, 'Folks may call this beautiful; but give me the beauty of the woods, of the tall tree, springing from the great trunk, and tapering up into the slender spire, which, like the good man's thoughts, point always to heaven; or even the beauty of our old log cabin, rough, uncouth, and, like a shapeless dwarf, a world too broad for its height, but covered all over with an evergreen coat made for it by the Creator.' This is what I thought; but as I sat there, the scaffolding seemed to fall away, the grass to spring up around, and the building to rise, like what it is now, — more beautiful than any work of man I have ever seen.

"Then it flashed upon me that the soul is like that building, half-finished, but rising from the earth to be a thing at which the man himself shall, some day, wonder. The evils around and in us are only the bricks and mortar, and other rubbish by which the soul is growing, and the body is only the scaffolding by which it is rising into the heavens. The rubbish will be cleared away, the scaffolding be thrown down, and then the soul will rise, a thing of grandeur and of beauty forever."

His eyes now gave out another light, his thin nostrils opened and shut, and his whole face was aglow with the strange enthusiasm that possessed him; but the woman said coolly, "And yet, John, some men haint never more'n half-finished. They go out of the world no higher to heaven nor when they come into it."

"So it seems to us, mother; but that is only because so much rubbish gathers about them that we can't see their growth. The soul, which is the workman, sometimes, too, sees so much rubbish around that it gets discouraged, and stops working, and as the building doesn't go up before our eyes, we forget that it has even a foundation. But it has; and the more rubbish there is about it, the higher and grander it will rise at last; for the rubbish — which is what we call evil — is only the material out of which the building is formed. It may not rise to its full height in this world, but it will in the world to come."

"No, no, my son! 'As the tree falls, so it lies!' 'There is no device, nor knowledge, nor wisdom in the grave!'"

"That is not the meaning of those words, mother. The tree does not lie as it falls; and all the wisdom of the ages is in the grave. The tree rots away, and springs up again in the green grass and the beautiful flower; and the soul, which only buds here, blossoms there, and sends out its fragrance forever."

"Ah, John, this comes on yer over-much reading and yer

day-dreamin'. Yer sorry wrong. Ye mustn't be wise above what is written."

"I am not wise above what is written, mother, — above what is written here, — in my soul. That is the true interpreter of God's word and works. The one who has not rightly read his own soul, cannot know God, or read one-half of the riddles that surround us."

"We carn't read 'em any way, John. Ye know what yer father says, — truth lies at the bottom of a well."

"Yes, I know; but when I look down the well, I see my own face in the water. When I try to find God in nature, or in the great world, I feel lost, — lost, as the worm does when he looks up at the stars; but when I look down the well, and see my own soul reflected there, I catch a glimpse of the Unknown; for we are made in the image of God."

"But ye don't s'pose God ar' a man? Ye don't s'pose ye kin measure him?"

"No, mother; no more than father, with his rod and chain, can measure yonder mountain. But with just such tools as his, other men have measured higher mountains, — put a girdle round about the earth, and found the distance of stars — suns like ours — which are so far away that imagination itself wearies in going the long journey."

"Ah, John, John, I wish ye'd put away sech thoughts. Come nigher the earth, and leave the stars alone. No one by searching kin find out God."

"Thar you are wrong, mother. Jesus found him out, shared his thoughts, probed his plans, and, with a single glance of his eye, took in the whole of history to the end of

6 *

time. Think upon the parables of the kingdom, and tell me if what I say is not true?"

"Yes, my son, it'r true; but Jesus was God."

"I know you think so, mother; and I am not sure that he was not; but you, and the rest of the world, forget that he was also man, — that he wept and prayed, was hungry and faint, felt grief and pain, like other men. God himself, if he took our nature upon him, could be nothing more than he was; but in exalting Jesus into God we only lower him as a man; for his real glory is that he was a man, and, that being a man, he lived the life he lived, and died the death he died. He came not so much to show us what God is, as what man may be; and when I think of his life, when I look on its dazzling beauty, though my eyes, like Paul's, are blinded with the sight, I catch a glimpse of the real grandeur of the human soul, — of the ineffable glory in which it will be clothed, when, like his, it shall have been made perfect through suffering."

As I write them, the man's words sound like the rant of a half-crazed fanatic; but, as he spoke them, they were the natural language of his thoughts, — of such thoughts as in the rugged prose of the old Cameronian would have had a rough force and eloquence that is something akin to the lofty grandeur of Milton.

"Ah, John, ye deny the Lord that bought ye. I weep, — I weep bitter tears when I think how far ye've strayed from the faith of yer fathers. What would they think — the old Jordans who gave their lives for the truth — if they know'd how ye dress up the Lord himself in the clo'es of a man, — how, with shod feet, ye go upon the mountain amid all the thunders of Sinai?"

"Think, mother! If they lived now they'd think as I do. The world has moved since their day. It was dark then. They saw only half the truth; but now the mists are clearing away, and the man with clean hands, and a pure heart, can look straight up to the sun in all his morning brightness."

"Ah, John! yer heart ar' right; but yer head ar' sadly wrong, — a'most turned with thinkin' overmuch on things as is above human reason. Oh! if ye'd only heared to me, only had put away such thoughts, and took the edication yer father offered ye, what a man ye moight have been, — what good ye moight have done in the world!"

"I could have done no good in the world, mother. None but an honest man can make other men honest; none but a good man can make them good. I should have been neither honest nor good if I had sold my conscience for a little learning, and preached as true what I knew to be false. But I don't blame father. He thought he was doing right, and for the best. And I don't forget, mother," and here he laid his hand upon hers, and his voice grew husky with an emotion his face did not express, "I don't forget how you took your scanty earnings to buy me books; how you begged Israel to teach me the little I know; and how you worked of nights, when father was asleep, to pay him his unfeeling price. No, mother, I don't forget this; and your work will not be thrown away. I shall do something yet. God never fits a man for work, but he gives him the work to do. He has fitted me for something better than I am doing; and my work will come, — it may be sooner than we know."

The woman's eyes were wet, and her voice trembled as she answered, "It may be, John, it may be. Ye has a wonder-

ful look inter things, and ye orter know. But I am paid,
John, for all I ever done, — more than paid. Ye has allers
been a lovin' son to me, and I knows ye has been to God; and
he looks onto the heart, and wont holt ye to account for things
of the head, that, maybe, ye can't hinder. But let us talk no
more on it, for, spite of all I kin do, it brings the old grief back,
— the only grief I ever bore from yer father." Then, after
a pause, she added, " But, Israel, did he die — die easy ? "

" No, mother," said the man, looking away, the fearful look
coming again into his eyes. " It was awful, — awful. He
thought they were thar, waiting to drag him down to the tor-
ments. With his last breath he begged, and prayed, and
shrieked in such a terrible way, that Rachel was half-dead
with fright, and her mother fainted. And, mother," he put
his hand again upon her arm, and his voice sunk again to the
low, broken whisper, " they *were* thar. I couldn't see, but
I could feel them, — feel their breath, their cold, clammy
breath. It loaded all the air, and almost stifled me with hor-
ror. I feel it *now ;* it fills the room, and seems to be creeping
into my very veins, as it did the moment I saw him wrestling
with the great terror."

Here he rose suddenly to his feet, and with a quick, nervous step, paced up and down the room. The woman gazed
at him with a look half of wonder and half of dread, and it
was some minutes before she said, —

" I reckon 'taint so, John. Ye don't s'pose sperets kin
make tharselves felt by mortals ? "

" Felt by mortals ! Why not ? Do you never feel people
without seeing them ? and what are spirits but people, — men
and women like ourselves ? "

"And who is they?"

"She, — the evil woman, and the man."

"Not the 'Squar' — the poor 'Squar'? — not him, ye think?"

"Oh, no, mother, not the 'Squire. I know him. His breath is as gentle as a child's. He never comes to me but he lifts me up, — makes me purer and better; but this, — it stifles me."

He took one or two turns up and down the room, and then, with perhaps the same instinct that led the servant of Saul to seek out a cunning player to charm away the evil spirit that troubled the wicked king, he took up the violin which lay on the bureau, and sat down again by the fire. Quickly he touched the strings, and then it spoke — spoke in that strange, weird language which is the essence of all music. Not every man or woman has an ear to catch the subtle spirit that slumbers in the soul of sound; but this man and this woman had such an ear, and to them the violin told a strange and awful story.

At first it gave out low, swaying sounds, as if echoing the tread of a weary man, who, with uncertain step, was groping his way over a rugged road in thick darkness. Then it uttered a short, shrill cry, like the alarmed shout of a surprised sentry on an outpost, and then a loud hail, a low reply, and another cry, which seemed to wake the dark army of the nether world; for at once there came the rapid tread of many feet, and the swift rush of hot breath, like that which rises from the pit that is bottomless. Then it gave out a quick, broken noise, like the startled cry of a man in some deathly terror; and then again the rapid tread of many feet, and a dull, rushing sound, like the slow falling of a dense body through air that is heavy with the fumes of charcoal.

Then again came the startled cry, changing now into a low wail, and then, into an earnest prayer, faint and broken, but rising soon, clear and loud, above the yell of the angry fiends, as once I heard a seaman's voice rise above the awful roar of the storm, on the deck of a ship that was thought to be foundering at midnight, in the mid-ocean. Then there came the melody of human voices, and a rush as of angel wings swooping down to rescue the soul which was lost in the dark abyss of evil. Faint and fainter it grew, until it sank into a far-off hail, and a low reply, which were followed by the clash of arms and the roar of conflict, as if the nether world, stirred to its depths, was rising with all its angry host and battling with the rescuing angels. But soon the din died away, and there again came the rush of wings, and the melody of human speech rolling up from the dark abyss in a glad song, near and nearer, and loud and louder, until it burst into a grand hallelujah. Then the man, who until then had sat as if entranced by the strange melody he was creating, raised his head, and with eyes uplifted, and hands still playing with the magic strings, he broke into a song that shook the rafters of the rude cabin, and floated off on the still air till the far woods echoed the mighty anthem of salvation : —

> " To HIM who loved us first,
> Before the world began ;
> To him who bore the curse,
> To save rebellious man ;
> To him who forms
> Our souls for heaven,
> Be endless praise
> And glory given.

" To Christ, the Lord of heaven,
The first-born from the dead;
The Prince of Life, be glory given,
And wide his kingdom spread;
Through earth's extent
His honors raise;
And all consent
His name to praise."

The last echoes were dying away, and the radiance the music had evoked was still lingering on the faces of the two who sat by the fire, when the inner door opened, and a tall, gaunt man, half-dressed, entered the apartment. His hair was gray, and a long stoop was in his shoulders; but a glance showed that he was the same stern, but canny Scotchman who, twenty years before, had bearded the first politician of the district, and stood, so like a man, by the broken Weddington.

" What's this, John? what's this?" he said. " You are making racket enough to raise the dead. Don't you know it's after four in the morning?"

" He is dead," said John, without looking up from the fire.

" Dead!" echoed the other, with a sudden start. " Then may God have mercy on his soul!"

" He will. He doesn't measure out his mercy by a narrow theology."

" Perhaps not; but you never knew Irving," said the other, seating himself by the fire. " There was an awful weight on his soul."

" I know. He told me all, — more than you ever dreamed of."

" More? I read him twenty years ago, as if he had been an open book!"

"No one ever read him. You don't know one-half of his crimes."

"Then the Lord pity him! I know he had a soul blacker than pitch darkness."

"It isn't for us to judge of his soul," said the younger man. "He has felt terrible remorse; and for years has been a penitent man."

"Penitent, John! Then you don't know him, as I do. I have known all from the first; but, out of love for the memory of the poor 'Squire, I have never opened my mouth. But now I will tell you *one* thing, and then think, if you can, that he was penitent. You know that after the mansion was burned, and when he was houseless and penniless, the hands set to work and built his cabin and barn, and got in the supplies I gave him for the winter. Well, then that scoundrel Cecil began the lawsuit, and served on me the injunction that stopped the removal of the negroes. I suspected that Irving knew all about the will, and could, by a word of evidence, enable me to remove the injunction. So I went to him. I told him I knew all his doings; but they would be as secret with me as the grave, if he would only say the word that would let those people go. He didn't deny a thing; but laughed in my face, and cursed the negroes, — cursed them when he was under their roof, and eating their bread! He seemed to want to make every one as miserable as he was. Twenty times since, as the suit has been carried up from court to court these twenty years,* I have gone to him, and have always had the

---

* Incredible as it may seem, this suit was in the Kentucky courts for more than twenty years, and the negroes were only, at last, liberated by the order of General Garfield, after he invaded Eastern Kentucky.

same answer. You think he was penitent! True penitence bears fruit, and its first fruit is good-will to one's neighbors, — particularly to one's poor neighbors."

The younger man made no answer; but the woman said, —

"Say no more of him. Let him rest. He is in the hands of God. But what is to become of Rachel and her mother? Jackson Weddington has sot eyes on the girl. Do yer think he means to marry her?"

"No, mother," said the son. "He would treat her as he did poor Lucy. Her father feared it, and so I promised him I would marry her."

"Marry her!" echoed the older Jordan, his florid face flushing a deeper red. "Marry the daughter of such a man — a low thief, and a"—

He checked himself, and the woman added, —

"And the darter of sich a 'ooman, — allers uncontented, allers flyin' in the face of Providence! The father was bad enough, but the mother is worse; and Rachel takes arter her. She cares fur nothin' but dress and show. John, she'd never make ye happy."

"Happy!" echoed the son. "The man who aims at happiness always misses his mark. Duty is the one thing to think of; and it is my duty to marry Rachel."

A short silence followed. It was broken by the older Jordan, who had sat with his head in his hands, as if repressing some deep emotion.

"I have nothing to say," he said. "You are obstinate, John, — obstinate as a mule; but you take it from men who died for their faith, — died to give freedom to Scotland. I've nothing to say, only I wish, — no matter to what it had

7

led, — I wish I had sent you away to get an education. Then this disgrace might not have come upon your old mother and father."

His head sank again into his hands, and no more was spoken.

And now having, during the twenty years that are covered by this chapter, nailed a few weather-boards upon our *one-story* building, and revealed enough of the inner life of our rustic hero to make credible the marvels of his future career, we will leave those three sitting there in the dim light of the early winter morning, and plunge into the thick-coming events that follow.

CHAPTER IV.

EATH comes seldom into this quiet valley; but when it does come, its voice echoes among its rustic homes like the sound of a great tree falling in a still forest, and now, though it is a week-day, and a heavy fall of snow obstructs the narrow roads, the simple dwellers of the district have gathered, from far and near, to pay the last rites to the dead at the lonely church at the cross-roads. It is a rude, unshapely structure of logs, but through its low doorway a nameless multitude have passed to the shadowy realm of the immortals; and now all that could die of another soul is waiting on that rude bench to join the silent throng who are sleeping the long sleep in the little graveyard.

The rude people are seated around on the rough benches, oppressed by the silent awe which all feel in the presence of death; and on low seats in front of the platform are two women decently clad in black, their faces hidden in the wadded hoods, which are the winter head-dress of their class in this region. These women are the mourners, and it may be that only they will drop a tear over the dark, unloved man, who soon will be at rest in the winter's snow forever. But no, — other eyes are wet, and another head is bowed in sorrow.

(75)

An old negro sits at the right of the platform, among the
choristers, his head resting on his hand, and his whole
frame trembling, every now and then, with suppressed emotion.   In one hand he holds a huge violoncello, worn, cracked,
and of a decidedly jaundiced complexion, but he clutches it
closely to his side, as if it were a living thing, — some old
friend, or near blood-relation.   Soon he lifts his head, and, as
he looks around in an absent way, we catch a glimpse of his
features.   They are broad, intensely black, and deeply furrowed; but in them, and in his deep, large eye, there is a sort
of slumbering power which at once strikes the beholder.   He
must be of great age, for his bushy hair is as white as wool,
and his flesh only thinly covers his bones in wrinkled layers;
but his large, almost massive frame is erect and apparently
as agile as that of a stripling.   Every square inch of his
body seems instinct with genuine manhood; and yet here,
where men are sold by weight, I doubt if he would, put up to
the highest bidder, bring a dollar a pound.

In a few moments the preacher advances to the little desk
which surmounts the platform, and, with a long prayer, opens
the services.   He is a gaunt, angular man, with a thin cadav-
erous face, and long bony arms, which, as he becomes
engaged in his work, flounder about the desk in the manner
of the finny tribe when first drawn from their native element.
The prayer is not a prayer; for it asks for nothing; and, indeed, the self-satisfied air of the man shows that he wants
nothing, at least nothing from any invisible region.   He
comes to an end at last, and then, in a strong, nasal drawl,
lines out a hymn, which is sung by the whole congregation.
The singing over, he begins the sermon.

It is an incoherent, almost blasphemous harangue, and unfit to be fully recorded. If dead men have to listen to what is said over their coffins, many a sensitive man would pray to have his eternity in the coldest corner of this world, rather than be condemned to hear the words spoken at his funeral. The preacher began by telling the Maker how he should govern the universe, and then he hinted at the disposition He should make of the sinful soul which had so recently gone to judgment. He was a bad man, — beyond a doubt he was a bad man, — everybody said so, though nobody know'd nothing certain agin him; but the preacher did know that fifteen years afore he had labored for his conversion, — labored like time, — and been met with a rude rebuff, which was the way sinners grieved away the sperit, and got lost forever inter the outer darkness. He trusted it warn't so with him; but if it war', he hoped the Lord would look with kind eyes on his sinful life, and deviate enough from his custom in such cases, to give him a place in Abraham's bosom. If he would, it would afford particular consolation to the mourning women who were weeping beside his coffin, and would, probably, not entirely derange the solar system.

The discourse contained, perhaps, a world of truth, but it certainly was little calculated to comfort the mourners. During its delivery the congregation listened with anxious and disturbed faces, and the two women sat with bowed heads, one of them weeping convulsively. The old black, however, was differently affected. He moved about uneasily on his seat, now and then clutching the violoncello as if he would crush it to atoms; and the sermon was no sooner over, than, springing suddenly to his feet, he gave vent to the fire

7 *

and fury which had been gathering within him. The scene that followed was one for a painter; and could have happened in no other than this primitive region.

While the people looked on with staring eyes, and the preacher stood, half-bending over the desk, transfixed with amazement, the old black drew up his majestic frame to its full height, and poured forth a torrent of impetuous words that would have entranced Demosthenes himself, — if he had been born with an ear for negro eloquence.

" 'Taint so!" he cried, " ladies and gemmen! 'Taint so! Parson Bradslaw don't know nuffin' 'bout it! 'Taint so; and 'taint fur him to come yere, and sit in de judgment on a feller-creeter as neber done him no wrong: and, p'raps, 'taint fur me to speak in meetin' to white folks; but ole 'Zeke wouldn't be de man as some on you hab know'd him fur nigh onter fifty year, if he sot still, and leff dis ig'rant parson send his pore massa, as is dead and gone, down among de hot debils. He haint dar! 'Zeke knows he haint dar; for warn't he wid him night and day for nigh onto twenty year, and couldn't he learn him all by heart in dat time? Maybe he done wrong, — dough 'Zeke don't say so, — but who don't done wrong? — not you, nor me, nor eben dis yere parson, who am paid to gib pore massa a decent berrying, but comes yere and sits down in de judgment on a feller-creetur. 'Taint Christian to git money under sech false pretensions, and pore Massa Israel — if he was a sinner — wouldn't have done no sech mean thing, no how. He neber done no mean ting, as I knows on; and I knows a heap he done like de good Samaritan. You've yeard ob him, — how when de priest and de Levite passed by on de oder side, he

went to de wounded man, bound up his hurts, laid him on
his own mule, and paid for his night's lodging. Now dat's
jest what Massa Israel done once to ole 'Zeke, who haint
nuffin' but a poor brack man. He war down sick wid dat
drefful sickness what kills all as comes nigh it, and de par-
sons and de doctors — dem am de priest and de Levite —
wouldn't come widin a mile ob him; but Massa Israel he
come, — he come, and he bound up his hurts, gabe him de cool
drink, and de hot broth, and tended him night and day till
dar warn't nuffin leff ob de dreffull sickness but de big scars
you kin see yit under dese wrinkles.

"Just tink ob dat, ladies and gemmen, — a gemman like
what Massa Israel was in dem days, a tendin' a poor brack
man, at de risk ob his own life, ebery night and day for a
whole fortnight! And what does ye spose he done den?
Why, dough it was agin de law, he larned him to read; and
it am all along ob him dat ole 'Zeke kin read de Bible, and
de hymns dat am sung in de great congregation. And does
you spose dat sich a man was a bad man, and am gone
down among de hot debils? I reckons not; and if you does,
you neber seed him, as ole 'Zeke hab seed him, a kneelin'
down in de woods, and a cryin' and a groanin' to de Lord till
de tears run down his cheeks, and he shook all ober like a leaf
in a gale ob wind, — a cryin' and a groanin' to de Lord to
tuck de burden off his soul, — to roll away de stone from
de door ob de sepulchre so he might come out inter de free air,
under de clar sky, and leab all his tattered, worn-out clo'es
ahind him.

"And now de Lord *hab* rolled away de stone from de door
ob de sepulchre, and massa hab comed out inter de free air,

under de c. ar sky, and am fass gwine up de ladder dat Jacob
seed in his dream, — dat ladder dat reach from de yearth to
de heaben, and on which de angels ob de Lord am allers as-
cendin' and descendin'.   P'raps he haint high up yit, —
p'raps he haint, — but afore he die he got his foot onter de
fuss round, and now it am on de second ; and dem as gits dat
high neber comes down agin, — neber comes down agin, but
goes on and up, till dey lands on de bery top, right in de
heabenly kentry.

"'S'cuse me, ladies and gemmen ; p'raps I've said what I
ortent to say to white folks ; but I couldn't holp it ; I couldn't
sot still, and yere my massa sent among de hot debils, — my
massa, as wid his dyin' breaf telled me he had made me a free
man, — made me a freeman, when he had nuffin' else in all de
worle, 'cept a ole cabin, and some sile as wont raise only rocks
and cow-peas, to leab to his wife and Missy Rachel.

"I know you don't tink sich a man as dat am gone among
de hot debils ; I knows you don't, ladies and gemmen, so I
wont say no more, — only dis : dat missus hab paid dis parson five dollar 'spressly to come yere from de village, and say
a kind word for pore massa ; and he haint done it.   He hab
done all he could to send him down among de hot debils ;
and arter doin' dat, he orter to guv back de money.   He
orter, and if he don't, some on ye gemmen, as is white, and
so kin be judge and jury, orter hev him up ter onct for gittin'
it under false pretensions.   I knows de law ; and it kin be
done ; for dem sort o' folks can't run loose in dis kentry, —
'cept on Sunday."

The negro sat down, and the preacher sprang to his feet,
fire and fury in his face and gestures.   While the black was

speaking, he might have driven a billet of wood into a solid rock more easily than have wedged a word in among his passionate sentences; but, when he had ended, the field was all his own, and he improved it in a singular fashion. He poured forth a torrent of denunciation which ended with, —

"I shake yer dust off uv my feet; I go, and I leave yer money with ye [here he suited the action to the word, throwing upon the floor a bank-note, which was instantly taken up by the negro]. I go, and I shall not return; for the Lord hath said, 'Let the dead bury the dead,' and 'Go thou and do likewise.'"

These irregular proceedings were so sudden, and so unexpected, that the congregation sat as if paralyzed till they were over; but when the excited preacher tore down the aisle toward the door-way, a number of persons rose to bring him to the pulpit and to reason; but the voice of the old black arrested any such intentions. Holding the bank-note aloft in his hand, he cried out, —

"Leff him go, ladies and gemmen! leff him go! He's leff more'n he'm worth ahind him. Massa Jordan'll go on wid de ex'cises, ef he wont; old Zeke don't want *his* massa buried as dat parson 'ud bury him."

Quiet was shortly restored, and the old Scotchman, entering the desk, concluded the services. Then the coffin was lifted upon the shoulders of four strong men, and, followed by the mourners and the rest of the congregation, was borne to the little graveyard on the other side of the highway. There it was placed on the snow, near an open grave, and the rude people gathered round to take a last look at its silent tenant.

The mourners stood apart, the older woman wringing her hands and weeping convulsively, and the younger silent and abstracted, as if her thoughts were far away in the dim region to which the spirit of the dead man had journeyed. So they stood while a hymn was sung, and the younger Jordan lifted the lid from the ground as if to nail down the coffin. The young woman then sprang forward.

"Not yet! not yet!" she cried. "I must see him once more."

Instinctively the people moved back from the grave, and left the dead and the living alone together. Kneeling down on the snow, she threw her arms about the stiffened corpse, and pressed her face against its pallid features. For a moment her lips moved as if in prayer; then she rose, and, turning to the young man, she said in a voice which had in it no trace of feeling, "You can go on, John, it is over."

They lowered the body into the grave, and as the first frozen sod fell upon the rude coffin, the young woman turned, and, with the other woman, and the old black, walked toward the highway. As she did so the wind blew back her hood and revealed her features. They were pallid, — pallid as those of the dead man, — but they wore a fixed, resolute expression, as if by some great effort of will she were keeping down her emotion.

She was tall, — somewhat above the medium height, — but of a slight and graceful figure. Her features were prominent, her chin was broad, and her face stern and almost hard in its outline ; but her forehead was full and wide, expressing benevolence and breadth of mind, and her large hazel eyes, though now burning with a sort of dead fire, had in them a

latent softness and warmth that showed she had the sensibility and tenderness of a true woman. She walked with a firm
and rapid step, holding the other woman by the hand, and
when she reached the highway, turned and said coldly to the
old black, "Bring the sled here, 'Zekiel. We will go home
now."

As the black went to do her bidding, two young men who
had followed them from the grave, approached the two women.
One was a short, squarely-built man of about thirty, with a
ruddy face, and an easy, good-natured expression; the other
a tall, spare, angular man, some years younger. He had
a dark skin, and coarse black hair, but regular, finely-cut
features, which would have been handsome, had they not been
overshadowed by large, sunken eyes of uncertain, if not sin-
ister expression. Like his companion, he was well-dressed,
and had the air of one who had mingled with the world.
Between him and the young woman there was a certain re-
semblance which would have struck even a casual observer.
It was not in the face, for hers was fair and open, with an expression which, though at the moment stern, had in it nothing
of evil; while his was dark and secret, as if he were nursing
thoughts too ugly to be allowed abroad in the daylight.
The likeness was in their general carriage, and in the whole
contour of their forms and features. He was evidently not
welcome; for, as he lifted his hat and met the eye of the
young woman, she turned away with a mingled look of dislike and terror.

"Had you not better go home in my sleigh?" he said, not
seeming to notice these signs of aversion. "The drifts are
heavy, and the road but poorly broken."

"Thank you," answered the elder woman, between her sobs, for she was still weeping. "We"—

Before she could say more the younger one interrupted her with "No, no, mother. We'll go alone; we'll not trouble you, Mr. Weddington." This she said in a low tone, with her face still averted, and a hard emphasis on the last words.

" It will be no trouble," he said, blandly, and moving a step or two forward to catch a glance at her features. "No trouble, I assure you."

"We knows it wont be," sobbed the elder woman. "Ye's allers *so* kind, Mr. Weddington. We'd better go, Rachel. 'Zeke ar' so blind, he'll tip us inter the first snow-bank."

" *You* can go, mother, if you like. I will ride with 'Zekiel," said the younger woman, now turning round and meeting the glance of the young man firmly; but her nostrils dilated, and she drew a quick breath, as if the words cost her an effort. " To-day I prefer to be alone."

"It is natural you should, and, believe me, I wouldn't obtrude my attentions on you," said the young man in a tone which was as soft as the gentlest zephyr.

" We is in great sorrer," moaned the elder woman, " great sorrer; and, O Mr. Weddington, what will become on us? —two lone wimmen, with not a dollar, and not a friend in all the wide wurld,—in all the wide, wide wurld!"

"Hush, mother," said the daughter, in the same low tone as before. "We have hands,—we can work,—God will not leave us friendless."

"Spoken like a true 'ooman," now said the older of the two men. "Keep up a good heart, Rachel. Ye'll not want a friend so long as Brad. Brown ar' above ground."

"Nor so long as I live," said Weddington, "shall you want anything that money can give you."

The young woman turned rather impatiently away, and the elder broke into a perfect hurricane of thanks, in the midst of which the old negro drove up with the rude sled which had conveyed them to the funeral. It was a rough box, supported on a couple of saplings, bent so as to serve as both shafts and runners to the vehicle; and it was attached by a rope harness to a quadruped old enough to have forgotten all about his colthood.

The old black sprang nimbly to the ground, saying "All a-ready, missus," and the younger man held out his hand to help the younger woman into the sled, whose sides were nearly as high as a five-barred gate. As he did so, the old negro brushed him rudely aside, and, catching his young mistress lightly in his arms, lifted her into the vehicle. The movement was so sudden, and so violent, that it well-nigh took the white man off his feet. In a moment he turned fiercely on the black, and, with a fearful oath, aimed at him a blow, which, if it had taken effect, would have laid the old man prostrate. But the black stepped nimbly aside, the other's clenched fist hit only the thin air; and, obeying the laws of motion, he went headlong into a snow-bank. Springing instantly to his feet, he was about to repeat the blow, when the younger Jordan, who had now come up, caught his arm, saying, —

"Think of it, Weddington! Only a coward will strike a negro."

Weddington's face, which when he rose was a flame of fire, now took on a dull, leaden hue, and quickly drawing a long

8

knife, he sprang upon Jordan.   The latter caught his de-
scending .hand, and the two struggled for a moment.   Then
the knife fell to the ground, and, with one lift of Jordan's
powerful arms, Weddington was again buried in the snow-
bank.

The old negro, as if unconscious of any personal concern in
these rude gymnastics, had, meanwhile, lifted the elder woman into the sled; but now he turned upon the prostrate
man, his black face glowing like burning anthracite.

"Massa 'Squire," he growled out, "you'm a coward and a villun to boot — you am!   Ole 'Zeke knows you, — know'd you
afore you was born.   You's a coward, or you wouldn't strike a
man as the law wont 'low to strike you back; and you's a villun, or you wouldn't ha' said to Missy Rachel what you said
lass night, — lass night wid her dead fader in de house.   But
jess you 'member, Massa 'Squar', I'se her fader now, — Ole
'Zeke,"— and he drew his six feet two inches of manly sinew
up to their full height, " and ef you eber comes nigh de cabin
agin, — ef you eber sots dem snake's eyes ob yourn onter
Missy Rachel, — 'spectful or not 'spectful, — ole 'Zeke 'll whale
you till you can't stand, — till you'll wish de Lord neber'd
make anoder darky.   He will, — shore as his name am 'Zeke,
— law or no law."

With this the old negro took the reins of the rude vehicle,
and drove away amid the smothered gratulations of the people
who had gathered round, attracted by the disturbance.   When
they were out of hearing, the elder woman, hushing her sobs
for the occasion, said to the negro in a sharp, gritty tone, —

"It war jest like ye, 'Zeke.   It war yer everlastin' querrel-
some speret.   Ye's allers gittin' us inter trouble.   Ye's mor-

tally 'fended that good man, Parson Bradslaw; and now ye's
lost us the best friend we's ever had."

The black turned about, and looking at the woman, a smile
of mingled contempt and pity on his features, he said,—

"What wud you hab, missus? What wud you hab?
Wud you pay five dollars to hab pore massa sent to de debil,
and den ax de young 'Squar' to make Missy Rachel a ting
as decent folk wont wipe dar shoes on ?"

"Mr. Weddington wouldn't do no sich thing," snarled the
woman. "He's our best friend. Rachel shill write him ter
onct, 'pologizen' for your conduct. If it hadn't been for him
we'd never hev got through with all the docterin' and 'spence
uv this winter."

"Yas, we would," responded the negro, turning about
again, and venting his feelings in a smart lash on the back of
the mule. "We'd ha' got fru, 'case, if he'd knowed it, pore
massa wud ha' died wid takin' the fuss dollar. He neber
wanted no money as wasn't his'n, and 'Zeke haint a gwine to
sleep more'n five hour a night 'fore he pay back dat ar' fifty
dollar."

"Fifty dollars haint nothin' to him," said the woman.
"He's plenty o' money."

"I knows," answered the black, "and dat am all he'm got.
And leff me tell you, missus, — I don't mean no 'fence; but
now dat massa am gone, it comes onter me to luck arter de
fambly, — you wont git Missy Rachel to 'pologize to de
young 'Squar' for nuffin', — 'case 'Zeke wont 'gree to it; and,
— you yered what I telled him, — ef he eber sots eyes on her
agin, I'll hab de black soul out ob his body, — I will."

The old negro accompanied this energetic speech with another energetic gesture directed to the back of the innocent mule ; but, instead of offending, his remarks seemed only to alarm his mistress. She was evidently accustomed to being ruled by a stronger will, and not unused to having such control asserted even by the old black. In a subdued but somewhat petulant tone she asked, " And what has he done that ye sh'ud speak so uv Mr. Weddington, as was allers sich a friend to yer master, — allers, ever sence he come to live in the new mansion ? "

" Wall," said the negro, " ef Missy Rachel hasn't tell'd you, 'Zeke can't ; but if he'd sot by when the 'Squar' done it, he'd a wrung his neck, — wrung it quicker'n he wrung de ole rooster's dat made de broth for massa's lass dinner."

" What was it, Rachel ? " said the elder woman, addressing the younger, who until now had sat with her hood drawn over her face, apparently unconscious of what was going on about her.

Without lifting her eyes, she answered, — " He has done nothing, mother ; he has said what no honest man would say to a woman, — what gives 'Zekiel a right to detest him ! "

" You's my own gal, Missy Rachel ! " exclaimed the old black, a tear glistening in his eye, and rolling, like a silver bead, down his dark visage ; " you's a credit to yer bringin' up, — old 'Zeke hasn't lubbed you, like he lubs his own soul, for nuffin."

The young woman raised her eyes, and a soft, gentle, almost tender look, came into her face, but she said nothing ; and the rest of the way the three rode along in silence.

Meanwhile the people at the little church had scattered to their several homes, and the two young men, in a richly-furnished sleigh, drawn by a pair of gayly caparisoned horses, were floundering along over the drifted road, on the way to a stately mansion at the head of the valley. For a time they rode on in silence; then the one who had christened himself Brad. — probably short for Bradley — said to the other, " Wed., what ar' atween ye and Rachel ? — what ha's ye said to the gal as has so riled the ole darky ? "

" Nothing," answered Weddington, " that you wouldn't say to any pretty woman ; — told her she is handsome, and that I would be glad, now her father is dead, to do her a service."

" If she paid ye the price ? " asked the other, with a curious smile.

" Why, yes. I didn't say that; but I suppose it was understood."

Brown was silent for a moment, then, with a strong savor of contempt in his voice, he said, " Well, Weddington, I used ter think ye a decent feller, ginerally ; but I begin to b'lieve ye's a d——d scoundrel. Ef ye done that, with the old man dead in the house, 'taint no wonder that even a darky dispises ye ! "

The other started as if stung by a wasp, and said, in a sudden rage, " How ? What is that you say ? "

" 'Taint worth sayin' over," answered Brown, coolly. " Them is my sentiments ; but — we has business together, and I never lets words come atween me and business."

The midnight lightning leaves the sky of a deeper blackness ; so the sudden flash which then lighted up the face of Weddington left it darker than before. A close observer would have seen danger in the look ; but Brown was not a close observer, — he was only one of those simple souls who

go through the world seeing nothing larger than a dollar, or a
glass of whiskey; and yet, if he had looked above his eyes,
even he might, at that moment, have beheld, suspended over
his head, the sword of Damocles, — that famous weapon
which, were it not of most wonderful metal, would long
ago have been worn out by the frequent handling of simile-
hunting writers.

Weddington's voice, when he spoke again, was as soft as the
low wind of summer, or as an April snow-flake when embrac-
ing a pool of water. "I've fancied, sometimes," he said,
"that you liked the girl."

"Well, p'raps I does," said the other, slowly, and as if he
preferred to change the subject.

"Then, why don't you marry her?"

"Well, I may hev thought uv that; but I reckoned ye hed
an eye to her; and, to talk squar, I feared ye mought put it
atween me and the business."

"Pshaw! you ought to know me better," said Weddington,
as if hurt in a sensitive quarter. "Friendship is friendship,
and business is business. Give me a lien on the other boat,
and I'll lend you another thousand."

"Ye will!" exclaimed Brown, his recent reserve disappear-
ing with the words. "It's jest what I wants; for the floatin'
debt is a-botherin' me. Will ye make it for a y'ar, and put it
all in black and white?"

"Yes, and extend the rest, so you'll feel easy."

"Well, ye is a trump!" said Brown, with enthusiasm.
"But," and now he spoke more slowly, as if he had some latent doubts of Weddington's sincerity, "does ye r'ally mean
. to give up the gal?"

"Give her up!" exclaimed the other, while again the lightning flashed, leaving his face again in deeper darkness. "You'd think so, if you'd heard her last night. Seven devils got into the girl. I believe she'd have turned me out of doors, man as I am, if I'd stayed a second longer."

"Well," said the other, "ye has the impudence uv the devil, or ye wouldn't ha' spoke to her agin."

"Pshaw, Brown, you're a fool! A man isn't a man if he can't pocket an insult," rejoined Weddington; adding, after a moment's pause, as if he feared so sublime a sentiment might not be appreciated by his companion, "from a woman."

Neither spoke for a little time; then the younger broke the silence. "When do you mean to pop the question?"

"Not just yit; I'd best wait till the old man's cold in his grave. To ax her now mought look like crowdin' the mourners."

"Perhaps it might," replied Weddington; "but you mustn't put it off too long. That fellow, Jordan, has an eye upon her. He's a dreamy fool; but he has wonderful power over the girl."

"Pshaw! he can't hev no showin' with a stylish gal like Rachel; but I wont put the thing off too long. Will ye make them papers out to-day, so I kin go back in the mornin'?"

"Yes, and give you the money."

By this time they had reached the mansion, — one of the better class of Southern houses, and located on a gentle knoll which overlooked a fine plantation of a thousand acres. A servant was at once despatched for a justice, and, that functionary shortly arriving, a paper was soon drawn up,

signed, sealed, and witnessed, which recounted, in the ver
bose language of the law, that "Bradley Brown, for, and in
consideration of the sum of four thousand dollars, lawful
money of the United States (the amount of the previous
debt and of the new obligation), to him in-hand that day
paid by Jackson Weddington, did sell, assign, transfer, and
make over to the said Weddington, as his rightful property,
the two stern-wheel steamers, then lying and being at the
wharf in the town of Paintville, in the State of Kentucky,
and intended to be employed in the navigation of a certain
river, called the Big Sandy; which said steamers were the
sole and only property of the said Brown; and were named
and known, as, respectively, 'The Transfer,' and 'The Potwin.' The said sale to vest the ownership of said 'stern-
wheelers' in the said Weddington absolutely, providing
the said Brown failed, within one year from the date of said
instrument, to repay to said Weddington the aforesaid sum
of four thousand dollars, with interest thereon, at the legal
rate current in the said Commonwealth of Kentucky."

When this was done, and the justice had gone, the two
men sat down at a table with a decanter of brandy before
them. Toward daybreak they rose, and Brown staggered to
his bed with the contents of the decanter in his head, and
a huge roll of bank-notes in his pocket. Brandy is com-
monly thought a bad thing for any but sickly people, and
money a good thing, — so good that sick or well can take it
in the largest doses; and yet, Brown might better have swallowed all that was set before him, brandy and decanter to
boot, than have gone to bed with those bank-notes in his
pocket.

Late one night, a week afterward, the same two sat together at the same table, with the same brandy-bottle before them. Weddington drank sparingly, — temperance is one of the cardinal virtues, and he was a temperate man, — but he plied his friend with glass after glass of the red fluid. "Pshaw!" he said, "don't run at the first fire. Try again, 'Faint heart never won fair lady.'"

"But, I tell ye," replied Brown, speaking thickly, — for brandy, taken freely, stiffens the tongue, as starch stiffens a shirt-collar, — "she refused me plump, and said, squar out, I hadn't money enough."

"Oh ho!" exclaimed Weddington, his eyes emitting a flash which, for a moment, encircled his dark face with a halo not altogether saintly. "Sits the wind in that quarter? Ask her again in a fortnight, and I'll bet a hat she'll say 'Yes,' and thank you."

"Why should she? I carn't make a fortin' in a fortnight."

"But I can make her think you have one in a day. I'll set the gossips upon her before the week is out, and make her believe you roll in money."

"No, no, Wed., that wouldn't be squar dealin'; and fa'r play ar' a jewul. I never sail under false colors; besides, she'd find it out, and the devil 'ud be to pay arterwards," answered Brown, who, though far gone from original righteousness, was not wholly given over to evil.

"Pshaw, you're a fool!" said the other. "Suppose she does find it out, she'll not blame you. The sin will be mine, — you'll have nothing to do with it."

"No, no; I carn't 'gree to it, Wed. Ye mean right, and

'twould be all for my advantage; but, if I let ye do it, I couldn't never look the gal in the face."

"You're more nice than wise. But never mind; pluck up courage, and ask her again in a fortnight."

"Well, I will," answered Brown, nerving himself with another glass of brandy. But, honor, Ned! Don't ye give the gal no false notions."

"Don't be alarmed," said his friend, "I'm not in the practice of lying, — unless something can be gained by it."

An hour afterward the two men went to their beds, — Brown tacking from side to side, as he was swayed by the troubled sea of fire in his stomach, and Weddington going straight on, with the firm and steady stride of a man who is moved by a resolute purpose.

CHAPTER V.

FORTNIGHT has gone by, and late at night a ruddy fire is blazing through the windows of Irving's cabin. A man opens the door, and pauses for a moment, with his hand upon the latch; then, with a slow, swaying step, he turns towards the highway. He stops in the road, and looks up at the ruddy moon, which is silvering the silent snow, and drawing strange pictures in the fields where the trees cast their shadows; then he sinks to the ground, his head falls upon his breast, and a great cry goes from him. It is the cry of a soul waking from a long dream, — waking to find that all is cold and dark in the universe.

Soon a man glides from around the corner of the cabin, and comes to the one in the highway. He lays his hand lightly on his arm, and in a deep voice says, —

"Don't you tuck it so to heart, Massa John; don't you. De good Lord am leff in the heabens!"

"I know, I know," says the other, rising. "He is there; but his face is behind the clouds. Good-night, 'Zekiel;" and with his swaying step, which now is almost a stagger, he goes again slowly forward.

The other follows, and in a moment speaks; his voice now being even yet gentler.

"No, no, not 'good-night,' Massa John! Old 'Zeke wont leab you now, when it'm so dark dat you can't eben see de Lord's hand afore you."

He said no more, but wound his arm about the other's neck, and so the two — the black, and the white — staggered along through the drifted snow-banks. At last the white man paused in the shadow of a great tree which cast its broad branches over the desolate highway.

"'Zekiel," he said, suddenly, "you love me, and — Rachel?"

"Lub you? Massa John!" exclaimed the negro. "Why, you'm my chillen — my chillen!"

"Then watch over her, — watch over her, day and night. It may be that God has put her very soul in your keeping."

"What does you mean, Massa John? What hurt kin come to Missy Rachel?" asked the negro, his voice trembling with a sudden emotion.

"I don't know, I only *feel* she's in danger. It's in the air. I scent it as the bloodhound scents a panther. Some terrible thing is following her."

As the moonlight fell on the old man's face, it was of a blue, livid color.

"I knows, I knows, Massa John," he said, earnestly. "You hab a mazin' feelin' ob tings as can't be seed, but am a comin'. And can't you scent de *way* it'll come? Can't you do dat, Massa John? Can't you do dat?"

"Yes, from Weddington."

"De good Lord!" and the negro started back in sudden terror. "Why, he'm her own " —

"I know," said Jordan, "and I wish I could tell him *all* I know. It might save her."

The negro's superstitious confidence in the prescience of the white. man had overcome him at the sudden announcement; but now his natural bravery and trust in God came back to him.

"Don't you say a word, Massa John. Not a word. Leab it in de grabe along ob pore massa. He suffered enuff, — don't leff it come outer Missy Rachel. And don't you worry 'bout de young 'Squar'. He'll neber come nigh her. He'm as feared ob me as he am ob de debil. I seed it in his eye at de meetin'."

"Don't be too sure, 'Zekiel. He'll burrow under ground. That is the way of such men."

"Under or 'bove ground, he wont root ole 'Zeke out ob de hole," and the old man laughed at his own grotesque imagery. "He'll freeze to Missy Rachel loike death froze to de dead herrin'. De Lord haint leff him outlast all ob his kin, and lib dese nigh onto eighty year, for nuffin', — it am fur Missy Rachel!" and here the old man threw back his broad chest, and drew up his great frame, till he looked like some gigantic statue moulded out of iron, and suddenly dropped there in the shadows.

"Don't be too sure, don't be too sure, 'Zekiel; there's something deeper here than you reckon. To-night she's told me that she is to marry Brown, and to live like a lady. Who told her Brown was rich? Nobody else thinks so."

"Why, bless you, it *am* so, Massa John! 'Zeke kin read,

9

and he hab seed de papers dat make ober dem two stern-wheelers to Missy Rachel."

A singular light flashed from Jordan's eyes; it was gone in a moment, and he said, as·if speaking to himself, but in his usual manner, "I see it all, — she can't be saved, — she will have to suffer. Oh, the ways of God are wonderful! The father plunged into unheard-of crimes, because he would be a gentleman; and now the daughter must drink of the bitter cup, because she would be a lady. Thus He visits the sins of the fathers upon the children! Only suffering will wash out the evil she has taken from him, — so she must go through the fire. I see it all; it is for this that she turns from me, and goes to that drunken fellow. And, O Father!" and here he looked up, and over his face came a radiance that was not of the moonlight, "forgive me, if, for one moment, I have questioned."

Along with his undoubting faith in the intuitions of the young man, the negro had a strong veneration for his singular but elevated character. This veneration usually led him to listen in silence to the strange rhapsodies which often broke up the other's ordinary speech, making it flow like a mountain brook, rippling over rocks and pebbles; but now anxiety for his young mistress gave him utterance.

"What am it you see, Massa John?" he said. "What am it?"

"What I should have seen an hour ago, — the hand of God, — which neither you nor I can turn aside or hinder."

"But mus' de pore chile suffer? Mus' she go fru de fire 'fore she kin come out cl'ar, and fit for de Lord?"

"She must. I never saw her soul till to-night. At bottom it is pure and clear, but it is crusted over with the same passions that ruined her father."

" And mus' de great sin come onto her? " asked the negro, his huge frame bowing down, as if a world were suddenly thrust upon his shoulders. " Oh, keep her free ob dat, Massa John ! keep her free ob dat ! Tell her — go back, and tell her to-night ! 'Zeke would — only it would break his old heart."

" No, no, 'Zekiel, tell her nothing. She'll be kept from that, if you are with her. The young 'Squire has over her the power that a snake has over a bird ; but he can't use it if a stronger love is round her. So you keep near her, and say nothing. Leave the rest to God. Now, good-night, — mother'll be waiting for me."

" Good-night, and bress you, Massa John ! De Lord bress you ! " .

Then the two went opposite ways; but now it was the young man who walked with a firm, manly stride, and the negro who staggered along under a load he had not the power of lifting.

Before another fortnight had gone away, Rachel Irving had become Rachel Brown, and, with her mother, had exchanged a mean hut of logs for a comfortable house in the village. There the older woman soon forgot her grief for her husband ; and, to tell the truth, that feeling had never been very deeply rooted. At best, it was only a wretched compound of regret for a man whom custom had made tolerable, and a selfish concern for her own future, — in which the latter feeling was much the larger ingredient. But now her future seemed assured; and she was too much engrossed in the excitements of her new life to waste a thought on the dead man who had for so many years been to her so strange a mystery. The world was giving her all that it has to give to such shallow natures, — attendants, friends, fashion. When she walked she had velvety carpets under her feet; when she slept, a gorgeous canopy over her head; and, when she took an airing, a gilded carriage, in which to flaunt the faded charms that had so long been wandering in the wilderness. What more could a reasonable woman, on the shady side of forty, ask for? To do her justice, she did not ask for more. She revelled in an excess of happiness. What a pity it is that such women cannot live here and roll in luxury forever! Here they do some good, — help to support those useful members in society, the pastry cooks and the men-milliners, — and they can be of no possible use in any other quarter of the universe.

But what of Rachel? How did she take to this life of gilt and gingerbread? Just as if she had been born to it. Before she had been a fortnight married, she lent more grace to a *moire antique*, cut in an ancient fashion, than many a town belle lends to the most modern costume, just from Paris. She did the honors of her husband's house, and spent his money beautifully. He was much away; for he was master of one of his " stern-wheelers," and with it made semi-weekly trips to Cincinnati and Louisville; but that made no difference to his wife. With visits and balls and parties, she got along very well without him, — in fact, better without than with him; for a troublesome fondness which he had for a full decanter made him, at times, too boisterous for the refined society of the high-bred people with whom Rachel was now familiar.

During the first three months of her marriage she saw nothing of Weddington; though her husband often spoke of him, and she learned that they had intimate business relations. Then, one day, they had an appointment together, and Weddington came to the house just in the edge of the evening. She was in the parlor when he entered. Their eyes met, and over her face came the look it wore that winter day, when she stood by the grave of her father. Rising suddenly to her feet, with the air of a queen, she swept out of the apartment.

The next day her husband — then in a sober mood — said to her, —

"Rachel, I'd like ter hev ye civil to Weddington. I knows he's spoken to ye as he ortent to speak to no 'ooman; but he's sorry for it, — and if ye haint, he mought trouble me; he mought ax me fur money as I can't pay him till times is better."

Poor Rachel had already learned that gold can gild bedroom and parlor furniture, but not the coarse natures of even those who love it best; yet until now she had not suspected her husband of downright baseness. A quick spasm shot across her face; but she only said, —

"Well, let him come, if you would have your wife insulted in your own house."

"Pshaw! he'll give you nary insult. He mought do that to a gal as had no father; but he'd be afeared to say a word to *my* wife. If he did, I'd have his heart's blood, and he knows it, — money or no money."

9 *

The blunt sincerity of the man reassured Rachel, and she said, —

"Well, let him come ; I have no fear."

He did come, and the door once open, he came often ; but, for a long time, always on some business with her husband. At last he called one day when Brown was away on the river. Ezekiel, who was a sort of major-domo to the establishment, saw him coming, and quietly took a seat outside the parlor door, in the hall-way. He did not listen to their conversation, — he did not care to, — but, somehow, the old fellow crossed the long bridge of years, and fancied that he was carrying her about in his arms, as he was used to in her childhood. Weddington did not stay long, but when he left, Rachel bowed him politely out of the parlor, and, as he closed the outer door, she turned to Ezekiel, and said, —

"'Zekiel, do you think this a cold day ? "

" Cold, Missy Rachel ! " echoed Ezekiel. " It'm de hottest day ob de whole summer. I'm a'most roasted."

" So am I ; but the 'Squire complained of the cold, — said he was nearly frozen ; and he did seem to be all of a shiver."

" He ! he ! " laughed the old black ; but, as his mistress went up the stairway, this natural expression of his race changed into quite another part of speech. " Ho ! ho ! " he said to himself, in an undertone, a look of curious wonder coming on his face. " It *did* fix him ! What a wonderful sight inter t'ings Massa John hab ! I b'lieve he know all de secrets ob creation. Jess leff dat ar Squar' come yere often enuff, and I'll froze him inter a icicle."

The 'Squire did come often enough, but was not frozen, though the winter came and went, and his visits grew all the

while more and more frequent. He never came when Brown
was away, but Ezekiel took his seat in the hall, and both by
his manner, and by that subtle will-power which Jordan had
told him to exert, tried to give the house the atmosphere of a
refrigerator. Weddington may have felt this, but it did not
hinder his coming; and yet who knows but the great love of
that faithful heart may have encircled her young soul with a
wall of ice, and so saved it from the clutch of the spoiler?
There is much in heaven and earth, reader, that you and I
have not yet fathomed; and this secret of the subtle power
of the human will is one of nature's deepest mysteries.

Mrs. Irving, as I have intimated, was, for the first time in
her life, perfectly contented. She thought she had all that
her heart could wish; but at last there came a slight ripple
on the calm sea of her enjoyment. One of the neighbors set
up a carriage. There had been carriages in Paintville before;
but none like this, with a footman's board, and a driver's seat
perched high up in the air, and looking for all the world like
an orthodox pulpit. She must have just such a carriage, or
die of chagrin, and — go back to be buried beside her husband in the vulgar graveyard in the wilderness. New horses,
too, they must have; for one of theirs was spavined, and both
had bobtails, and necks that needed a constant check-rein.
She wanted animals with long tails, nimble legs, and that
would hold up their heads among folks. Such could not be
had about Paintville, though one-half of the district grew
nothing but mules and horses. They must send to Cincinnati
for a complete turn-out. She lay siege to Rachel; and Rachel,
after some hesitation, — for she knew he was up to his ears in
debt, — lay siege to her husband. Brown objected; Rachel

persisted; and at last he said, — he had just taken an extra glass or two of brandy, — "You shall hev them. I'll fix the thing somehow; if I don't, I'll be d—d."

His boat lay at the wharf, ready to sail at evening; and it was at once decided that Ezekiel should go along, and take charge of the new equipage. The old black heard the summons with absolute consternation. He stuttered, stammered, and went through all manner of guttural gyrations; but, at last, he managed to eject the words, —"I can't, Missy Rachel. I haint well; I'se too ole; I neber was so fur away in all my life."

He was told that that was a good reason why he should go, — he would see the world, and he ought to see something of it before he died. Then he grew suddenly lame, — "de rheumatics was a troublin' him bad;" but Rachel had no mercy on so sudden an attack; and finally, looking her full in the face, the old man said, —

"Wall, Missy Rachel, 'Zeke'll go, on one condition, and only on dat; and, if you don't promise dat, dey'll hab to tote him out feet foremose; and *den* he wont go."

"What is that, 'Zekiel?"

"Dat you don't speak to Massa Weddington while 'Zeke'm away; and dat, if he come to de house, you send word you'se 'gaged."

"And why shouldn't I speak to him?" asked Rachel, in a tone of only slight impatience; for she was accustomed to the freedom of the old man, and loved him with some of the great affection had for her.

"'Case, when 'Zeke am yere, de Lord kin tuck keer ob his little gal; but, if 'Zeke am 'way, p'raps de Lord can't do it."

She promised; and then, but with a heavy heart, the old man started on the journey.

The boat went down the river by night, stopping only to take in and land passengers and freight, at Catlettsburg, — a small town at the junction of the Big Sandy with the Ohio. The old man was accustomed to going early to bed, and he had not been long on board before he sought out his berth, and fell into uneasy slumbers.

His life had been one long prayer, and often by day he would lift up his voice "to Him who dwelleth in the heavens;" but it was only at night that he could come so near to God as to talk to him as one friend talks to another. Then, something in the stillness and darkness seemed to open the gates of his being, and to let into his soul the unseen world, whose pulses thrill with the heart-throbs of the Great Author of the universe. But this night he prayed; and the golden gates turned not on their hinges. All about him was darkness, and a thick shadow glided in between him and his Maker. At last it took shape, — huge, weird, unearthly, — and its form was that of Weddington! A blazing fire was in its eyes, and its long arms were reached out to clutch a sleeping victim. The victim was Rachel. The old man uttered a low cry, and with that cry, which held in its bosom the mighty breath of prayer, the figure faded. Then, in its place, came another, — a dark, silent man, wrapped about with grave-clothes. An unutterable look was in his hollow eyes, and with his skeleton hand he pointed southward. "Go," he said. "Upon the wind! She is in danger!"

With a sudden start, the old man awoke, and, springing out of bed, threw on his clothing. He went on deck; the

boat was just rounding to at Catlettsburg, and, hidden by
the darkness, he stepped off upon the landing. In a few
hours the consort of the "Potwin" came in on her return trip.
The old man went on board, and about an hour after noon
was again at Paintville. Springing ashore, he hurried to the
house of Rachel.

He entered softly, and, the parlor door being ajar, had a
view of the inmates. They were seated on the sofa. His
arm was about her waist, his hot breath in her nostrils; and
she was struggling in his grasp, as a tired bird struggles in
the net of the fowler. The old man looked for but a moment,
then with one bound he was upon them. Lifting Weddington in his brawny arms, he threw him, as if he had been a
man of cork, out of the open window. Then Rachel fell at
his feet, clasped his knees, and cried out, —

"O 'Zekiel! 'Zekiel! God has sent you!"

He lifted her up, and drew her closely to him on the sofa.
She wound her arms about his neck, put her soft cheek
against his; and so they sat there an hour together. When
he got up to go away, he said, —

"My little gal, say nuffin' ob dis. If massa should yere
it, he'd hab his life. Leab it all to ole 'Zeke."

In a few days Brown returned from Cincinnati. He had
missed Ezekiel, and had concluded he had not gone on board;
but he was rather glad of that, for it gave him an excuse for
not buying the turn-out. He had not been long at home, .
however, before he heard of the old man's assault upon
Weddington. Boiling with rage, he went to Ezekiel, and
demanded to know why he had laid his hand upon his best
friend.

"Don't you 'member, massa," said the old man, with immense deference, "what I say to de young 'Squar' dat day Massa Irving was buried?"

"Yes; but what has that to do with it?"

"Eberyting; 'case 'Zeke allers keep his word. You sees, when you'se to home, you rules de house; but when you'm away, ole 'Zeke, he'm de massa. Den he neber leffs de young 'Squar' show his face yere 'cept on good behavior. Wall, de lass time he come, 'Zeke didn't like his looks, — he'm allers stuck-up, you knows, — so he jess up and frowed him out ob de winder."

With this Brown exploded: "You d——d nigger, I'll teach you manners! You shall hev fifty lashes."

Ezekiel heard this with perfect coolness, but Brown set about putting the threat in execution. Rachel, however, learning of his intention, told him all; and this gave another turn to the proceedings. Instead of scoring the old black, the whip made acquaintance with the back of Weddington. Meeting him in the public street, Brown left him there so badly beaten as to be incapable of motion.

Disaster quickly followed. The boats were seized for the debt; and Brown's splendid furniture went under the hammer. In one day he was reduced from comparative affluence to abject poverty. But, to do him justice, he bore up bravely.

"Never mind, Rachel," he said. "I hev health and strength; you shill hev another kerridge. Go back, for a time, to the old cabin in the woods, and I'll go onter the Ohio. In a y'ar I'll be on my feet agin."

So Rachel went back to her father's mean hut; and so ended her short dream of living like a lady.

CHAPTER VI.

A WINTER NIGHT.

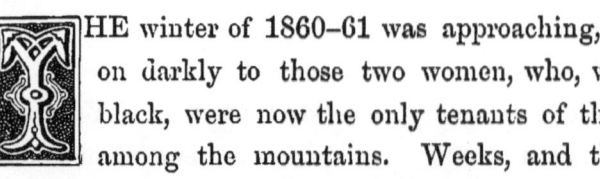HE winter of 1860–61 was approaching, and it came on darkly to those two women, who, with the old black, were now the only tenants of the lonely hut among the mountains. Weeks, and then months, had gone away, and no word, and, what was more important, no money had come from Brown; and now, with the cold weather upon them, not a pound of provisions was in the pantry of the comfortless dwelling. Ezekiel, in the early autumn, had got in fuel enough for the winter, and plastered up the chinks which else had let volumes of cold air into the scanty lower room of the long-deserted cabin; but even he could not make corn grow in the snow, or coin money from frozen sand-hills. When the single barrel of meal had dwindled to less than a single bushel, he went for assistance to the elder Jordan, — the younger having long been away, following his business of dealer in mules and horned cattle. The old Scotchman received him kindly; but when the negro, with moistened eye and a stammering tongue, disclosed the destitute condition of the two friendless women, he answered coldly, —

" The girl should not have married such a worthless fellow.

She should have learned to work, and not have set up for a lady. But I will not see you starve. How much bacon and corn-meal will you need a week?"

The old black was about to speak; but the words stuck in his throat, and, brushing a tear from his cheek, he turned and walked away, leaving the cold Scotchman lost in wonder at a revelation which is not so much as hinted at in the system of narrow, but even-handed, theology, that had been the constant study of his lifetime.

This was at the close of a stormy day in mid-winter, and the fire-light was blazing brightly through the windows of the little cabin when the old man opened the door and entered the desolate apartment where dwelt the two women. Rachel was spreading the table for their scanty evening meal, and her mother, lying on a poorly-furnished bed in the corner, from which she had scarcely risen since her return to their meagre home, was complaining, in low, querulous tones, of the hard fate that had reduced her to the wretched fare which Rachel had just set before her, when the old black, throwing off his ragged top-coat, turned to the elder woman and said, in a cheerful, sympathizing voice, —

"Say no more ob dat, missus. De Lord knows you's had a sorry bad time; but it'm ober now. He'm put an idee inter ole 'Zeke's head that'll keep us jess like we was in clober all de way till de nex' harvest, and longer'n dat, if 'Zeke haint able to get in a good crap. So you say no more, missus. 'Zeke'll fix de libin'. You leab him alone for dat; he haint read de Bible day and night, for dese more'n twenty year, widout findin' out how de Lord kin manage tings, when we gits to the end of de rope, and 'cludes we is gone up,

10

for sartin. And jess to think! it was pore massa dat larned
'Zeke to read, and so, it'll be *him*, dough he'm cold in de
grabe, as'll be savin' dem as he lubed from starvin', and not
his old darky, after all! He! he!" and the old man sat
down on the rude settle before the hearth, rubbed his hands
together, and stretched his huge feet out to the fire, with the
air of one who had suddenly come into a fortune.

The elder woman raised herself up in the bed, and said in
a whining tone,—

"Then, old Jordan'll holp us! I allers helt he was the
meanest, stingiest man I ever know'd; but I'll never say
ill of him agin — never agin."

"Wall, I wouldn't, missus," said the old negro ; "I wouldn't;
'case it haint de Bible way. But 'taint ole man Jordan as'll
holp us; it'm de Lord; and he'm a gwine to do it jess loike
he done wid 'Lijah in de Bible — only he feed 'Lijah wid de
ravens, and he'm a gwine to feed us wid de crows — de
woolly crows! He! he!" And he laughed heartily at his
own sorry witticism.

Rachel came to him, and putting her hand gently on his
shoulder, said, —

"How is it, 'Zekiel? If Mr. Jordan is not willing to
help us, how are we to be helped?"

The old man drew her down near to him on the settle, and
said, in a tone of inexpressible tenderness, —

"Massa Jordan was a willin' to holp us, missy. 'Zeke
tells you dat, fur he don't want you to do him no wrong, —
but 'Zeke wouldn't tuck his holp, 'case he find fault 'bout
you marryin' Massa Brown! — jess as if *he* had a right to
complain ob dat, when 'Zeke neber done complain, and neber

would, not if you'd a married de bery ole debil hisself, —
neber ; for you's his own little gal."

Here the old man's head sank forward upon his hands, and
two great tears rolled down from under his half-closed eyelids.
The young woman's arms twined themselves about his neck,
and in low, broken words, she said, —

"O 'Zekiel, 'Zekiel! how can I ever pay you for all
your love ? "

"Pay!" ejaculated the old black, looking up tenderly in
her face. "You hab paid me — paid me ebery day sense you
was born. But say no more ob dat,— jess leff 'Zeke tell you
de idee de good Lord hab put into his head, and den you'll see
how we'm a gwine to git fru de winter ; how de Lord am
a gwine to feed us like he feed 'Lijah — only wid de crows —
de woolly crows! He ! he!" And again he laughed, so
heartily as to choke, for a time, his utterance.

With a smile half of trust, half of incredulity, Rachel
drew herself back on the settle, and said, —

"Tell me, 'Zekiel, tell me."

"Wall, Missy Rachel, you knows dem Levites in de Bible,
— sorry bad set dey was, I reckon, de most ob 'um, — loike de
one dat go down to Jericho on de oder side, — but dey was de
Lord's chosen for all dat, and he gabe 'um de right to lib
scot free onto oder folks; and to hab ten dollar out ob
ebery hun'red; dough dey neber done a honest day's wuck
in all dar lives. Wall, jess now, when Massa Jordan was a
axin' how much corn an' bacon we'd eat a week, and ole Zeke
was jess a gwine to tell him, it comed into his head all to
onct, loike a flash, dat he'd ben a Levite to dese brack
Israelites on dis yere plantation for nigh onto forty year, and

neber got a cent; but hoed his own row, loike all de rest ob
dem. Wall, you see, dat comed to him, and he made up his
mind to onct jess to tell 'em at de next meetin' dat dey owes
ole 'Zeke board and lodgin' fur forty year; but he'll leff 'em
up on dat, if dey'll jess fork ober a tenth of all dey hab, till
de next harvest. Dey'll do it, — dey'll jump to do it; and,
bein' dar's more'n a hundred ob 'um, you knows enuff ob
figgers, missy, to count how much it'll come to, — why! it'll
keep us fur de year, buy a set o' 'hogony cheers, a new bed
fur de missus, a carpet fur de floor, and dress you up loike a
lady agin."

In his warm burst of enthusiasm, the old man had not observed the face of the young woman; but now he looked up,
and noticed the strange, almost despairing, expression on her
features. "What am de matter, missy? what am de matter?" he cried, in an earnest, anxious tone, the glow going
from his face in an instant.

Her head fell upon his shoulder, and she said, almost sob-
bing, —

"O 'Zekiel, 'Zekiel! To think I should come to this! —
to think I should come to this!"

The old man folded his arm about her, and drawing her
closely to him, said, in tones in which there was a strange
blending of rebuke and tenderness, —

"Dat am it, Missy Rachel; dat'm de pride de Lord meant
to git clean out ob both on us 'fore he'd holp us. It was in
ole 'Zeke. It stuck in his froat, loike it was a alligator, 'fore
he go to Massa Jordan; but he make up his mind to swaller
it down for de sake ob his little gal; and den de Lord, he
make up *his* mind to holp us, 'case 'Zeke had been and done

crucified dat ar ole Adam. And, honey, you do loike ole 'Zeke done, and de Lord, he'll turn round, and not send onto us no more truble; but lift up de clouds, and show us de sun, dat'm allers a-shinin' on de 'tother side ob Jordan. And dis yere haint loike gwine to dat ole Scotchman, dat was a beggin'; dis yere am only takin' what belongs to us; it'm only sayin' to dese yere folks, as hab owed 'Zeke for forty year, 'We'll forgib you de ole debt; but you must pay up in de futer'; if you don't, you can't hab no more preachin',' — and dey can't, not so long as ole 'Zeke am 'bove ground."

"Oh! but 'Zekiel, to take so much from such poor people!"

"Lor' bress you, missy, dey haint poor; dey's rich, — richer dan we am. But it needn't be so much, missy. If you says so, 'Zeke'll leff 'um up on de carpet, and de bed, and de 'hogony cheers, — only you and de missus must hab some warm clo'es fur de winter. 'Zeke am afeard she'm got her death wid dat ar' cold a'ready."

At the mention of her mother, the young woman rose, and said, in a subdued voice, —

"Well, 'Zekiel, let us say no more about it. It is the Lord's will. His hand I have not always seen; but now I see it. I will put away pride, and try to be a better woman."

Quietly then she took up the meagre loaf of corn-pone, which was baking before the fire, and placed it upon the table. Then, going to a closet in the chimney-corner, she brought out a plate, and a cup and saucer, and laid them opposite similar pieces of crockery ware which already adorned the scanty board. Then she turned to the old man and said, cheerfully, —

10 *

"Now, 'Zekiel, bring up your chair; let us eat our supper."

"Eat supper!" exclaimed the old man, shaking his head. "Not wid you, Missy Rachel. 'Zeke haint got to be so bad as dat yet."

Before Rachel could answer, her mother, who had been a silent but attentive listener to the preceding conversation, cried out, in an angry, querulous tone, —

"What do ye say, Rachel? Eat with 'Zekiel! — eat with a old black! I hope ye haint come to that! I'd starve fust!"

"Mother," answered the younger woman, in a firm but mild voice, "for twenty years you have been telling me that I am better than other people; and all that time God has been showing me that I am not, — that I am not half, no, not nearly half, so good as this poor old man. Now I mean to listen to God, and not to you or my own false pride. I mean to treat 'Zekiel like what he is, — our only true friend. Come, 'Zekiel, bring up your chair."

Without a word the old black rose, and came forward to the table. Then, brushing away a tear, he bent down his head and said a few low words. He meant them as a grace over the frugal meal; but, before he was aware of it, they had become a simple thanksgiving to the Great Father, who had touched his young mistress' heart, not to exalt him, but to humble herself, and to cast away that pride which had shut her eyes to the beauties of all but this world, and been a wall between her and Him, and the good angels who would come and be with her alway.

When the meal was nearly over, a knock came at the door,

and a tall, ungainly man entered the apartment. A huge
slouched hat half hid his face, and it was not till he had
spoken her name that Rachel recognized him as the younger
Jordan. Then she sprang suddenly to her feet, and a deep
crimson suffused her features. They had not met since her
marriage, and old memories may have come rushing on her,
or some lingering remnant of the pride she meant to conquer
may have revolted at being thus discovered at table with the
old negro. Whatever it was, the feeling vanished in a moment, and, extending her hand to the new-comer, she
said, —

"John, is it you? I am very glad to see you."

"I am glad to see you, Rachel," responded Jordan, a slight
tremor in his voice; "and 'Zekiel, how are you, — and you,
Mrs. Irving?"

"Poorly, right poorly," squeaked the older woman, raising
herself in the bed, and taking Jordan's offered hand; "and
O John! who'd ha' thought we'd ever come to this? — not
a bushel of meal in the house, and Rachel got to eatin' with
sarvints."

"She might do worse than that," answered Jordan, smiling, but with a strange gleam in his eyes. "I have had
many a dinner of cold bacon and hickory nuts with 'Zekiel,
and I hope to have many another."

The crimson glow again suffused the face of Rachel for a
moment; but she only said, —

"Sit down, John. You have been a long time away."

"Yes," he answered, seating himself by the fire. "After
selling the mules, I was kept at Frankfort, nearly a month,
by the lawsuit."

" And have the poor people at last got their freedom ? "

" No; the case was decided in their favor; but Cecil managed to get in something that will probably secure another
trial."

" It is a great wrong.   I don't see how such men can hold
up their heads among people."

" Cecil is a bad man; he would do anything for money.
He is the only one I know for whom I have a natural dislike.
But I have this moment got home, and have not eaten since
morning.   Don't you mean to ask me to supper ? "

" If you will take our poor fare, John," she answered, rising, and placing another plate upon the table.   " We are
very poor, — we hardly know how we shall get through the
winter."

" So father has just told me," said Jordan, seating himself
beside the negro.   " That is why I have come so soon; he
wants to help you."

" We doesn't want his holp, Massa John. 'Zeke hab
made oder 'rangements," said the negro, leaning back in his
chair with the air of an African king.

" Father was afraid he had offended you.   He is blunt, you
know; but he means kindly."

" 'Zeke doesn't know what he means, — he only know what
he say, — and he say to-night what 'Zeke don't leff no one
say 'bout his young missus.   'Zeke gub him a chance to do
a good action, and he'll neber hab anoder sich a chance if he
libs to be as old as Mathuselum."

" I am sorry you are offended, 'Zekiel."

" 'Fended, Massa John !   I'se wuss dan 'fended, — I'se
riled way down to de bottom.   And, leff me tell you, Massa

John, 'Zeke haint no patience wid dese folks dat make sich great pretensions, and doles out de good dey does wid a peck measure. De Lord don't do dat; if he did, dar haint a Scotchman livin' dat wouldn't starve 'fore de week was out."

"That's so, 'Zekiel," said Jordan, laughing at the earnestness of the negro. "But let us say no more about it. What arrangements have you made for the winter?"

"Neber you mind, Massa John — ' Zeke's made 'em, and you neber know'd him to broke down when he went 'bout a ting."

Jordan made no reply, but looked inquiringly at Rachel. Her face took on again a crimson hue; but she said, quietly, —

"He means to tithe the negroes; and, John, I have consented to it."

The strange gleam came again into the young man's eyes, as he answered, —

"Ah, Rachel! God teaches us in strange ways; but you have learned His lesson, and I am thankful."

No one spoke for some minutes; then the young man said,—

"'Zekiel must not apply to the negroes. It is as much as they can do to live. Here is enough to keep you through the winter."

With this, he drew from his pocket a leathern money-belt, such as is sometimes worn by travellers, and laid it upon the table. A sudden glow lit up the face of the negro, as, opening it quickly, he ran his eye over its contents.

"Fru de winter, Massa John!" he exclaimed, with not a trace of his recent dignity; "fru de winter! Why yere'm 'nuff to keep us fru twenty winters! 'Zeke kin count — yere'm more'n a t'ousand dollars!"

Rachel had sat without speaking, as if moved by contending emotions; but now she said, —

"No, no,. John, I can't take it — not from you, after " —

She said no more, but in her face the young man read the remainder of the sentence.

" You *can* take it, Rachel," he said.   " It is not a gift, but a debt.   For ten years your father taught me, — mother paid him all she could; the rest I promised to pay you, when he was dying."

She made no reply for some moments; then, the crimson glow again on her face, she said, —

" John, your mother more than paid my father, but I mean to have no false pride; I will take the money,— enough to carry us through the winter."

" Take the whole," he answered.   " I have no use for it. It is the capital on which I have traded; but now I have given up trading, — so I have no need of money."

" Given' up tradin' !   What am you gwine at, Massa John ? " asked the negro, still running the bank-notes through his fingers, with a look as gleeful as that of a child over a parcel of new playthings.

" Whatever is given me to do.   The South is threatening disunion, and the leading men are already rousing the people. Cecil has made appointments to stump the district, and they hope to carry out Kentucky.   I shall do what I can to pre-vent it."

" But what can you do, John ? " asked Rachel.

" Speak wherever he speaks; show the people it is for their interest to stay in the Union."

"And can you argue with such a man? You know he is one of the best speakers in Kentucky."

"I know. I have heard him; but I shall have truth on my side; and, Rachel, you know all my ancestors were preachers. Such things run in the blood; so it may be I have the gift of talking."

A look of pride came on the face of Rachel; but she said nothing.

The old black exclaimed, —

"'Zeke knows you hab, Massa John! He allers helt you'd orter to ha' been a preacher. But don't you trust in yourseff; jess you look to de Lord — He'll gib you de words, and de wisdom. He will! 'Zeke knows; fur, many and many a time, he's stood up in de little church, widout a word to say, and, 'fore he's sot down, he's had de whole house a groanin'."

"Well, this is the Lord's work," answered Jordan, smiling. "I know He will help me."

"And when do you begin?" asked Rachel.

"At once. Cecil speaks at Piketon to-morrow; and then, somewhere else, nearly every day during the winter."

"Well, the Lord be with you; I shall pray for you, John."

"I thank you, Rachel. It will help me."

Their eyes met; but it was his that now were dimmed with moisture.

"About the money, John," she said, taking the roll of bank-notes from the hand of the negro. "I will take enough for the winter."

"No, no," he said, quickly, "take the whole. You may want it. I fear terrible times are coming, — and I may not be here to help you."

"What do you fear, — not war?" she asked, eagerly.

"Yes; it must come, if the Cotton States persist in going out of the Union, — and they will."

"But you wont go into it, John? You wont go into it?" she said, her face turning to an ashy color.

"I must, Rachel, if it comes. The true work of my life will be in it. Ever since I balked father's plan of making me a preacher, I have known I had something to do in the world; and now my work is coming."

"But you will be in danger, John; you may not live through it."

"I shall not live through it."

Rachel started, and her face grew even more pallid than before. He noticed this, and said in soft, subdued tones, —

"Don't be alarmed, Rachel. Death must come to us at some time. I shall not die till my work is done."

The color came again into her cheeks, as she answered, —

"But you do not know that you will die. I have had such presentiments, and they have oftener been false than true."

He shook his head as he answered, —

"This is no presentiment, — it is knowledge. I have seen the shadows of the future. The other night, when I sat in the court-room hearing Cecil talk away the freedom of better men than himself, a cloud gathered round him, and in that cloud I saw — not with my eyes, but with my mind — the outlines of what is coming. He seemed to stand at the entrance of a long avenue which stretched out dimly beyond him. His hands were dripping with blood, and blood was on the hands and garments of nearly all that were about him. Soon I saw myself. My hands were clean, but blood was on my clothing. Then, again, I was far down the avenue in a prison, my hands as red as Cecil's; and then, again, I was farther down, — at the very end of the avenue. My hands were white, and a great light was breaking over my head; but I was on the ground, and — dying."

"And whar was Missy Rachel? Did you see her, Massa John?" asked the old black, who had listened with breathless attention.

"Yes, — she came to me in the prison;" and he bowed his head upon his hands, and no one spoke for many minutes. At last Rachel broke the silence, —

"Ah! John!" she said, "this is all imagination. You had been over-anxious about the trial and the country, and things have got mixed up in your mind so as to make this dreadful picture."

She said these words; but her face spoke quite another language. That told that she believed the vision.

"No, no, Rachel," he answered; "I have had such visions before, and the events have always followed. All men and all events cast their shadows before them. Few can read these shadows; but I can, and so could some of my ancestors."

"You have told me so, John; but you've said you never saw yourself in your visions."

"I never did before. This has been shown me for a purpose, — to prepare me for what is coming, — to fit me for the work I have to do."

"And what work do you see you have to do?"

"I do not see the work; I only see the end; but then my hands are clean, and I die for my country, as did the old Jordans."

11

As he said this, his gray eyes gleamed, and his dreamy face lighted up with a glow that outshone the fire-light. No longer able to restrain herself, the young woman buried her face in her hands, and sobbed out, —

"O John! John! to think that you must die, — you who are so good, so noble!"

He rose from his seat, and paced the room for a while in silence. Then he said, as if unconscious of any but her presence, —

"It is best, Rachel, — best for us both. God is good; he has opened your eyes, and that was all I wanted. Now the end may come, and the sooner it comes the better."

She made no answer, but kept her face buried in her hands. For a while longer he paced the room, then he came to her, and, reaching out his hand, said, —

"Good-by. I must go."

She looked up; her eyes were streaming with tears; but she took his hand, and said, —

"Good-by, John. You will come to see me when you can?"

"Yes, when I can. Good-by, 'Zekiel."

"Good-by, Massa John, good-by. De good Lord be wid you."

"He will be; for I shall try to do his work;" and, turning away, he left the apartment.

Half an hour later, when Rachel rose from her seat before the fire to clear away the tea-things, she saw the roll of bank-notes and the leathern belt on the table. Taking them up, she turned to Ezekiel, saying, —

"Why, look here, 'Zekiel! We have forgotten the money. Take it to him at once. He'll go away in the morning."

The old man looked into the fire, as if to ask counsel of the backlog, and then he said, —

"No, no, missy. Massa John am right. 'Twont be ob no use to him; and dar's no tellin' what'm comin'. Ole 'Zeke'll buckle de belt round his body, and de money'll be safer dar dan anywhar in creation."

CHAPTER VII.

HAT night Rachel did not sleep. She lay awake re-
volving the strange revelations of the strange man
who had been so great an enigma to her from her
girlhood. His earnest manner, and his own firm faith
in his singular vision, had at first inclined her to believe that
the terrible things he predicted were in truth coming; but
now, when the darkness brought calm thought, and she no
longer felt the powerful magnetism of his presence, her mind
revolted from its former conclusions, and she came to regard
it all as the dream of an excited imagination, the disordered
working of a sensitive nature, overwrought by anxiety, and
thrown from its true balance by the disturbing influences of
the excited court-room. She knew little of mental philoso-
phy; but she had often watched the workings of her own
mind; and could her own eyes pierce the shadows that shroud
the future? and, too, was it not said that since the last Evange-
list looked within the vail on the unacted realities of the life
to come, the vision and the prophesy had been sealed to mortal sight forever?

With these thoughts she rose when the first sunlight
touched the windows of the little cabin, and, going to the
head of the stairway, called the old negro.

(124)

" What am it, missy ? " he asked, thrusting his head from under the clothes of a scanty pallet that occupied one corner of the attic. " What'm broke loose so airly? "

" Nothing; only that money. John will need it; and I am afraid, if you don't go at once, he'll be gone before you get there."

" Lor' bress you, Missy Rachel, he *wont*. He'm right, — he'll neber need no more money ! 'Zeke knows; he seed it all lass night in a dream."

" What did you see ?" she asked, in a startled way.

" Jess what Massa John say. 'Zeke seed it all, way down to de lass, jess as he done."

" Of course you did," she answered, turning away with a gesture of impatience. "Your mind got absorbed in his story, and so you dreamed just what he told us."

" No, no, missy," and now his voice sunk to a low, husky whisper, as if some terrible dread had suddenly taken possession of him, and was half smothering his utterance. "'Zeke seed more, — seed it all, — and it all went afore him loike it went afore John, and Daniel, and ole 'Zekiel in de Bible; only it wasn't in blind figgers, but in plain folks, — me and you, and Massa John, and ole Massa Jordan, and de whole kentry, and all plowed up wid de red-hot cannon ob de battle-field. But 'Zeke'll neber leab you, missy, — neber! He'll stand by you if de lass day am a-comin', and — he reckons it am ! "

It is singular the magnetic force which dwells in some minds, and not in others, equally as earnest and equally as powerful. Ezekiel's will was strong; his convictions were earnest; but his nature lacked that subtle element which,

11 *

in Jordan, had transfixed the mind of his young mistress,
and made his dreams seem to her, while she was in his presence, to be living realities.

Giving no heed to the old negro's words, Rachel turned to
go down the stairway, saying, as she did so, —

"Well, 'Zekiel, get up; I shall send back the money."

"Not de whole, missy, not de whole? You wont make ole
'Zeke ax de toll ob dem ar' pore folks, as, wid de hard winter
and de eberlastin' lawsuit, haint more'n half a moufful fur
darselves."

Smiling at his sudden recollection of his constituents, Rachel answered, —

"No, we'll keep a hundred dollars. John would feel hurt
if we didn't; and that will support us till harvest."

The old black had scarcely turned into the high-road which
led to the house of the Jordans, when Rachel heard a low
rap at the door of the cabin. Wondering who could be coming to see her so early, she said, —

"Come in;" and a strange serving-man entered, bearing a
letter. Bowing to her, and handing her the missive, he was
turning to leave the room, when she said, quickly, "Who is
this from? Does it need an answer?"

"No, missus," answered the man. "Dat'm all I was telled
to say;" and he went as suddenly as he came.

She opened the letter, and a mingled look of dread and
loathing came over her features.

"Who ar' it from, Rachel?" asked her mother, whom the
coming of the man had awakened.

"Jackson Weddington," said the younger woman, catching her breath, and sinking down on the settle before the fire.

"From him! — the mean scamp! — I thought he was away out of the kentry."

"No; he is here, and I am to be persecuted by him again;" and she rested her head on her hand, and over her face came a look which was half despair, half indignation.

"What need ye to fear of him?" asked the older woman, in the querulous tone which had become habitual to her. "He ar' a coward. He went away only 'case he war afeard of another beatin' from Bradley."

"But Bradley is not here; and somehow, mother, he has over me a strange power. When he is near me, there come upon me the queerest feelings, — I lose all strength, and it seems as if I should smother."

"Never you worry, — he wont come nigh you. 'Zeke ar' yere, an' he ar' more afeard of him nor he ar' of Bradley;" and the old woman laughed a croaking, disdainful laugh, which plainly said that in her mind the white man who could fear a negro was the most contemptible of bipeds.

Rachel made no reply, and it was not long before the old negro entered the apartment. His glance fell upon Rachel, and in an instant, with the quick eye of affection, he detected her unusual emotion.

"What'm it, missy?" he said. "What'm broke loose now?"

"O 'Zekiel," she answered, looking up, and handing him the letter, "read that!"

He took the letter, and, as he slowly opened it, a bank-note fell from it upon the floor. Taking it up, he said, —

"Gor-a'massy! It sort ob rain money dis mornin'. A hun'red dollar! Wall, if Massa Jackson war only brack, he wouldn't fotch dat much under de hammer nohow. But leff 'Zeke see what he say." [Reads.]

"'MISSUS BROWN, — 'Spected madam (Ob course, "'spected," and s'pectable, too, Massa Jack : you'll find dat out 'fore you'm much older): I hab jess return to de mansion, and I jess yere dat you's in distress (not nigh so bad off as you, Massa Jack, wid all your money). I beg (he orter beg, and he *will*, in dat kentry whar ebery one'll git 'cordin' to his doin's) dat you'll 'cept dis triflin' ("triflin'!" wall, it am triflin'; 'Zeke hab got ten times dat, all his own, in his pocket; and ebery dollar ob it honest money) 'sistance.

"'From your true friend,

"'JACKSON WEDDINGTON.'"

The old man laid the letter and the money on the table, and, sitting down by the fire, looked fixedly into the blaze, and was silent for many minutes. At last he turned to Rachel, and, with an alarmed, but grotesque expression on his wrinkled features, said, —

"It'm a comin', Missy Rachel, it'm a comin'! what 'Zeke hab feared all his life, — eber sense he was a child, — eber sense his poor mudder die, as come from de kentry far ober de great sea."

"What is coming, 'Zekiel?" asked Rachel, catching a portion of his intense feeling.

"Blood, Missy Rachel! 'Zeke can't die wid clean hands, — can't die wid clean hands! His pore mudder say so, — and it'm true, — it'm true."

"But how could she know? How could she tell so many years ago?"

"She seed it, — seed it in 'Zeke's hand when she was dyin' in de ole cabin down in Virginny. You see she was born whar de sun shine more brighter dan it do yere, and whar de brack folks hab dat wonderful eyesight."

"Don't feel so, 'Zekiel. She couldn't see, — no one can see into the future."

"Oh, yas dey kin, Missy Rachel,—yas dey kin! Massa John am right, — ebery man and every ting frows his shadder afore him. All he'm to be and to do am writ on de a'r dat's born wid him; and dem as hab de eyes kin read de writin'. She seed on 'Zeke's hand de shadder ob de blood, and she say he couldn't neber die 'fore he'd sent a bad man to de judgment-day, — and it'm him, — dat letter show it'm him."

"But you wouldn't hurt him, 'Zekiel. He'll never dare to come here; so, he'll never give you occasion."

"He *will* come yere; he *will* gib 'Zeke 'casion, — de letter show dat; and dough 'Zeke wouldn't hurt a flea, he couldn't holp hisseff, if he comed round you ag'in, Missy Rachel."

"Never you fear, 'Zeke," said the older woman, now, for the first time, interrupting the conversation. "He's mortal afeard of ye. He'll never come."

"Don't you be ober sure ob dat, missus," answered the black. "Cowards am allers fools, and he'm a coward, sartin."

After a moment's pause, he added, —

"But it can't be holped; 'Zeke wont git inter his way; and he can't be 'sponsible fur what'm writ in de shadders."

With this crude fatalism the old man dismissed the subject, and, turning to his young mistress, said, —

"I seed Massa John. He was jess gwine 'way on de bay mar', wid Massa Robin, and a lot of young gemmen, all ob 'em armed way up to de teeth wid knives and 'volvers — 'cept Massa John. He say he'm gwine to talk, and not to fight, and he wouldn't tuck a thing."

"Why, is there danger?" asked Rachel, turning suddenly pale.

"So Massa Jordan tink; and he wouldn't leff Massa John go widout Massa Robin, and de ress goed wid him. He say dat ar' ole Cecil am desput bad, and wont stop fur nuffin', if he's git floored. And he'm sure Massa John'll took 'um all down, case he hab de tongue, so Massa Jordan tink, of de ole Jordans as was drowned in de deluge."

"Well, you gave him the money?"

"No, 'Zeke didn't; he wouldn't tuck it. To de fust he say you muss keep it; but when he know'd, fur sartin, dat you wouldn't hab only de hun'red dollars, den he gub it to ole 'Zeke, all for hisseff. Fac', missy — ebery word; and who'd a thought," — and here he drew the money-belt from his pocket, and fondled it affectionately, — "who'd ha' thought ole 'Zeke would ha' lived to die a rich man! Who'd ha' thought it! He! he!"

"But you will give it back to him, 'Zekiel, as soon as he comes home for good, and these troubles are over?"

"Gib it back to him! 'Zeke reckons he wont. He make a fa'r trade, and he reckons he'll stick to it. You see 'Zeke 'greed to do jess what Massa John want him, jess so long as he lib, — and dis am de price." Here he tossed the money-belt up and down, and laughed gleefully, — "and dis am de price, missy — twelve hun'red dollar — and a mighty good price it am for a ole darky as'm nigh onto eighty; but 'Zeke allers helt Massa John had too big a heart in him to be right smart at tradin'."

Rachel smiled pleasantly at the facetiousness of the old man; but in a few moments she said, gravely, —

"Well, 'Zekiel, you'll take this letter and money back to Jackson Weddington to-day?"

"No, missy, 'Zeke couldn't do dat to-day. He darsn't trust hisseff in sight ob dat snake jess yit — not jess yit. 'Sides, he want to pay dat ar' fifty dollar we owes him fur de docterin' 'spences ob pore massa. We'll go down to de village, and buy suffin' to eat, and suffin warm for you and de missus; and den, 'Zeke'll broke one ob dese hun'red dollar-bills, and squar' up wid de young 'Squar', foreber."

Mrs. Irving had kept her bed almost constantly since the catastrophe which had ruined her son-in-law. She had no natural force of character; but she might have held together some years longer, had she not been so suddenly lifted from years of poverty to the dazzling heights of a gilded coach and long-tailed horses, and as suddenly let fall into the amazing depth in which she now was grumbling and grovelling. Her nervous system was not strong enough to rally from the last shock, and slowly, but surely, she had for months been sinking. The anxiety and excitement of the past two days had weakened her greatly, and, on the morning following the conversation just recorded, she was too ill to be left alone; and so Rachel was obliged to defer her intended visit to the village. Another day passed, and she was no better; but then not a pound of meal was left in the cabin. Food must be had at once, and at last Rachel decided that Ezekiel should go alone for clothing and provisions. Getting in the day's fuel, and harnessing the old mule, — which, by some strange Providence, had been saved from the wreck of their fortunes, — he set out soon after daybreak. He took no breakfast, and it was a twelve-mile ride by a very slow conveyance ; but the old man said cheerfully, as he took his seat in the crazy sled, —

"Neber mind de breakfust, missy ; dar'll be de more for you. 'Zeke eat ob de fat ob de land, and smoke some 'backer to boot, when he git to de village."

The old man had been gone a couple of hours, Rachel was quietly clearing away the breakfast things, and her mother, after a restless night, was sleeping soundly in the low bed in the corner, when the door suddenly opened, and a man entered the apartment. His face was muffled in the cape of his overcoat, and it was not till he had spoken her name that Rachel discovered that it was Weddington ! Then, springing back, and almost panting with a sudden fear, she said, —

" Why are you here ? What do you want ? "

Glancing quickly about the room, he uncovered his head, and unmuffled his face ; and then, advancing a few paces, he fixed his eyes intently upon hers, and said, in a voice as low and plaintive as the coo of a hurt pigeon, —

" Rachel, is this the way you receive an old friend ? "

" Friend ! You are no friend of mine ! Leave me, — I beg of you leave me ! "

" Then you would rather *hear* from me than see me ? " he said, his voice even more plaintive than before, but his eyes still fixed upon her with a cold, serpent-like stare.

It was true, she had kept his letter two days, and he had a right to misconstrue her intentions. The thought shot through her like an arrow, a sudden faintness came over her, and she sank down on the settle.

"It is nothing to what I would do for you. I would lift you above every want! I would make you always happy;" and again he advanced a few paces, his cold, serpent-like stare still upon her.

"Go away, oh, go away from me!" she gasped, faintly, and with a weak, repellent gesture.

"Go away, and leave you starving in this wretched hovel!• you, who would grace any palace in the world! Oh, no, Rachel! I cannot do that! If I did, I should not be the friend you have known me."

And now he sat down beside her, and placed his hand on hers, as it rested on the edge of the settle. She attempted to draw it away, but his grasp was firm, and her muscles were powerless.

A moment he sat so in silence, then he said, and his voice now was as soft and musical as the strings of the Eolian when stirred by the gentlest wind that ever came from heaven, —

"Rachel, some one has belied me; I am your friend, — your best friend. It goes to my heart to have you meet me so coldly. Believe me, I am your friend; and I would be more;" and here his arm crept about her waist, while his hand still grasped hers, and his serpent-like stare — no longer stealthy and cold, but fierce and hot with the very fire of hell — was still fixed on her eyes. "I would be more, — I would make you my wife. Your husband has deserted you; in a few months more you can be free by the law; then I will

12

make you my wife. I *will*, believe me; and, meanwhile, your every wish shall be gratified; you shall have a home, servants, friends, all, and more than all, that your sot of a husband lost by his folly."

It is said that the poor bird, caught by the spell of the serpent, circles about the creature's head, gasping and fluttering, but drawing nearer and nearer, till, at last, it darts, a willing prey, into the very jaws of the monster. So it was with Rachel. She gasped for breath to cry out; but the words would not come. She struggled to get upon her feet, and throw off his hold; but her strength was gone, her limbs refused to obey her will, and, at last, her head sank upon his shoulder, and, panting and powerless, she lay at his mercy.

But there is a force in this world that is mightier than the power of evil. It is the love of even the weakest of men or women. That force now came between Weddington and his victim. Half-dressed, her hair falling loosely about her, her eyes glaring, her cheeks hollow, but glowing with the hectic fire that was burning at her vitals, the mother of Rachel stood before him. Stamping her foot on the floor, she lifted her skinny hand and pointed to the door.

" Begone!" she cried; " wretch — man of hell — begone!"

He bounded to his feet, and staggered a step or two backward, startled from his self-control by the sudden interruption. In an instant he recovered himself; but in that instant he had lost all power over his victim. The charm broken, Rachel rose suddenly from the settle, and, seizing a rusty shot-gun which hung in the corner, turned upon him, her face and her eyes blazing.

"Go — go," she cried, "this instant — or I shall do a murder."

He grew very pale; but taking up his hat from the table, and fixing on her his basilisk eye, he said, coolly, —

"I'll have you yet. I haven't followed you so long to be balked at last."

The older woman had stood supporting herself by the table; but now she turned suddenly, and, snatching the shotgun from the hand of Rachel, levelled it at Weddington. In a moment it exploded; but the man had bounded, unharmed, through the door-way, — a little longer to go at large, a little longer to do, on this planet, the deeds of his father, the devil.

Rachel sprang to bar the door, and as she did so the gun dropped from the hand of her mother, and, staggering a step or two, she fell at full length upon the floor. She had not fainted; but reaction had come, and it was only with superhuman effort that Rachel half-dragged, and half-carried her to the bed in the corner. Then, smoothing back her tangled hair, she said, —

"O mother! mother! I am so afraid this has hurt you."

"No — matter — if it has! — you is safe! — but Rachel — promise me — never let — let 'Zekiel out of yer sight — ag'in — not — not — while *he's* a livin'."

"I never will, mother — never! But don't you look so, mother; it frightens me! Oh! I am so afraid you are hurt!"

"No, child! I don't feel no pain; but it's growin' dark; put — some more wood on the fire, — make it burn up a little — little brighter."

"It burns brightly, — and it's broad day, mother!" Now a terrible fear came upon her. "O mother! mother!" she cried, "are you dying?"

"No, no! child! — only tired, — he waked me up, you know; but — it's gittin' very dark, child. Do put — a little more wood — on the fire."

Rachel clutched the thin, skinny fingers, and put her hand upon the cold, pale forehead.

"Do you feel my touch, mother?"

"Oh, yas, — you's a darlin' chile; — *you's* allers borne with — your pore mother, — though she's been so peevish — and so — ongrateful. Bless you for it, — darlin', — bless you; — God" —

Her hand clutched her daughter's tightly; her head fell over toward the wall of the hut; and then, her soul left this world for another.

The shadows had begun to creep around the desolate room, when a heavy step sounded outside, and a heavy hand lifted the wooden latch which closed the rude door-way.

"Missy, missy! It'm me, ole 'Zeke, — so don't you be afeard. You done right to bar de door, — you did. 'Zeke meant you shud, — dough he didn't tink a word ob it till five mile away. But, he know'd you wud, — he know'd you wud, — for you's de sensiblist, and best lookin', too, ob any young missy in all Kaintucky."

The last words were spoken as Rachel undid the barred door, and let the old man into the room. He bore in his hands two immense baskets, filled with sundry bundles, and a variety of hams, chickens, turkeys, and other defunct barn-yard commodities. Placing the baskets on the floor, he went on, —

"Christmus hab come rader late dis y'ar, missy, — way onto de middle ob Febrary, — but it hab come at lass, and ole 'Zeke hab got 'um all yere, right in dese baskets, gowns and shawls and hoods and hams, and 'nuff chicken fixins to keep missus clar fru de winter. Wid sich broth as you kin make out ob dese, we'll hab her well in no time;" and the delighted old black held a brace of fat pullets up before the eyes of his young mistress.

"She needs nothing now, 'Zekiel," said Rachel, turning away, and resuming her seat on the settle.

"Needs nuffin' now? What does you mean, missy?"

She made no answer, and he stepped softly to the bed of the dead woman. He lifted her hand, and for a moment, bent over her cold features. Then, without a word, he turned away, and sat down in his leather-bottomed chair in the chimney-corner. Long he sat there, gazing intently at the fire, and apparently unconscious of the presence of Rachel. At last he looked up, and said, —

"We'se alone now, missy, — alone, wid nuffin' in de wurle, 'cept de Lord, and de good angels. But don't you greab, missy, don't you greab. De Lord he hab a big heart; and he'm weepin' fur you now, jess loike he weep fur Lazarus. 'Zeke knows he'm a big heart, and dat he weep ober we pore folk dat am 'flicted, 'case y'ars and y'ars ago he come and weep ober 'Zeke, when his own mudder was dead in her bed, loike you's am now in de corner."

Rachel covered her face with her hands; but said nothing, and in a moment the old black continued, —

"Don't you greab, missy; she'm better now, — better 'an she was dis mornin'. 'Zeke 'members when she was young as you, — and how handsome she was den! how beautiful! But she'm handsomer now; she'm younger now. Massa John say dat dey grow younger up dar ebery day, till dey gits to be jess so young and handsome and innercent as little chillen. So don't you greab no more, missy. Tink no more 'bout it; but jess you git 'Zeke his supper, like a good missy. He haint had a mossel to eat since dis time lass evenin'."

"Nothing to eat!" said Rachel, rising, and hanging the kettle over the fire. "Why! didn't you have your breakfast and dinner in the village?"

"No, missy. 'Zeke hadn't more'n druv inter de village 'fore he seed a great crowd of folk gwine inter town meetin'. He axed what it all was 'bout, and dey say it was Massa John as was a gwine to gib de Secesh hail, fire, and brimstun, — he'd done it, dey say, de day afore, at Piketon. Wall, arter dat, 'Zeke forgot all 'bout de gowns, and eben de chicken fixins for de pore missus; and he hitched de ole mule under a shed, and went inter de court house. It was cram jam full, all wid white folk, but 'Zeke he wedged fru 'um, and close up to whar Massa John and a whole lot ob big gemmen was a-sittin' on de platform.

"Fuss dat ar' ole debil, Cecil, he got up, and talked 'way 'bout de rights of de Souf, and how dey was a-trod on, — he mean de big planters, as neber done a stroke ob work, neber was ob no use to nobody, and allers had a hun'red darkies to tend on 'um. Dat was 'bout all he say; but he stormed 'way for a hour like a wild critter, and den he sot down, and Massa John he come to de front ob de platform. He look jess

loike he done when he was yere, wid his homespun clo'es,
his long hair, and his great white forrard. Wall, he come to
de front ob de platform, and de fuss word he say was, ' De
wrong haint no rights dat eider man or de Lord am bound to
'spect; and you go out ob de Union, and you's in de wrong,
and you's outlaws.'

"He go on wid a good deal more ob dat sort, and den he
come onto some argumens dat 'Zeke neber yered afore. He
say, fuss, dat de Lord hab made dis one kentry, and dat man
couldn't make it two nohow. Dat all de big ribers and all de
big mount'ins dey run norf and souf, and dar was nowhar
dat you could run a line east and west, dat eben de bery
smallest debil couldn't git over; and he say, ' Jess you try
to run sich a line, and de little debils dey'll allers be a-gittin'
ober, on both sides, and keepin' up a war all de time.' Den
he say, second, dat union was de bery order ob natur' ; and
dat dis Union was a-fashioned jess as de Lord fashioned de
universe. Dat ebery whar dar was big and little, centre and .
s'cumference; and dat all creation was only a great wheel, wid
a hub in de middle, spokes on de sides, and a felly round de
whole, and dat it would all fall to pieces and go to rack and
ruin if you took out de hub or de spokes, or tore off de felly.
And den he 'lustrated de idee by de solar system. He say de
sun gib light and heat to all de planets, and holt 'um all togedder, so dey neber stray away, but hab reg'lar summer and
winter, and seed-time and harvest allers. Wall, he say, ' De
gubment at Washington am de sun to dis Union ; it gibs
light and heat to all de States and de territories; and you
blot dat out, and you'll all go wand'ring off, lost inter de outer
darkness.'

"'Zeke neber yered sich talk, — it was chain lightnin'; and Massa John, his face was a bonfire, and his eyes, dey was two blazin' knots of light-wood. De folks dey neber said a word, but was as still as mice de whole time he was a-talkin'; but when he got fru, you neber yered sich a noise. Dey got up, and dey shouted, and dey cheered, and lots ob ·'um comed up, and hugged him, and a'most killed him wid kindness. Finarly de meetin' it broke up; but ole 'Zeke he stayed, and at lass Massa John he got his eye onto him. Den he beckoned to 'Zeke to come, and he went up dar, 'mong all de big gemmen on de platform; and den Massa John telled dem who 'Zeke was, and dat he lubed him loike he done his own fader. He did, missy, and 'Zeke had to cry, right out dar 'fore all dem big gemmen."

Here the old man pulled out a great red handkerchief, wiped his eyes, and, for a few moments, was unable to go on with the narrative. At last he said, —

"Dat was all, missy, 'cept he say I muss tell you he was well, and his fader dat *dey* was wid him, — he mean de ole Jordans as had de fiery tongues and was drowned in de deluge. Wont de old man be proud ob him, Missy Rachel?"

"Oh, yes, he will be! *I* am proud of him; we all are proud of him, 'Zekiel."

An hour later the two went to their beds, — his, a blanket before the fire; hers, the negro's scanty cot in the corner of the attic.

CHAPTER VIII.

ITHIN the thirty days that followed the events recorded in the last chapter, the quiet district, which is the scene of our story, felt the first rising of the great tide that had already swept the Gulf States from their moorings in the Union. At its every cross-roads began a war of words, which was soon, very soon, to become a war of a much more deadly character. At the outset, the two principal speakers who canvassed the district, conducted the wordy contest with an order and decorum which does not always accompany similar controversies; but soon Cecil, mortified beyond endurance by the frequent discomfitures he received from his homespun opponent, resorted to personal threats, which so exasperated the friends of Jordan, that actual violence followed on several occasions. On one of these occasions, at an open-air meeting near Jordan's home, knives were drawn, and revolvers fired, and to such a length did the disturbance go, that the life of Cecil might have been sacrificed but for the timely interference of Jordan. When the excitement was somewhat allayed, the young man mounted the platform, and said to the multitude, —

"I regret the violent words into which Judge Cecil has

been betrayed; and I do not intend to retort in similar language. I came here to speak for peace, — to appeal to the reason, and not to the passions, of my fellow-citizens; and I now give notice, that if similar language is again employed, or a similar disturbance again occurs, either here or elsewhere, I shall give up the discussion and go to my home, leaving the public to come to its own conclusion as to who does, and who does not, desire the best good of the country."

Goaded by these words beyond all sense of prudence, Cecil rose, and turned upon the auditory, his face pale, and his eyes blazing with passion.

"Who cares," he cried, "whether the fellow goes on with the discussion, or goes home to his shanty, and his dunghill? Does he suppose that other men estimate him as he estimates himself? I have consented to bandy words with the low fellow only out of respect to the people, and because I think a man may be a man even if he is a horse-trader. But now I give notice that I will discuss with him no longer. If the other side wants to be heard in these meetings, it must select a speaker in some way my equal, — one who is a gentleman."

The meeting was crowded with Jordan's neighbors and personal friends, and this indiscreet speech renewed the tumult, and might have cost Cecil dearly, had not Jordan sprang quickly to his feet, saying, —

"No violence, my friends, no violence! Every man here who loves order, or his country, will now go quietly to his home, and take no notice of the insulting language of Judge Cecil. I shall not continue the discussion; it might lead to bloodshed; and *I* shall not be the first to light the fire which, I see, must soon sweep over Kentucky."

Saying this, he descended from the platform, mounted his horse, and with his younger brother, and a score of his neighbors, rode away to the rude cabin among the mountains. There he remained for a time, — a silent but interested spectator of the thick-coming events which soon involved the country in one of the most gigantic and bloody struggles that redden the pages of history.

All discussion had ceased; but the dragon's teeth had been sown, and they brought forth a harvest of discord. Father became arrayed against son, family against family, neighborhood against neighborhood; and soon the district experienced all the evils of civil strife, except its rapine and carnage. Men had for months been mustering for both sides of the conflict; and directly over the river, the brave Rosecrans had for months been fighting the brilliant series of battles which saved West Virginia to the Union; but not till the middle of summer did the red devil of war begin to sprinkle this peaceful region with his fiery baptism.

Kentucky had assumed the attitude of mock neutrality, by which its leading men hoped to cloak their hostility to the government, and most effectually serve the South; and early in August the governor issued a proclamation, commanding all persons having arms belonging to the State to deliver them up immediately. This gave opportunity to the State Guard, a secession organization, to enter the houses of Union men, and, under color of law, to take away their rifles and shot-guns, — in fact to disarm every loyalist in the Commonwealth.

The natural result followed. The Union men of nearly every county met and banded together to resist these high-handed proceedings. One of these bands, numbering about a hundred men, was organized by Jordan; and late in September, about an equal number of the State Guard having entered the district to disarm the inhabitants, a collision ensued between the two forces, in which one man was killed, and two were badly wounded. One of the wounded men was a nephew of Judge Cecil.

A writ was then issued by Cecil, charging Jordan and a dozen others with murder; and a body of three hundred was despatched to take them into custody. Hearing of their coming, and being too weak to make a successful resistance, Jordan and the others named in the indictment took to the woods, and remained secreted until the departure of the rebels. Balked in the intended arrests, the party of Cecil turned upon the inhabitants, and took away the arms of every loyal man in the district.

Meanwhile, though the country people generally remained loyal, the residents of the towns had become thoroughly inoculated with the virus of secession, and large bodies of armed men had gathered in the principal places. Early in September, the force collected near Piketon numbered nearly two thousand; and then the rebel leaders, emboldened by the defenceless condition of the Unionists, ventured upon an act of general conscription. Orders were published, summoning every able-bodied man in the district, between the ages of eighteen and forty-five, to report for military duty, within ten days, at the camp of Colonel John S. Williams, in the vicinity of Piketon.

Seeing that neutrality was no longer possible, numbers of loyal men, who had not already volunteered in the army that was mustering across the Ohio, at once repaired to the various rendezvouses where Union regiments were being formed, and offered their services to the government. Jordan, meanwhile, had been lying out in the woods, to escape a rebel band of two hundred which, under Weddington, was scouring the district to effect his arrest; but now he appeared openly, one morning, in the little hamlet, and in half an hour a dozen horsemen were riding over the hills, calling all loyal men to a meeting at the little church on the Weddington plantation. They came armed with clubs, staves, scythes, and the few rifles that had been saved from the clutches of the State Guard, and by nightfall fifty had assembled. Then, led by Jordan, they set out to join the Fourteenth Regiment of Kentucky Infantry, which, under Colonel Moore, was mustering at Louisa, twenty miles distant.

They had proceeded about half way, and were, at midnight, watering their horses at a stream near the little hamlet of Peach Orchard, when the troop of Weddington suddenly issued from the woods that lined the road, and surrounded them. The rebel had been apprised of their destination by a mounted spy; and, outnumbered four to one, and poorly armed as they were, they had no alternative but surrender. They were conveyed at once by forced marches to the rebel camp near Piketon.

There the larger number, intimidated by threats of a criminal trial for their participation in the skirmish of September, enlisted in the rebel ranks, and took the oath of allegiance to the Confederacy. A few, however, steadily refused the overtures of the secession leader, and among these few was Jordan. When informed of his refusal, Colonel Williams directed him to be brought into his tent, and something like the following conversation ensued between them.

Looking at his manacled limbs, the colonel said, —

"Mr. Jordan, I am sorry to see you in irons;" then, turning angrily to an aid, he added, "By whose order was this done, sir?"

"Judge Cecil's," was the answer.

"Ah!" said the colonel to Jordan; "Judge Cecil is not your friend, I have discovered."

"No, sir," answered Jordan. "For twenty years he has been my father's enemy; now he is mine."

"Well, I command this camp," said the colonel to his aid, "Take off Mr. Jordan's irons. Do it at once. Sit down, Mr. Jordan."

Jordan seated himself on a camp-stool, and no more was spoken until the manacles were removed. Then Colonel Williams said, —

"Now we can talk together like gentlemen. We are strangers to each other, Mr. Jordan; but I have heard of you, and I have a high respect for your talents and character. This induces me to make you a proposition I would make to few men, who, like you, were under arrest for a capital crime."

Jordan answered, —

"I thank you, colonel, for your good opinion, and will be glad to hear any proposition from so courteous a gentleman."

"Thank you, Mr. Jordan," replied the colonel. "I wanted

to say, that with your talents, and influence in your district, you could, in the troubles that are now upon us, greatly serve your native State, and rise to almost any position in the army. Take the oath, and go home and recruit for us, and I will make you a captain on the spot, and, if you raise five hundred volunteers, will pledge my word that you shall have a colonel's commission from Richmond."

"I thank you, colonel," answered Jordan, coldly. "I would sooner fight you as a private in a Union regiment."

"But that is not the alternative, Mr. Jordan," said the colonel, with the same bland civility. "It is trial for murder; and you know before whom, — Judge Cecil. He has already opposed my making you this proposition."

"That does not surprise me, sir," answered Jordan, "and I know that a trial before him would be a conviction; but that does not alter my decision."

The colonel now rose to his feet, and taking two or three turns up and down the tent, he said, with a warmth that was in striking contrast with his previous cool civility, —

"You are a splendid fellow, Jordan; but listen to me! It would be death! certain death! Now, your life is in my hands; but let me once turn you over to the civil authority, and I couldn't save you. All Kentucky couldn't save you; you would surely die."

Jordan's face was as impassive as marble; but his deep gray eye gave out the singular light which has already been mentioned. With his usual coolness, he said, —

"You are mistaken, colonel. My life is not in your hands. Eighteen hundred years ago, one man said to another, ' You could have no power over me, were it not given you from above.' Those words are as true now as when they were spoken."

The colonel paused in his hurried walk, and looked at Jordan for a moment. Then he said, —

" They *are* true, and you have found out the secret of real bravery. I would not have the blood of such a man as you on my hands, for the universe. There is the book we both venerate." And he drew from his left breast pocket a small and well-worn Bible. " It was given me by my mother, who is now in heaven. Promise me, upon it, that you will not bear arms against the Confederacy, and that you will leave Kentucky within a fortnight, and though it may cost me my commission, — for the eyes of some of our leaders are on you, — you shall go as free as I am."

" Colonel, you are a true man, but I cannot make that promise. If I live, I shall do all I can for my State and my Country."

" You would ruin both them and yourself. Don't be rash. Take time to think of it, — a day, a week, a month, — and in the mean while you shall have respectful treatment."

"I need no time. A year would not alter my decision," said Jordan, rising from his seat, and straightening up his bent form with the air of quiet dignity that was natural to him.

" Then may God forgive you, Jordan, for you will do self-murder. It is painful to me, very painful; but I must do my duty."

"Do it, colonel. I acquit you of all blame. Now let me go back to the guard-house."

"No, you will have to go to the jail at Piketon. The

moment you leave this tent you are out of my hands; and
then — think of it again — I can do nothing."

"I know, colonel; but — good-by," and Jordan held out
his hand, which the other grasped, and held while he was
speaking. " Strange things sometimes happen; and we may
meet again; if we do, I shall try to return your courtesy."

The colonel wrung his hand, but made no reply, and
within an hour, Jordan, though not as yet declared guilty,
was loaded with irons, and a tenant of the condemned cell in
the prison in Piketon.

His trial took place in about a fortnight. It was shown by
the testimony of two rebel officers, who had taken part in the
skirmish, that he did not fire a shot; but, on the contrary,
exerted all his influence to prevent a collision between the
two forces; but Cecil was judge, and it was a packed jury, —
packed, because the town was in the possession of the Confederates, and not a man had the courage to give his vote
against the prevailing sentiment. The verdict was "guilty,"
and the sentence, the gallows the following Friday.

Jordan was taken again to the jail, thrust again into the
condemned cell, and now, to make escape impossible, was
chained to the stone floor of the prison. No one was allowed
to visit him ; but, at last, on the evening preceding the appointed Friday, a short, thick-set, red-faced man, who had
been employed by Colonel Williams in gathering beeves for
the army, presented himself to the jailer with a note from
that officer, requesting that he might be allowed to take the
prisoner's last words to his father and mother.

The jailer at first protested that his orders were strict, —
no one could be admitted ; but the man found a ready mode

13 *

of overcoming his scruples, and soon entered the prison, his pocket the lighter by a few half-eagles. Once within its walls, he was turned over by the honest jailer to as honest a turnkey. What message the prisoner gave the man was not known; but when he came out an hour afterward, he was sensibly affected. Wringing the jailer's hand, he said, in words which were half choking with emotion, —

"I'd hang, myself, sooner'n see that man hung. My God, sir! last winter he kep' my wife from starvin'. I only yered on it to the trial."

The next morning the jailer, making his accustomed round, looked in at the cell, and found it vacant. A rickety cot, an empty tin pan, a broken stool, and a huge heap of chains were in their accustomed places; but the prisoner had gone, — no one knew whither.

An angel once opened the doors of Peter's prison; so one came that night and did a like service to Jordan; but, to be historically correct, I must add that this angel wore seedy butternuts, chewed tobacco, drank poor whiskey, and swore like a pirate. It was the turnkey; for he, too, had flown, and, what was quite as singular, it soon was ascertained that the fine bay mare, which Jordan had ridden for some years, but which now was the property of the Confederate commander himself, — and could not, therefore, possibly be bribed, — had, during the night, also absconded.

The next morning, Judge Cecil presented himself at the head-quarters of the colonel commanding, and demanded a force of three hundred men to go in pursuit of the prisoner.

"Three hundred to capture one!" exclaimed the officer. "Why, you are crazy."

"Not crazy, sir," answered the judge, tartly. "It's an Union nest, and we are liable to fall in with scouting parties from Louisa."

"Well, I can't afford any men go that distance. Nelson has moved into Kentucky, and may advance upon me at any moment."

"And for that reason a reconnoissance might do you a service. I will go along with the troops and see that you get correct information."

"No, no; I have twenty scouts at Nelson's heels at this moment. In a week I shall know all about his movements. He is recruiting for the grand army forming in Ohio."

Balked in this direction, the judge adopted other tactics.

"Pardon me, colonel; but ugly whispers are afloat about a horse being missing that once belonged to the prisoner. The animal, it is thought, could hardly have been taken from your very head-quarters without the help of some one connected with your stables. It is said, too, that you have censured the proceedings at the trial, and expressed strong sympathy for Jordan."

The colonel looked at the other in a kind of blank amazement.

"My God, sir!" he said, "would you intimate that I know anything of his escape?"

"Not by any means; but if you refuse my request, ugly remarks will be made, most certainly."

"You have said enough, sir," answered the colonel. "You can have two hundred mounted men, — in an hour they shall be ready."

It was noon of the following day, when this body of men

rode up the narrow valley of the Blaine and quietly surrounded the cabin of the elder Jordan. A dozen then dismounting, Cecil advanced with them to the door-way. His
summons was answered by the customary " Come in, gentlemen," and, opening the door, the party entered. It was
early in October, but it was a cold day, and a bright fire was
blazing on the hearth, before which the family — the elder
Jordan, his wife, and Robin, the younger son, a manly lad of
about seventeen — were assembled at dinner. They all rose
on the entrance of the soldiers, and the eye of the elder Jordan falling on Cecil, he drew himself up rather stiffly, and
said, —

" To what do I owe this visit, sir ? "

" To your traitor of a son. Is he here ? "

" No, sir."

" When was he here ? "

" He left about an hour before daybreak."

" Where is he now ? "

" I can't tell you, sir."

" Do you mean that you do not know; or that you do, and
are not willing to tell ? "

" I know where he intended to go; but I am his father,
sir, — you can't expect me to tell when his life is in question."

" I do expect you to tell; if you do not, your own life may
be in question."

" I understand you, sir. I decline to betray my own flesh
and blood."

Cecil had entered the room with a revolver in his hand,
the others with their pistols in their belts, and their swords
in their scabbards, and they had not yet drawn them. Cecil

now cocked his revolver, and, placing it close to the ear of Jordan, said, —

"I will ask you once more. Tell me where your son is concealed?"

As he said this, the wife of Jordan, who had stood till now apparently stupefied with the sudden proceedings, sprang forward, and falling at Cecil's feet, and clasping his knees, she cried out, frantically, —

"O Judge Cecil! Judge Cecil! do not hurt him! Oh, have mercy! as you expect mercy of God, have mercy on my husband!"

Cecil did not seem to hear her. Jordan had not answered his question, and now he repeated it.

"Will you tell me where your son is?"

"I will not," said Jordan.

The pistol exploded; and the man who, five short minutes before, had been quietly eating in peace at his own fireside, lay mortally wounded on his own hearth-stone.

In another instant another shot was fired, then another, and another, and another, and three of the rebels fell to the floor, — two of them dead, the other severely wounded. The wounded man was Cecil; and, though the boy Jordan's hands were now pinioned to his side by the strong arms of three of the troopers, he still clutched the revolver which had worked such sudden and terrible vengeance.

"Secure him! Don't shoot him! — hang him, — hang him before his own door-way!" cried Cecil.

"You'd better not!" yelled the boy. "It will take five minutes to do that; and if I live that long I will have your life, certain."

The smoke had now somewhat cleared away, showing the wife of Jordan kneeling by the side of her fallen husband. He was shot through the brain, but was still living, though breathing short and brokenly.

"Die like a man, my boy," he gasped. "Ruth, good-by. Robin, we'll go together. Ruth, tell John to be worthy of his ancestors."

The hand that held hers then relaxed its hold, and the everlasting gates opened to the old Scotchman.

I have no heart to dwell on what followed. There are some deeds at thought of which one stands aghast when he remembers that he too is a man, and that slumbering in his own soul are the passions which at times transform other men into incarnate devils. This was one of those deeds. While this mother was kneeling and pleading by the side of Cecil, they took her son, — her youngest born, the joy of her life, the hope of her old age, the one thing that, next to God, she loved better than she loved all else in the universe, — and before her very eyes they hanged him to the great tree in the little court-yard.

CHAPTER IX.

" THE BEGINNING OF THE END."

T is the night of this day, and it has come on with heavy clouds, which hide the moon and stars, and shroud the lonely valley in thick darkness. A low fire is burning on the hearth of the little cabin, and Rachel sits by it, her head upon her hand, and her face shadowed by troubled and anxious thoughts. The dinner things are untouched on the table, and about the whole room is an air of careless disorder, which shows that its occupant has been drawn away from her daily cares, and, for the time, paralyzed by the dark tragedy, which, echoing along the little stream, has already filled the far mountains with sounds of horror.

After a while the door opens, and the old negro enters, the shot-gun in his hand, and in his belt a revolver. Rachel looks up, and, springing to her feet, she says in a quick, eager way, —

" Have you seen him? Is he coming?"

" Yas, missy; he'll be yere in a jiffin; he'm to Massa Jordan's."

" How did you tell him? How does he bear it? Where did you find him? Tell me all; but don't speak loud, or you will wake her."

She said this in low, but rapid tones, and glanced hastily round at the rude bed in the corner.

"And how am she, missy?" asked the black, not heeding her questions. "Hab she got all ober dem dreffel histerics?"

"Yes; the opiate began to work just after you went away, and ever since she's been sleeping; but every now and then she tosses her arms about, and moans piteously. Oh, it is dreadful! dreadful!" and she clenched her hands together, and turned her face away for a moment. "To think that God, who they say is so good, should allow such wickedness!"

"Dat'm jess what show He am good, missy. Dat idee used to bother 'Zeke, till he read in de Bible dat in de oder worle He gibs ebery man 'cordin' to his deeds, — sots de sheep on de right han', de goats on de leff."

"I know; 'there the wicked cease from troubling, the weary are at rest.' But what kept you so long? — you've been gone at least four hours."

"I knows, missy, and I was afeard you'd be troubled; but I forgot to tell you 'fore I go away. You sees it wouldn't do to go a huntin' Massa John in broad day, widout knowin' de coast was cl'ar. Dis comed to 'Zeke, so he went up de valley to Massa Campbell's, and got him and some ob de folks as had comed dar to talk ober de drefful ting, to scour de kentry, on all de roads, fur five or six mile all round. 'Zeke was fur gwine hisseff, too; but de men-folks dey say 'twould look suspicious loike for him to be scoutin' round, and Missy Campbell, she wouldn't yere to it nohow, — she say 'Zeke should stay dar, and hab suffin to make him warm and strong; and de fac' am eber sense he cut de pore chile down, and lay him dar, 'longside ob ole Massa Jordan, 'Zeke hab been jess as weak as a rat, — weaker'n dan dem rats in de barn as make dar dinner uv nights off de hind legs ob de ole mule. He ! he !" and the old man laughed ; but his voice was forced and hollow, — more like a wail than a laugh.

"Well, well ; did they find all clear ? "

"Yes, missy; nobody stirrin', and all de folks eberywhar a'most gone dead wid de drefful news as de wind had toted all ober de kentry. Well, dat tuck two hours; fur it was dat long 'fore de lass one comed back, and 'Zeke darn't start afore. Den he sot out fur de big cave up on de mountin, whar Massa John hided when dem rebel sodgers was in de valley. He warn't dar; but he'd a-been dar widin a hour or so, fur de fire was a-burnin', and some on his dinner was a-hangin' ober de coals, not yit burnt to nuthin'. Den 'Zeke he looked round outside de cave, and found dar tracks,— Massa John and de mar's, — he gwine ahead, and de knowin' critter follerin', and steppin' right onto his footprints, loike as if she knowed dat if dey was seed it mought git him inter trouble. Dis idee 'peared to come to Massa John at lass; fur, haff way down de mountin, he turned out ob de path inter de openin's, and dar, in de dead grass, 'Zeke lost 'em. Den fur a minnit, he didn't know what to do, or which way to turn, so he kneeled down to pray, and right off to onct it comed inter his head to follow stret on down de mountin. Dat would tuck him right to Massa Jordan's, and it didn't stand to reason dat Massa John would go dar in broad day ; but 'Zeke 'membered him to say onct dat atween dem as love one oder dar am a sort ob telegram wire dat leffs one know when de oder am in trouble. Massa John had

14

a felt a blow on dat wire, and so he'd a-gone down wid his
dinner half eaten. Well, 'Zeke went to Massa Jordan's —
inter de room whar dey am, and all ober de house, and den
round de barn, and de yard; but Massa John warn't dar, and
hadn't been dar. Dar was a plenty ob tracks; but dey all
was de rebels', as had stole de wagin to tote off dat ar' ole
Cecil and de two dead ones. 'Zeke knowed, 'case Massa
John hab a foot dat covers nigh onto a haff acre, and de mar',
she hab a 'quar shoe on 'count ob de cracked hoof she got by
gwine too fass in de hot sand. Wall, ag'in 'Zeke didn't know
which way to turn, and dis time, as Massa Brown would say,
he was all out ob his reckonin'. He kneeled down to pray,
but somehow he couldn't git at de Lord, — couldn't git his
mind onto Him ; fur dar kep' runnin' fru his head dem words
de poor 'Squar' write in de sand, down dar by de run, and
dat de rain wouldn't wash out till dey was larned by heart by
de whole plantation. Seein' 'twarn't no use tryin' to pray,
'Zeke got up, and den suffin' 'peared to tote his legs right off
to whar Massa John was a-hidin'."

"And where was it ?" asked Rachel, who had listened
patiently to the old man's prolix narrative, knowing very well
that it was the shortest way to arrive at the essential facts
she was so eager to learn.

"Right dar whar de pore 'Squar' die twenty year ago, —
in de little wigwam. Massa John was dar and de mar'; and
he was a-lyin' on de ground, and she was a-holtin' him in her
arms loike she'd a-been his mudder."

"Holding him in her arms! What do you mean ?"

"Why, you sees, missy, Massa John must hab made de
mar' lay down to keep her quiet, and to keep hisself warm

he lay down aside ob her. He had his head on her neck, and she, dat game fore leg ob hern doubled up ober him, and a-huggin' him down to her as if she'd tuck all de breff out ob his body. But she didn't mean dat; she knowed he was in trouble, — de tender, pitiful look in her eyes said so; and when 'Zeke seed dem a-layin' dar so lovin' tugedder, and thought ob how Massa John, — now when he need so much lub, — hab no one to lub him in all de worle but dat ar' poor dumb critter, he burst right out a-cryin', he did, he couldn't holp it, dough he had sot his mind hard, to gib Massa John comfort, and not add to his great sorrer."

Here the old man's head sank upon his breast, and he sobbed convulsively. Rachel covered her face with her hands, and, for a moment, her frame shook with some hidden agony. Then she said, with a trembling voice, and words that were broken and quivering, —

"Oh, yes; he has! All the world loves him ! '"

Nothing more was said for some minutes; then the old negro looked up, and went on with his story.

"Massa John bounded to his feet, when ole 'Zeke goed inter de wigwam, — he comed onto him so sudden, — but when he seed who it was, he said, cooler'n 'Zeke says it, 'It hab come, 'Zekiel, — my wuck; dis am de beginnin' ob de end.' "

"Then he knew ; — he had been to the cabin ? "

"No, missy, he didn't know a ting; he'd only felt de blow on de wire, and de great shadder dat'm come onto de fambly. But he'd tuck it all in, like dey does in de oder worle. Up dar, you knows, dey don't talk loike we does. Dey jess gin a look or speak a word, so Massy John say, to leff 'em git hold

ob de end ob de tread, and den dey hab it all unwound in a
twinklin'.   Dar sense and 'telligence am so 'cute, he say,
'case dey hab brung dar natur's inter 'cord wid de. Lord's
natur', and de true order ob creation.   Dat'm why Massa
John hab sech a wonderful look inter tings, 'case he hab
brung his natur' so inter 'cord wid de Lord's natur'.   It'm
so; for Massa John say dat ar' sort ob eyesight hab growed
on him jess so fast as he hab growed more and more like de
Lord Jesus, and now he'm got so much loike him dat he can
feel dem fine strings dat run all fru all tings, and am sort ob
nerves to de great Lord ob de universe.   Dat'm de reason,
too, Massa John say, why de Lord Jesus could see so fur inter
de futur', and do dem great miracles, — 'case his natur' was so
in 'cord wid de Lord's natur' dat de Lord could wuck wid his
nerves, and use his hands and feet loike dey was his own.
If anybody else had such a natur' as de Lord Jesus, dey
might see and do jess what he done; but dey haint, and dey
neber will hab, 'case He was de only begotten, — born to be
de Lord ob all dis part ob creation."

"Well, well," said Rachel, with a slight gesture of impatience.   "How did he bear it, when you told him all?"

"'Zeke didn't tell him, missy; he hadn't de heart to tell
him.   He jess sot down onto de ole stool as used to be the
poor 'Squar's, and cried; dat was all 'Zeke done, and all he
could do."

"And what did John say?"

"Nuffin'; only he telled de mar' to lay right dar till he
comed back, and den he sot out to go to Massa Jordan's.   It
was haff a hour by sun, and 'Zeke was afeard he'd be seed,
so he run'd arter him, and at lass got him to come back,

and sot down in de wigwam. Den he say ag'in that his wuck had begun, dat he was a gwine off dis bery night, — 'Zeke don't know war, — but 'bout some great ting, dat'll cl'ar ebery rebel out ob all dis region."

"Going away to night!" exclaimed Rachel, in an alarmed, excited tone. Soon, however, she asked, calmly, "When did you go to the cabin?"

"Jess arter sundown Massa John opened de door, and he and 'Zeke goed in turgedder. De fire hadn't gone cl'ar out, and dar was 'nuff light to see all in de room. Dey laid right afore de fire, — Massa Jordan on de h'arth, and Massa Robin 'longside ob him, wid his arm round his fader, — you sees when 'Zeke leff de chile down on de floor, de arm fell so, and he hadn't de heart to tuck it away; but he jess leff 'em dar, in one anoder's arms, loike as if dey was sleepin'. When Massa John seed 'em, he sunk down onto de floor, and gave out sech a cry, — sech a cry as 'Zeke neber yered, — never but onct, missy, and dat was from him, off dar in de snow, dat cole night when you telled him you and Massa Brown was to be married."

Rachel uttered a stifled moan, clenched her hands tightly above her head, and then, in sharp, piercing tones, cried out, —

"Oh, don't! 'Zekiel, don't! Spare me! I well deserve it all; but, O 'Zekiel, don't! it will kill me!"

The old man rose, and sat down on the settle beside her. Then he wound his arm about her waist, and drew her head down upon his shoulder; but he said nothing. They sat so, neither of them speaking, until they heard the cry of an owl, sounding some distance away, in the direction of Jordan's

14*

cabin. Rising quickly to his feet, Ezekiel went out of the house, and in a moment sent up an answering hoot from in front of the doorway. Another then sounded, not so far away, and in a few minutes the door opened, and Jordan entered the cabin.

His face was very pale; but the singular light was in his eyes, and a hopeful, almost radiant, look was on his features. Rachel sprang from her seat and bounded toward him. Their four hands met, and so they stood for many minutes, looking into each other's eyes, and saying only, "John!" "Rachel!"

At last Jordan glanced about the room and asked, —

"Where is she?"

"There;" and she pointed to the bed in the corner.

He went to it, and, bending down over the sleeper, kissed her on the forehead. Then, touching her gently on the shoulder, he said, —

"Mother, mother, wake up! It is me, — John; in a few minutes I must be going."

She opened her eyes, and gazed vacantly at him for a few moments. Then, rising on the bed, she threw her arms about his neck, and cried, —

"O John! John! Is it you? I thought it war Robin, and he war a callin' me."

"It *is* Robin, mother. I will be Robin to you now; and what I can't be, Rachel will, — she will never leave you."

"Leave me! You're not going away, — you can't go away, and leave me all alone. Haint you yered about your father and Robin?" and she clung to him wildly.

"Yes, mother. I have been there. I know it all, — all!

But, come, try to get up. Muster all your strength, and be as calm as you can, for I have much to say; and time is pressing. I must be thirty miles away before daylight."

She rose feebly to her feet. Her face was ghastly white, and she tottered like a young child as he supported her to a seat on the settle. As they went forward, he said to the old man, —

"'Zekiel, bar the door, hang something before the windows, and put out some of the logs, so the fire wont blaze so brightly. There may be prowlers about, and, just now, my life is worth something to Kentucky."

As the negro did as he was bidden, Jordan said to Rachel, —

"Rachel, have you any brandy in the house?"

"Yas, Massa John," quickly responded the old man, drawing a flask from his breast-pocket. "Yere'm some. Missy Campbell guv it to ole 'Zeke, and it put de breaf ob life inter him when he feel a'most as bad as Missy Jordan."

When his mother had swallowed some of the stimulant, she said, —

"I feel stronger now. Go on, John — I kin yere ye; and I know ye wouldn't go away without ye was obleeged to."

"No, mother, I wouldn't; and I hope to come back soon — within a month at the latest. In the mean time, I want you to stay here with Rachel. She will take good care of you, and, when I come, I will take you both to Ohio, with 'Zekiel; and, 'Zekiel, the negroes can then go along, too, for the court has removed the injunction, and they are as free now as I am."

"Free, Massa John! Free!" cried the old man, springing to his feet, and bounding into the air as if he were
a boy practising for a leap over a five-barred gate. "Free,
Massa John! Den why can't dey go now, to onct? 'Zeke
don't want to wait a minnit."

"But you must. The district is full of rebels. Weddington and his band are here, and I suppose are now lying out
for me between here and Louisa. You couldn't go a rod
while there is a rebel in this part of Kentucky."

"But, de law, Massa John,— de law! Don't you say de
court hab gib up de 'junction?"

"Yes; but Weddington would care nothing for that; he
robs and murders peaceable white people, and he cares no
more for negroes. You must stay quietly at home, and say
nothing — not even to the negroes — till I am ready. When
I am, I will come and see you safely into Ohio."

"But whar is ye a gwine to-night, John?" asked his
mother.

"To the Union head-quarters at Louisa."

"O John, inter danger! What should I do if you, too,
was took from me?"

"I may be going into danger, mother, but I shall be safe.
God will be with me, for I go about his work. I can't die
till it is done, and these incarnate devils are driven from Kentucky."

"God will be with you!" exclaimed Rachel, her eyes
beaming with inexpressible tenderness. "He *is* with you;
or you never would have escaped from that dreadful prison."

"You are right, Rachel; and then he made an enemy
serve me. If he can do that, he can keep me safe, and

so incline the heart of the Union general that I shall succeed in what I am going about."

"An enemy, John! Who was he?"

"I am not certain, and if I was it would not do to mention his name. All I know is that the turnkey came to my cell about midnight, unlocked my chains, and led me into the Confederate camp, where a man met us with the mare and another nag ready saddled. The turnkey had the countersign, and, after going all about the camp, we came away together. After we left the lines he told me he was paid for what he did, and that it would cost him his neck if he was found in Kentucky. He didn't know who hired him, nor even the name of the man who paid him the money. It was some considerable sum, and I can think of no one who would have paid it, but an officer, who, before my trial, spoke to me very courteously."

"But why did you go about the camp, John? Wasn't that useless danger?"

"No, Rachel; for then came to me my real work in the war. But my time is short. I must soon be going."

He drew from his breast-pocket a large wallet, and, after taking from it some folded papers, handed it to his mother, saying, —

"There, mother; I took that from father's drawer. It is yours, — ten Kentucky bonds. They will make your old age comfortable. These, 'Zekiel," handing the other papers to the negro, "are for you and Rachel. They are what came to me from your dead master."

The negro took the papers, and said, with a ludicrous

grimace, which he meant should hide his really deep emotion, —

"'Zekiel keep 'um along ob de ress, Massa John, and dat he totes 'bout under his cloes, allers; and nobody'd eber tink ob looking dar for money, — leastways, not fur a t'ousand dollars. 'Zekiel keep 'um fur you, Massa John, ag'in the war am ober, and we'm all fixed in de 'Hio, — dat free kentry."

" Well, any way you like, only keep them safely; and remember your promise about father and Robin."

" Yas, yas, Massa John, 'Zeke'll do dat."

"Now I must go," said Jordan, rising. The others also rose, and taking Rachel by one hand, and his mother by the other, Jordan said, —

" Good-by to both of you. Keep up good heart, for in less than thirty days I shall be back, and then " —

He paused suddenly, for the tread of a horse sounded outside, and in a moment a loud knock came at the door-way.

CHAPTER X.

HE four looked at one another in silence, then Jordan said, in a low voice, —

"Rachel, ask who it is; but don't open the door."

"Who is there?" she asked, raising her voice so as to be heard above the wind, which now was moaning loudly among the trees.

"Me, — Bradley — Bradley Brown," was the answer.

Rachel turned to Jordan, with a surprised and questioning look, but said nothing. He shook his head, as he answered, in the same low tone as before, —

"I fear it is a trap, Rachel. He has been for months with the rebel army; I heard so at Piketon. They may have sent him here to track me."

"What shall I do?" she said, her face turning to a deathly pallor.

Jordan put his hand to his forehead for a moment, then he said, quickly, —

"I have it. Ask him if he is alone?"

"Is any one with you?" said Rachel, going close to the door-way.

"No. It'r only me — Bradley; and, Rachel, don't ye shut

(167)

me out, don't ye, if I has been a villun. I mean to be a
decent man in futur'; and I'se comed back with a pocket full
of money. Ye shall ride in yer kerridge, and be a lady
ag'in."

"It'll be all right," said Jordan, in the same low, quick
tone. "Tell him you'll open the door in a moment. Then
pour the kettle upon the backlog, to make the room a little
darker. 'Zekiel and I will go into the loft. I will keep him
only a few minutes. Don't be afraid. It will all be right.
Come, 'Zekiel."

As Rachel answered her husband, Jordan and the negro
went quickly up the ladder which led to the attic. Rachel
then partly extinguished the already smouldering fire, and
a moment afterward the fugitive husband and the deserted
wife stood face to face together.

Brown held out his hand to her, saying, — "Rachel, how
d'ye do?"

"Very well," answered Rachel, her voice trembling
slightly, and the hand she held out as rigid and cold as an
icicle.

Brown noticed her agitation, and said, quickly, —

"Don't ye be afeard, Rachel. I'se come onto ye sudden;
but I'se come for good. I mean to be a decent man in
futur'."

"I am not afraid," said Rachel. "Are you well?"

"Yas, — never better." The dim light of the smouldering
logs revealed only the outline of his features; but his full
face, and stout, burly form plainly indicated that he spoke the
truth. "But, Rachel," he added, "ye's very cold to me.
I'se been a sorry feller; but wont ye forgive me?"

" Yes; if I have anything to forgive; but I don't know that you have done me any wrong."

" I haint meant to, but some o' the time I'se been in bad ways, and I couldn't come back till I had money ; for, Rachel, ye knows, ye allers counted-on that."

" I do not now. I have no need of money. 'Zekiel and I earn what little we want."

" I know ye does ; ye's a brave gal. I'se yered all about ye to the camp from sum of the neighbors. But, Rachel, I'm in great business; I kin keep you loike a lady ag'in, and — ye'll take me back, and be my wife ag'in, wont ye ? "

All this while they had stood by the door-way, Brown unconscious of the presence of a third person ; but now Rachel, stepping aside a few paces, said, —

" We will talk of that hereafter. You have not yet spoken to Mrs. Jordan."

The elder woman had sat in the shadow of the chimney, her hand behind her ear, and her head bent forward, eagerly weighing every word and gesture of Brown, to catch some token of the real motive of his visit. Now she said, in a kindly tone, as if assured that he had no covert purpose, —

" How d'ye do, Mr. Brown ? I'm glad to see ye."

" I'se glad to see ye, Mistress Jordan," said Brown, advancing to the hearth, and taking her hand warmly.

" 'Scuse my not gettin' up," said the widow. " I'm not very strong."

" It can't be expected ye'd be," said Brown. " It'r a terrible blow yese had, Mistress Jordan. I'se yered all about it. But ye bear it bravely ; and yer son John, how do he stand up under it ? "

15

"Like a man. John knows the Lord does all things well."

"And whar ar' he now? They's scourin' heaven and yerth to find him. They's offered a thousand dollars to the man as brings him in dead or alive."

The widow gave him a quick, suspicious glance, and answered coldly, —

"He's safe; the rebels will not catch him."

Just then a heavy step was heard overhead, and in a moment the old negro came down from the attic. As his huge frame revealed itself upon the ladder, Brown looked up, and said, cordially, —

"Upon my word, thar's 'Zeke! How d'ye, old boy? A little frosty at top; but as warm underneath as ever, I'll warrant."

"Egzac'ly, Massa Brown," answered the old man, taking the other's extended hand. "'Zeke am a little frosty at de top; but all his friends knows he'm a warm heart, if his head am cobered all ober wid de snow ob nigh onto eighty winters. When did you leab Piketon, Massa Brown?"

Brown gave a sudden start, but answered good-humoredly, —

"How did you know I'd been to Piketon?"

"Oh, 'Zeke yered it from a friend as said you'd been dar fur months, doin' a mighty stroke of business as — what am de big name? — commissy, or suffin' loike dat, for de brute critters ob de rebel army."

"It'r true, 'Zeke," said Brown, with a glowing face, "and I'se made a pile at it; it'r better'n follerin' the river."

"So Zeke yeres," answered the old man, with a sarcastic

grin, " a sight better.   But Massa Brown, you wont mind if
'Zeke jess bars you in; dese am ticklish times, and we don't
sleep no more wid de latch-string out."

"Oh, no!   Bar the door if ye loike; but I'm armed, —
you needn't hev no fear."

"We haint afeard, massa," said the old man, coming to the
fire after fastening the door, " fur 'Zeke keeps loaded.   And
p'raps 'twont 'sturb ye if he sots down yere in de corner, and
primes up his 'volver.   It'm darker dan a pocket up dar in de
loft."

Brown moved away his chair, and the old man sat down
and drew the revolver from his belt.   As he did so, Rachel
exclaimed, —

"Why, 'Zekiel! where did you get that?"

"Oh, 'Zeke got it, missy, — got it honest; *he* neber steals.
Haint it right han'some, Massa Brown?" and he held the
weapon close to the flickering flame.

Brown bent over to more closely examine the weapon, and
then suddenly grasping it, exclaimed, —

"Why, 'Zeke, I know that pistol!   It'r Captain Hart's, of
the Third Kaintucky.   Thar's his name on the stock.   I'se
been onto many a scout with him."

"Wall, 'Zekiel owns it now," said the old man, coolly taking the pistol from the other's hand, " and he reckons Cap'n
Hart wont use it no more ag'in honest folks; for, Massa
Brown, dat rebel hab gone to kingdom come, — sent dar wid
his own 'volver!"

"Dead!   Hart dead?   I'se sorry," exclaimed Brown.   "He
war a clever feller, — one uv the cunnel's staff.   I owe him
for a good turn, and — he's dead!"

"What pistol is that? How did you come by it?" asked Rachel, quickly.

"I cornfiscated it, missy. Dis am de 'volver dat de pore chile sole his life wid, — fur two sorry rebels, and a shot at de ole debil, Cecil."

The widow sank suddenly down upon the settle, and would have fallen to the floor but for Rachel. Springing forward she caught her in her arms, saying, —

"Put it away, 'Zekiel. Come, ma'am, take a little more of the brandy."

"No, Rachel, no more. Only let me get to the bed. I would lie down now."

She rose feebly to her feet, and staggered a step or two forward. Rachel caught her, and, putting her arm about her, said, —

"Lean on me, mother. You will let me call you mother now, — I will be a daughter to you."

"Oh, yes! and you's a good chile. I never knowed what you was afore to-day."

Reaching the bed, she lay down upon the outside, and then drawing Rachel's face close to hers, said, in a low tone, —

"Oh! will he ever get away?"

"Oh, yes, mother! don't be alarmed. He's given 'Zekiel his lesson, — that's the reason he acts so strangely."

Meanwhile the old black, giving no apparent heed to the two women, had been rapidly loading the revolver. When it was done, he tapped it lovingly on the hilt, and said to Brown, with a significant look, —

"'Zeke hab christened dis de 'rebel-killer;' dar's no tellin', — it mought do some mo' ob de wuck it was born to."

" Ye don't seem to loike the Secesh, 'Zeke," said Brown, laughing.

" Wall, I don't, Massa Brown. I neber loiked no one as don't know de diff'rence between dar own and oder folks' plun- der." Rising, then, he turned toward the ladder, saying, " Good-night, Massa Brown, 'Zeke muss go to bed. But bress his soul, he'd loike to hab forgot his pipe, — he couldn't sleep widout dat, nohow. Ye see, massa, 'Zeke hab growd stravagant in his ole age. He'm tuck to both 'backer and brandy."

Brown expressed the opinion that a moderate use of those articles is not hurtful to a good constitution, and then Ezekiel, taking a smouldering coal from the hearth, bore it away up the ladder, — to light his pipe in the attic.

When he had gone, Rachel came to the fire, and, seating herself on the settle, said quickly, as if to direct the conver- sation away from an unpleasant subject, —

" What have you been doing all this while, Bradley ? Why have I never heard from you ? "

" Wall, the truth ar', Rachel, I darn't come back till I'd some money. Ye knows ye allers sot high on that," said Brown, demurely.

" I know, — too high," answered Rachel, a little impatient- ly. " But why didn't you write to me ? "

Brown hesitated a moment, then, looking up with a frank expression on his ruddy features, he said, —

" Well, Rachel, I'll tell ye all, no matter what ye think uv me. Ye see, arter I goed away, I thought the whole thing over, and it troubled me so bad, that to drown it, I tuck to

15 *

drinkin' loike a fish, and for long, jest laid round, not fit fur nothin'.''

"But you bore up well at the time; why did it trouble you so afterward?"

"'Case I warn't nigh ye. When I was, I could be a man, for, somehow, a look at ye guv me courage; but when you was clar out o' sight, the whole thing came onto me, — how I'd stood atween ye and some better man; how by fraud I'd got ye to be my wife, when, if I hadn't, ye mought, at that minute, hev been as well off and happy as ary woman in Kaintucky."

"By fraud?" said Rachel, quietly, and without looking up from the hearth.

"Yes, Rachel, by fraud. I didn't do it myself, but Weddington did; and when I'd every reason to think he'd got lies into yer ears, I warn't man enough to tell ye the truth. It warn't the loss o'the money, fur that I could make ag'in; but it war the conscience uv that thing as come onto me in so terrible a way that it tuck the manhood right out o' me, and made me sink down jest good for nothin'."

Rachel's eyes were still bent upon the fire, but neither surprise nor displeasure was in her voice as she said, —

"I have thought this, Bradley. But why does the young 'Squire pursue me with such a bad, vindictive purpose?"

"'Case ye didn't consent to him when he axed ye, — yer dead father in the house." Here a slight shudder came over the stout frame of the man, and a deeper glow settled on his features. "It'r his natur'; he never guvs up arything he's sot his heart on, and never forgives ary man or woman as comes atween him and his hellish doings. I orter hev know'd this long ago; but I was a fool, and sense then I've been worse nor a fool, or I wouldn't hev staid away, and left ye to his mercy. I've yered it all, Rachel, — how yer mother shot at him, and how the shock and 'citement killed her."

Rachel said nothing for some moments, then she looked up and spoke in a quiet, pleasant way, —

"Well, Bradley, let it rest. We will say no more about it."

"As ye loike, Rachel; but I shall do suthin'. When he and I come together he ar' a dead man, if it ar' in the tent of Cunnel Williams hisself."

"No, Bradley," she said, quietly but firmly, "I shall nòt allow it; your own conduct gives you no right to call him to account for his; and I would leave him to God."

The man turned his face fully to hers, and a look of pain was on his features as he answered, —

"Then ye don't forgive me, Rachel? I thought ye said ye did."

"I do, fully and freely, — if I have anything to forgive; but I have not, — you have not meant to wrong me. God has used you only as an instrument to open my eyes, — to bring me to my true senses."

"Wrong ye, Rachel! I hev, but I hevn't meant to, — I hevn't been myself; if I had, I'd not hev left ye for a hour."

"I don't believe you would; but say no more about it. What induced you to join the rebels?"

"Wall, ye see, whoile I was a-layin' round Cincinnati, Captain Hart — him as the pore boy killed — was a runnin' a boat to Memphis, and he come onto me, — I'd knowed him afore on the Sandy, — and got me to go with him as second mate on the steamer. He treated me right well, though I was drunk half the time, and so, when the war broke out, and he jined the army, I went along with him to Piketon. Thar he got onto Cunnel Williams' staff, and fixed me into the berth of commissary, — to go round and get up the critters for the camp. I've been at it nigh onto four months, and made a pile, Rachel. Here it ar'," — and he drew from a side-pocket a well-filled bag, and laid it on the settle,— "all in half-eagles,— and, Rachel, thar's enough thar to set ye up ag'in as a lady."

Rachel turned musingly toward the fire, but made no reply. In a moment a heavy step was again heard overheard, and soon a tall, uncouth form and black face came down the stairway.

"Lor' bress me," said the new-comer, "'Zeke am a-gittin' to be a ole fool, — gwine to bed and neber once tinkin' dat de pore old mule haint had his fodder."

"Speak lower, 'Zekiel," said Rachel, turning round and looking toward the bed in the corner; "you may wake Mrs. Jordan; I reckon she is asleep."

"No, I'm not asleep," said a voice from the bed; "'Zekiel'll not 'sturb me."

"Not asleep yit, missus!" exclaimed the black man, going towards the bed. "Yous orter be, or dis trouble will a-wear you out. Hab some tea, missus, — dat'll shot you' eyes in a jiffin; and de kittle am a boilin' hot ober de fire."

A smothered scream was the only answer from the woman, and, turning quickly round, the two by the hearth saw the black bending over her, his face against hers and her arms about his neck in a close, convulsive embrace. Springing to her feet, Rachel hurried to the bedside.

"What is the matter?" she cried. "What is the matter, mother?"

The woman made no reply; but, turning her face away, sobbed hysterically. The black said, earnestly, —

"Get de lod'num, missy, quick! it'm de old stitch de missus use to hab in her side, and we muss git her ober it right off."

Rachel went to the cupboard, and in a moment came again to the bedside, with a broken glass and a small vial of laudanum. Pouring some of the opiate into the glass, the black man held it to the lips of the sick woman, and then, with his great, bony hand gently stroked her forehead.

"Neber fear, missus," he said, in a soft, musical voice; "it'll all come right. The Lord is in heaven, — he ruleth over all. John will come back. His time is not yet; and when he goes, it will only be to meet his father and his ancestors. He will die worthy of them." Then his voice sank, and his tone changed, as if he suddenly remembered that others were within hearing. "Massa John'll come back, shore, missus; and Missy Rachel'll tend you till den; she will, for 'Zeke knows she lubs you loike she was you' own chile."

"I do," said Rachel, pressing the hand of the widow. "I will be a daughter to you; you shall never know a want or a sorrow, if I can help it."

"Ye'r a good chile," said the widow, with returning composure; "kiss me, dear. And ye, 'Zekiel, kiss me 'fore ye go. I shan't see ye ag'in to-night, for the lod'num will put me to sleep in a minnit."

The black man bent down and pressed his lips to those
of the woman; then saying, " Good-night! good-night!" he
turned away, and, with a swaying, uncertain step, went out
into the storm, which now was raging furiously around the
lonely cabin.

For long after he went, Rachel sat on the side of the bed,
holding the hand of the sick woman, and every now and then
looking toward the door-way, as if wondering at his prolonged
absence.   But at last she rose, and going forward to the fire,
said to Brown, —

" She is asleep; but what can keep 'Zekiel so long at the
barn ?   He's been gone half an hour."

" Oh, it'r nothin'; the ole feller allers was slower'n tar in
January," answered her husband.   " He'll be back soon.
But sot down, Rachel.   Now she's asleep I want to talk to
ye.   I want to git out o' this suspense.   Ye's kind to me,
Rachel; but ye's cold, — colder'n an icicle.   Don't ye mean
to tuck me back ?   Wont ye be my wife ag'in, now when I'se
come to ye with a pile o' money, — a pile, — every dollar as
I've made, 'cept a few hundred that I *had* to spend t'other
day, to luck myself in the face.   Tell me, Rachel, wont ye
tuck me back ? " and the man's eyes met hers with a pleading, almost agonized, look, that had in it the depth of pathos;
for nothing is more pathetic than the sight of a strong
man, under the pressure of some great yearning of the soul,
going back to the simple humbleness of childhood.   His
emotion affected Rachel; for she turned her face away, and
said nothing for some moments.

" Tell me, Rachel," he said again, " wont ye tuck me
back ? "

"I feel kindly to you," she said, in a low, gentle voice, "very kindly; but I can never be your wife again."

"Why not?" he said, rising from his chair, and standing before her. "Ye don't mean ye's married ag'in! I haint heard o' that."

"No," she answered, quietly; "I am not married again. I do not intend to be married again; but there are reasons why I never can be your wife. Sit down quietly, and I will talk to you."

He sat down in the chair over against the settle, and she went on.

"When I married you, Bradley, I was a weak, silly girl; now I am a woman. I knew then that I did not love you as I should to be your wife; but mother said the love would come, and I hoped it would; but it did not, and now I know the reason."

"What war the reason?" asked Brown, anxiously.

"No matter. It would do you no good to know, and might do you harm. It is enough, Bradley, that I do not love you; and with the notions that I now have of marriage, I should not respect myself, — I should be sinning against my own conscience, — if I became again your wife. I feel very friendly to you. I do not forget how kind you always were to me; how patiently you bore with all my follies and extravagances, and that shuts my eyes to the low trick by which you made me marry you; but, — let us say no more about it. The sin and folly are both past, and nothing — nothing — will induce me to repeat them."

Brown buried his face in his hands, and, for a time, made

no reply. At last he looked up, and, in a voice so soft and gentle that it seemed scarcely his own, said, —

"I wont urge ye ag'in yer will, Rachel. I love ye too well for that. Ye'r the only thing I ever did love, and if ye'd now only love me a little, I mought be a better man. But I know I haint worthy uv ye; and I deserve this; yit it comes hard, hard," and again he buried his face in his hands, and his frame shook with a strong emotion.

Neither spoke for many minutes, then he rose to his feet, and said, with a forced calmness, —

"Wall, I'll go, Rachel. I wont be in yer way. Keep the money. It'll keep ye and 'Zeke till I kin guv ye more. Think kindly uv me, Rachel. I'se been a sorry feller; but I haint meant to wrong ye."

"But you'll not go such a night as this," she said, also rising. "It is storming furiously, and is near upon midnight. Stay till morning; you can sleep in the lean-to."

"And is ye willing I should?"

"Certainly."

"And ye will keep the money; ye'll let me wuck for ye, if I aint your husband?"

"No, Bradley. I will take care of it for you, if you like; it may be safer with me than with you, till you get over this. But I'll not use it. 'Zekiel and I can take care of ourselves. But what has become of him? Wont you go to the barn? I fear something has happened to him."

As Brown went towards the door, a heavy tread sounded again in the attic. It arrested his steps, and turning suddenly, his face aglow, and his eyes blazing with angry fire, he said to Rachel, —

"Ah! thet's it! Ye hev another man! Thet's why ye wont tuck back yer husband! I'll hev his life, if he's my own brother!" Drawing a long knife he started for the garret.

With one bound Rachel was between him and the ladder, but, seizing her by the arm, he was thrusting her aside, when he was suddenly lifted from the floor, and thrown headlong to the centre of the apartment. Before he could regain his feet, a heavy hand was at his throat, and an angry voice cried out, —

"You low, skulkin' tief and villun! Does you dar to tetch my missy! You'll neber do it ag'in, you rebel devil!" and the old negro's grasp tightened about the neck of the prostrate man, till his face assumed a deeper purple than was habitual to it.

"How came you in the attic, 'Zekiel?" cried Rachel. "Where is John?"

"Gone," said the negro, still keeping his hand on the neck of Brown. "Gone out to fodder de mule! He! he!"

"Let Bradley up, then. Let him up, I say!" she repeated, as the old man showed no inclination to heed her words. Then he released his hold, Brown rose to his feet, and the three stood face to face with one another.

Brown's eyes were blazing as he turned upon Rachel, —

"So, it's Jordan," he said, — "Jordan, as, warn't it for me, 'udn't be livin'."

"For you!" exclaimed Rachel. "Did you help him out of the jail?"

"I did. But, if I'd knowed this, I'd let him hung, if he *did* keep ye from starvin'."

16

"It was a noble act, Bradley. I thank you for it. There is nothing wrong between John and me. 'Zekiel, tell your master that you are sorry for what you have done."

The old black had stood speechless with amazement at this sudden revelation; but now he found words to stammer out, —

"'Zeke *am* sorry, Massa Brown. He 'udn't hab laid hands on you ef he'd knowed dat, — nudder 'ud you on Missy Rachel."

"Sit down, Bradley," said Rachel, with more warmth of manner than she had shown during the interview. "I assure you there is nothing wrong between John and me."

Brown stood for a moment, as if but half convinced of the truth of his wife's words; then, with a sudden movement, he took a seat in the chimney-corner, saying, as he did so, —

"I b'lieve ye, Rachel; and I'll tell ye all about it, so ye'll b'lieve me."

"Wait a minnit, Massa Brown," said the old man; "'Zeke wants to yere dat, and he muss put a log on de fire fuss. You sees, massa, — he! he! — you sees, Massa John kept you in de dark, so you moightn't see de shape ob his nose fru de charcoal. Didn't he do ole 'Zeke mazin' well? 'Zeke could ha' said on his Bible dat he was a down yere, and sayin' all dem fine words to Missy Jordan. Pore ting! dat gub her dat ar' stick in de side so sudden."

While the old man was delivering himself of these remarks, he raked together the coals on the hearth, and heaped upon them a few billets of light wood. The juicy pine, blazing up quickly, threw a broad light over the gloomy room, and then Rachel suddenly exclaimed, —

" Why, 'Zekiel, have you got on John's clothes ? "

The old man drew himself up, and, glancing down at his extremities with a look of comic satisfaction, said, —

"Sartin, missy! 'Zeke˜ and Massa John make a trade. 'Taint de fust one dey's made, and you knows 'Zeke allers gits de best end. Don't dey fit right smart? All but de legs, and dem 'Zeke is gwine to splice out wid de fust haff-dollar he kin come by. Dar wont no rebs come round yere now, missy. Dey'll run at de berry sight ob Massa John's clo'es. He! he!"

" But you don't mean to wear them? Put on your Sunday suit, and lay them away until John comes again."

" Wall, missy, 'Zeke reckons he wont! A trade am a trade, and dis was a fair one, dough done in de dark. But, missy," and his voice now lost its tone of grotesque humor, "'Zeke reckons dem ragged old clo'es of his'll serve Massa John a good turn to-night. Who knows but dis bery minnit dey'm fendin' off de arrers ob de Philistins ? "

" P'raps they is," said Brown, who had listened with curious interest to these disclosures; " the kentry ar' full uv Secesh, lookin' fur him. They know he'll head fur the Union camp, and, ten to one, he'll fall in with some on 'em. But he'll git through; fur he's the best darky uv ary white man I uver know'd."

The conversation then turned upon Jordan's escape from prison, and Brown related the part he took in the transaction, which, not to weary the reader with a long repetition of Kentucky vernacular, I will condense into a few sentences of ordinary English.

Soon after the trial and sentence of Jordan, Brown heard

of the relief he had given Rachel in her extremity, and at once determined to effect his release, even at the cost of his accumulations in the rebel service, — the precious gold with which he hoped to buy back the favor of his deserted wife. His first thought was to bribe Colonel Williams, and, with this object in view, he went to Captain Hart, who has already been mentioned, and, stating to him the circumstances, asked him to approach that officer. Hart had been present at the interview between Jordan and Colonel Williams, and sympathized with the prisoner. He entered heartily into the project for his release; but explained to Brown that the rebel commander had no control over his fate, and could not be bribed, if he had.

Hart then suggested the plan, with the working of which the reader is already acquainted; and it was he, aided by his orderly, who abstracted the horse of Jordan from the stable of his commander, — the animal being considered indispensable to Jordan's successful flight.

Brown did not see Jordan while he was within the prison, but spent his whole time there in undermining the principles of the turnkey. The reason he did not acquaint Jordan with his visit was, that he did not know him well enough to trust him with a secret on which his own life depended.

On the following day Hart informed Brown of the intended departure of the two hundred cavalry in pursuit of Jordan, and Brown at once suggested that Hart should accompany the squad, to thwart, if possible, the purposes of Cecil, while he himself followed on, and, through his wife, or the old negro, conveyed warning to the fugitive. He left the camp only a few hours after the cavalry, but lingered at Paintville till after nightfall, to escape observation from the rebel soldiers, who, he feared, would suspect his design, if they saw him in the neighborhood. While there, he learned of the fearful tragedy already enacted at the cabin; but not of the sad mischance by which the younger Jordan had taken the life of perhaps the only man among the two hundred who would have shown his hunted brother either mercy or humanity.

When he finished the recital, Brown looked up at Rachel, and said, a moisture gathering in his eyes, —

" Ye b'lieve this, Rachel ? "

" Yes, Bradley. I think you would not tell a falsehood about such a thing, — not to me."

" And ye don't b'lieve I'se altogether a bad man ? "

" No, Bradley; I always knew you to be capable of generous, noble impulses. If you would only leave drink alone " —

" I has, Rachel! Sense pore Cap'n Hart tell'd me that was the way to make ye a lady ag'in, I haint tetched a drop. And so ye wont throw me off? Ye'll alter what ye has said ? "

" No, Bradley," she answered, a saddened look coming upon her features, "I can't alter it. I said what I did, not on account of what you are, or what you have done; but because — I was not meant to be your wife."

He rested his face on his hand, and made no reply for some minutes; then he rose, and taking up his hat from the table, said in slow, subdued tones, —

" Good-by, Rachel. If ye's ever in ary trouble, ye'll send for me ? "

Rachel also rose to her feet, as she answered, —

16 *

"But you are not going, — in this storm and after midnight! Stay at least till morning."

"No, Rachel, I'll go. I don't keer now fur the dark or the storm."

"But you say the rebels are lurking about; you may fall in with some of them; they may find out what you have done, and take your life for it."

"No matter if they does, — my life haint worth nothin' now. Good-by, Rachel."

Then, strange to say, this man, who loved nothing in the world but that woman and the gold which lay on the table, opened the door, and went out into the storm, leaving both behind in the cabin.

CHAPTER XI.

HE night was dismally dark, and the rain was falling in torrents, when, in the guise of the old negro, Jordan emerged from the cabin, and, with rapid steps, made his way to the rude log-barn which stood, surrounded by a high worm fence, in the centre of the little clearing. As he softly lifted the heavy wooden latch, a low whinny, followed by the quick pawing of steel-clad hoofs, sounded from the inside of the barn, as if to welcome his coming. It may be that, with the acute ear of her species, the mare recognized the tread of her master, and gave vent to these expressions in token of satisfaction at the prospect of being relieved of the companionship of the ancient mule that was snoring soundly in the adjoining stall. Horses, doubtless, regard mules very much as the negro regards that other hybrid, the mulatto.

"Be quiet, Beauty! be quiet! Not a word!" said Jordan, in a hoarse whisper, as he entered the barn, and softly closed the door behind him. While he was doing this the animal backed out of the stall, and, stepping as if she were treading on eggs, came toward her master.

"We've a long road before us, Beauty; have you had

enough to stand it till morning?" whispered the man, putting his mouth close to the ear of the mare. She raised her head, and placing it gently over the man's shoulder, embraced him; but gave out no sound, brute or human.

"The night is dreadful dark, — my life may hang on your eyesight, — will you be careful?" Another and warmer embrace was the answer.

"Well, then, let's be going; but step softly, till we're out of hearing."

Then the man undid the door, and with the horse went out into the darkness. Closing the door again, he turned to the animal and said, again in a whisper, —

"Now, Beauty, keep your eyes open; you shall have a bushel of oats in the morning."

Again the mare answered, — this time by rubbing her nose against the man's features.

"Don't do that, you fool!" exclaimed the man; "you'll rub off the charcoal."

The mare hung down her head, and patting her on the neck, and speaking quickly, as if fearful of having wounded her feelings, Jordan said, —

"Never mind Beauty; it don't matter; but it shows your eyes are only half open; open them wide if you want to help me save Kentucky."

Again she put her head over his shoulder, and then, as he bounded into the saddle, she walked slowly and softly away from the clearing. When they had gone about a quarter of a mile, the man resumed the conversation. Bending down over the saddle-bow, he said, in his usual tones, —

"Now, Beauty, eyes and ears both open, but give them your heels, — show them you had a great-grandfather."

The mare gave a low whinny, and then flew forward like the wind, — or like the lightning, which every now and then lighted up the desolate highway.

To account for the readiness with which the mare understood her master, it is not necessary to suppose that she was acquainted with the English language. Any one who had listened to the whispered colloquy between the two would have observed that the man conveyed his meaning, not by his words, but by the different inflections of his voice, which, delicately modulated, could, like the notes of a cultivated singer, express ideas without the aid of language. The trained ear of the horse understood these sounds, and this shows her wonderful intelligence. I have hesitated about bringing a brute creature into my story, — romance-writers generally do hesitate to describe exceptional characters, — and I do so only in justice to this noble animal, that, like her master, gave her life for Kentucky.

Avoiding the direct road which threads the valley of the Blaine, and which he concluded would be guarded by the rebels, Jordan took a by-way leading eastwardly toward the Big Sandy, and was rapidly approaching the little hamlet of George's Creek, when the mare all at once slackened her pace, and soon stopped in the road suddenly. Leaning forward, Jordan said, in a low voice, —

"What is it, Beauty? What do you see?"

The mare uttered no sound; but, by the slackening of the reins, the man knew that she was turning her face toward him. Dismounting, and leading her into the timber which skirted the road, he went slowly forward along the edge of the highway, cautiously feeling his way with his hands before him. He had not gone far before he came upon an obstruction, — a stout rope stretched across the highway. The storm was still raging furiously, and the night was still pitchy dark, — so dark that no object smaller than a forest could be distinguished at a yard's distance. Sight, therefore, was of no avail; he must depend on his hearing. Stepping softly in among the trees, he slunk behind a huge oak, and, bending his ear to the ground, held his breath and listened. Soon the impatient pawing of a horse sounded from the other side of the road, not ten rods from the obstruction, and the smothered voice of a man said, —

"Quiet! quiet! Devil!"

Jordan rose to his feet, and, going closer to the road, again posted himself behind a tree and listened. Soon a vivid flash of lightning lighted up the narrow by-way, and revealed the figure of a man enveloped in a large cloak, and astride of a powerful horse, standing a little way within the timber. The end of a rifle-barrel protruded from the folds of his cloak, and this and the obstruction showed that he was lying in wait for some one whose coming he expected.

All this Jordan took in on the instant, and, stepping boldly into the road, he accosted the horseman, —

"Why, Lor' bress me, Massa Bent, am dis you? Out yere dis time ob night, in sich a storm as dis?"

The horseman started; but, quickly recovering himself answered, rather abruptly, —

"Is that you, 'Zeke? What are *you* doing here, — so late, and in such a storm?"

"Comin' from meetin', Massa Bent, and we'se had a high time, — a high time, Massa Bent; and 'Zeke don't mind de rain so long as he kin git nigh de Lord. He haint nudder sugar nor salt; he wont melt."

"No, you never melt except you git nigh de Lord," responded the man; "but I do. I'm melting now, 'Zeke. All the water in me is running into my boots, and there'll be nothing left of me if I have to stay here much longer. How much water does John say there is in a man?"

"Six buckets and a few lumps ob sugar for sweetnin', Massa Bent. But dar haint dat much in you. De mos' ob you am whiskey. O Massa Bent, you'm a sorry man to drink so much, and to call your nag arter your best friend, de debil! Nobody else wud do sich a ting as dat. 'Zeke know'd you so soon as you spoke de name ob de critter."

"Well, go home, old man; you've staid here long enough. Your noise may interfere with my business."

"And what am you' business, Massa Bent, yere dis time ob night? 'Zeke tort you was away wid de sodgers. Hab de Unions comed down from Louisa?"

"No, — but go along, old man, and mind, don't you tell a soul that you've seen me; if you do, I'll break your head the next chance I get."

"Oh, neber you f'ar, Massa Dick; 'Zeke knows you too well fur dat; jess you gib him a chaw ob 'backer, and he'll go."

"I can't; both my hands are full; and 'Devil' is as restive as Cain, standing here in the storm."

"Jess you leff 'Zeke holt you' gun, Massa Dick — den you kin git into you' pocket fur de 'backer."

"Well, here then," said the man, handing down his rifle; "but keep your hand over the trigger, — don't let the cap get wet."

Jordan took the weapon, and, placing it quickly against the man's breast, said, in his usual tones, —

"Now, Dick Bent, say a word, or make a movement, and you're a dead man. Tell me why you are here, — away from the Union army."

"Why, how is this?" stammered the man. "Who the devil are you?"

"*You* ought to know. Tell me your business at once; but speak low, or you'll be neither water nor whiskey in another moment."

"Why, bless your soul, John, is it you?" exclaimed Bent, in an excited tone, but still heeding the warning of the other. "You are just the man I am after. I heard from a scout, not two hours before day, that you had escaped from the rebs. I thought you'd know all about them, so I told the general, and he posted a dozen of us off at sun-up to find and bring you in. We had to come by a bridle-way over the mountain, for they hold all the roads between here and head-quarters. Cecil's squad, and Weddington's gang, are both out, and they'd have had you, sure. It occurred to me to rope up all the roads in their rear, and stop all passers till daylight, to head you off. So I've got you. But come, we mustn't waste time,— jump up behind me, and let us travel."

"Which way would you go?"

"The way I came, — up the valley to the bridle-path beyond your house, and then over the mountain, and down on the other side till abreast of Louisa. The coast there is clear, or it was this morning. But where's that old darky? He wanted some tobacco."

"No, tank you, Massa Bent," said Jordan, laughing; "'backer am a bad ting, — a'most as bad as whiskey."

"The devil, John! Were you that old nigger preaching to me about drinking whiskey? Well, it's like you; you're always preaching. But get up behind me, and let's be off."

"No, Beauty is here," said Jordan, giving a low whistle. It was answered by as low a whinny, and in a moment the mare, leaping the rope, was beside him. Bounding into the saddle, Jordan said to his companion, —

"Take away the barricade, Dick; some poor fellow might break his neck over it before morning."

The other did as requested, and a moment afterward the two were riding rapidly along the road by which Jordan had come from the cabin.

As they emerged from the wood which girdles the rude dwelling, and came in sight of the bright light which shone from its windows, Jordan suddenly halted his horse, and said, as if speaking to himself, —

"He's there yet. I wonder if she'll take up again with the wretched creature."

"Who's thar, John?" asked his companion, also reining up his animal.

"Brown, — Rachel's husband."

"The devil he is! Do you know he's joined the rebs, and been plundering every poor widow in all south-east Kentucky. They say he's robbed both sides, and made a pile of money."

17

"I reckon it's so. He brought a bag of gold to the cabin."

"He did! Then I'll have both him and his money," said Bent, spurring his horse forward.

A dozen bounds of the mare brought Jordan to the side of his companion, and, seizing his bridle with a force that threw "Devil" back upon his haunches, he said, —

"What would you do, Dick! You'll risk everything; we can't afford to lose a moment!"

While he said this, the door opened, and a man emerged from the cabin. In another moment the same man, mounted on a horse, rode rapidly past the lighted window.

"Back, Dick! He'll come this way! Into the timber!"

The other said not a word, but quietly let Jordan lead his horse among the trees which skirted the road. There Jordan let go his rein, and the two waited the coming of Brown, whose horse's hoofs were now clattering noisily over the sand of the rain-hardened highway.

The new-comer was nearly abreast of the two horsemen in the wood, when Bent gave a quick yell, and his horse bounded suddenly into the road, with his huge bulk nearly blocking the narrow passage.

"Halt!" cried Bent. "You d—d rebel! halt and surrender!"

Brown had reined in his horse at the first sound; but now he came to a full halt, and said, coolly, —

"Who is ye that asks me to surrender?"

"Captain Bent, of the Union army, by —! and you're my prisoner!" cried Bent, in excited tones.

"Not egzactly, Mr. Bent. I knows ye, and I'm good fur

ye ary day. But, let me pass, — I'm in no mood ter-night fur blood-sheddin'."

"No; you'd rather rob women than fight men; but you'll get your deserts. Surrender at once, or I'll put a bullet into you."

"No, no, Dick," said Jordan, spurring his mare in between the two; "don't be rash. Mr. Brown, we are two against you; but give your word you'll say nothing of this meeting, and you may go unmolested."

"And who is ye as knows me?" said Brown.

"No matter, — only promise, and you may go."

"By the Lord!" cried Brown. "It'r Jordan! I want to thank ye, Mr. Jordan, for the way ye's stood by Rachel."

"Never mind, — that's past. I wish I could thank *you* for the way you've stood by other defenceless women."

"Wall, I *has* done some mean things, Mr. Jordan. I own it; but I haint half so bad as they tell on."

"You're a d—d thief and scoundrel, that's what you are! and there's no discount upon it," cried Bent, angrily.

"Mr. Bent," said Brown, through his grated teeth, "ye couldn't hev said that, and lived, on ary night but this in the whole year. But I knows ye, — ye's a honest man, and that's what I mean to be, if I live. Then I'll fight ye fa'r, man ag'in man, when we come together."

"Say no more, Dick, we are wasting time," said Jordan. "Mr. Brown, you will give me your word you'll not mention this meeting?"

"I will. I wouldn't hurt a hair uv yer head fur all Kentucky."

"I'll trust you.   Now, Dick, move aside, and let him pass."

"You don't mean to let him go," said Bent, standing stock still in the road.   "What the devil's got into you, John?"

"Only a little sense, and that you never had.   Stand back, I tell you, and let him go."

The last sentence was uttered in a voice that either "Devil" or his rider understood, for both went aside, and gave Brown the whole highway.

Spurring his horse a little forward, Brown said, —

"Mr. Jordan, I shan't forget this, and I'll let ye know 'fore I die that Brad. Brown can be a gentleman."

The words came to Jordan on the wind; for, with his companion, he was already galloping rapidly up the deserted highway.

CHAPTER XII.

A MARCH AND A BATTLE.

IT was nine o'clock on the morning of the following day when Jordan and his companion rode up to the head-quarters of the Union general at Louisa. Dismounting at the door-way, they gave their horses in charge of an orderly, who was lounging near, and then, drenched to the skin and mud-bespattered as they were, entered the parlor of the mansion, — the deserted residence of a well-to-do rebel, who, a short time before, had "left his country for his country's good." Two young men in showy uniforms were seated by a window, but, giving them no heed, Bent rapped heavily at the door of an inner apartment. Soon a stout, burly man, half clad, with one boot on and the other off, and a white foam clinging to one half of his face, appeared in the door-way.

"What the devil's the matter?" he asked, in a strong, guttural voice.

"Nothing, general," said Bent, removing his hat; "only we've had a life-and-death ride of forty miles, and are in a hurry to see you."

"Well, what luck? Did you find Jordan?"

"Yes, general, and his news will put us into the saddle to-morrow."

" And why the devil didn't you bring him with you ? Fetch him at once ; don't lose a moment."

" He *is* with me.   This is Mr. Jordan," said Bent, pointing to his companion, and breaking, after a moment, into a boisterous peal of laughter.   In their haste to obtain audience of the Union commander, the two travellers had forgotten Jordan's unpresentable appearance, and it now rushed in all its forlornity upon the mind of Bent. ᴗIn truth, as he stood there, arrayed in the tattered garments of the old negro, his forehead densely black, and the charcoal lying in grimy streaks on the rest of his face, Jordan was a somewhat ludicrous object.   Nelson looked at him from head to foot, and managed to articulate, soberly, —

" I'm glad to see you, Mr. Jordan."   Then his mirth overcame his good-breeding, and, joining heartily in the laugh of Bent, he cried out, " And this is the man who floored old Cecil ? "

Jordan's impassive features expressed neither mirth nor displeasure.   He only said, coolly, —

" I have come with important information, sir ; but I will wait till you can give me attention."

" I'll give it now.   Come in, and close the door.   And, pardon me, Mr. Jordan, but you do look like the devil.   Close the door, and sit down ; I can talk and shave at the same time.   You've got out of rather a tight box, Mr. Jordan," he said, resuming his work before the looking-glass.

" Yes, sir, rather close quarters."

" How was it ? "

" I don't know, general.   The turnkey came to my cell

about midnight, took off my irons, and let me out of the jail. Then I went through the rebel camp, and came away."

" Went through the rebel camp!" Here the general laid down his razor, and turned with a look of surprise at Jordan. " How could you do that?"

" The turnkey had the countersign from the man who bribed him to release me ; with that it was easy."

" Yes, but ticklish; you had a rope round your neck."

" Yes, sir; but what I learned was worth the risk."

" What did you learn?"

" That Williams has three thousand men, and in thirty days will have ten thousand.   Recruits are coming in rapidly from the southern counties, and he is daily expecting reinforcements, by the way of Pound Gap, from Virginia."

" The devil he is!   What does he mean to do then?"

" March northward, and drive you from the State.   Then Kentucky will be lost."

The general by this time had scraped the last flake of foam from his upper lip, and now, laying his open razor upon the table, he sat down, in his shirt-sleeves, and looked intently at Jordan for some moments.   Then he said, —

" And what would you do to save it?"

" March at once upon Williams with every man I could muster."

" And how long should we be in getting there?"

" Perhaps twenty days."

" But then he would have an army of nearly ten thousand."

" Very likely, but poorly armed and equipped.   With three

thousand such troops as yours, you could drive him into Virginia, and keep him there."

"And so save Kentucky."

"Not only save Kentucky, — cut the Confederacy in two, and give a crushing blow to the rebellion!"

"How so?"

"Recruits would flock to you from all quarters. In thirty days you would have twenty thousand. With them you could march into East Tennessee, capture the salt-works in Smythe county, get possession of the Knoxville railroad, and so cut Kentucky and Tennessee off from Richmond."

"Mr. Jordan, you have a head on your shoulders; but you forget one thing, — I couldn't subsist an army in that region ten days."

"You could, for ten years, general. The region is full of live stock, and the country people would give you their last bushel of corn. One man has gathered a thousand beeves there, in one week, for the rebels."

"But how shall I get there? The roads are impassable."

"They are along the river; but by the way of Peach Orchard and Liberty you could get through with .a light train; your first supplies should go up by boat to Prestonburgh, — the country would do the rest."

"But the boats would be taken by the guerillas."

"Not if guarded. Weddington's is the only considerable gang, and he is between here and Liberty. You would drive him before you by taking that route."

"Give me two hundred men, general," said Captain Bent,

"and I'll bag that 'bird' by this time to-morrow. I surrounded him last night."

"Not so fast, Dick," said Nelson. After a moment's pause, he added, — "Tell a boy out there to bring me a cigar and a glass of brandy. By the way, have you had breakfast?"

"No, general," answered Bent, "not a mouthful since yesterday noon. I'll order an extra glass, if you don't object."

"Order breakfast for three, and, Mr. Jordan, be good enough to wash the black off your face; you do look like the devil."

While Bent went out to order breakfast, and Jordan introduced his face to the wash-basin, Nelson sat before the fire, gazing intently into the blaze, apparently forgetful of his half-shod, half-clad condition. When the table had been some time spread, Bent touched him on the shoulder, saying, —

"General, the brandy is waiting, and I'm as hungry as a bear."

Then he rose, drew on his coat, and sat down to breakfast; but throughout the meal uttered not a word, — not even an oath; and this, to those who knew him well, may seem not altogether characteristic. When the meal was about over, he turned to Jordan, and bringing his hand down upon the table, by way of additional emphasis, said, —

"By ——, sir, when I bag 'old Cerro Gordo,' I'll have you made a colonel."

"Then you mean to act on my suggestion?" said Jordan.

"Yes, sir! I'll set out as soon as I can get my men ready and hear from Sherman; but I shan't wait for him. He has

already proposed the movement; all that staggered him
was how to get supplies´ in that God-forsaken region.   Are
you *sure* about that? "

"I've been over every foot of the whole region.   You will
not only have supplies, but the moment you touch Tennessee,
reinforcements will pour in upon you by the thousand.   Before
January you will have an army of fifty thousand, and with
that force among those mountains you could hold out against
the world.   I will go ahead, burn the railroad bridges, and
rouse the whole Piedmont region."

"By ——, Jordan! you are a trump.   But how will you
get through?"

"After you have driven Williams that will be easy."

The events which followed have already gone into history,
and only such brief mention of them need here be made as is
necessary to preserve the thread of our narrative.

On the 20th of October General Nelson put his army in
motion.   On the morning of the 23d his advance guard, under Colonel Marshall, came up with the gang of Weddington at West Liberty.   After a short conflict the rebels fled,
leaving twenty-one dead and thirty-four wounded in the
hands of the Federals.   Pressing on, they encountered the
same evening, at Hazelgreen, the remnant of the gang, reinforced by the squad sent out in pursuit of Jordan.   Another
short conflict ensued, resulting in the capture of thirty-eight
of the rebels.   Weddington himself escaped, and Cecil, severely wounded by the younger Jordan, had previously been
removed to his home at Piketon.

Halting at Hazelgreen to get his men together, Nelson in

a few days resumed his march, and, on the 5th of November, entered Prestonburgh, driving the rebels before him. Here he divided his army into two bodies, and at once advanced upon Piketon. Despatching a force of sixteen hundred, under Colonel Sill, by the way of Jones' Creek, to cut off the retreat of the rebels, he, with the rest of his command, — eighteen hundred infantry, — advanced by the direct road along the Big Sandy. The advance guard of this body, under Colonel Marshall, was ambuscaded by the enemy in a strong natural position, twelve miles south of Piketon; but, after standing their ground for a while, they gave way, and scattered in the surrounding forest. Pressing on with his whole column, Nelson attacked the main body of the enemy at nine o'clock the following morning, and in an hour the rebels were fleeing in all directions. "Cerro Gordo" Williams and eleven hundred of his army made good their escape into Virginia, but the State was, for a time, freed from rebel dominion.

The history of the expedition cannot be better told than in the following address of General Nelson to his troops, which was issued after the battle :

"HEAD-QUARTERS, CAMP HOPELESS CHASE,
PIKETON, KY., Nov. 10, 1861.

"SOLDIERS, — I thank you for what you have done. In a campaign of twenty days, you have driven the rebels from Eastern Kentucky, and given repose to the State. You have made continual forced marches over wretched roads, deep in mud; badly clad, you have bivouacked on the wet ground in the November rains without a murmur. With scarce half rations, you have pressed forward with unfailing perseverance. The only place that the enemy made a stand, though ambushed and very strong, you drove him from in the most brilliant style. For your constancy and courage I thank you, and with the qualities which you have shown that you possess, I expect great things from you in the future.

W. NELSON."

CHAPTER XIII.

MONG those captured by the Union forces was **Judge Cecil**, — who, though convalescent, was unable to bear the fatigue of a hasty march into Virginia, — and **Bradley Brown**, who had returned to Piketon, but had not enlisted in the rebel ranks, or resumed his previous occupation of cattle-stealer for the rebel army. As soon as Jordan learned of Brown's capture he sought him among the rebel prisoners; but, failing to find him in the prison-quarters, he went — led by a sort of instinct — to the dingy public-house which still affords accommodation to such unfortunate men and beasts as an inscrutable destiny consigns to the tender mercies of its surly, whiskey-drinking landlord. There he found him, seated in a corner of the smoke-beclouded bar-room, his head swaying to and fro, and his senses half drowned in the frequent potations in which he had been indulging. Touching him on the shoulder, Jordan said, —

" Mr. Brown, I want you to go with me."

" Go wi' ye!" said Brown, looking up with unsteady gaze, and speaking thick and brokenly, " I reckon I wont. I guv my word to Dick Bent, — and he's a gentleman, every inch of him, — and I reckon I wont. I wont stir from yere till

18   (205)

I'm tuck out dead — dead; and the sooner that happens the better."

"You needn't speak of death," said Jordan; "you are not going to die, — not till you've kept your word to me, and shown yourself a gentleman."

Brown looked up again with the same meaningless stare; but in a moment staggered unsteadily to his feet, and, holding forth his hand, stammered out, —

"Why, Mr. Jordan, is it ye? Is it ye? But I might hev know'd it; nobody else would speak kind to a pore broken devil loike me; nobody but ye and Dick Bent; and he's á gentleman, Mr. Jordan, — every inch a gentleman."

"I know," answered Jordan; "when he lets brandy alone. And so can you be, if you'll keep sober. But, come, I want you to go with me, — I want you to do something for me."

"Do suthin' fur ye!" exclaimed Brown, again clutching Jordan's hand. "I'll do arything fur ye, — I'd die fur ye, — I *would*, Mr. Jordan! I'd let 'em draw my blood drop by drop, if 'twould do ye ary good."

"I believe you," said Jordan, putting his arm within that of Brown, and leading him out of the room.

"What ar' it, Mr. Jordan?" said Brown, somewhat sobered by the pure air of the open street. "What kin I do fur ye?"

"I'll tell you in the morning. Come to my tent, and sleep off the effects of the liquor, then I'll tell you."

On the following morning, thoroughly sobered by a night's sleep, Brown said to Jordan, —

"I'm ashamed, Mr. Jordan, to hev ye find me as ye done;

but I couldn't help it, — I couldn't help it. If I didn't drink,
I should go crazy wi' all the trouble thet's on me."

"I know you have trouble, and I'm sorry for you," said
Jordan, whose keen penetration had already detected the
secret of Brown's depressed feelings. "But I have work for
you that will keep your mind busy, and — take you back to
Rachel."

"Hev ye? I'll do it, Mr. Jordan; but — gwine back to
Rachel! There's no chance uv that, — no chance, Mr. Jordan. She's said the word, and nothin' 'll turn her. If ye
thinks so, ye don't know her as I does."

"I didn't refer to that," said Jordan, with some hesitation.
"That is between yourselves. What I want you to do is to
help me to remove the negroes into Ohio. They have been
declared free, and now can go; but 'Zekiel is too old to attend
to everything, and I have to be away for a fortnight, — perhaps for a month. I want you to get their things to Paintville, hire some flat-boats to take them down the river, and
have all in readiness against my return, when I will go with
them."

"I'd do it, Mr. Jordan, willin'; but I'se a prisoner yere on
parole. I can't stir out o' Piketon."

"I will get your release from the general," said Jordan.

"Then I'll go, — go to-day," answered Brown.

Knowing the commanding general's pro-slavery proclivities,
Jordan omitted, in his application for the release of Brown,
all mention of the real object for which he was going, and
merely stated that he desired him to superintend some business which might suffer if not at once attended to. The
request was readily granted, and the general added, —

" Ask anything of me, Jordan.   I have not forgotten my promise to see you made a colonel."

Brown started that day for the little hamlet among the mountains, and on the same evening Jordan set out on his long and perilous expedition into Tennessee. The country was still infested with straggling bands of rebel guerillas, but he made his way over the mountains in safety, and soon the results of his journey were known to the whole country. Every bridge between Knoxville and the Cumberland Gap, on the great line of railway which connects Richmond with the south-west, was, within a fortnight, destroyed, and the Confederacy, for the time being, as effectually cut asunder as if an earthquake had suddenly put an impassable gulf between its two sections. Nothing remained to insure the permanent dismemberment of the South but for Nelson to march with his whole force — now sixty-five hundred strong — to the occupation of Knoxville.

But this was not to be.   The country was not yet ready to do equal and exact justice to all men ; and so its heroic sons were yet to march over the burning ploughshare, and, with bleeding feet, to tread the wine-press of His wrath in the weary years that were coming.

Nelson had received his superior's approval of Jordan's great project, and was just on the eve of setting out on the expedition, when, with the bulk of his forces, he was suddenly recalled to Louisville, and East Kentucky was once more laid open to the inroads of the enemy.

One of those little events had occurred which so often changed the destinies of the war.   Tired out with the tardy and inefficient measures of the general government, Sherman, on the very day that Jordan set out for Tennessee, had resigned, and Buell had succeeded him in command of the department. This altered the whole programme of operations. East Tennessee was left to its fate; the campaign which resulted in the barren and bloody battle of Shiloh was decided on, and the troops in East Kentucky were ordered westward, to take part in the monster expedition which, it was hoped, would open the Mississippi from the Ohio to the Gulf of Mexico.

On his return, rather more than a fortnight after setting out on the expedition, Jordan learned these facts, and that Piketon was again in possession of the rebel forces, who, re-entering the State at Pound Gap, were already rapidly recruiting in the disaffected southern counties. With a heavy heart he turned his horse to the westward, and, after a perilous ride of two days and nights, entered Paintville at early dawn on the morning of the first of December. The place was held by a portion of the Fourteenth Kentucky (Union) regiment, and was the most southerly point then in possession of the Union forces. So soon had all the fruits of Nelson's toilsome march been thrown away by the blundering policy of Buell and the officials at Washington!

18*

CHAPTER XIV.

THE REMOVAL.

HE day succeeding Brown's arrival at the plantation was Sunday, and then, to the survivors and descendants of the fifty slaves originally liberated by Weddington's will, — now numbering, of men, women, and children, a hundred and twenty, — Ezekiel announced from the pulpit of the little church that the glad day which, through twenty years of deferred hope and ceaseless struggle, they had longed and prayed for, had at last come, and they were about to be led out of the land of Egypt, out of the house of bondage, into a fair country, flowing with milk and honey, beyond the Ohio.

A time of mingled grief and rejoicing followed; for some must go and some must stay, and ties of a lifetime were to be rudely sundered; but on the following morning they set about preparing for the journey. Every little article of furniture, however poor, had to be gathered up, and carried along, and thus more than a fortnight went away before they were ready to go; but at last they set out, — a motley caravan, laughing, and weeping, and singing, and shouting by turns, on the road to Paintville. A dozen heavy wagons, bearing their household goods, led the way, and two lighter vehicles followed.

(210)

In one of these, drawn by the old mule, rode Ezekiel and the widow Jordan; in the other, Brown and his wife Rachel. They had met but once since his arrival at the plantation, and he had avoided her on the plea that he must be away at Paintville most of the time in making arrangements for the removal of the negroes; but now he asked permission to drive her to the village, determined to make one last effort to induce her to fulfil the promise she had made to "love, honor, and keep him, in sickness, and in health, and, forsaking all others, to keep only to him, so long as they both should live."

As the little cabin went out of sight among the trees, he turned to her and said, in a voice husky with emotion, —

"Rachel, ye's gwine 'mong strange folks, inter a strange kentry, — wont ye be lonely thar?"

"Oh, no," she answered; "Mrs. Jordan will be with me; and, besides, I shant have time to be lonely, — there will be so much to do for the negroes."

"Yes, at fust; but as soon's they's settled they'll do fur tharselves; then ye'll have time to think, — then ye'll be lonely, and, 'sides, ye'll have no one to keer fur ye."

"Yes, I shall; 'Zekiel will care for me."

"But 'Zekiel carn't live forever."

"He may outlive me. He's not eighty, and he says his grandfather lived to be more than a hundred."

"Wall, ye don't tuck my meanin', Rachel. Wont ye let me go with ye? Wont ye be my wife ag'in? I'se been a readin' the good Book lately, and ye know it say them as God has jined together haint to be put asunder, but fur one thing, — and I'se allers been true to ye, Rachel."

"I know what the Bible says," she answered, somewhat

impatiently, "but I have given you my answer, — I cannot be your wife again."

"But wont ye let me go wi' ye?" he said, after a pause, and in pleading tones, — "not to be yer husband; but to be nigh ye, — whar I kin see ye, and work fur ye, and know yer happy? Somehow, I carn't stand up and be a man, when I'se away from ye, Rachel; I haint no backbone. I fall into bad ways, and I shill be lost, body and soul, — I knows I shill be lost, if I carn't be nigh ye, see ye once in a while, and know ye think a little uv him as cares more fur ye nor he does for all the rest uv creaytion."

Her words had a harsh, gritty tone, as if she had steeled her mind with a fixed purpose, when she answered, —

"No, Bradley, we each must stand alone. The sight of you is a trial to me; it brings back things I would forget; makes me discontented with the lot my own folly has made for me. We cannot live near one another!"

He drew a long breath, and his ruddy face took on a deathly pallor, as with these words his last hope went out, and he saw stretching before him a lonely, dreary lifetime. It was many minutes before he spoke; then, in a low, tremulous voice, he answered, —

"God forgive ye, Rachel! May ye never know what it ar' to love only one thing in the world, and to hev that one thing turn inter an icicle!"

Her face was as pallid as his; but she made no reply, and in another hour, during which neither spoke, they parted at the door-way of the mean public house at Paintville.

The negroes were soon housed in a deserted building, in which Brown had fitted up rude but comfortable quarters,

and the same day they began loading their household goods
upon one of the uncouth flat-boats he had chartered for their
voyage down the river. It was tedious work; for they handled each poor article of furniture as if it had been a piece
of porcelain; but by midnight all was on board, and they
went back to their quarters, to patiently await the coming of
Jordan.

In the morning he came, and, hearing of the presence of the
negroes, went at once to the landing. There he was met by
Brown, who explained to him all his arrangements.

"You have managed admirably, Mr. Brown. How much
money have you expended?" said Jordan, drawing out a
leathern wallet.

"I haint kep' no 'count," answered Brown, "and I carn't
tuck no pay; I warn't to do this much fur ye, — ye kep' my
wife from starvin'."

"Never mind that; I would rather pay you, though the
negroes have none too much to set them a-going in Ohio."

"Wall, let it go fur them, then; 'taint much, and they's a
decent set uv darkies."

Jordan thanked him, and then Brown, holding out his
hand, said, —

"Good-by, Mr. Jordan. If I kin ever do ye a good turn,
I'll do it. Brad. Brown never forgets a kind thing, if he ar'
a drunken critter."

"Where are you going?" asked Jordan. "Wont you
come with us, and help me get the flat down the river? I
know nothing of navigation."

"No, Mr. Jordan, I carn't. Thar's been a exchange, and I
must go back to the rebels."

"Not to fight again against the Union?"

"I never fout, — I only stole!" said Brown, bitterly; "but now, I reckon, I'll guv up stealin', and go to foutin'; fur it'll keep me busy, and ar' man's business."

"I am sorry, — you will fight against your friends and your country."

"Friends! I haint no friends, Mr. Jordan; and as for the kentry, it'r which and t'other whoever whips. The durned 'ristocrats'll rule, whether it'r rebel or Union; and a pore man haint no chance with nuther."

"That is too true — on this side of the border," said Jordan; "but why not go to Ohio with Rachel?"

"Rachel! Don't ye speak uv thet! She's said a'ready she warn't willin'. Good-by, Mr. Jordan."

Saying this, he turned and walked rapidly away from the landing.

At the stable of the tavern, where he went for the horse he had ridden from Piketon, and which, if the truth must be told, still rightfully belonged in that vicinity, he was met by the old negro.

"Whar am you a-gwine, Massa Brown?" asked Ezekiel, as he saw him preparing to mount the animal.

"To the devil, 'Zeke, — put a beggar on horseback, ye knows, and he's shore to go thar."

"Yas; 'Zeke knows," answered the old black, laughing; "but you haint a beggar, Massa Brown; nor you wont be, so long as you keep dis;" and he drew the bag of gold from his capacious pocket.

"Then your missus wont keep it?" said Brown, bitterly.

"No, Massa Brown. But 'taint dat, — 'taint 'case she

don't loike you, Massa Brown. It'm 'case we's enuff wid her hands and 'Zeke's, — and p'raps wid dis you kin git anoder home and anoder 'ooman."

Brown said not a word, but, leaning over his saddle-bow, took the bag of money, and then, burying the rowels in the flanks of his horse, turned up the mountain road that led to the rebel camp which again was forming at Piketon.

CHAPTER XV.

N the following morning the negroes were embarked on an 'empty flat-boat that was moored to the dock near their lodgings, and, going upon another, which was freighted with their household goods, Jordan, his mother, Rachel, and the mare, "Beauty," set out on the voyage down the river. Their way was slow, for the water was low, and the channel narrow and difficult of navigation; but at nightfall they rounded-to at the wharf at George's Creek, only thirty miles from the longed-for Ohio. Here Jordan went on shore to gather further information about the river, before venturing down by moonlight. He was away only half an hour, but, on his return to the boats, found them in possession of a squad of soldiers, and the negroes huddled together, like frightened sheep, upon the landing. As he approached, Ezekiel, his furrowed face wet with tears, came forward to meet him.

"It'r all up, Massa John," he said; "all up. Read dese. We muss go back inter bondage."

Jordan glanced at the two papers the black handed him. One was a writ from the court of Johnson county, restraining him, or any other person, from removing out of the State certain negroes, who were claimed as the property of Jackson Weddington, Esquire. This was signed by Judge Cecil. The other was an order to the same effect, addressed, "To all whom it may concern;" and this was signed by "William Nelson, Commander of the Department of East Kentucky." This last made no mention of Jordan, which rendered it probable that the general had given it in ignorance of his connection with the negroes. Both bore date ten days previously, showing that, with a refinement of cruelty worthy of savages, the men-hunters had purposely delayed the execution of the papers until the blacks had removed their little store of worldly wealth, and were almost within sight of their long-hoped-for freedom.

Jordan's first thought was to go to Nelson, at Louisville, and, by an appeal to his humanity, induce him to countermand his order; but Nelson was strongly pro-slavery in sentiment. He feared the war would induce a stampede among the negroes of Kentucky, and this was a first step in that direction. Besides, he would not be likely to annul the order of a court, the reëstablishing of which had been a part of his plan for pacifying the district.

Uncertain what to do, Jordan was turning away to take counsel of himself in silent reflection, when his arm was touched lightly by the young officer in command of the squad of soldiers.

"Mr. Jordan," he said, "this is unpleasant business; but my orders are strict, — these negroes must be at the head of Blaine by this hour to-morrow morning."

"By to-morrow morning!" exclaimed Jordan. "You certainly can't mean that these women and children, half-clad as they are, shall be made to march twenty miles over the frozen ground, on such a night as this, in winter!"

"Those are my orders, — they are strict; the negroes must be at the Weddington plantation by daylight to-morrow. And I must tell you further, Mr. Jordan, my orders are to scuttle and sink both of the boats. I will give you two hours to remove the furniture."

"Very well, sir," said Jordan, without turning round. "That is enough. Come, 'Zekiel, and bring every man and woman with you."

The negroes ceased their lamentations, and, going to work with a will, soon had the furniture unladen, and stowed away under the roof of a half-vacant building which served as a storehouse for passing steamers. Then the soldiers scuttled and sunk the boats; and then, escorted by the whole squad, now mounted on stout horses, the old negro led his flock back into the wilderness.

When they had gone, Jordan applied at every one of the half-dozen houses which compose the little hamlet, to get lodgings for his mother and Rachel; but at none of them could they be admitted. Jordan was known to be a Union man, proscribed, and under sentence of death by the Confederates, and not one of the inhabitants would risk the wrath of the rebels, — who, it was rumored, were gradually driving the Union troops from the mouth of the river, — by giving shelter to the two houseless women with whom he was connected.

With a heavy heart he went back to the storehouse. There was no fire, and no means of making one in the building; but opening the negroes' stores, he spread before the two women a scanty meal, and then arranged for them a bed in the most sheltered corner of the storehouse. When this was done, he went out upon the landing to get strength, — strength from the Source that never faileth. For the first time in his life, his mental vision was clouded, and his heart, as it were, lead in his bosom.

The freedom of these negroes had been the great purpose of his father's life, and his own dream from early boyhood. Often had the old Scotchman said to him, as year after year he had gone on with the well-nigh hopeless legal struggle, —

"John, I 'may not live to get through it; but don't you die till you see these poor people safely settled in Ohio."

This the boy had promised, and when, after long years, he had set about carrying the promise into execution, he felt that he was doing that for which the brave old man, who had given his life for him, would, when they should meet in another world, bless him. But now all his plans were crushed, — crushed by his own friends, — by the very man whom he had aided to what many a soldier values most, — reputation; and who had professed to owe him a lasting debt of gratitude. As he thought of all this, a feeling of bitterness came over him, and for a moment his heart wavered in its love — pure and unselfish till now — for his State and his Country. Why should he spend his strength for such returns? Why give his time, perhaps his life, to secure peace and safety to a people who seemed destitute of every feeling of justice and humanity?

The night was dark and cold. A thin coat of snow covered the ground, and a misty veil of clouds shrouded the sky, letting the stars shine but dimly. But in the cold and the darkness he stood there, now looking up at the sky, and now down along the windings of the gloomy river. At last he sank to his knees, his hands clenched together, and his head bent downward. Long he prayed, pleading with God as a child pleads with its father; asking help, guidance, and strength to do the work which it was his to do for his country.

As he finished, a soft arm wound itself about his neck, and a wavy head sank down on his shoulder. Kneeling beside him was Rachel.

"O John!" she said, "I know it all. I know how you feel. I know you are throwing your strength and your life away. But let us go, — let us go to some free State where we can live in peace together. I will go with you; I will be your wife. You shall never know a care or a sorrow;" and she pressed her cheek against his, and clung to him with a strange, convulsive energy. He put his arm about her, and, bending down, kissed her on the forehead. Then he rose to his feet, and, putting away her soft brown hair, drew her gently to him.

"I knew the truth would come to you, Rachel," he said, tenderly; "but it can't be in this world; it will be in the other. Then you will be mine forever."

"And why not in this world, John?" she said. "Only *he* is in the way, and the law will free me from him to-morrow."

"Yes, I know;" and now, with his great hand he gently stroked her forehead. "But I have work to do, Rachel; work which I must do, to stand where you would have me when I change this world for the other. That work I can't do, if my little girl is with me; — can't do, unless she learns to stand alone and be a true woman."

"But I can't stand alone, John. I can't live without you. I so long for you, at times, that it seems I shall die if you are kept from me any longer."

"And so do I for you, Rachel; but I go to God, and he gives me strength, — strength to do my work, and to bear all He lays upon me. Go to Him, my darling!"

Her arms twined again about his waist, and her head sank again upon his shoulder; and so they stood there for many minutes, neither of them speaking. At last she looked up, and said, —

"O John, I *will* pray; I *will* try to be a true woman."

"You are my own Rachel," he said, bending down, and again placing his lips to her forehead. "You are my own Rachel, and there will be a recompense for all this, — for all this, in the hereafter."

The next morning, mounting Rachel and his mother on the back of "Beauty," Jordan led them slowly and wearily back to the little cabin among the mountains. There he remained for a fortnight, superintending, at first, the bringing back of the household goods of the negroes, and then lying out in the woods, to escape the murderous gangs of rebels, who again were overrunning the whole district.

Then a new actor appeared on the scene, and Jordan was again able to do some service to his State and Country. This new actor was a young Ohio officer, who now took command of the Union forces in Eastern Kentucky.

19 *

CHAPTER XVI.

HIS young officer had a character that peculiarly fitted him for the arduous work which was before whoever attempted to retrieve the fortunes of the Union arms in Eastern Kentucky.

Born in a log hut, in the depths of the Ohio wilderness, he was the younger son of a poor widow, and his early life had been one of great hardship and poverty. Until he was sixteen, he gained a livelihood by working on a farm, and in a dry saltern, doing odd jobs of carpentering, and by driving the horses of a boat on the Ohio and Pennsylvania Canal. While on the canal, he fell in with another boy, some years his senior, who was named Bradley Brown, and whose dissolute habits might have led him into bad courses, had not a singular event occurred, which changed the whole current of his life, and turned a new page in his history. This event was a narrow escape from drowning.

One rainy midnight, as the boat on which he was employed was leaving one of those long reaches of slackwater which abound in the Ohio and Pennsylvania Canal, the boy was called out of his berth to take his turn in tending the bowline. Tumbling out of bed, his eyes heavy with sleep, he took his stand on the narrow platform below the bow deck, and began uncoiling a rope to steady the boat through a lock it was approaching. Slowly and sleepily he unwound the coil, till it knotted, and caught in a narrow cleft in the edge of the deck. He gave it a sudden pull, but it held fast; then another and a stronger pull, and it gave way, but sent him over the bow of the boat into the water. Down he went into the dark night and the still darker river; and the boat glided on, to bury him among the fishes. No human help was near. God only could save him, and he only by a miracle. So the boy thought as he went down, saying the prayer his mother had taught him. Instinctively clutching the rope, he sank below the surface; but then it tightened in his grasp and held firmly. Seizing it hand over hand, he drew himself up on deck, and was again a live boy among the living. Another kink had caught in another crevice and saved him. Was it that prayer, or the love of his praying mother, which wrought this miracle? The boy did not know, but long after the boat had passed the lock, he stood there, in his dripping clothes, pondering the question.

Coiling the rope, he tried to throw it again into the crevice; but it had lost the knack of kinking. Many times he tried, — six hundred, says my informant, — and then sat down, and reflected.

"I have thrown this rope," he said to himself, "six hundred times; I might throw it ten times as many without its catching. Ten times six hundred are six thousand; so there were six thousand chances against my life. Against such odds, Providence only could have saved it. Providence, therefore, thinks it worth saving; and if that's so, I wont

throw it away on a canal-boat. I'll go home, get an education, and become a man."

Straightway he acted on the resolution, and not long afterward stood before his mother's log cottage in the Cuyahoga
wilderness. It was late at night, the stars were out, and the
moon was down; but by the fire-light, that came through
the window, he saw his mother kneeling before an open book,
which lay on a chair in the corner. She was reading, but her
eyes were off the page, looking up to the Invisible.

"Oh, turn unto me," she said, "and have mercy upon me!
give Thy strength unto Thy servant, and save the son of
Thine handmaid!"

More she read, which sounded like a prayer, but this is all
that the boy remembers.

He opened the door, put his arm about her neck, and his
head upon her bosom. What words he said I do not know;
but there, by her side, he gave back to God the life which he
had given. So the mother's prayer was answered. So sprang
up the seed which in toil and tears she had planted.

Then the boy went to work in earnest. With a saw and a
jack-plane he fitted himself for college; and, borrowing
money upon a policy of insurance on his life, partly worked
and partly paid his way through an eastern university. At
the age of twenty-four he graduated, a man, with a body
hardened by toil, and a mind strengthened and energized by
early struggles, and a fixed purpose — born of his experience
on that rainy midnight — to give all his strength and all his
life to the work that fell to him for God and humanity.

The blood of the Ballous was in his veins; so at first he
took to preaching, as naturally as a duck takes to water; but

soon he was made President of the Collegiate Institute at Hiram, Ohio, and within three years was elected to the Senate of his native State. A man of nearly thirty, he was serving in that body when the war broke out, and it was he who sprang to his feet, when the President's call for seventy-five thousand men was announced to the Ohio Senate, and, amid the tumultuous acclamations of the assemblage, moved that twenty thousand troops and three millions of money should at once be voted as the quota of the State.

Not many months afterward Governor Dennison offered him command of a regiment. He went home, opened his mother's Bible, and pondered upon the subject. He had a wife, a child, and a few thousand dollars. If he gave his life to the country, would God and the few thousand dollars provide for his wife and child? He consulted the Book about it. It seemed to answer in the affirmative, and before morning he wrote to a friend, —

"I regard my life as given to the country. I am only anxious to make as much of it as possible before the mortgage on it is foreclosed."

To this man, who thus went into the war with a life not his own, was given, on the 20th of December, 1861, command of all the Union troops in Eastern Kentucky; and thus it was that he became an actor in our brief history.

He knew nothing of war beyond its fundamental principles; which are, I believe, that a big boy can whip a little boy, and that one big boy can whip two little boys, if he take them singly, one after the other.

He knew no more about it, and yet he was selected by General Buell — one of the most scientific military men of his

time — to solve a problem which has puzzled the heads of
the ablest generals; namely, how two small bodies of men,
stationed widely apart, can unite in the face of an enemy
and beat him, when he is of twice their united strength,
and strongly posted behind intrenchments. With the help
of many "good men and true" he solved this problem; and
in telling how he solved it, I shall resume the direct thread of
my narrative.

In the months of October and November, this graduate
from the Ohio and Pennsylvania Canal, with the aid of Judge
Sheldon, of Elyria, Don A. Pardee, of Medina, Ralph Plumb,
of Oberlin, and other patriotic citizens of his district, had
raised the Forty-second Regiment of Ohio Volunteers.
Taking its command, he repaired with it to Camp Chase,
and at once set vigorously to work to master the art and mystery of war, and to give to his men such a degree of discipline
as would fit them for effective service in the field. Bringing
his saw and jack-plane again into play, he fashioned com-
panies, officers, and non-commissioned officers out of maple
blocks, and, with these wooden-headed troops, thoroughly mas-
tered the infantry tactics in his quarters. Then he organized
a school for the officers of his regiment, requiring thorough
recitation in the tactics, and illustrating the manœuvres by
the blocks he had prepared for his own instruction. This
done, he instituted regimental, company, squad, skirmish, and
bayonet drill, and kept his men at these exercises from six
to eight hours a day, until it was universally admitted that
no better drilled or disciplined regiment could be found in
Ohio.

While thus employed, he was suddenly ordered to move his

regiment, by the way of Cincinnati, to Catlettsburg, Kentucky, a town at the junction of the Big Sandy and the Ohio, and to report immediately, in person, to the department head-quarters at Louisville.   Arriving at Louisville just at sunset on the 19th of December, he at once sought an interview with General Buell, and was told by that officer that he was to be sent against the rebel General Humphrey Marshall, who had invaded Eastern Kentucky, from the Virginia bor-der, and had already advanced as far north as Prestonburg, driving the small Union force before him.

How many men Marshall had was not known ; but he was rapidly gathering an army, and, if unmolested, would soon have a large force, with which he could hang on Buell's flank, and so prevent his advance into Tennessee, or, if he did ad-vance, cut off his communications, and, falling on his rear, while Beauregard encountered him in front, crush him, as it were, between the upper and nether millstones.   This done, Kentucky was lost, and that, occurring so early in the war, the dissolution of the Union might have followed.

To check this dangerous advance, meet Marshall — a thor-oughly educated military man — and the uncounted hordes whom his reputation would draw about him, the inexperienced Ohio colonel was offered — what ? Twenty-five hundred men, — eleven hundred of whom, under Colonel Cranor, were at Paris, Kentucky, the remainder — his own regiment, and the half-formed Fourteenth Kentucky, under Colonel Moore — at Catlettsburg ; a hundred miles of mountain country, overrun with rebels, being between them ! This was the problem of the big boy, — of uncertain size, but known to be skilled in war, — and the two little boys, who were to whip him, when, only by a miracle, could they act together, and when they knew no more of war than can be learned from the posturing of wooden blocks, and the crack, perhaps, of squirrel rifles.

"That is what you have to do, Colonel Garfield, — drive Marshall from Kentucky," said Buell, when he had finished his view of the situation; "and you see how much depends on your action. Now, go to your quarters, think of it over night, and come here in the morning, and tell me how you will do it."

On the way to his hotel, the young colonel bought a rude map of Kentucky, and then, shutting himself in his room, spent the night in studying the geography of the country in which he was to operate, and in making notes of the plan which in the still hours came to him as the only one feasible, and likely to secure the objects of the campaign.

His interview with the commanding general, on the following morning, was, as may be imagined, one of peculiar interest. Few army officers possess more reticence, terse logic, and severe military habits than General Buell, and as the young man laid his rude map and roughly-outlined plan on his table, and, with a curious and anxious face, watched his features to detect some indication of his thought, the scene was one for a painter. But no word or look indicated the commander's opinion of the feasibility of the plan, or the good sense of the suggestions. He spoke, now and then, in a quiet, sententious manner, but said nothing of approval or disapproval; only, at the close of the conference, he did make the single remark, —

"Your orders will be sent to you at six o'clock this evening."

Promptly at that hour the order came, organizing the Eighteenth Brigade of the Army of the Ohio, Colonel Garfield commanding; and with the order came a letter of instructions, in Buell's own hand, giving general directions for the campaign, and recapitulating, with very slight modifications, the plan submitted by Garfield. On the following morning he took leave of his general, and the latter said to him, at parting, —

" Colonel, you will be at so great a distance from me, and communication will be so slow and difficult, that I must commit all matters of detail, and much of the fate of the campaign, to your discretion. I shall hope to hear a good account of you."

Garfield set out at once for Catlettsburg, and, arriving there on the twenty-second day of December, found his regiment had already proceeded to Louisa, — twenty-eight miles up the Big Sandy.

A state of general alarm existed throughout the district. The Fourteenth Kentucky — the only force of Union troops left in the Big Sandy region — had been stationed at Louisa; but had hastily retreated to the mouth of the river during the night of the nineteenth, under the impression that Marshall, with his whole force, was following to drive them into the Ohio. Union citizens and their families were preparing to cross the river for safety; but with the appearance of Garfield's regiment a feeling of security returned, and this was increased when it was seen that the Union troops boldly pushed on to Louisa, without even waiting for their colonel. This, however, was only in pursuance of orders he had telegraphed on the morning after he had formed the plan of the

20

campaign by midnight, in his dingy quarters at the hotel in Louisville.

Waiting at Catlettsburg only long enough to forward supplies to his forces, Garfield appeared at Louisa on the morning of the twenty-fourth of December, and thenceforward he became an actor, in all its circumstances considered, one of the most wonderful dramas to be read of in history.

CHAPTER XVII

ARFIELD had two very difficult things to accomplish. He had to open communications with Colonel Cranor, while the intervening country, as has been said, was infested with roving bands of rebels, and filled with a disloyal people. He had also to form a junction with the force under that officer, in the face of a superior enemy, who would, doubtless, be apprised of his every movement, and be likely to fall upon his separate columns the moment that either was set in motion, in the hope of crushing them in detail. Either operation was hazardous, if not well-nigh impossible.

Evidently the first thing to be done was to find a trustworthy messenger to convey despatches between the two halves of his army. To this end, Garfield applied to Colonel Moore, of the Fourteenth Kentucky.

"Have you a man," he asked, "who will die rather than fail or betray us?"

The Kentuckian reflected a moment, then answered, —

"I think I have. John Jordan, from the head of Blaine."

Jordan was sent for, and soon entered the tent of the Union commander. The young colonel was at once impressed with his appearance. He describes him as a tall, gaunt, sallow man, of about thirty, with gray eyes, a fine falsetto voice, pitched in the minor key, and a face which had as many expressions as could be found in a regiment.

To him he seemed a strange combination of cunning, simplicity, undaunted courage, and undoubting faith, but possessed of a quaint sort of wisdom, which ought to have given him to history. He sounded him thoroughly, for the fate of the campaign might depend on his fidelity; but Jordan's soul was as clear as crystal, and in ten minutes the young colonel had read it as if it had been an open volume.

"Why did you come into the war?" at last asked the commander.

"To do my part for the country, colonel," answered Jordan; "and I made no terms with the Lord: I gave him my life without conditions, and if he sees fit to take it on this tramp, why, it is his. I have nothing to say against it."

"You mean that you have come into the war not expecting to get out of it?"

"I do, colonel."

"Will you die rather than let the despatch be taken?"

"I will."

The colonel recalled what had passed in his own mind when poring over his mother's Bible that night at his home in Ohio; and it decided him.

"Very well," he said, "I will trust you."

The despatch was written on tissue-paper, rolled into the form of a bullet, coated with warm lead, and put into the hand of Jordan. He was given a carbine, and a brace of revolvers, and, mounting his mare when the moon was down, he started on his perilous journey. He was to ride at night, and hide in the woods, or in the houses of loyal men, in the daytime.

It was pitch dark when he set out, but he knew every inch of the way, having travelled it often, driving mules to market. He had gone twenty miles by early dawn, and the cabin of Rachel was only a few miles beyond him. His mother was there, and there he would hide till nightfall. He pushed on, and tethered "Beauty" in the timber; but it was broad day when he rapped at the door and was admitted.

He was received joyfully, and, after breakfast, was conducted by Rachel to the guest-chamber, where, lying down in his boots, he soon fell into a deep slumber.

The house, as has been said, was a log cabin in the midst of a few acres of deadning, — ground from which trees have been cleared by girdling. Dense woods were all about it; but the nearest forest was a quarter of a mile distant, and had Jordan been tracked, it would be difficult to get away over this open space, unless he had warning of the approach of his pursuers. Rachel thought of this, and sent Ezekiel up the road, on the old mule, to watch and give warning. It was high noon when the mule came back, his heels striking fire, and the old man's eyes flashing, as if ignited from the sparks the steel had emitted.

"Dey'm comin', missus," he cried, — "not half a mile away, — twenty Secesh, — ridin' as ef de debil was arter 'em!"

Mrs. Jordan was paralyzed, but Rachel barred the door, and hastened to the guest-chamber.

"Go," she cried, "through the window, — to the woods. They'll be here in a minute!"

20 *

"How many of them?" asked Jordan, rising to his feet.

"Twenty. Go — go at once, or you'll be taken."

"Yes, I hear them. There's a sorry chance for my life, already. But, Rachel, I've that about me that is worth more than my life; that, it may be, will save Kentucky. If I'm killed, will you take it to Colonel Cranor, at McCormick's Gap?"

"Yes, yes, I will. But go; you've not a moment to lose, I tell you."

"I know; but do you promise to take this to Colonel Cranor, before the Lord who hears us?"

"Yes, yes, I do," she cried, clutching the bullet. But horses' hoofs were already sounding in the door-yard. "Oh, it's too late!" she cried, wringing her hands. "Why did you stop to parley?"

"Never mind, Rachel," answered Jordan. "Don't feel badly. Take care of the despatch. Value it like your life, — like Kentucky. The Lord is calling for me, and I am ready."

He was mistaken. It was not the Lord, but a dozen devils at the door-way.

"What do you want?" said Rachel, in answer to the summons from outside.

"The man as came from Garfield's camp at sun-up," answered a voice; "John Jordan, from the head of Blaine."

"He's not to be taken alive," said Jordan. "Go away, or some of you are dead men."

"Pshaw!" said another, — one of the chivalry. "There are twenty of us, Jordan. We'll spare your life if you give up the despatch; if you don't, we'll hang you higher than Haman."

The reader will bear in mind that this was in the beginning of the war, when swarms of spies infested every Union camp, and treason was only a gentlemanly pastime, not the serious business it was before traitors were dangerous.

"I've nothing but my life that I will give up," answered Jordan, "and if you take that, you will have to pay its price, — at least six of yours."

" Fire the house ! " shouted one.

" No, don't do that," said another. " I know him, — he's cl'ar grit, — he'll die in the ashes; and we wont git the despatch."

This sort of talk went on for half an hour, all which while the mother of Jordan was by her bedside, bent down in prayer.

At last there came a dead silence, and Rachel went into the loft, whence she could see all that was passing on the outside. About a dozen of the horsemen were posted around the house; but the remainder, dismounted, had gone to the edge of the wood, and were felling a well-grown sapling, with the evident intention of using it as a battering-ram to break down the front door.

Coming down from the attic, Rachel, in a low tone, explained the situation, and, after a moment's reflection, Jordan said, —

" It is my only chance. I must run for it. Bring me a red shawl, Rachel."

She had none, but she had a petticoat of flaming red and yellow. This she brought, and, handling it as if he knew

how such articles can be made to spread, Jordan softly un-
barred the door, and said, in a low whisper, —

"Good-by, mother. Good-by, Rachel. It's a right sorry
chance; but I may get through. If I do, I'll be in the
woods to-night; if I don't, take the despatch to Colonel Cranor. -Good-by."

The barn stood to the right of the house, midway between
it and the wood. That way lay the route of Jordan. If he
could elude the two mounted men at the door-way, he might
escape the other horsemen, for they would have to spring two
barn-yard fences, and their horses might refuse the leap. But
it was foot of man against leg of horse, and "a right sorry
chance."

He grasped Rachel by the hand, then suddenly opened the
door, and dashed at the two horses with the petticoat. They
reared, wheeled, and bounded away like lightning just let out
of harness.

In the time that it takes to tell it, he was over the first
fence, and scaling the second; but a horseman was making
the leap with him. Jordan's pistol went off, and the rebel's
earthly journey was over. Another followed, and his horse
fell mortally wounded.

The rest made the circuit of the barn-yard, and were rods
behind when Jordan reached the edge of the forest. Once
among those thick laurels, nor horse nor rider can reach a man,
if he lies low, and says his prayers in a whisper.

The rebels bore the body of their dead comrade to the barn,
and one of them, going to the house, said to Rachel, —

"We'll be revenged for this. We know the route he'll
take, and will have his life before to-morrow; and you, —

we'd burn your house over your head, if you weren't the wife of Brad. Brown."

"And he?" asked Rachel; "is he among you again?"

"Yes, he's enlisted, like an honest man, with Marshall."

Soon the rebels rode away, taking Rachel's only wagon as a hearse for their dead comrade.

Night came, and the owls cried in the woods in a way they had not cried for a fortnight. "T'whoot, t'whoot!" they went, as if they thought there was music in hooting. Rachel listened, put on a dark mantle, and followed the sound of their voices. Entering the wood, she crept in among the bushes, and talked with one of the owls as if he had been human.

"They know the road you'll take," she said; "you must change your route. Here is the bullet."

"God bless you, Rachel," responded the owl; "you are a true woman;" and he hooted louder than before, to deceive pursuers, and keep up the music.

"Is "Beauty" safe?" she asked.

"Yes, and good for forty miles before sun-up."

"Well, here is something to eat; you'll need it. Good-by, and God be with you."

"He be with you, for he loves true women."

Their hands clasped, and then they parted; he to his long ride, she to the quiet sleep of those who, out of a true heart, serve their country.

The night was dark and drizzly, but before morning the clouds cleared away, leaving a thick mist hanging low on the meadows. Jordan's mare was fleet, but the road was rough, and a slosh of snow impeded the travel. He had come by a strange way, and did not know how far he had travelled by sunrise; but lights were ahead, shivering in the haze of the cold, gray morning. Were they the early candles of some peaceful village, or the camp-fires of a band of guerillas? He did not know, and it would not be safe to go on till he did know.' The road was lined with trees, but they offered no shelter, for they were far apart, and the snow lay white between them. He was in an "opening" of the blue-grass region. Leading "Beauty" into the timber, he climbed a tall tree by the road-side, but the mist was too thick to admit of his discerning anything distinctly.

The fog, however, seemed to be breaking away, and he would wait until the road was clear before him; so he sat there one hour, two hours, and ate his breakfast from the satchel Rachel had slung over his shoulder.

At last the mist lifted a little, and he saw close at hand a small hamlet, — a few rude huts clustered about a cross-road. No danger could lurk in such a place, and he was about to descend and pursue his journey, when suddenly he heard, up the road by which he had come, the rapid tramp of a body of horsemen. The mist was thicker below, and might conceal him; so half-way down the tree he went and awaited their coming. They moved at an irregular pace, carrying lanterns, and pausing every now and then to inspect the road, as if they had missed their way, or lost something. Soon they came near, and were dimly outlined in the gray mist, so that Jordan could make out their number. There were thirty of them, — the original band, — and a reinforcement. Again they halted when abreast of the tree, and searched the road narrowly.

"He must have come this way," said one, — he of the chivalry. "The other road is six miles longer, and he would take the shortest. It's an awful pity we didn't head him on both routes, just this side of the clearing."

"We kin come up with him yit, if we turn plumb round, and foller on t'other road, whar we lost the trail, back thar, miles to the deadnin'," said another, — Parson Bradshaw, now in arms for the Lord's anointed, — slavery.

Now another spoke, and his voice Jordan recognized as that of a private in the company he had recently joined in the Fourteenth Kentucky.

"It's so," he said; "he has tuck t'other road. I tell ye I'd know that mar's shoe 'mong a million. Nary one loike it was ever seed in all Kaintucky; only a d——d Yankee could ha' invented it."

"And yere it ar'," shouted the parson, who held one of the lanterns, "plain as sun-up."

The Fourteenth Kentuckian clutched the light, and, while a dozen dismounted and crowded round, closely examined the shoe-track. The ground on the spot was bare of snow, and the print of Beauty's foot was clearly cut in the half-frozen mud. Narrowly the man looked, and Jordan's life or death hung on his eyesight. He took out the bullet and placed it in a crotch of the tree. If they took him, they should not take the despatch. Then he drew a revolver. The mist was clearing away, and he would surely be discovered if the men remained much longer; but he would have the value of his life to the uttermost farthing.

Meanwhile, the horsemen crowded eagerly around the footprint, and one of them inadvertently trod upon it. The

Kentuckian looked long and earnestly, but at last he said, —

" 'Taint the track. Thet ar' mar' has a sand-crack on her right fore foot. She didn't tuck kindly to a round shoe; so Jordan, he guv her one with the cork right in the middle of the quarter. 'Twas a durned smart contrivance; fur, ye see, it eased the strain, and let the nag go nimble as a squirrel. The cork haint yere, — 'taint her track, and we're wastin' time in luckin'."

The print of the cork was not there, because the trooper's tread had obliterated it! Let him be remembered for that one good step, if he never took another; for it saved Jordan, and, may be, it saved Kentucky. When Jordan returned that way, he halted his mare abreast of that tree and examined the ground about it. There, in the road, was the mare's track, with the print of the man's foot still upon the inner quarter! He uncovered his head, and from his heart went up a simple thanksgiving.

The horsemen gone, Jordan came down from the tree, and rode on into the misty morning. There might be danger ahead, but there surely was danger behind him. His pursuers were only half convinced they were on his trail, and some sensible fiend might put it into their heads to divide, and follow, part by one route, part by the other.

He pushed on over the sloshy road, his mare every step going slower and slower. The poor animal was jaded out; for she had travelled fifty miles, eaten nothing, and been stabled in the timber. She would have given out long before had she not had a grandfather. As it was, she staggered along as if she had taken a barrel of whiskey. But five miles further on was the house of a Union man, and she must reach it or die by the way-side. Even the merciful man regardeth not the life of his beast when he carries despatches.

The loyalist did not know Jordan; but his face secured him a friendly welcome. He explained that he was from the Union camp on the Big Sandy, and offered any price for a horse to go on with.

"Yer nag ar' wuth ary two of my critters," said the man. "Ye can tuck the best beast I've got; and when ye'se ag'in this way, we'll swop back even."

Jordan thanked him, mounted the horse, and rode off into the mist again, without the warm breakfast which the good housewife had half cooked for him in the kitchen. It was eleven o'clock in the morning; and at twelve that night he entered Colonel Cranor's quarters at McCormick's Gap, — having ridden nearly a hundred miles with a rope round his neck, for thirteen dollars a month, hard tack, and a shoddy uniform.

The colonel opened the despatch. It was dated Louisa, Kentucky, December 24th, midnight; and directed him to move his regiment at once to Prestonburg. He would encumber the men with as few rations and as little luggage as possible, bearing in mind that the safety of his command would depend on his expedition. He would also cause the despatch to be conveyed to Lieutenant-Colonel Woolford, at Stamford, and direct him to join the march with his three hundred cavalry.

Hours now were worth months of common time, and on the following morning Cranor's column was set in motion. Worn out with fatigue, Jordan lay by till nightfall, then he

21

set out on his return, and at daybreak swapped the loyalist's now jaded horse for his own fresh " Beauty," even.   He ate the housewife's breakfast, too, and took his ease with the good man till dark, when he again set out, and rode through the night in safety.   After that his route was beset with perils; but an account of them must be reserved for another chapter.

CHAPTER XVIII.

E must now leave Jordan to pursue his perilous way alone, and, for a time, go back to the Federal camp at Louisa. The contents of the bullet which Jordan has conveyed to Colonel Cranor, indicate that it is the intention of the Union commander to move at once upon the enemy. Of Marshall's real strength he is ignorant; but his scouts and the country people report that the rebel's main body — which is intrenched in an almost impregnable position near Paintville — is from four to seven thousand, and that an outlying force of eight hundred occupies West Liberty, — a town directly on the route by which Colonel Cranor is to march to effect a junction with the main Union army. Cranor's column, as has been said, is eleven hundred strong, and the main body under Garfield now numbers about seventeen hundred; namely, the Forty-Second Ohio Infantry, ten hundred and thirteen strong, and the Fourteenth Kentucky Infantry, numbering five hundred rank and file, but imperfectly armed and equipped. All told, therefore, Garfield has a force of only twenty-eight hundred, in a strange district, and cut off from reinforcements, with which to meet and crush an army of at least five thousand, familiar with the country, and daily receiving recruits from the disaffected southern counties. Evidently a forward movement is attended with great hazard; but the Union commander does not waste time in considering the obstacles and dangers of the expedition. On the morning following the departure of Jordan he sets out up the river with such of his command as are in readiness, and halting at George's Creek, — only twenty miles from Marshall's intrenched position, — prepares to move at once upon the enemy.

The roads along the Big Sandy are impassable for trains, and the close proximity of the enemy renders it unsafe to make so wide a detour from the river as would be required to send supplies by the table-lands to the westward. In these circumstances, Garfield decides to depend mainly upon water navigation for the transport of his supplies, and to use the army train only when his troops are obliged, by absolutely impassable roads, to move away from the river.

The Big Sandy is a narrow, fickle stream, and finds its way to the Ohio through the roughest and wildest spurs of the Cumberland mountains. At low water it is not navigable above Louisa, except for small flat-boats, pushed by hand; but these ascend as high as Piketon, one hundred and twenty miles from the mouth of the river. In time of high water small steamers can reach Piketon; but heavy freshets render navigation impracticable, owing to the swift current, filled with floating timber, and to the overhanging trees, which almost touch one another from the opposite banks. At this time the river was of only moderate height; but, as will be readily seen, the supply of a brigade at mid-winter, by such an uncertain stream, and in the presence of a powerful enemy, was a thing of great difficulty.

However, the obstacles do not intimidate Garfield. Gathering together ten days' rations, he charters two small steamers, and impresses all the flat-boats he can lay hand on, and then, taking his army wagons apart, he loads them, with his forage and provisions, upon the flat-boats. This is on the first of January, A. D. 1862, and the day before a little event happens, which has a decided influence on the result of the expedition. This is the appearance, at the Union head-quarters, of Bradley Brown, who, on his stolen horse, has ridden the previous night all the way from Marshall's camp near Paintville.

"Colonel," says Captain Bent, of the Fourteenth Kentucky, entering Garfield's tent in the early gray of the morning, "there's a man outside who says he knows you, — Bradley Brown, a rebel thief and scoundrel."

"Brown?" says Garfield, rising, half-dressed, from his blanket, "Bradley Brown? I don't know any one of that name."

"He has lived near the head of Blaine, — been a boatman on the river, — says he knew you on the canal in Ohio."

"Oh, yes," answers Garfield, "bring him in; now I remember him."

In a moment Brown is ushered into the colonel's quarters. He is clad in country homespun, and spattered from head to feet with the mud of a long journey, but, without any regard to the sanctity of rank, he advances at once upon the Union commander, and, grasping him warmly by the hand, exclaims, —

"Jim, ole feller, how ar' ye?"

21 *

The colonel receives him cordially; but, glancing at his ruddy face, says, —

"Fifteen years haven't changed you, Brown, — you still take a glass of whiskey. But what's this I hear? Are you a rebel?"

"Yes," answers Brown; "I belong to Marshall's force, and" — this he prefaces with a burst of laughter — "I've come stret from his camp to spy out yer army."

The colonel looks surprised, but says, coolly, —

"Well, you go about it queerly."

"Yes, quar, but honest, Jim, — when yer alone I'll tell ye 'bout it."

As Bent was leaving the tent he said to his commander in an under tone, —

"Don't trust him, colonel; I know him, — he's a thief and a rebel."

The disclosures of Brown, condensed into a few sentences, were as follows : —

Hearing a short time before, at the rebel camp, that James A. Garfield, of Ohio, had taken command of the Union forces, it at once occurred to him that it was his old canal companion, for whom, as a boy, he had felt a strong affection. This supposition was confirmed a few days later by his hearing from a renegade northern man something of the antecedents of the colonel. Remembering their former friendship, and being indifferent as to which side was successful in the campaign, he at once determined to do an important service to the Union commander.

With this object he sought an interview with Marshall, stated to him his former acquaintance with Garfield, and proposed that he should take advantage of it to enter the Union camp, and learn for the rebel general all about his enemy's strength and intended movements. Marshall at once fell into the trap, and the same night Brown set out for the Union army, ostensibly to spy for the rebels, but really to tell the Union commander all that he knew of their strength and position. He did not know Marshall's exact force; but he gave Garfield such facts as enabled him to make, within half an hour, a tolerably accurate map of the rebel position.

When this was done the Union colonel said to him, —

"Did Bent blindfold you when he brought you into camp?"

"Yes, gin'ral; I couldn't see my hand afore me."

"Well, then you had better go directly back to Marshall."

"Go back to him! Why, gin'ral, he'll hang me to the first tree!"

"No, he wont, — not if you tell him all about my strength and intended movements."

"But how kin I? I don't know a thing. I tell ye I war blindfolded."

"Yes; but that don't prevent your guessing at our numbers; and, about our movements, you may say that I shall march to-morrow straight for his camp, and in ten days be upon him."

Brown sat for a moment musing, then he said, —

"Wall, gin'ral, ye'd be a durned fool, — and if ye'r thet ye must hev growed to it, — ef ye went upon Marshall, 'trenched as he is, with a man short uv twenty thousand. I kin 'guess' ye's thet many."

"Guess again, — I haven't that number."

"Then, ten thousand."

"Well, that will do — for a Kentuckian. Now, to-day I'll keep you under lock and key, and to-night you can go back to Marshall."

At nightfall Brown set out for the rebel camp, and on the following day Garfield put his little army — reduced now by sickness and garrison duty, to fourteen hundred — in motion.

It was a toilsome march. The roads were knee-deep in mire, and encumbered, as it was, with only a light train, the army made very slow progress. Some days it marched five or six miles, and some a considerably less distance ; but on the sixth of January it arrived within seven miles of Paintville. Here the men threw themselves upon the wet ground, and Garfield laid down in his boots, in a wretched log hut, to catch a few hours of slumber. About midnight he was roused from sleep by a man who said his business was urgent. He rubbed his eyes and raised himself upon his elbow.

"Back safe ? " he asked. " Have you seen Cranor ? "

"Yes, colonel; he can't be more than two days behind me."

"God bless you, Jordan ! You have done us great service," said Garfield, warmly.

"I thank you, colonel," answered Jordan, his voice trembling ; " that is more pay than I expected."

He had returned safely ; but the Providence which so wonderfully guarded his way out, seemed to leave him to find his way back ; for, as he expressed it, " The Lord cared more for the despatch than He cared for me ; and it was natural He should, because my life only counts one, but the despatch, it stood for the whole of Kentucky."

Be that as it may, his road was a hard one to travel. The same gang which followed him out waylaid him back, and one stormy midnight he fell among them. They lined the road forty deep, and, seeing he could not run the gauntlet, he wheeled his mare and fled backward. The noble beast did her part, but a bullet struck her, and she fell in the road disabled. Then — it was Hobson's choice — he took to his legs, and, leaping a fence into a wood undergrown with thick laurels, was at last out of danger.

For two days and nights he lay there, not daring to come out; but hunger finally forced him to ask food at a negro shanty. The dusky patriot loaded him with bacon, brown bread, and blessings, and at night piloted him to a rebel barn, where he found his own mare, wounded, but still fit for service.

With her he set out again, and after various adventures and hair-breadth escapes, too numerous to mention and too incredible to believe, had not similar events occurred all through the war, he reached in safety, that rainy midnight, the little army encamped seven miles north of Paintville.

In the morning another horseman rode up to the Union head-quarters. He was a messenger direct from General Buell, who had followed Garfield up the Big Sandy, with despatches. They contained only a few hurried sentences from a man to a woman, but their value was not to be estimated in money. It was a letter from Marshall to his wife, which Buell had intercepted, and it revealed the important fact that the rebel general had five thousand men, — forty-four hundred infantry and six hundred cavalry, — with twelve pieces of artillery, and was daily expecting an attack from a Union force of ten thousand!

Garfield put the letter in his pocket, and then called a council of his officers. They assembled in the rude log shanty, and the question was put to them, —

"Shall we march at once, or wait the coming of Cranor?"

All but one said, "Wait." He said, "Move at once. Our fourteen hundred can whip ten thousand rebels."

Garfield reflected awhile; then closed the council with the laconic remark, —

"Well, forward it is. Give the order."

Three roads led to the rebel position :—one at the east, bearing down to the river and along its western bank; another, a circuitous one, to the west, coming in on Paint Creek, at the mouth of Jenny's Creek, on the right of the village; and a third between the two others, a more direct route, but climbing a succession of almost impassable ridges. These three roads were held by strong rebel pickets, and a regiment was outlying at the village of Paintville.

The diagram on the opposite page will show the situation.

To deceive Marshall as to his real strength and designs, Garfield orders a small force of infantry and cavalry to advance along the river road, drive in the rebel pickets, and move rapidly after them, as if to attack Paintville. Two hours after this small force goes off, a similar one, with the same orders, sets off on the road to the westward; and two hours later still, another small body takes the middle road. The effect is, that the pickets on the first route, being vigorously attacked and driven, retreat in confusion to Paintville, and despatch word to Marshall that the Union army is

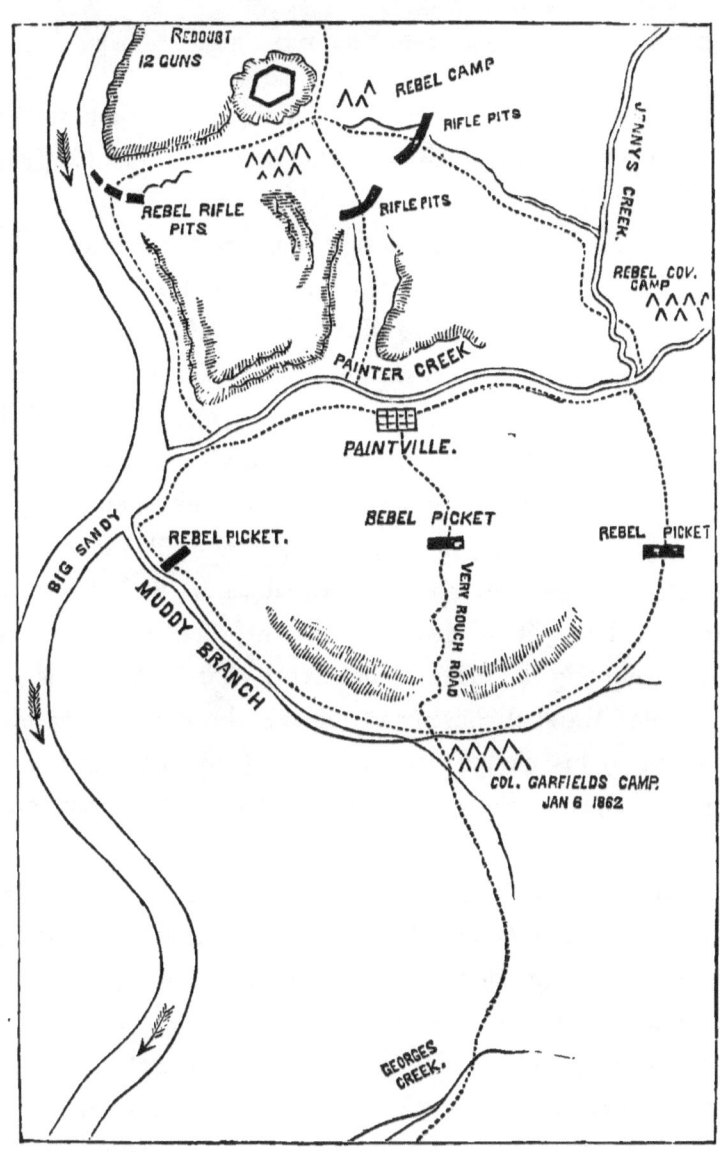

(251)

advancing along the river. He hurries off a thousand infantry and a battery to resist the advance of this imaginary column.

When this detachment has been gone an hour and a half, Marshall hears, from the routed pickets on his left, that the Union forces are advancing along the western road. Countermanding his first order, he now directs the thousand men and the battery to check the new danger; and hurries off the troops at Paintville to the mouth of Jenny's creek to make a stand at that point. Two hours later the pickets on the central route are driven in, and, finding Paintville abandoned, they flee precipitately to the fortified camp, with the story that the whole Union army is close at their heels, and already occupying the town. Conceiving that he has thus lost Paintville, Marshall hastily withdraws the detachment of a thousand to his camp; and, then Garfield, moving rapidly over the ridges of the central route, occupies the abandoned position.

So affairs stand on the evening of the eighth of January, when a rebel spy enters the camp of Marshall with tidings that Cranor, with thirty-three hundred (?) men, is within twelve hours' march at the westward.

On receipt of these tidings the rebel general, conceiving himself vastly outnumbered, breaks up his camp, — which he might have held for a twelvemonth, — and retreats precipitately, abandoning or burning a large portion of his supplies. Seeing the fires, Garfield mounts his horse, and, with a thousand men, enters the deserted camp at nine in the evening, while the blazing stores are yet unconsumed. He sends off a detachment to harass the rebel retreat, and waits the arrival of Cranor, with whom he means to follow, and bring Marshall to battle in the morning.

In the morning Cranor comes; but his men are footsore, without rations, and completely exhausted. The most of them cannot move one leg after the other. But the Union commander is determined on a battle, so every man who has strength to march is ordered to come forward. Eleven hundred — among them four hundred of Cranor's tired heroes — step from the ranks, and with them, at noon of the ninth, Garfield sets out for Prestonburg, sending all his available cavalry to follow the line of the enemy's retreat, and harass and destroy him.

Marching eighteen miles, he reaches, at nine o'clock that night, the mouth of Abbott's Creek, three miles below Prestonburg, — he and the eleven hundred. There he learns that Marshall is encamped on the same stream, three miles higher up; and throwing his men into bivouac, in the midst of a sleety rain, he sends back an order to Lieutenant-Colonel Sheldon, who has been left in command at Paintville, to bring up every available man, with all possible despatch, for he shall force the enemy to battle in the morning. He spends the night in learning the character of the surrounding country, and the disposition of Marshall's forces; and then again Jordan comes into action.

A dozen rebels are grinding at a mill, and a dozen honest men come upon them, steal their corn, and take them prisoners. The miller is a tall, gaunt man, and his "butternuts" fit Jordan as if they were made for him. He is a rebel, too, and his very raiment should bear witness against this feeding of his enemies. It does. It goes back to the rebel camp,

22

and Jordan goes in it. That chameleon face of his is smeared with meal, and looks the miller so well that the miller's own wife might not detect the difference. The night is dark and rainy, and that lessens his danger; but still Jordan is picking his teeth in the very jaws of the lion.

Jordan's midnight ramble in the rebel ranks gave Garfield the exact position of the enemy. They had made a stand, and laid an ambuscade for him. Strongly posted on a semi-circular hill, at the forks of Middle Creek, on both sides of the road, with cannon commanding its whole length, and hidden by the trees and underbrush, they were awaiting his coming.

Deeming it unsafe to proceed further in the darkness, Garfield, as has been said, ordered his army into bivouac at nine in the evening, and climbing a steep ridge, called Abbott's Hill, his tired men threw themselves upon the wet ground to wait for the morning. It was a terrible night, — a fit prelude to the terrible day that followed. A dense fog shut out the moon and stars, and shrouded the lonely mountain in almost Cimmerian darkness. A cold wind swept from the north, driving the rain in blinding gusts into the faces of the shivering men, and stirring the dark pines into a mournful music. But the slow and cheerless night at last wore away, and at four in the morning the tired and hungry men, their icy clothing clinging to their half-frozen limbs, were roused from their cold beds, and ordered to move forward. Slowly and cautiously they descended into the valley, feeling, at every step, for the enemy.

About daybreak, while rounding a hill which jutted out into the valley, the advance guard was charged upon by a body of rebel horsemen. Forming his men in a hollow square, Garfield gave the rebels a volley, that sent them reeling up the valley, — all but one; and he, with his horse, plunged into the stream, and was captured.

The main body of the enemy, it now was evident, was not far distant; but whether he had changed his position since the visit of Jordan was yet uncertain. To determine this, Garfield sent forward a strong corps of skirmishers, who swept the cavalry from a ridge which they had occupied, and, moving forward, soon drew the fire of the hidden rebels. Suddenly a puff of smoke rose from beyond the hill, and a twelve-pound shell whistled above the trees, then ploughed up the hill, and buried itself in the ground at the very feet of the adventurous little band of skirmishers.

It was now twelve o'clock, and, throwing his whole force upon the ridge whence the rebel cavalry had been driven, Garfield prepared for the impending battle. It was a trying and perilous moment. He was in presence of a greatly superior enemy, and how to dispose his little force, and where first to attack, were things not easy to determine. But he lost no time in idle indecision.

Looking in the faces of his eleven hundred, he went at once into the terrible struggle. His mounted escort of twelve men he sent forward to make a charge, and, if possible, to draw the fire of the enemy. The ruse worked admirably. As the little squad swept round a curve in the road, another shell whistled through the valley, and the long roll of nearly five thousand muskets chimed in with a fierce salutation. Then began the battle.

CHAPTER XIX.

T was a wonderful battle. In the history of the late war there is not another like it. Measured by the forces engaged, the valor displayed, and the results that followed, it throws into the shade the achievements of even the mighty hosts which saved the nation. Eleven hundred footsore and weary men, without cannon, charged up a rocky hill, over stumps, over stones, over fallen trees, over high intrenchments, right into the face ·of five thousand fresh troops, with twelve pieces of artillery !

A glance at the ground will best show the real nature of the conflict. It was on the margin of Middle Creek, a narrow and rapid stream, and three miles from where it finds its way into the Big Sandy, through the sharp spurs of the Cumberland mountains. A rocky road, not ten feet in width, winds along this stream, and on its two banks abrupt ridges, with steep and rocky sides, overgrown with trees and underbrush, shut closely down upon the road and the little streamlet. At twelve o'clock Garfield had gained the crest of the ridge at the right of the road, and the charge of his handful of horsemen had drawn Marshall's fire, and disclosed his actual position. It will be clearly seen from the subjoined diagram.

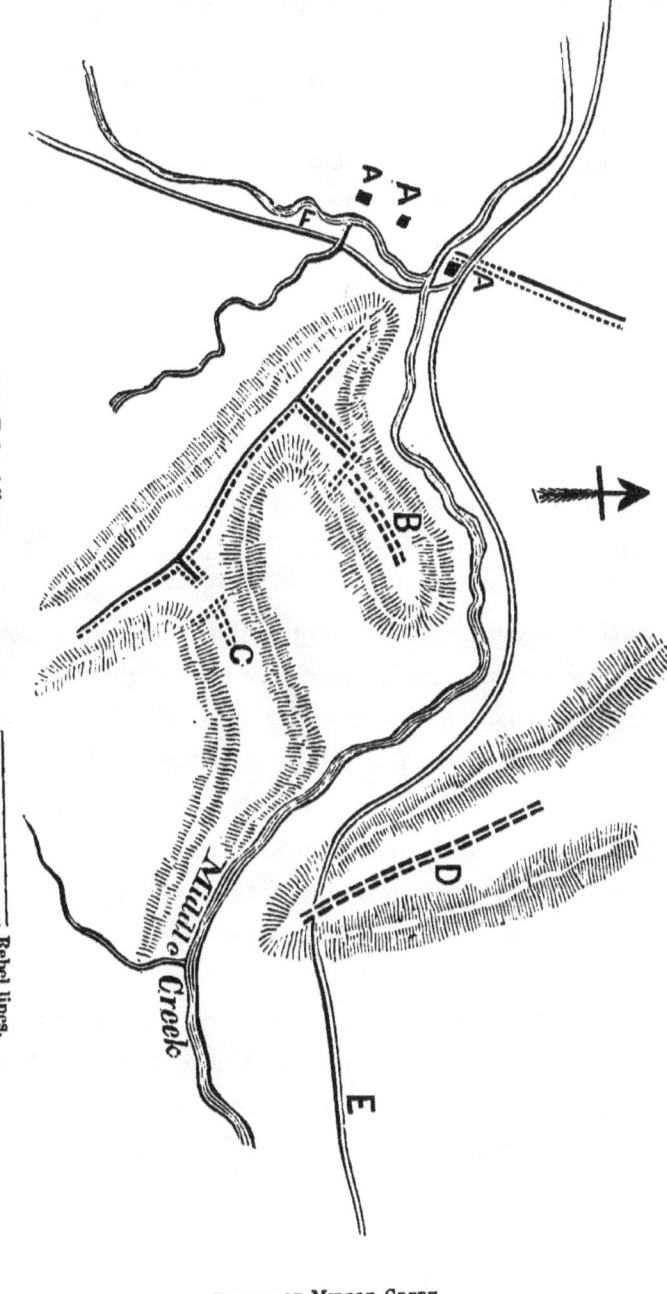

A — Rebel Artillery, 6 and 12 pounders.
B — Ridge taken by the Ohio boys.

·········· Federal lines.

C — Ridge taken by the Kentuckians under Monroe.
D — Garfield's reserve.

———— Rebel lines.

E — Approach of reinforcements under Col. Sheldon.
F — Road by which the enemy retreated.

BATTLE OF MIDDLE CREEK.

The main force of the rebels occupied the crests of the two ridges, at the left of the stream, but a strong detachment was posted on the right, and a battery of twelve pieces held the forks of the creek and commanded the approach of the Union army.   It was Marshall's plan to lure Garfield along the road, and then, taking him between two enfilading fires, to surround and utterly destroy him.   But his hasty fire betrayed his design and unmasked his entire position.

Garfield acted with promptness and decision. A hundred undergraduates, recruited from his own college, were ordered to cross the stream, climb the ridge whence the fire had been hottest, and bring on the battle.

Boldly the little band plunge into the creek, the icy water up to their waists, and, clinging to the trees and underbrush, climb the rocky ascent.   Half-way up the ridge, the fire of at least two thousand rifles opens upon them, but, springing from tree to tree, they press on, and at last reach the summit. Then suddenly the hill is gray with rebels, who, rising from ambush, pour their deadly volleys into the little band of only one hundred.   For a moment they waver, but their leader calls out, " Every man to a tree !   Give them as good as they send, my brave Bereans ! "

The rebels, behind rocks and a rude intrenchment, are obliged to expose their heads to take aim at the advancing column, but the Union troops, posted behind the huge oaks and maples, can stand erect, and load and fire, fully protected. Though they are outnumbered ten to one, the contest is, therefore, for a time, not so very unequal.

But soon the rebels, exasperated with the obstinate resistance, rush from cover, and charge upon the little handful

with the bayonet. Slowly they are driven down the hill, and
two of them fall to the ground wounded. One never rises;
the other — a lad of only eighteen — is shot through the
thigh, and one of his comrades turns back to bear him to a
place of safety. The advancing rebels are within thirty feet,
when one of them fires, and his bullet strikes a tree directly
above the head of the Union soldier. He turns, levels his
musket, and the rebel is in eternity. Then the rest are upon
him; but, zigzagging from tree to tree, he is soon with his
driven column. But not far are the brave boys driven. A
few rods lower down they hear again the voice of their
leader.

"To the trees again, my boys!" he cries. "We may as
well die here as in Ohio."

To the trees they go, and in a moment the advancing
horde is checked, and then rolled backward. Up the hill
they turn, firing as they go, and the little band follows.
Soon the rebels reach the spot where the Berean boy lies
wounded, and one of them says to him, —

"Boy, guv me yer musket."

"Not the gun, but its contents," cries the boy; and the
rebel falls mortally wounded. Another raises his weapon to
brain the prostrate lad; but he, too, falls, killed with his comrade's own rifle. And all this is done while the hero-boy is
on the ground, bleeding. An hour afterwards his comrades
bear him to a sheltered spot on the other side of the streamlet,
and then the first word of complaint escapes him. As they
are taking off his leg, he says, in his agony, —

"Oh, what will mother do?"

A fortnight later his words, repeated in the Senate of Ohio,

rouse the noble State to at once make provision for the widows
and mothers of its soldiers. I do not know whether he be
now dead or living; but his name at least should not be forgotten. It was Charles Carlton, of Franklin, Ohio.

Meanwhile, Jordan is standing by the side of the Union
commander, upon a rocky height on the other side of the
narrow valley, and his quick eye has discerned, through the
densely-curling smoke, the real state of the unequal contest.

"They are being driven," he says. "They will lose the
hill, if they are not supported."

Instantly five hundred of the Ohio Fortieth and Forty-
second, under Major Pardee and Colonel Cranor, are ordered
to the rescue. Holding their cartridge-boxes above their
heads, they dash into the stream, up the hill, and into the
fight, shouting, —

"Hurra for Williams and the brave Bereans!"

But shot and shell and canister and the fire of four thousand muskets are now concentrated upon the few hundred
heroes.

"This will never do," cries Garfield. "Who will volunteer
to carry the crest of the other mountain?"

"We will!" shouts Colonel Monroe, of the Twenty-second
Kentucky. "We know every inch of the ground."

"Go in, then," cries Garfield, "and give them Hail Colum-
bia."

Jordan goes with this second column. Fording the stream
lower down, they climb the ridge at the left, and in ten
minutes are upon the enemy. Like the others, these rebels
are posted behind rocks, and their uncovered heads soon become ghastly targets for the unerring Kentucky rifles.

"Take good aim, and don't shoot till you see the eyes of your enemy," shouts the brave colonel.

The men have never been under fire, but in a few moments are as cool as if shooting at a turkey-match.

" Do you see that reb ? " says one to a comrade, as a head appears above a rock. " Hit him while I'm loading."

Another is bringing his cartridge to his mouth, when a bullet cuts away the powder, and leaves the lead in his fingers. Shielding his arm with his body, he says, as he turns from the foe and rams home another cartridge, —

"There ! see if you can hit that ! "

Another takes out a piece of hard tack, and a ball shivers it in his hand. He swallows the remnant, and then coolly fires away again. One is brought down by a ball in the knee, and, lying on the ground, rifle in hand, watches for the man who shot him. Soon the rebel's head rises above a rock, and the two fire at the same instant. The loyal man is struck in the mouth; but, as he is borne down the hill, he splutters out, —

" Never mind; that Secesh is done for."

The next morning the rebel is found with the whole upper part of his head shot away by the other's bullet.

The brave Kentuckians climb or leap up along the side of the mountain. Now they are hidden in the underbrush, now sheltered by the great trees, and now fully exposed in some narrow opening; but gradually they near the crest of the ridge, and at last are at its very summit.

Then comes a terrible hand-to-hand struggle, and the little band of less than four hundred, overpowered by numbers, are driven far down the mountain.

A ball pierces Jordan's hat, three go through his clothing, but he is uninjured.

Soon the men rally, and, as they turn, a bullet grazes Jordan's side, and buries itself in the breast of a man whom he has seen send five rebels to the great accounting. Blood will have blood, and so he, too, goes to the judgment!

Meanwhile, another cannon has opened on the hill, and round shot and canister fall thickly among the weary eleven hundred. Seeing his advance about to waver, the Union commander sends volley after volley from his entire reserve, at the central point, between his two detachments, and for a time the enemy's fire is silenced in that quarter. But soon it opens again, and then Garfield orders all, but a chosen hundred, upon the mountain. Then the battle grows terrible. Thick and thicker swarm the rebels on the crest; sharp and sharper rolls the musketry along the valley, and, as volley after volley echoes among the hills, and the white smoke curls up in long wreaths from the gleaming rifles, a dense cloud gathers overhead, as if to shut out this scene of carnage from the very eye of Heaven.

So the bloody work goes on, so the battle wavers, till the setting sun, wheeling below the hills, glances along the dense lines of rebel steel moving down to envelop the weary eleven hundred. It is an awful moment, big with the fate of Kentucky. At its very crisis two figures stand out against the fading sky, boldly defined in the foreground.

One is in Union blue. With a little band of heroes about him, he is posted on a projecting rock, which is scarred with bullets, and in full view of both armies. His head is uncovered, his hair streaming in the wind, his face upturned in the

darkening daylight, and from his soul is going up a prayer, —
a prayer for Sheldon and reinforcements. He turns his eyes
to the northward, and his lip tightens, and he throws off his
coat, and says to his hundred men, —

"Boys, *we* must go at them."

The other is in Rebel gray. Moving out to the brow of the
opposite hill, and placing a glass to his eye, he, too, takes a
long look to the northward. He starts, for he sees something
which the other, on lower ground, does not distinguish. Soon
he wheels his horse, and the word "RETREAT" echoes along
the valley between them. It is his last word; for six rifles
crack, and the rebel major lies on the ground, quivering.
The one in blue looks to the north again, and now, floating
proudly among the trees, he sees the starry banner. It is
Sheldon and his forces! Jordan's perilous ride is at last doing its work for the nation. On they come, like the rushing
wind, filling the air with their shouting. The rescued eleven
hundred take up the strain, and then, above the swift pursuit,
above the lessening conflict, above the last boom of the wheeling cannon, goes up the wild huzza of Victory.

As they come back from the short pursuit, the young commander grasps man after man by the hand, and says, —

"God bless you, boys! you have saved Kentucky."

While war is the greatest of earthly enormities, it is strange
the interest which a battle-field always awakens. We go
over the ground, marking the spot where occurred some fearful struggle, or where some noble regiment went down to a
swift destruction, and we do not see the pallid faces of the
dead, or hear the moans of the wounded. But this is when

the grass has grown green, and the smoke has cleared away, letting in the light of heaven. But when the ground is red, when the unburied dead lie in heaps, and the wounded are stretched around on the trodden grass, rending the air with cries for succor, then it is that we realize the real horrors of the battle-field. It was thus that Jordan saw it when, with a water-bucket on his arm, he walked slowly along the mountain-side, on the evening of this fearful conflict. Twenty-seven rebel dead lay unburied on the ground, and sixty more, hastily thrown together, and only loosely covered with a few leaves and underbrush, were at the bottom of a ravine. Leaning against a tree was a fair-haired youth, his hands clasped across his knees, and his head slightly bent forward. His face was flushed, and his eyes gleamed bright in the moonlight. Baring his breast to stanch the still-flowing blood, Jordan spoke to him gently. The eyes looked out in a mute appeal, but the still lips gave no answer. With him the battle of life was over forever.

A little farther on five dead and one wounded lay behind a rock, two of the dead fallen across the living. The living man's leg was shattered, but his wound was not mortal.

"You must be in great pain, — can I do anything for you?" asked Jordan.

"There are others worse off," said the man; "tend to them; then you may look after me."

Moving the dead from his crushed limb, Jordan went forward.

One had received a ball through the neck, which destroyed the power of speech, and he made frantic signs for water; another, a dark-hued man, was lying under a tree, his thigh broken. He was stern and morose, asking only one thing, — that Jordan would kill him. Jordan said, kindly, —

"You will soon be taken to a surgeon; he will relieve you."

Then the man faltered out. " I thank you."

An old man sat at the foot of a stump, with a ball directly through the base of his brain. A ghastly smile was on his face, his eyes looked wildly out upon the night, and his breath was rapid and heavy. He was a breathing corpse, — dead and yet living.

The atmosphere of death was on the earth; it was a scene on which one needs look but once to remember it forever.

23

CHAPTER XX.

NOTHER night on the frozen ground, and, during it, the Union commander pondered the situation. Marshall's forces were broken and demoralized. Though in full retreat, they might be overtaken and destroyed; but his own troops were half dead with fatigue and exposure, and had less than three days' rations. In these circumstances Garfield prudently decided to occupy Prestonburg, and await the arrival of additional supplies before dealing a final blow at the enemy.

On the day succeeding the battle, he issued the following address to his army, which tells, in brief, the story of the campaign : —

"Soldiers of the Eighteenth Brigade, — I am proud of you all! In four weeks you have marched, some eighty and some a hundred miles, over almost impassable roads. One night in four you have slept, often in the storm, with only a wintry sky above your heads. You have marched in the face of a foe of more than double your number, led on by chiefs who have won a national renown under the old flag, entrenched in hills of his own choosing, and strengthened by all the appliances of military art. With no experience but the conscious-

(260)

ness of your own manhood, you have driven him from his strongholds, pursued his inglorious flight, and compelled him to meet you in battle. When forced to fight, he sought the shelter of rocks and hills. You drove him from his position, leaving scores of his bloody dead unburied. His artillery thundered against you, but you compelled him to flee by the light of his burning stores, and to leave even the banner of his rebellion behind him. I greet you as brave men. Our common country will not forget you. She will not forget the sacred dead who fell beside you, nor those of your comrades who won scars of honor on the field.

"I have recalled you from the pursuit that you may regain vigor for still greater exertions. Let no one tarnish his well-earned honor by any act unworthy an American soldier. Remember your duties as American citizens, and sacredly respect the rights and property of those with whom you may come in contact. Let it not be said that good men dread the approach of an American army.

"Officers and soldiers, your duty has been nobly done. For this I thank you."

Meanwhile Bradley Brown had not been idle. Making his way back to Marshall's camp, he had filled the ears of that officer with exaggerated accounts of the strength of the Union forces, and thus materially aided in the success of the expedition. It was wonderful that his double-dealing was not suspected, for three days before the battle Marshall had intercepted a despatch passing between Garfield and Colonel Cranor, which disclosed the fact that the Union commander was fully informed of the strength and disposition of the rebel forces, and had thoroughly mapped all the roads, hills, streams, and fortifications in and around his position.

"How he got the facts," said Marshall to the rebel Colonel Gregg, "I cannot tell; but we are certainly outnumbered and outgeneralled."

Hearing, while yet at Paintville, of the rapid approach of Cranor from the westward, Marshall, a few days before the battle, despatched Brown to learn his strength and the route by which he was advancing.

This was welcome work to the ex-boatman, for the nearness of the Union forces made it daily more and more likely that his false reports would soon be sifted, and his head had begun to feel uneasy on his shoulders. He set out with alacrity, and at the end of two days rode boldly up to the lines of Cranor, and demanded to see the "gineral." Being led into the presence of that officer, Brown disclosed his name and the ostensible object of his visit, but was astonished to find that his tale was met with a cautious incredulity.

Either his appearance, or the improbability of the exploit of which he boasted, impressed Colonel Cranor unfavorably. He ordered him into close custody, and in vain Brown affirmed and reaffirmed that he knew Garfield when a boy, and that his old love for him had led him to run the risk of a halter. Cranor was not to be convinced, and Brown was made to march to Paintville, strapped upon the back of his own confiscated horse, and with an armed cavalryman at his either elbow.

Arriving at the village in the early gray of the winter morning, the weary column was met by the Union commander. When the cheering which greeted him had somewhat subsided, a voice was heard to shout from the ranks, —

"Gineral — Gineral Jim, tell that skeery cunnel that Brad. Brown ar' as true a man as he ar'."

Garfield turned his eyes toward the speaker, and, taking in at a glance the circumstances, ordered him to be set at liberty. When his cords were unloosed, Brown rode coolly up to the two officers, and said to Cranor, with an air of intense disdain, —

"Another time, p'raps, ye'll tuck the word of a gentleman! Didn't I tell ye I knowed him, — knowed him ever sence he war a boy?"

He bore himself bravely in the battle, and, when it was over, again did important service to the little army. The men, as has been said, had less than three days' rations, and supplies must be at once brought up from Louisa, where a depot had been established.

The rainy season had set in, and the roads had become impassable for any but horsemen. The river was the only resource; but the Big Sandy was then swollen beyond its banks, and its rapid current, filled with floating logs and uptorn trees, rendered navigation a thing of great danger and difficulty. The oldest boatmen of the district shook their heads, and refused to attempt the perilous voyage. But Brown said to Garfield, —

"It's which and t'other, Gineral Jim; starvin' or drownin'. I'd ruther drown nur starve. So guv the word, and, dead or alive, I'll git down the river."

Garfield gave the word, and within four days the hearts of the little army were gladdened with full rations.

23*

CHAPTER XXI.

STATE of general alarm existed throughout the district. The retreating rebels had spread the most exaggerated reports of the strength and character of the Union forces, and the simple country people looked for a reign of terror which would deprive them all, loyal and disloyal, of life and property. The result was that, fleeing from their homes, they hid away in the woods and mountains, and the towns, for a time, were well-nigh deserted. To allay this alarm, and to restore society to more of its normal condition, Garfield, during the week following the battle, issued the following proclamation:—

> " HEAD-QUARTERS, EIGHTEENTH BRIGADE, }
> PAINTVILLE, KY., Jan. 16, 1862. }

" CITIZENS OF THE SANDY VALLEY,— I have come among you to restore the honor of the Union, and to bring back the Old Banner which you all once loved, but which, by the machinations of evil men and by mutual misunderstandings, has been dishonored among you. To those who are in arms against the Federal Government I offer only the alternative of battle or unconditional surrender; but to those who have taken no part in this war,— who

(270)

are in no way aiding or abetting the enemies of the Union, even to those who hold sentiments adverse to the Union, but yet give no aid and comfort to its enemies, I offer the full protection of the government both in their persons and property.

"Let those who have been seduced away from the love of their country to follow after and aid the destroyers of our peace, lay down their arms, return to their homes, bear true allegiance to the Federal Government, and they also shall enjoy like protection. The army of the Union wages no war of plunder, but comes to bring back the prosperity of peace. Let all peace-loving citizens who have fled from their homes, return and resume again the pursuits of peace and industry. If citizens have suffered from any outrages by the soldiers under my command, I invite them to make known their complaints to me, and their wrongs shall be redressed and the offenders punished. I expect the friends of the Union in this valley to banish from among them all private feuds, and to let a liberal-minded love of country direct their conduct toward those who have been so sadly estranged and misguided. I hope that these days of turbulence may soon end, and the better days of the Republic soon return.

"(Signed,)   J. A. GARFIELD,

"Colonel Commanding Brigade."

Encouraged by this promise of protection, the people soon issued from their hiding-places, and began to flock about the Union head-quarters. From them various reports were received of the whereabouts and intentions of Marshall. By some it was said that, reinforced by three Virginia regiments

and six field-pieces, he had made a stand, and was fortifying
himself in a strong position about thirty miles above, on the
waters of the Big Beaver; by others, that he was merely col-
lecting provisions and preparing to retreat into Tennessee as
soon as the runs and rivers should become passable.

All the information, however, indicated that Marshall had
made a stand, and was still within the limits of Kentucky.
It was to Garfield of the first moment to learn his exact position, and to this end he despatched a body of a hundred
horsemen, under Captain Jenkins, of the Ohio Cavalry, with
orders to go up the Big Sandy as far as Piketon, and not
to return until they had ascertained the position and intentions of the enemy.

Jordan accompanied the squadron as guide, and, proceeding
cautiously up the narrow road which winds along the river,
they surrounded the town just as a dozen mounted rebels
were fleeing from it in the opposite direction.   Lieutenant
Lake, of Wooster, Ohio, being in the advance, called to two of
his men, and, putting spurs to his horse, followed in a break-
neck chase of four or five miles.

During the pursuit they killed one rebel, and severely
wounded another; but they kept on, — for a short distance in
advance were two others, one of them evidently a man of
some consideration.   The two were mounted on one horse,
which they were urging to his utmost speed, and, as they
turned a bend in the road, came within range of the guns of
their pursuers.

Private Boone, of the Forty-second Ohio, being for the moment in advance, levelled his carbine, and fired as he ran; but
the ball struck the saddle of the rebels, and glanced off harm-

less. Lieutenant Lake then drew his revolver, and brought the horse to the ground so suddenly that the two riders turned a somersault over the head of the animal, and landed in the creek which bordered the highway. When they recovered their feet they were prisoners.

Jordan had seen the reckless daring of the little party in setting out to pursue more than twice their number, and, fearing for their safety, had called a half-dozen cavalrymen to his aid, and followed only some ten minutes in the rear. He came up while Lake and his prisoners were still standing in the highway.

Reining up his horse, he turned to the two rebels, and, his eyes giving out a lurid glare, suddenly exclaimed, —

"Ah! it is a long road that has no end." Leaning over his saddle-bow, he almost hissed the remainder, "And at the end of all roads there is retribution!"

The other's face grew livid, but he said, with some appearance of coolness, —

"I am your prisoner; but I am ready to take the oath."

"Take the oath!" exclaimed Jordan. "Do you expect to atone for your crimes by a little false swearing? Do you expect to live while there is timber for a gallows in all Kentucky?"

"I do," answered the other, with a mocking smile. "I expect to live, and to pass sentence on a good many more scoundrels."

"Not while so much sacred blood cries from the ground against you," cried Jordan.

Not another word was said, but there was a sudden upward

movement of Jordan's hand, then his pistol exploded, and Cecil fell dead in the highway.

"My God, Jordan!" cried Lake, who had stood a silent listener to this conversation. "What have you done? He was unarmed, and a prisoner."

A strange, wild light was in Jordan's eyes as he answered,—

"So was an old man he shot down on his own hearth, — so was a young boy he hanged before the very eyes of his mother. Blood will have blood. This world couldn't hold him and me, lieutenant, — no! not this world, nor any other."

"I know, and I pity you, Jordan," said Lake; "but the colonel will have to hang you. Go, — get away. Get away at once. Not a man of us will lift a hand against you."

"No," answered Jordan; "I shall not run; I will answer for what I have done."

Then, turning his horse's head, he led the column, which bore the lifeless body of Cecil, back to Piketon.

CHAPTER XXII.

CONDEMNATION.

HE killing of Cecil was the source of much embarrassment to the Union commander. He was the leading man of the district. His death would be known far and wide, and, if it went unpunished, it would show the people of the district, and of all Kentucky, — whom it was then the policy of the government to pacify and conciliate, — that no trust could be put in the friendly professions of the Federals. Policy, therefore, required that his slayer should be severely dealt by. But, on the other hand, Jordan had done important service to the Union cause, and on the lone and toilsome marches had so often ridden by the side of Garfield, that he now seemed to him more a friend than a subordinate. His release might spread a feeling of insecurity throughout the district, and lose one of the objects of the campaign. His trial for murder, by court martial, might forfeit the life of a man whose services had entitled him to great reward, and whose wrongs at the hand of the murdered man would secure him acquittal by any civil jury in Kentucky.

While the commander was undecided which course to pursue, Bradley Brown rather unceremoniously entered his tent one morning.

(275)

"General," he said to him, "ye orter to let Jordan off. He's done a heap fur the kentry, and the best thing he ever done was riddin' it uv ole Cecil!"

"I know Cecil was a bad man, and Jordan had received great provocation."

"Provercation!" exclaimed Brown. "If Jordan hadn't a killed him, he'd not ha' been a man. Let him go, general."

"I don't see how I can without a trial. If he is court-martialed, he may not be convicted."

"May not!" echoed Brown; "but them ar' ugly words, general, when a man's life ar' at stake. Let him go, and put it to my account. I've done ye a good turn or two, and I'd ruther hang myself than hev thet man's neck get inter a halter."

"I can't let him go, Brown, without a trial," answered the general. "The forms of justice must be complied with; but I hope he will not be convicted."

A court, composed mostly of Kentucky officers, was convened within a few days, and Jordan was brought before it. He sat among the few soldiers who were detailed as his guard, and nothing in his appearance indicated that he was about to be tried for taking the life of a fellow-being. His face wore its usual dreamy expression, but some deeper lines about his mouth told that the fearful tragedy had made its impression on his soul.

The court was opened in the usual manner, the charge read, and then the witnesses were examined. Each of the half-dozen present testified to hearing the discharge of the revolver, and to seeing Cecil fall, without a word, suddenly dead in the highway; but not one could swear positively who fired the fatal shot, or remember any act that would fix the deed upon the prisoner.

At this point in the proceedings, the Judge Advocate smiled, and Brown, who sat at his elbow, drawing a long breath, exclaimed, —

"I'm durned ef ye haint a decent set, anyhow. Count on Brad. Brown if *ye* uver git inter trouble."

The words had scarcely left his mouth when the prisoner rose, and turned toward the witnesses.

"Gentlemen, I thank you," he said. "You mean to do me a kindness, and I thank you. But I prefer the truth should be told. I fired the shot which killed Judge Cecil. For a moment I forgot that vengeance belongs only to God, and I stained my hands with a crime which all the water in the world cannot wash away. For that I expect justice, not mercy. Whether you deal it to me or not, it will come. I could not, if I would, escape it, for, as night follows day, so retribution follows crime. It is already on me, bearing me down, and bringing darkness between me and my God. You could not save me from it if you would; and, with the hand of God on me, why should I fear the hand of man? No, gentlemen, let justice be done, — I killed Judge Cecil."

He sat down, rested his head upon his hand, and with sad, dreamy eyes looked out upon vacancy.

For a few moments not a word was uttered in the assemblage; then the Judge Advocate rose, and in a husky voice said to the presiding officer, —

"Nothing remains but to pass sentence upon the prisoner."

The sentence was passed: it was, — subject to the approval of the colonel commanding, — death on the following Friday.

24

CHAPTER XXIII.

T is the night before the fatal Friday, and Jordan is alone in the dreary log-shanty, which has been his prison-house since he received the sentence of the court-martial. Without, the moon is shining brightly, and the measured tread of the guards is making a sort of doleful music on the frozen highway; but within, all is gloom and silence. A low fire is burning on the hearth, casting a dim halo round the solitary man, but leaving the most of the room in darkness.

He sits before the hearth, gazing intently into the blaze, and now, as a slight puff of wind fans the almost dying flame, we get a view of his features. They are strangely altered. His cheeks are hollow, his eyes sunken; his sandy hair is turned to a sort of flaxen whiteness. There have been men whose heads grief has turned white in a single night; but it is not grief which has made this young man an old one. It is the shadow of his crime, that, settling on his soul, has brought around him the thick night in which he has stood face to face with the Unseen in all its terrors.

As he sits there gazing into the fire, the door opens, and, with a hurried step, a woman enters the apartment. She

(278)

falls at his feet, clasps his knees, and, in a voice laden with the despair which it echoes, says, —

"O John! John! There is no hope! Nothing — but death to-morrow!"

He lifts her gently from the floor, draws her near to him on the rude bench, and, putting away her tangled hair, tenderly kisses her on the forehead. Then he says, —

"I knew it would be so; but never mind, my little one. It is all well, — all well now. The darkness has cleared away, and it will all be bright in the great to-morrow."

She twines her arms about his neck in a convulsive embrace as she cries, —

"Oh, no! It can't be; you shall not die! Oh, it would kill me, John, — me, your poor Rachel!"

His great hand toys with her flowing hair, and he softly answers, —

"I know it will be hard; but I want you to be a brave woman, Rachel. I want you to be worthy of me; and I, Rachel, — though the blood I told you of is on my hands, — *I* have tried to be worthy of my ancestors."

"And can't they help you?" she cried, looking up, wildly. "Can't they save you from this dreadful death? O John, if you have to die, I shall think there is no God, and no goodness or truth in all the universe!"

Then again her head sank upon his breast, and her arms twined about him convulsively.

He was silent for a few moments, and when he spoke his voice had in it even a deeper tenderness.

"Listen to me, Rachel," he said. "I have done a great crime, — taken what I cannot give, — the life of a fellow-being. I have usurped the right of God, — wrought the vengeance that belongs only to Him. It was the thought of this that bowed me down. But now it is over; for He, — the Jesus I accounted only a man, and with my weak wisdom tried to measure, — He has been to me, and in my inmost soul has whispered, 'Son, be of good cheer; your crime is forgiven you.' He can forgive, for He is the Great Ruler; but men cannot forgive, because society, for its own security, must punish the criminal. If they should let me go, people would say there was no law and no safety in all Kentucky."

"I know," she sobbed, "it is the hard-hearted reason they give for taking your life. They forget that weren't it for you, there might be no law and no safety for even themselves this side of the Ohio."

"No, they don't forget it. How Buell feels I am not certain; but Garfield, I know, would make any sacrifice to save me. He knows that, if I were let go, it would give the lie to his promise of protection, and perhaps make impossible the pacification of the district; but still, I think, he would release me if he could."

"But he says he can't, — the messenger has come back from Buell, — the order has already been given for the execution;" and again she clutched him with a strange, convulsive energy.

"And how am I to die? Not — not by the gallows?"

"No. He says you shall die like a soldier, — as a man should who has risked his life for his country."

"Then the end has indeed come, Rachel. It was this death I saw in the vision at Frankfort. Armed men were about me, and I was bleeding from a rifle-bullet."

"Then it is so! But you shall not go alone. I will die with you."

"No, Rachel, you must live, — live for her, — my mother."

She made no reply, but, slowly rising to her feet, paced up and down the room, now and then tossing her arms into the air wildly. Jordan said nothing, but his eye followed her, and his whole frame shook with repressed emotion. At last she came to him, sat down again at his side, and twined her arms again about him.

"I *will* live, John," she said, "live for you; but you will let me stay here till they take you away to-morrow?"

"No, darling," he answered, "you had better not. She needs you now. Go, and bring her with you in the morning."

She rose, bent down over him for a moment, and then, drawing her outer garment over her uncovered head, staggered, without a word, out of the door-way.

An hour, two hours he sat there after she went away, and the fire died out, leaving the dreary room in thick darkness. Then he rose, and stretched himself upon a blanket before the hearth to wait for the morning. Soon sleep crept over him, — the deep sleep which is born of great sorrow. Gradually the darkness went out of his eyes, and there opened to him a scene which his boyhood's dreams had made strangely familiar. It was the mountains he had pictured in all their Alpine grandeur. Far below was the arid plain, with it's grovelling horde, and far above the cloudy summits, along which the angel messengers were passing and repassing on their missions of love and mercy. One came near, and Jordan, stretching out his arms, cried to him, —

24*

"Come, oh, come, and take me to yonder land of peace and rest eternal."

"Not yet, — not yet," the angel answered. "Look around you."

He looked. He was on a narrow island, between which and the base of the mountain a wide sea was rolling. It was an arid desert, overgrown with thorns and thick briers, and its only inhabitant was a man, bent nearly double with a heavy load, his clothes in rags, and his eyes ever looking downward. Jordan went near, and saw it was — Cecil !

"You sent him here, and you must raise him up, and lift the burden from off his shoulders," said a voice from out the gloom, — for the clouds had gathered round, and shut out alike the angel visitant and the far-off mountain summits.

Jordan essayed to speak, but a heavy hand was on his shoulder, and he was awake again in the darkness of the dreary cabin.

"Be as still as death; but come quick, put on this uniform," said a voice which sounded familiar.

"Who are you?" asked Jordan, rising, and running his hand over the man's face in the darkness.

"Brad. Brown. But put on the uniform quick; if ye don't, ye carn't git beyont the outside pickets."

"But you are running yourself into danger," said Jordan, undecidedly, standing with the new accoutrements in his hands.

"D——n the danger! Don't stop to parley. It'r arter midnight, and at four the guard'll be changed, and they'll larn ye're missin'. Ye must be miles away 'fore then, for the gineral'll hev to hunt ye down, to save 'pearances."

"Then he knows of this?" said Jordan, beginning to don the disguise.

"No, he don't, — not a thing. It's only me, the old sargint, and some of the Fourteenth, as is on guard from now till four in the morning."

"And you have bribed them to shut their eyes to their duty?"

"Not a bribe! I offered it, but they wouldn't tuck a red; they's the decentest set I've come onto in all Kaintucky."

"But they'll surely get into trouble. Garfield will have to hold them to account for letting me go."

"Don't be too shure uv thet. Don't I know him? — haint I knowed him ever sence he was a boy? He'd give all his old boots to be well rid uv ye. But come, hurry up; I've left Ole 'Zeke asleep into my tent to prove an alibi, and swar I warn't out o' doors all the night-time; and if the old fellow should wake up and find me gone, he wouldn't swear it to save me frum a halter. Come!"

By this time Jordan was arrayed in the new regimentals, and, taking him by the arm, Brown led him out of the cabin. Not a sentinel was in sight, but when they had proceeded a few rods Jordan heard a low whistle; and, turning round, saw about a dozen men emerge from the rear of the low cabin.

Without a word, the two walked rapidly on until the last house on the outskirts of the village was behind them. Then Brown led the way into a belt of trees, and said to Jordan, —

"I carn't go no furder, — I musn't be seed by the pickets. One on 'em ar' 'bout a hundred rods ahead, t'other 'bout as fur ag'in, stret horrard; and ye'll find 'Beauty' a half a mile

down thar, hitched in a laurel thicket. The fust word ar
'Conciliate,' the t'other 'Kaintucky;' and, ha! ha! it war
them two words as was a gwine to be the death uv ye to-
morrow."

"I thank you, Brown," said Jordan; "at bottom you have
a noble heart."

"I don't know 'bout that, Mr. Jordan; but I never forgits
a debt, and I owe ye a big one. P'raps this oughter pay it,
but ye'll need suthin' to begin the world on whar ye's a gwine.
Yere's a thousand hard rocks, and with yer talents, they'll
sot ye up well in 'Hio."

"I thank you," said Jordan, his voice trembling slightly;
"but I shall not need money, — I shall not leave Kentucky."

"Not leave Kaintucky! Why, yer mad. If the gineral
catches you, he will *have* to hang ye. I yered him say it
war awful hard, but thar warn't no holp fur it; fur the guv'-
ment thought it necessary to keep good faith about the
proclamation."

"I know; but I shall not go. I shall die here, if I have
to be buried under a gallows."

"Then ye will be; for both the Confederates and the Unions
will have death and a thousand dollars onto ye. Why, Mr.
Jordan, ye're atween two fires, — thar's a halter hangin' fur
ye from every tree in Kaintucky."

"I know it; but I shall cheat them all, and die with my
back to the earth and my face to heaven."

"Wall, I hope ye will, fur yer one of the heroes. Good-by,
and God bless ye."

"God bless you, Brown! I shall never forget this, and it

may be you will be repaid, even here, where good deeds are not always rewarded."

Then they parted, Brown to his quarters, Jordan to a long ride among the thickets and ravines of the almost inaccessible mountains.

When the guard was relieved, the prisoner's absence was discovered, and at once reported to the colonel commanding. An expression of satisfaction at first unguardedly escaped him; but, instantly remembering his duty, he summoned to his quarters all the sentinels on guard at the cabin.

They came, and with them came Captain Bent, the men being members of his company. Each was separately examined, and all denied any knowledge of the escape of the prisoner. Not one had seen him, either inside or outside of his quarters.

This was all that the men said, but the sergeant volunteered a few additional words of explanation.

"Why," he said, "thar warn't but one door and one winder to the cabin. He couldn't hev got out o' them, and he couldn't hev gone up the chimley; so he must hev turned inter a sperit, — he must, certain!"

The colonel had listened with becoming dignity to the meagre reports of the men, but this wordy explanation of the sergeant was too much for his gravity. Laughing heartily, he said, —

"You are more knaves than fools, every one of you; and if we were not to march to-morrow, I'd find a way to get the truth from you."

"No, you wouldn't, colonel," now said Captain Bent. "You might put them to the thumb-screw, and not get another word. There's not a man in the Fourteenth Kentucky but would die to save John Jordan."

No more was said; and so Jordan went at large, outlawed by both his friends and his enemies.

CHAPTER XXIV.

T was late at night, on the third day after the escape of Jordan, when a low rap came at the window of the lonely cabin in the wilderness, and, roused by the sound, Rachel raised herself on her elbow and listened. Soon the rap was repeated, and then came a low, peculiar cry, like that of a wounded bird struggling in the death-agonies.

Lifting the sash, Rachel leaned out into the darkness, and said, in quick, eager tones, —

"John! John! is it you?"

"Yes, Rachel. Go round to the door and let me into the cabin."

"No, John, not by the door; you would disturb mother. Come in here; not at this one, — my bed is here, — at the other. I will open it in a moment."

Letting the sash down softly, she sprang out of bed, and, throwing a loose robe over her night-clothing, went to the other window. In a moment more Jordan was in the room, and enclosed within the arms of the wildly joyful woman.

"O John! John!" she cried, "to have you once more! Oh, I shall die with this great joy! You safe and back again!"

"Calm yourself, my little one," he said, bending down and kissing her on the forehead. "God is good; He gives us some moments which make up for years of suffering."

"But we will have no more suffering," she said, clinging closely to his neck, and pressing her lips to his wildly. "I will never let you go away again; you shall stay with me now always."

He made no reply, but, putting back her flowing hair, kissed her again and again on the forehead. Then he said, —

"And how is mother? Has she got over the terrible shock it gave her?"

"Oh, yes; but she almost died of joy when she heard of your getting away. I believe she would have died if we hadn't made her sleep. She needs it now, so you mustn't disturb her; and, besides, I must have you all to myself for a little while." And again she pressed her lips to his frantically.

He held her so for a while; then, placing her gently in a chair near the hearth, he raked up the smouldering fire, and hung some thick blankets before the windows. When this was done, they sat for many minutes, neither of them speaking. At last she said, softly, —

"O John! I so thanked God when they told me you were outlawed by both sides; for then I knew you would go, and we could go together, and be all in all to each other forever."

She leaned forward, and pressed her lips to his again, wildly.

He made no reply, but turned his face away towards the the fire-light. Some great struggle seemed to be going on within him. At last he said, his face still averted, —

"No, no, Rachel. I must go, — I must be about the Master's business."

"What can you do? Where can you go? What now should keep us apart? Are you not hunted down by both your friends and your enemies? You must flee to some strange country. I will go with you, and be your wife forever."

She paused for a while, and then she added, —

"Oh, I so yearn for you, John! so long to be with you always!"

He was silent for a time, and again he turned his face to the fire-light. The old gleam was on it when he answered, —

"Rachel, I love you better than I love my life, and I will put my soul itself into your keeping. You shall hear what I say, and then I will do as you bid me, let come what may come hereafter. Every man has a work to do in the world. If he does this work, he grows; his whole nature expands, and he enters upon the other life, ages, it may be, in advance of the one who turns his back upon his duty. The work of some men is hard, — of others, easy. My work has been hard, Rachel. It has required me to crucify one half of my nature, to live in constant peril of my life, and, since I knew you did not love Brown, to bear a heavy cross daily."

"But it is over now, John," she said, looking up, with a

25

tender gleam in her eyes. "With a price set on your head, what more can you do for Kentucky?"

"What, perhaps, no other man can do," he answered. "I will tell you. Garfield has beaten Marshall, but has not driven him from the State. He still holds Pound Gap, and his guerillas are still overrunning all the lower counties, robbing and murdering defenceless men and women. Garfield has moved on to Piketon, in the hope of bringing him to battle; but Marshall will not fight until he can bring up strong reinforcements from Virginia. Then he will sweep down upon Garfield, and drive him from the State within a fortnight. In that event, Kentucky and the Union may be lost forever. Garfield cannot bring Marshall to battle, because he is entrenched in a position from which a force five times as strong as his could not dislodge him by direct assault. Some one must enter Marshall's camp, learn his exact strength and position, and then guide Garfield over the mountains to the rear of the rebel entrenchments."

"But you can't do that, John."

"I can, Rachel. I can go into Marshall's camp, and get safely out, for nature made me an actor. Then I can guide Garfield, for I know every rod of the mountain."

"But you would be taken, you would be shot! Garfield himself told me that if you were captured he would have to carry out the sentence of the court-martial."

"I know; but not a man in his army would be willing to do these things. If I do not do them they will not be done, and if they are not done Kentucky will be lost."

"Oh, but you will lose your life, John, — you will surely

lose your life!" and her head sank to his shoulder, and her arms twined about him convulsively.

"Rachel," he answered, "it is more than likely that I shall. It is for you to say whether I shall or not, — whether I shall die a brave, true man, and leave a memory that you will be proud of, or whether I shall skulk away into some free State, and, with the wife of the man to whom I owe my life, live the rest of my days in open violation of the laws of both God and man."

"O John, I had not looked at it so. Do not ask me. I cannot decide."

His voice was very soft, and very gentle, as he answered, —

"You must, Rachel. To your unselfish love I commit my very soul."

She raised her head from his shoulder, and, looking into his face with eyes that had in them a strange radiance, she said, —

"Then die, John ; and wait there till my life here is ended. I will do my humble work and live upon your memory, until you come and take me to you forever."

He clasped his great arms about her, and, drawing her to him yet more closely, he said, —

"Oh, my guide, my hope, my comfort! Now you are indeed mine ! Now no shadow can come between us, — between your soul and my soul."

Long they sat there, she in his arms, and neither of them speaking. At last he said, —

"I had a strange dream the other night, Rachel, — a dream that was a revelation. It showed me a new truth, —

gave me a new insight into the moral government of the Creator."

"What was it?" she said; "tell me."

"The curtain was drawn aside. I saw the delectable country. But it was far away, and between me and it a wide sea was rolling. I wanted to go to it, but a voice said, 'Not yet; look around you.' I looked, and saw that I was on a desert island. No one was near but a wretched man, his clothing in tatters, and he so bowed down with a heavy burden that he could not stand upright. It was Cecil."

"Cecil, that bad man! Oh, what could be its meaning?"

"That the voice told me. It said I had sent him there, and I could not reach the beautiful land till I had raised him up and lifted the burden from off his shoulders. And this was the truth it taught me, — that we ourselves cannot rise until we lift those who are brought down by our crimes or our neglect of duty. Think of this, my darling. I will say no more; but some day it will come to you, — my meaning."

She turned suddenly pale, and her voice was almost husky, as she asked, —

"What do you mean, John? You surely would not have me go back to that man, — have me become a wanton?"

"No, Rachel. I would have you do nothing against your conscience. If that says you have done all you can do, it will all be well hereafter."

"O John, you put a dagger through me. He has told me that only with me could he stand upright and be a man, and I did promise to keep to him through all things. It was an idle promise, got from me by deceit; but it may be that, to punish me for breaking it, God has put his very soul into my

hands. Oh, the idea is too horrible! Since I woke to know
I loved you, the very thought of him has been to me a terror
and a loathing."

" Well, think no more of it now, Rachel. Some day your
duty will be plain to you."

They sat for a while longer in silence; then he suddenly
sprang to his feet, exclaiming, —

" Hark! What is that? The sound of horses?"

She sprang to the window, threw up the sash, and looked
out into the darkness.

" Yes," she cried, in a moment; " twenty horsemen coming
up the highway, — now they are turning into the path. Run,
John, this way, through the window."

But he was too late, for already the shadow of one of the
troopers was against the half-open casement.

25 *

N a moment a heavy pounding was heard at the outer door, and the widow Jordan, awaking, cried out, —

"Who is there? What is wanted?"

"Rachel Irving," said a voice which Jordan recognized as that of Weddington.

"Thank God, it is me and not you," said Rachel, in a whisper. "Keep quiet, and you will not be discovered. I will go and open the door. They will not try to harm me; if they do, this will protect me;" and she took a long knife from Jordan's girdle.

"Do not open the door," said Jordan. "Do nothing. Leave all to Providence. He will, I know, bring us out of this danger."

By this time the summons for admission had been repeated, and it was Ezekiel's voice that now answered, —

"You carn't come in, Massa Jack, and you'd better go away mighty sudden; for 'Zeke's got suflin' yere as'll settle you' hash so quick it'll make you' head swim."

Nothing more was said, but a heavy blow came against the door, starting the half-rotten plank from its hinges. Then came another blow, which drove the whole frame, with a loud crash, into the apartment. A half-dozen pistol-shots were fired in quick succession, and then half a score of armed men rushed into the room, one of them crying out, —

"Secure the old nigger. See he does no more mischief."

In a few moments the smoke cleared away, showing the old black held to the floor by four strong men; and Rachel, standing against the door of the lean-to, with the naked knife in her hands.

"Do not harm him," she cried; "do not, on your lives! Jackson Weddington, what do you want with me?"

"Not much, my pretty one; only I am going away for a while, and a short journey with me will do you good."

"Are you a man, or a brute?" cried Mrs. Jordan, advancing upon him, her eyes blazing. "Do you think these ways will always prosper?"

"Peace, mother!" said Rachel, with an imperious gesture. "I know him. Your words are thrown away." Turning to Weddington, she added, "Release 'Zekiel, and, with your men, leave the house this instant, and I will go with you."

"Go with him! Why, child, are you crazy?" cried the widow Jordan.

"No, mother, not crazy. Do you consent, Mr. Weddington?"

"Consent! of course I do. You are a sensible woman, Rachel."

When the old negro had risen to his feet, and one half of the horsemen had left the apartment, the door of the lean-to suddenly opened, and, a revolver in his either hand, Jordan stepped directly in front of Rachel.

Weddington sprang a step or two backward, and drew a pistol.

"Put up your weapon, Mr. Weddington. I can fire before you," said Jordan, coolly. "I have twelve shots, and the first of you who move are dead men."

"What brings you again in my way?" asked Weddington, pale with rage, or — cowardice.

"That I will tell you, if you send your men into the road, and go with me out of all hearing. I will tell you of something that will keep you from a crime too terrible to think of."

"Ha, ha! Do you think I am a fool? You would have me where the odds will not be against you," said Weddington, half-raising his revolver.

"No, I would not. But lower your pistol, or I shall fire."

The pistol was lowered, and Jordan went on, —

"Send your men away, and give me your word to listen to what I may say, and you shall have my arms as a pledge of good faith."

"Why not speak here, before these witnesses?" asked Weddington, his color changing with an ill-defined fear of some bad tidings.

"Because I am under oath to tell no one. I tell you only to save you from a crime that would embitter your whole life."

Weddington stood undecided for a few moments, then he said to a man in the door-way, —

"Sergeant, take all the men into the road, — not more than a quarter of a mile away."

"Now, Mr. Jordan, where would you lead me?"

"To the barn; that is far enough."

"Very well; give me your weapons. I will go with you."

The troop mounted and rode off, and, handing Weddington his revolvers, Jordan said, —

"Good-by, Rachel; good-by, mother," and led the way in the direction of the out-building. He did not pause till they had reached an open space not far from the forest; then, pointing to a fallen log, he said, —

"Sit there, Mr. Weddington, and you will have the moonlight on my face. No man can deceive me when I see his features."

Without a word, and, as if only mechanically obeying another's will, Weddington sat down, and Jordan began to pace to and fro before him. In a moment he said, —

"It is a long story; but, if I tell a part, I must tell the whole. It concerns you to understand it in all its bearings."

"Go on," said Weddington, with an impatient gesture.

"Well, many years ago, far at the North, there lived an orphan boy, who had no friends or near relations. He was born, it was thought, in a poor-house; at any rate, he was taken from one when very young, and adopted by a good old man, who was a teacher. The old man had no children of his own, and all his life had been a sort of good Samaritan, going about doing good to the poor. He gave largely in charity, but was a frugal man, and so accumulated quite a little property. The boy he loved as if he had been his own, and he educated him, and made him his assistant; but the lad never took to teaching, nor to any work, except dressing fine and being a gentleman. The old man knew this, and partly to get these fine notions out of his head, and partly to have something solid to leave him, he determined to buy a farm, which should be the boy's when he died. He told him of this intention, and that he wouldn't have long to wait; for his time, he thought, was soon coming. You see, he had a foreknowledge of his death, not fixed and certain, but that sort of foreknowledge which some have of great events in their lives, — such men as live near enough to God to feel the pulses of the great spirit-world that is all about us.

"I reckon the old man lived so. At any rate, he knew his work here was about over. He had always lived sober and natural; so he was hale and hearty, and the boy thought he would last ten or fifteen years longer. He couldn't endure the idea of being that long in the school, and was determined not to go upon the farm; but he encouraged the old man to buy it, because it would bring his money into the house, when he could get it into his hands, make away to some far country, and live at his leisure. He knew his going away would break the old man's heart; but he didn't heed that, he thought only of himself, — thought only of himself, when he was certain the old man loved him too well even to follow, and try to get back the money."

"This is indeed a long story," said Weddington; "and on my life I can't see how it concerns me."

"You will see, shortly," said Jordan, pausing in his measured walk. "So have patience, and let me go on in my own way."

"Go on," said the other.

"Well, the old man bought the farm, and, the day before he was to receive the deed, drew his money from the bank, and went to sleep with it under his pillow. The two lived by themselves, in a large house, with only an old house-keeper, — and she was half deaf, and slept in the farther end of the building. The boy — he was twenty then — waited until the old man was asleep, and all around was still, and then he went to his bed and began to search for the money, which he knew was under his pillow. It woke the old man. He sprang up, grappled the boy, and they struggled, — the old man not knowing who it was for the darkness. He was very strong, and soon was getting the better of the boy; then all at once it flashed upon him that he would be discovered and ruined, — so he drew his knife, and gave the old man his death-blow."

"It was a terrible deed," continued Jordan, pausing and looking the other full in the face, "and yet not half so terrible as what followed; but I'll tell you the whole, that you may know just how much and how little to blame him."

"The old man was dead, — dead, but living; living in that room, and knowing that his own adopted son had killed him. The boy thought of this, and the thought overcame him. He sank down on the floor, and groaned in agony, and something within — it was his good angel — said to him, —

"'Go out. Confess the crime, and take the consequences.'

"But in a moment the devil that had led him on to the deed came back, and said, —

"'What's done can't be undone. Cover up the crime, and profit all you can by it.'

"Then the boy set about hiding the trace of his hand in the dreadful business.

"The bag of money he put up the chimney, and, catching some of the old man's blood in a basin, sprinkled it along the stairs, and out at the front way. Then he fixed the outer door so that the house would seem to have been entered from the outside. This took an hour, and it was as much as he could do to get through it, for, at his every step, the spirit of the old man followed him. It glared on him out of the darkness when he kneeled down to catch the blood that was flowing from the body, and went with him, step by step, down the stairs, through the hall, and out at the door-way; and there it stood right before him in the moonlight, looking so sad and pitiful, and yet so yearning and so forgiving, that the boy was tempted to drive the knife into his own heart, and go at once to the great accounting. But he did not. Something held his hand, and said, —

"'Don't be weak *now*. Finish what you've undertaken.'

" Going back into the house, he burned his bloody clothes, and, it being still early in the evening, put on another suit, and went off to the house of a young woman, whom he was to have married. He stayed there all night, and, it appearing that he was away when the deed was done, he was not even suspected when the cook found the old man's body in the morning.

" Then began his retribution. The old man was dead; his work was over, or, rather, he had gone to work where work is only playing. But the young man was haunted by a devil that gave him no rest, but followed him day and night like his own shadow, — only it always went before, keeping between him and the sunlight. Day and night it was at his elbow, and day and night he kept doing over again the murder, and seeing the old man as he saw him in the dark room, and out there in the moonlight.

"At last, he could endure this no longer, and he tried to kill himself, but he couldn't. The same devil again held his hand, and again spoke to him, this time saying that he could not die till he had expiated his crime by long years of suffering.

"He thought the old man haunted the house, and often would wake up at night and fancy he was standing by his bedside. Then he would rush out into the open air, and go wandering round until morning. But nothing gave him any rest, and at last even the sight of his best friends became a torment. He determined to go away, and, in some strange place, try to escape the memory of his crime and his terrible visions. He sold the house and the school, — for the old man had left him all, — and then went off on a journey. For a year he wandered about from place to place, and then came to Lexington, when the court was in session.

"A middle-aged man was there attending court, with a young wife, to whom he had been married some years without children. The young man got acquainted with them, and the Kentuckian, who was a desperate hand at those things, led him deeply into drinking and gaming. Well, he won the young man's money, and the young man won his wife; and so one crime was made to punish the other. This was about a year before you were born, Jackson Weddington."

Weddington's face turned to a livid hue, but he said nothing, and Jordan went on, —

"The poor woman, however, wasn't so much to blame, — *he* told me she was not. He had the power over her that a snake has over a bird. Often she tried to get away, but could not, and he kept the spell upon her until she died."

26

"It was horrible," now stammered Weddington. "Had the man no soul?"

"Yes,— a soul; but one hardened and encrusted with crime. It's the nature of sin, Weddington," answered Jordan. "We open the door to one devil, and seven come in, worse than the first. This was worse than the murder. That was sudden and unthought of; this he planned, gloated over, and, for years and years, rolled like a sweet morsel under his tongue.

"Well, the Kentuckian knew nothing of all this, and about a year afterward a son was born in his family. This seemed to change his whole nature. He threw off his bad habits, and became a man. He knew his wife did not love him; but this gave him something to live for.

"But the Northerner still darkened his door-way, and one day was seen by a servant in doubtful relations with his mistress. The negro had been brought up with his master, and, presuming on their long connection, he cautioned him about having his friend longer in the family. His master took offence, and sold him; but the next year the negro came back to the plantation, and then told the overseer the whole facts; and these he had not disclosed to his master.

"The overseer at once told the Kentuckian; for the Northerner was still at the mansion. He stormed, and affected to disbelieve the story, and the two parted in anger; but that night the Kentuckian charged the crime upon his wife. She confessed it, and a duel between the two men followed. They fought with swords in the billiard-room in which they had gambled together, and the Northerner disarmed the Kentuckian. He gave him his life, and then left the plantation.

The other went away the next day, and the woman fell dangerously sick. While she was on her death-bed, and *he knew it,* the Northerner came back to the house, and told her to rob her husband. She did so, and in a little time she died.

"But retribution again followed. His ill-gotten gains went in a night, and, after twenty years of wretched life, he died, mourned only by his innocent daughter."

Jordan paused, and for a time, paced to and fro in silence. Then stopping directly before Weddington, he said, —

"That man was your father, his daughter is your sister; and now tell me if you will not thank me for this through all eternity?"

He laid his hand gently on the other's shoulder, as he said this, and his voice was strangely soft and musical.

Weddington's head sank upon his breast, and, in hollow tones, he muttered, —

"It can't be true, — it can't be true!"

"It *is* true. He told me when he was dying. Look at your sister, and see if she is not yourself, — only more of her mother, and less of her father. Think of all this, Weddington, and remember, retribution followed him; let it not follow you. Now I must go; give me the pistols."

Weddington mechanically held out the revolvers. Jordan took them, and, turning away, was soon lost in the forest. A moment later a shrill whistle was heard in the wood. It was answered by a low whinny, and soon afterward a horse's hoofs echoed along the narrow road which led to the far-away southern mountains.

CHAPTER XXVI.

HE traces of Jordan's subsequent career are dim and shadowy. He was never again seen in the vicinity of the cabin, and to only a very few was it known that he had not left Kentucky. How and where he lived was a profound mystery, even to Bent and the half-dozen members of his regiment with whom Jordan's self-imposed mission brought him in almost nightly contact.

On one occasion a small party of Ohio soldiers, crossing the mountain on a hunting expedition, soon after the army encamped in the vicinity of Piketon, came upon a dilapidated hut, buried in the deepest recesses of the forest. It was a rude shanty of rough logs, and had been the temporary home of some hunter, who, before the war, had trapped for furs in that wild region; but now was so fallen into decay as scarcely to afford shelter to the untamed creatures that frequent the dense thickets of those well-nigh inaccessible mountains. The soldiers were about to pass the place without special notice, when their attention was arrested by a thin column of smoke curling lazily up from the half-ruined chimney. Cautiously approaching the hut, they looked in at the open door-way. The cabin was without door or window,

(304)

and the cold wind, which swept through the interstices in the walls, half-filled the desolate room with the smoke of a fire that was smouldering on the decayed hearth; but through the cloudy atmosphere the soldiers soon got a view of the occupants of the cabin. They were a man and a horse, stretched on a bed of dry leaves and sleeping soundly. The man lay near the fire, his head resting on the neck of the horse, and his body extended between the fore-legs of the animal, one of which was coiled about his waist, as if it were the arm of a mother encircling a sleeping child. His skin was densely black, but he had straight, European features, and long gray hair that might have belonged to a white man.

One of the soldiers touching him on the shoulder, the man and the horse rose to their feet at the same instant.

The man stepped back a few paces, and suddenly drew a revolver, but as suddenly he put it back into his belt, and said,—

"Ah, dar's no f'ar ob you! Ole 'Zeke know you, — you'm ob Cunnel Cranor's regimen'."

"And who are you, and what are you doing here?" asked one of the soldiers.

"Why, don't you know?" exclaimed the negro. "I'se ole 'Zeke — friend to de Unions. I scouts it fur Cap'n Bent ob de ole Fourteenth. You ax him, an' if you wont tuck de word ob Cap'n Dick, jess you ax de gineral. He'm yeard ob ole 'Zeke, dough he haint de honor ob his pussonal 'quaintance."

"Well," now said another of the soldiers, "come with us, and we'll give the 'gineral de honor ob your pussonal 'quaintance.' The fact is, old man, we can't allow prowlers so near the lines."

The old black hesitated a moment, then he answered, —

"Dar haint only free ob you, so 'Zeke haint obleeged to go; but he will, jess to keep de peace, — only you sot out to onct, case he muss be twenty mile away by midnight. Tuck him to onct to Cap'n Bent, — Cap'n Dick, of de Fourteenth Kaintucky."

"We don't know Captain Bent. We'll take you to the colonel himself."

" 'Scuse me, gemmen, but bein' we'se too fur away, it'd tuck too long, and me and de mar muss get some sleep ag'in de night's journey. You jess go to Cap'n Dick, — 'Zeke wont go no whar else."

The resolute manner of the negro decided the soldiers. They conducted him at once to the head-quarters of the Kentucky regiment; but, to their surprise, both Captain Bent and Colonel Moore at once denied all knowledge of the old negro. When he was at last taken into the tent of the latter officer, Captain Bent said, —

"Now, old man, speak the truth. Who are you, and why are you hanging about the camp?"

"Jess 'case, I couldn't git inside, Massa Dick. You sees, I hadn't de word, and widout dat you wont leff in eben a ole darky."

"And why did **you** want to come in?"

"Jess to git dat 'backer you promise ole 'Zeke, dat night he cotched you down dar by Peach Orchard."

"The devil!" exclaimed Bent, springing to his feet, and going closely to the negro. "How dare you come here?"

The negro laughed, as he answered, —

"Why, what wuss am it comin' yere dan layin' out on de

mountain? It'm full of rebs, Massa Dick. Dar's a nest ob 'em not twenty mile away, and ef you'll tuck fifty calvary, and foller ole 'Zeke, you'll hab 'em all 'fore mornin'."

"What do you say, colonel?" asked Bent, turning to another officer. "Can I have the men? The negro can be trusted."

"Who is he?" asked Colonel Moore.

"An old fellow I've known since I was born," answered Bent. "I'd trust my life with him."

"Then why is he in danger in our lines?" asked Moore, with a look of incredulity.

"I'll tell you."

Bent took the other aside, and for a while the two conversed together in whispers. Then Colonel Moore approached the negro, and, taking him cordially by the hand, said, —

"I am glad to see you safe; but the blood-hounds are after you. It's a dangerous game you are playing."

"I know, Massa Moore," answered the black; "dar'm danger eberywhar; but it'm all one to a ole darky. All he wants am to die in de harness."

Moore wrung his hand for a moment without speaking; then he said, —

"Bent shall go with you. Meet him somewhere outside the lines after nightfall."

"Bery well," said the other. "Now 'Zeke'll go. He don't tuck ober strong to any sogers, — rebs or Unions."

The old man was soon conducted outside of the army lines, and not long after dark was met at an appointed place by Captain Bent and the fifty horsemen. In the morning the party returned without the guide, but with a score or more of rebel guerillas, whom they had captured at midnight.

A few nights later, as a sentinel was pacing his round on the outer picket line of the army, he caught sight of a man moving quickly along the edge of the wood which skirted the foot of the mountain.

"Halt!" he cried. "Who goes there?"

"A friend," was the answer.

"Advance, friend, and give the countersign," said the sentry.

"Freedom for Kentucky."

"All right," answered the soldier. "I've orders from the captain. Take my musket and stand guard. I'll have him here in ten minutes."

The old negro — for it was he — mounted guard, and soon the soldier returned with the officer. Leading him in among the trees, the old man talked for a while with him earnestly. Then, saying "I'll be dar," he turned away and disappeared in the darkness.

Half an hour later, Bent left camp with a party of horsemen. In the morning he returned with another score of rebel guerillas, whom he had surprised and captured at their hiding-place on the mountains.

Scarcely a night followed, for nearly a month, that the same old man did not make his appearance at the same picket-station, always giving the words, "Freedom for Kentucky," and always walking the sentry's beat while the latter was away in search of his superior officer. Some midnight movement always followed these visits, and soon the region was cleared of the roving bands of marauders, who, issuing from their hiding-places among the mountains, had descended into the valleys, and spread terror and death among the defence-less dwellers of the district.

Toward the close of February, the midnight visits of the old black suddenly ceased, and Moore said to Bent, —

"What has become of him? — not, I hope, taken by the rebels."

"I hope not," answered Bent; "but he's off on a desperate expedition, — gone into the rebel camp at Pound Gap. If they suspect him he's a dead man, certain."

A fortnight later, a white man presented himself at the line of pickets held by the Fourteenth Kentucky, giving the old negro's password, "Freedom for Kentucky," and demanding an interview with Captain Bent, of that regiment.

"Who are you? Whar's the old man? How came you by his countersign?" asked the sentry, who had often met the old negro on his midnight visits.

"Ah! my name ar' Bradslaw," said the man, speaking with a strong nasal drawl, and turning up the whites of his eyes in the moonlight. "They call me Parson Bradslaw, ah, 'case, ah, I'm one of the Lord's chosen, ah, chosen to give milk to his babes, ah, strong meat to his older children, ah. The negro man " —

He was going on, but was here interrupted by the soldier, who assured him, in not very courteous terms, that he was a liar and a hypocrite, to boot, — the said Bradslaw being, to his certain knowledge, then an inmate of the jail at Piketon.

In vain the parson insisted that the Bradslaws were a numerous family, and that more than one of them had been servants of the Lord, and preachers of his gospel, and in vain he protested against being taken within the lines, and begged to be allowed to meet Captain Bent there "by moonlight alone." The soldier was deaf to both remonstrance and entreaty, and, calling to a companion to relieve him of sentry-duty, he marched the reluctant parson off to the head-quarters of the regiment.

At the quarters of Colonel Moore, a number of officers, among them Captain Bent and the colonel commanding, were assembled to deliberate on some intended movement of the army, when the canting parson was brought before them. As he stalked into the centre of the tent, and the light fell full on his face, they had a view of his personal appearance. It was entirely nondescript, and of a character never seen east of the Cumberland mountains.

He was tall, above six feet in height, with long, stooping shoulders, and gaunt, bony arms that extended nearly down to his knees. On his head, when he entered, was a broad, slouched hat, half hiding his face; but this he soon removed, revealing a pair of deep-gray eyes, a heavy, projecting brow, and a dark, sallow skin, begrimed apparently with the smoke of a curing-house. His beard was not heavy, but long and intensely black, and his hair was also long and black, and came forward of his ears in an exact line with the outer angle of his eyes, unclipped by shears, except straight across, half an inch above his eyebrows. He was dressed in the common butternut jean of the district, his coat much too long in the skirts, and his trousers much too short in the legs; and as he turned to the assembled officers, and, describing a half-circle with his enormous beaver, addressed them in a shrill nasal drawl, he was a sound to hear, as well as "a sight to behold."

"My friends, ah," he said, "I must call ye friends, ah — for I ar' one of the anointed, and ye is a-wieldin' the sword of the Lord and of Gideon. Ye is a-fightin' the battles of the right ag'in the hosts of Belial ; and so ye is my friends, ah, ye is my friends ; but it is my duty, ah, — bein' as I ar' a free citizen of old Kaintuck, — it is my duty, ah, to let ye know, ah, this shinin' evenin', ah, that ye is a doin' violence to the great principles to w'ich I do believe, ah, — principles w'ich rest, ah, at the very foundation of all things, — w'ich is the chief corner-stone of all human freedom, ah, — w'ich will stand when man that is born of woman, with a few days to live, w'ich is full of trouble, shall hev gone back to dust, — shall hev turned inter the unresolvable elements, of w'ich, ah, Shakespeare wrote, ah. It is my duty, ah, to say unto you that you hev done violence to them great principles for the w'ich our foreancestors fout, bled, and died, under William the Conqueror, and William Penn, and loikewise under Gineral Jackson at the battle of Bunker Hill. Ye hev done violence to them great principles, ah, by a draggin' me yere, — yere among yer men of war, — me, a messenger of peace, a ambassador of the Lord, a minister of the Gospil in good standin'. And now, with all due deference to the presence into w'ich I am fotched, ah, I must ax, ah, that ye let me go the way I come, — that ye let me return to my flock upon the mountains, — my flock that ar' a-strayin' without a guide, ah, — that ar' a-nibblin' the short grass, and lookin' with strainin' eyes and bleatin' hearts for thar shepherd as haint forthcomin'."

The officers listened with ill-restrained mirth during the delivery of this unique harangue, but at its close they burst into a merry peal of laughter, and, as soon as he could, Bent shouted, —

"Why did you come to the lines, and who the devil are you?"

Without turning his head, the preacher rolled his great gray eyes upon Bent, and, in the same sanctimonious drawl, answered, —

"I ar', Richard Bent, ah, what I fears ye never will be, — a chile of the Lord, a sarvint of the Most High; and I ar' loikewise, ah, a watchman on the walls of Zion, a' shepherd of Israel, tending the Lord's flock that is a wanderin' in the wilderness; and as sich it ar' my duty, ah, to tell ye, ah, that ye is one of the profane, ah, — for out of ye flows words that shock the ear, and into ye flows whiskey that ruins the stomach, and'll bring ye to an untimely eend, if ye don't turn from yer ways, take to readin' yer Bible, and drinkin' spring water, ah!"

Bent joined less heartily in the laugh that followed; but he soon again demanded, —

"Who are you, and what brought you here?"

The preacher now drew a' roll of paper from an inside pocket, and his whole manner suddenly, and, as it were, unconsciously, changed, as he quickly answered, —

"My name ar' Bradslaw; they call me Parson Bradslaw, and I ar' yere to do ye a good turn, — mayhap, to save Kaintucky."

As he handed the roll to Bent, the colonel commanding said to the stranger, —

"Speak the truth, my friend, — you are not Bradslaw; we have him safe under lock and key at the village."

Resuming his drawling tone, the preacher answered, —

"That may be, gineral. Thar war but one Adam, and he war shot out o' Paradise. Thar war but one Noah, and he war saved in the deluge. Thar war but one Jacob, and he wrestled all night with the angel, and did prevail, though his withers was unstrung, and he went a cripple all his life arterwards. But thar is two Bradslaws. One, like Esau, has sold his birthright for a mess of pottage, and in yonder jail is a-gittin' the due reward of his doin's. The other is yere afore ye, and he ar' a cl'ar, free man, as would, this night, lay down his life for his kentry; as would lay down his life, for the time ar' nigh, the time of w'ich the Scripture speaks, — the time as tries men's souls. Ah, and he reckons we orter all to do our duty to our kentry, ah, 'fore thet time comes, thet time, and the great con-flag-a-ration of the universe — ah " —

He was suddenly interrupted by Bent, who, rising to his feet, and holding the open paper before him, said, in an angry way, —

"Tell me, you canting devil, where did you get this, and where is the man that made it?"

"Richard Bent," said the preacher, again rolling his eyes upon him, with a look half of reproof and half of concealed merriment, "ye is one of the profane! But I will answer yer question. This hand made it, this foot trod every rod of thet sile, — trod it thet *ye* might tread it, and not stumble; and ye kin go the way I went, and come in and go out in safety; ye kin, as sure as my name ar' Bradslaw."

27

Bent grasped the preacher by the hand, and was about
to speak; but, at a significant look from him, he turned away,
and, throwing the paper upon the table, said, —

"Colonel, here is a complete map of the rebel position,
with full directions how to turn it, and how to bag them all
within forty-eight hours."

As each one in the room clustered eagerly about the table,
Bent turned to the preacher and spoke a few hurried words
in a whisper.

After a long and close scrutiny of the paper, the colonel
commanding looked up, and said to Bent, —

· "Do you think this can be relied on?"

"Implicitly," answered Bent; "he has been among them
for a fortnight."

"Well, my man," continued the colonel, looking round for
the preacher. He suddenly paused, for that individual was
no longer visible. "Where is he?" he added. "Bring him
here; I must question him."

"Well, you can't, colonel," said Bent; "I gave him the
word, and he's beyond the lines by this time. Don't you
know? It was Jordan!"

CHAPTER XXVII.

OUND Gap is a wild and irregular opening in the Cumberland Mountains, about forty-five miles southwest of Piketon. It is the only channel of wagon communication between the southerly portions of Virginia and Kentucky, and takes its name from a fertile tract of meadow-land which skirts the southerly base of the mountains, and is enclosed by a narrow stream called Pound Fork. In the early history of the district this mountain locality was the home of a tribe of Indians, who made periodical expeditions into Virginia for plunder. Returning with the stolen cattle of the settlers, they pastured them in this meadow enclosure, and hence it acquired the name of the "Pound," which in time it gave to both the Gap and the streamlet.

In this "Pound," and on the summit of the gorge through which the road passes, the rebels had built log huts, capable of quartering nearly a thousand men; and across the opening of the Gap they had erected a formidable breastwork, that completely blocked the passage, and which five hundred men could hold against five thousand.

For several weeks Pound Gap had been garrisoned by about six hundred rebel militia, under a Major Thompson, and

though incapable of effective service in the field, they had
held this gateway into Virginia, and maintained a constant
reign of terror among the Union citizens of all the lower
counties. Issuing from their stronghold on the mountains,
small parties of this gang would descend into the valleys, rob
and murder the peaceable inhabitants, and, before pursuit
could be begun, would be again behind their breastworks.
Many of these predatory bands had been captured, in conse-
quence of the vigilance of Jordan, and the ceaseless activity
of the Kentucky cavalry; but as soon as one party was made
prisoners another would appear in the valley, until it was evident that the only way to effectually stop their incursions was
to break up their nest on the mountain. This Garfield had
long determined to do. He had waited only for reliable information as to the strength and position of the guerillas, and
for a definite description of the route to be taken to get in the
rear of their intrenchments.

This information the map of Jordan supplied, and it added
a significant fact which decided Garfield to at once set on foot
the intended expedition.

On the margin of the map, in Jordan's own writing, were
these words : —

"General Marshall has issued an order for a grand muster
of the rebel militia on the fifteenth of March. They are to
meet at the 'Pound,' in the rear of their intrenchments, and
it is expected they will muster in sufficient strength to enter
Kentucky, and drive the Union forces before them."

It was this indorsement only which had enabled Bent to
penetrate the disguise of the counterfeit preacher.

Garfield at once determined to forestall the intended gathering, and to disperse the entire swarm of guerillas. With two hundred and twenty of the Fortieth Ohio, under Colonel Cranor; two hundred of the Forty-second Ohio, under Major Pardee; one hundred and eighty of the Twenty-second Kentucky, under Major Cook; and a hundred cavalry, under Major McLaughlin, he set out on the following morning, with three days' rations in the haversacks of the men, and a quantity of provisions packed on the backs of mules.

The roads were deep in mud, and the countless rivulets which ramify through this mountain region were filled with ice, and swollen into rushing torrents; but pressing on over the rough roads, and in the midst of a drenching rain, the little army, late on the night of the second day, reached Elkhorn Creek, — a small stream which flows along the northern base of the mountains, and empties into the Big Sandy, only two miles below the rebel position. There they went into camp on the wet ground, and waited for the morning.

Garfield's plan was to send his small party of cavalry up the road to make a demonstration against the enemy's intrenchments, and to engage his attention, while, with the infantry, he should climb the steep side of the mountain, and, filing along a narrow ledge of rocks on its summit, reach the gap, and attack the flank of the rebel position. To prove successful, the movement must be executed with the utmost secrecy, and a guide must be obtained to guide the infantry over the mountain. To these ends every male resident of the vicinity was brought into camp, where he was detained to prevent his carrying information to the enemy, and questioned as to some practicable route to the rear of his intrenchments. There was no route. The mountain was steep, and in some places precipitous, and it was tangled with dense thickets, obstructed with fallen logs, and covered with huge boulders, which, coated with ice and snow, formed an almost impassable barrier to the passage of any living thing save the panther and the catamount. But if, in the face of all these obstacles, the mountain summit were at last gained by the adventurous band, they would be obliged to thread for a long distance a narrow ledge, buried three feet deep in yielding snow, where one false step would be death, and ten men could dispute the passage of an army.

Though tempted with liberal offers of money, not one of the "natives" would undertake to guide the expedition. In these circumstances, Garfield laid down at midnight on the floor of a wretched log shanty near the foot of the mountain. The prospect was in no way encouraging; in fact, it seemed that Jordan had carefully concealed the real difficulties of the expedition. But turning back was out of the question. Even if he failed, the Union commander would attempt to scale the mountain in the morning.

These thoughts in his mind, he fell into a light slumber; but before morning he was roused by a number of men entering his apartment. One of them was Captain Bent. Approaching his commanding officer, he said, —

"Colonel, this old fellow has just come into camp, and offers to guide us over the mountain. He says he knows every rod of all this region, and can lead us to the rebel nest safely."

Garfield raised himself on his blanket, and, by the dim light of the logs that were smouldering on the hearth, looked narrowly at the old "native." He was apparently not far from seventy, with a tall, bent form, and long hair and beard, which were of almost snowy whiteness. He wore the common homespun of the district, and over his shoulder carried, slung by a stout leather thong, a brightly-burnished squirrel rifle. His enormous beard and huge slouched hat more than half hid his face, but enough of it was exposed to show a tawny, smoke-begrimed skin, and strongly-marked, determined features. Hastily scanning him from head to foot, the Union officer said, smiling, —

"You!— old man, do you think *you* can climb the mountain ? "

"I hev done it, gineral, many and many a time," said the "native," in a voice that sounded much like a cracked kettle.

"I know ; but in winter, — the slope a sheet of ice, and three feet of snow on the summit ? "

"I comed down it not ten days ago. Whar I kin come down, ye kin go up."

"I should think so, up or down. Is there a bridle-path we can follow ? "

"Yes ; eight miles below. But ye'd better make yer own path. Ye must come onto 'em unbeknown and sudden, and to do that, ye must foller the route the squirrels travil."

"What route is that ? "

"The one over the rocks and along the edge of the presurpiss. They has pickets on every other path. On that they look for nothin' but wild critters."

"And do you think we can git over it safely ? "

"Yes, if ye's men of narve, as means to do what they has come about."

"Well," said Garfield. "What induces an old man like
you to undertake a thing so hazardous ? "

"The hope to rid the kentry of a set of murderin' thieves,
as is carryin' terror and death inter every pore man's home in
all the valley."

"And what reward do you look for ? "

"Nary reward, — only yer word that I shall go as I comed,
with no one to let or hinder me."

At this the Union officer gave him a quick, suspicious
glance, and the old man turned his face aside, and slunk
back a little into the darkness. Bent said, hastily, —

"I know him, colonel. You can stake your life on him.
He'll guide us safe or die in trying."

"Very well," answered Garfield; "I'll trust him. Let
him be here early in the morning."

In the morning the snow was falling so thickly that objects
only a few rods distant were totally invisible; but at nine
o'clock the little body of cavalry was sent up the road to engage the attention of the enemy, and draw him from his
intrenchments ; and then the infantry was set in motion.
In a long, bristling, serpent-like column, catching at every
twig and shrub and fallen log that lay in their way, they
clambered slowly up the icy mountain-side, the old guide
leading the way, and steadying his steps by the long, iron-
shod staff in use among mountaineers. The ridge at this
point rises two thousand feet above the valley, and half-way
up breaks into abrupt precipices, which seem to defy the approach of any foot but that of the deer or chamois. Thus far
the guide had gone on with tottering steps, stopping often for
breath, and to see that he was closely followed; but now

planting his staff firmly in the icy slope, he leaped from rock to rock as agile as if he had been a stripling. His altered gait caught the quick eye of the Union commander, and, suspecting treachery, he hailed him, demanding he should go no further. The old man kept on, giving no heed to the summons, and then the officer cried, —

"Halt! or I'll put a bullet through you."

This brought the guide to a stand, and clambering up to him, Garfield said, —

"Who are you? Tell me the truth, or I shall hang you to the first tree."

The other lifted his hat, and putting aside his long snowy hair, showed the officer the gray locks, and wide, white forehead of Jordan!

"I suspected as much. You have my word. Go on; we will follow," said the Union commander.

Without a word, the guide again led the way through the tangled thickets, over the ice-coated rocks, and along the steep ridge which crowns the summit of the mountain, and then, turning sharply to the left, said to the officer, —

"You are now within half a mile of the rebel position. Yonder is their outside picket; but the way is clear; — press on at the double-quick, and you have them."

The picket had now descried the advancing column, and, firing his gun, he set out at the top of his speed for the rebel intrenchments. A dozen bullets made shrill music about his ears, but he kept on, and the eager blue-coats followed. When within sight of the rebel camp, a line was thrown down along the eastern slope of the mountain, and, pressing rapidly forward, was formed along the deep gorge through which the

high-road passes. Up to this time the rebels had been skir-
mishing with the cavalry in front of their breastworks; but
now they gathered on the hill directly opposite the advanced
position of the Union infantry.

To try the range, Garfield sent a volley across the gorge,
and, as the smoke cleared away, he saw the unformed rebel
line melt like mist into the opposite forest. The enemy's
position being now understood, the Fortieth and Forty-second
Ohio were ordered to the already formed left wing, and then
along the line rang the words, "Press forward; scale the hill
and carry it with the bayonet!"

A ringing shout was the only answer, and then the long
column swept down the ridge, across the ravine, through the
rebel camp, and up the opposite mountain. The rebels fell
gradually back among the trees, but when the Union bayonets
clambered the hill, they broke and ran in the wildest confusion.
The Unionists followed, firing as they ran, and for a few moments the mountain echoed with the quick reports of the Ohio
rifles; but pursuit in the dense forest was impossible, and
soon the recall was sounded.

Only one was killed, and seven were wounded; but this
well-nigh bloodless victory rid Eastern Kentucky of rebel
rule forever. When all was over, and the tired men had
gathered in the comfortable quarters of the beaten rebels,
Garfield said to Bent, —

"Where is Jordan?"

"Ten miles away, I reckon, by this time. He took to the
woods before we charged down the mountain."

CHAPTER XXVIII.

THE DEATH OF "BEAUTY."

T nightfall, not many days after the events related in the preceding chapter, the old black entered the lonely cabin where Rachel and the Widow Jordan were looking and listening for his coming. As the door opened, they both rose from before the fire, and, in one breath, exclaimed, —

"Have you seen him? Is he safe?"

"Yas, missy, safe and comin', but not yere. De brute beasts am a huntin' him down. He fall inter de trap, but de dumb critter she seed de lion in de way, and de Lord he led him safe ag'in to de mountains."

"And can't they let him alone? After all he has done, must they hunt him down as if he were a wild animal?" said Rachel.

"No, missy, 'taint dem. De gineral hisseff telled 'Zeke to git him out ob Kaintucky, whoile he got pardon and reward for him from de big 'uns down tew Washington. No, missy, 'taint dem; it am the debil's own chile as he saved from hangin' a millstone round his neck, and gittin' his feet fast in de mire foreber."

"Not Jackson!" said Rachel, her face turning to a deathly pallor.

"Yes, missy, it am dat debil; he hab put on de angel's clo'es 'spressly to hab Massa John's life 'fore he kin git out ob Kaintucky. But neber you f'ar, missy, dey as am wid him are more dan dey as am ag'in him; de chariots and de hoss-men am round him, and dey'll git him safe wid us inter de land ob Canaan. So, neber you f'ar, missy, de Lord'll luck arter Massa John; jess you git 'Zeke some supper, fur he haint had a morsel sense de lass sundown."

While he said this, the old black removed his travel-soiled hat and outer garment, and, seating himself in the leather-bottomed chair, stretched his huge feet and mud-bespattered brogans out toward the backlog. As Rachel went about preparing a hasty meal, the older woman said, —

"And whar ar' he now, 'Zekiel? Kin he go with us to the 'Hio?"

"Yas, missus, he says he will, if de Lord am a willin'; for he reckons he hab done all he kin for Kaintucky. 'Zeke am a gwine to git his black sheep — he! he! — togedder, and den Massa John'll come onto us down de riber, and see us safe cl'ar ober Jordan."

"Then you got the gineral's permission to tuck all the folks inter the 'Hio?"

"Yas, missus, all de free folks, — all as ole Massa Jordan 'lotted on to go dar, wid dar chillen and gran'-chillen. De ress, de gineral say, wont hab to wait long, 'case slavery am a'ready more'n half dead in Kaintucky."

"Then it is true," said Rachel, "that the rebels are driven from Pound Gap, and far back into Virginia?"

"Yas, missy, and Massa John done it. He jess goed inter dar nest, played off dat he was Parson Bradslaw as was safe in de jail at Piketon, and den he guided de Unions to de rout ob de Philistines. De Yankee gineral he say dar haint sech anudder brave man as him in all Kaintucky."

The remainder of the old black's prolix narrative may be condensed into a few sentences of ordinary English. He had arrived at the Union head-quarters just as Garfield — who had been made brigadier-general for his important services in Eastern Kentucky — was on the eve of departing to join the army of Buell, then on its march to Shiloh. Obtaining at once the permission of that officer for the removal of the negroes, he had remained in camp for a few days in the hope of learning the hiding-place of Jordan, who he desired should accompany his flock in their exodus from Kentucky. Bent was ignorant of Jordan's exact whereabouts, but at once sent scouts to all his former haunts, and encouraged the old man to believe that a very few days' search would discover him.

While awaiting the return of the scouts, the old negro was not a little astonished one morning by encountering Weddington at the head-quarters of Colonel Cranor, who had been placed in command of the handful of troops that were left behind to hold the Sandy Valley. The ostensible object of Weddington's visit to camp was the taking of the oath of allegiance. This he was allowed to do by Colonel Cranor, and he was also given a safe-conduct by that officer on condition of his remaining peaceably on his own plantation. On meeting Ezekiel, Weddington inquired most eagerly after Jordan. His manner excited the suspicion of the old man, — led him to fear that his visit to camp and taking of the oath

2S

boded no good to Jordan, who he knew was in possession of a secret whose disclosure would bring lasting disgrace on Weddington and his family. Might he not be seeking his life in the hope that the secret would be buried with him ? This the old man feared, and he communicated his fear to Bent, whose search for Jordan had been unsuccessful. Bent advised him to return to the valley of the Blaine, seek Jordan among the mountains, and warn him to at once leave Kentucky.

Mounted on the old mule, the old man set out on the following morning. His way was slow, but at nightfall he had gone one-half the distance, and was approaching a friendly house, where he purposed to pass the night, when he was overtaken by a single horseman. The man was black, and was arrayed in a tattered suit of ."butternuts"; but the horse was a spirited animal, and evidently belonged to the better sort of four-footed society. In the dim light the old negro failed to distinguish the features of the rider, but the horse he at once recognized as the mare, "Beauty."

"Am it you, Massa John ? " he cried, as the other made as if he would pass him.

"Yes, 'Zekiel," was the answer. "I thought you wouldn't know me."

" 'Zeke know'd de nag, Massa John, and he's afeard she'll git you inter trouble. De young 'Squar' am out, Massa John ; he's been done whitewashed with a oath, 'Zeke fears, 'spressly to hunt you down, and hab you' life, 'fore you kin git out ob Kaintucky."

He then recounted his meeting with Weddington, and the suspicions his manner had excited.

Jordan listened in silence to the disclosures of the negro, but after a time he said, —

"It may be that the end will come in that way; but, however it comes, I am ready. You got the safe-conduct and the permit for the removal of the negroes?"

"Yas, Massa John."

"Well, you had better make all haste to get them ready for the journey. I will go on with you, and lay out in the mountains till you set out, then will see you safely out of Kentucky."

At the suggestion of Jordan, it was decided to travel all night in order to reach the Blaine by early morning, and they pressed forward as rapidly as the old mule could be induced to travel. They had gone on about two hours, and were approaching a dense wood that lined both sides of the highway, when Jordan's mare stopped suddenly in the road, and gave a low whinny. The old black drew up his mule, and asked eagerly, —

"What am it, Massa John? What'm de matter wid de critter?"

"She sees something that I can't make out in the darkness. Be quiet and listen."

The words were scarcely spoken, when a rifle-shot echoed from the edge of the wood, not a hundred yards distant, and the mare, with a frantic bound, fell suddenly dead in the highway. A moment later a dozen horsemen sprang into the road, and moved suddenly down upon Jordan and the old negro. Quickly disengaging himself from the fallen animal, Jordan cried out, —

"To the woods, 'Zekiel, — back with the mule into the timber."

Saying this, he leaped a narrow stream which skirted the road, and was lost in the dense shadows of the forest.

"Never mind the old black. Dismount every one of you, and into the wood after Jordan. A thousand dollars to the man that kills him," said the voice of Weddington.

The troops dismounted, and for half an hour their shouts echoed here and there through the forest. Then one by one they returned to the highway, and from the babel of curses which arose on the night the old negro knew that the pursuit had been unsuccessful. Then he thought of his own safety, and, dismounting, led the old mule still farther into the forest. There he remained over night and till the last guerilla had disappeared down the highway. Then he slowly resumed his journey, and, without further incident, reached the valley of the Blaine on the following day at nightfall.

"The Lord is with him; he will never be taken," said Rachel, as the old man concluded his story.

"So 'Zeke reckons, missy; but he'd feel ten year younger if Massa John was only safe out ob Kaintucky."

"And Bradley?" asked Rachel; "did you see him at the army?"

"No, missy, he'd gone, and nobody know'd nothin' about him. He'd fell into bad ways, and done suffin' dey shot him up for; but he broke out ob de guard-house, and goed off, — whar no one know'd for sartin."

CHAPTER XXIX.

" THE LAST OF EARTH."

HE ensuing fortnight was spent by the negroes in again preparing for the journey into Ohio. At its close they set out in a long cavalcade, led by the old mule, and a wagon containing 'Zekiel, Rachel, and the widow Jordan. On the following morning they embarked with their household goods on a couple of flat-boats moored to the dock at Paintville, and before many hours were moving rapidly down the river. They had not proceeded many miles when a small canoe put out from the western bank, and Jordan, disguised as before, boarded the leading flat-boat. When the old negro's somewhat boisterous greeting was over, Jordan said to him, —

" 'Zekiel, send one or two of the men back at once to Captain Plumb, at Paintville. Weddington and a dozen of his gang are lying in wait further down the river. He seeks not only my life, — he means to prevent the negroes leaving Kentucky."

" But he can't do dat, Massa John ; we've de general's permission."

" I know ; but he has in some way managed to get a counter order from Colonel Cranor. The court, too, has issued

another writ for their detention.   If the general were here it
would be all right, but he is gone, and our only course is to
fight our way down the river.   Once across the Ohio, you can
defy all the courts in Kentucky."

"I knows, I knows, Massa John; but how many ob dem
am dar?"

"About a dozen, I am told, strong men, and all armed with
rifles and revolvers."

"And we haint more'n six sorry shot-guns among us!"

"For that reason you must send at once to Captain Plumb
for assistance.   He has a few men with him, and — I know
him — will come at once to the rescue.   Meanwhile, we
had better tie up the boats, and land in some position that
can be easily defended."

In a few minutes the canoe in which Jordan had come was
sent back to Paintville, and not long afterwards, the boats
were halted and moored to the shore, at a point where a steep
bank shuts down upon the river.   A couple of deserted shan-
ties occupied the summit of the bank, and in these the
women and children were soon collected.   Then the men
felled a number of trees, and, forming a rude breastwork,
gathered behind it to await the coming of their friends, or
their enemies.

They had not to wait long.   An hour had not passed before
Jordan, from a lookout in the top of a tree, discovered two
row-boats, filled with armed men, rapidly ascending the river.
They were Weddington and the handful that was left of his
gang of guerillas!

The boats bore directly for the point where the negroes

had landed, but, as they came within speaking distance, were suddenly brought to by a summons from Ezekiel, —

"Halt!" he cried, "not another rod, or ole 'Zeke'll send some ob you to de judgment."

"Push on. Never mind the old fool," cried Weddington, seizing an oar and driving the forward boat directly under the lee of one of the flats. A shot whistled over his head, but, rising above the gunwale, he fired at a man who stood at the barricade.

The man was Jordan. A low sound escaped him, he staggered back a step or two, and fell to the ground, mortally wounded. A moment of frantic confusion followed among the negroes, and in that moment, with wild shouts, Weddington and his gang sprang ashore and climbed half way up the bank towards the barricade. The shouts recalled 'Zekiel to the danger, and, rising to his full height, he cried out, —

"Massa Jack, you knows me, — you knows I tell you de truth. Come up yere, and I'll shoot you, shuah."

Weddington sank behind a fallen log, and, firing quickly, lodged a bullet in the old man's shoulder. He fell, badly wounded, but in a moment was on his feet again, with his shot-gun levelled at the breast of Weddington. The latter was now at the barricade. The old man fired. The ball passed through the thighs of Weddington, but he kept his feet, and raised his revolver. At this moment the old man, clubbing his gun, felled him to the earth, not to rise again forever. But now the brave old man could do no more. Sick and faint with the loss of blood, he fell again to the ground, crying out, —

"Beat 'em back, my chillen, — pay 'em for Massa John, and ole 'Zekiel."

The guerillas pressed on, firing indiscriminately among the women and children, and a desperate hand-to-hand conflict ensued between them and the negroes. It had lasted only a few moments, when loud shouts were heard coming down the river. It was a canoe pulling rapidly towards the landing. In it were Captain Ralph Plumb, Captain Joseph Heaton, and the solitary soldier who had been left with them at Paintville. With loud shouts they came on, and, seeing them, the guerillas fled to their boats, leaving the body of their leader to negro burial.

Arrived at the barricade, a melancholy scene met the eyes of the Union officers. Lying on the ground, which was red with the blood that was flowing from his neck and shoulder, was the old negro. His breath was short and labored, but, in broken words, he gasped out, —

"Neber mind me, save Massa John, if you kin, gemmen."

Jordan's head was resting on his mother's lap, and beside him Rachel was kneeling. Her hand was clasped in his, and his eyes were fixed on hers with a strange, unearthly gleaming.

"Remember," he said, in a low, faltering whisper, "whoso turns a sinner from the error of his way, saves a soul from death, and hides a multitude of sins. Remember, Rachel!"

Then a smile passed over his face, his head sank back, and, tranquilly and slow, his soul crossed the silent river.

And now a few words will tell all that remains to be told of this short history. The next day they buried Jordan among the mountains he had done so much to make free; and, a few days following, the negroes, with their wounded patriarch, were embarked on a government transport, furnished by Captain Plumb, and conveyed to Portsmouth, Ohio; thence they were removed to Jackson county, and settled in comfortable houses, under the care of old Ezekiel and his young mistress. There Rachel, in quiet work, found the peace which comes at last to all souls, who, in patient waiting, look for the rest which is hereafter.

So two years went away, and, during these, Rachel heard nothing of her husband. Then, one day, taking up a paper, she noticed that Garfield, returned with honor from the war, had visited and made an address to the prisoners at the Ohio Penitentiary. Among the prisoners, it was stated, was one who had been his companion and friend in boyhood. The meeting between the two men was described, and some comments were made on the strange fortune which had so brought together a convict and a major-general. The man, it was added, though a confirmed sot and notorious horse-thief, had done some service to his country in Kentucky. Something within told Rachel that it was Brown, her husband. Instantly she set out to see the governor, and before many days, with a pardon in her hand, was at the gateway of the prison.

In the years that have followed, she has learned that "he who turns a sinner from the error of his way, saves a soul from death, and hides a multitude of sins."

THE END.